Praise for Ward Larsen

"It's always a pleasure to read an author who knows his stuff." —Kyle Mills, #1 *New York Times* bestselling author, on *Assassin's Edge*

"There's no denying that Ward Larsen is one of our best modern thriller writers, and he's at the top of his game in *Deep Fake*." —William Martin, *New York Times* bestselling author of *The Lost Constitution* and *December '41*

"Larsen is not just a dazzling new talent; he's a dazzling new superstar!" —Stephen Coonts, *New York Times* bestselling author, on *Assassin's Silence*

"Ward Larsen is bound to attract devotees." —Ralph Peters, *New York Times* bestselling author, on *Assassin's Game*

"Be prepared to be fabulously faked out." —Whitley Strieber, #1 *New York Times* bestselling author of *Communion* and *The Grays*

BOOKS BY WARD LARSEN

*Published by Forge Books

DEEP FAKE

WARD LARSEN

Tor Publishing Group
New York

DEEP FAKE

A Forge Book
Published by Tom Doherty Associates/Tor Publishing Group
120 Broadway
New York, NY 10271

www.tor-forge.com

Forge® is a registered trademark of Macmillan Publishing Group, LLC.

ISBN 978-1-250-79821-3

Our books may be purchased in bulk for promotional, educational, or business use. Please contact your local bookseller or the Macmillan Corporate and Premium Sales Department at 1-800-221-7945, extension 5442, or by email at MacmillanSpecialMarkets@macmillan.com.

First Edition: March 2023
First Mass Market Edition: January 2024

Printed in the United States of America

0 9 8 7 6 5 4 3 2 1

For Dane and Jack.
All the adventures you will have.

1

MISTED AWAY

Sarah read the words never realizing how apt they would prove: The End.

A wave of cool air brushed over the bed and she sank deeper beneath the covers. She looked accusingly at the window, saw the left-hand frame hanging crookedly on its hinge. Every time a door opened downstairs, a tiny blast of hard November air sucked in.

One more thing for Bryce's honey-do list.

She put down the short story and capped her red pen, glad to be done. She'd given up late last night, not quite able to finish—hardly a vote of confidence for the poor author—but after the first clatter this morning she was hopelessly awake. *Five a.m.* She'd made the best of it, editing the last twenty pages. The ending was decent, or at least it hadn't put her back to sleep. She'd begun picking up freelance work eight years ago, a perfect job for a stay-at-home Army wife with a sharp eye for detail. Today she was getting all the work she wanted. Magazine articles, fiction, the occasional memoir. Nothing lucrative, but it paid the bills. Or at least some of them. Phone, electric. Gas in a good month.

Another bang from the kitchen storm door. Another microburst of chilly outside air.

With a sigh, Sarah threw off the covers and pulled

herself up. She went straight to the closet, shrugged a waffle robe over her nightshirt and knotted the sash tight. Then a precautionary inspection in the dressing mirror: her shoulder-length sandy hair was mussed but not tangled, and she gave her front teeth a perfunctory finger-brush.

She padded downstairs feeling chipper, ready for whatever the day might bring. At the midpoint on the staircase she noticed the doorbell chime—mounted high on the wall over the front door, it appeared crooked. Bryce had been busy lately, but it was time for a nudge.

Where was that list?

Fortunately, the house was a good house. Not new, but endowed with good bones, or so the realtor had said. Sarah supposed that meant the rafters weren't creaky, the studs not rotted. She loved the place because it was theirs. After fifteen years of Army-issue family housing, with its white-popcorn ceilings and painted-over black mold, she and Bryce finally had their names on a real deed. Right next to the bank's.

She reached the kitchen, her favorite room of the house and where her nesting instincts were most evident: sunny yellow accents on the walls between cabinets, a tasteful backsplash behind the counter, pots hung functionally near the stove. It was all bright and organized, a place where comfort food was served.

At first, she saw no sign of Bryce. Then a flash of motion at the storm door. He hooked it open with one foot, his arms laden with firewood. Still wearing his heavy backpack, he looked like a bad juggling act. Before she could go to his aid he was stomping inside, the door crashing shut behind him.

"Good morning," he said. "Is Alyssa awake?"

"If she wasn't, she is now."

He shot her a sideways glance. "Oh . . . sorry."

"Don't worry. It's after six—she ought to be getting ready for school." More racket as he dumped the logs next to the fireplace. Sarah checked the floor—a bit of mud, but for once he'd remembered to wipe his feet. He returned to the kitchen, a portrait of fitness in running shoes, shorts, and a moisture-wicking pullover. He was perspiring despite the morning chill.

"How was the run?" she asked.

"Better than yesterday."

This was his stock answer, a domestic version of the outlook beaten into him at Army Ranger school. *No easy day* and *Hoorah* and all that crap. Those days were behind them now, and as much as Sarah wanted to blame the Army for what had befallen her husband, she knew better. At every turn, Bryce had made his choices. Now they would live with them. And by her account, they were doing just fine.

He shrugged off a backpack holding thirty pounds of sand and an empty water bottle.

"What time did you get up?" she asked.

"A little before five. Today was a long run, twelve miles."

"I thought a 'long' was ten."

"That was last month. I'm making progress."

"Toward what? Masochism? You're not training for a marathon and you're not in the Army anymore. You're a first-term congressman from Virginia's Tenth. Extreme fitness doesn't get you votes."

"Don't be so sure. There's a big track club in Fairfax." He moved toward the gurgling coffee machine, sideswiping a wet kiss on her cheek as he passed.

"Yuk," she said with faux disgust, wiping away the wetness.

"It's drizzling outside."

Sarah popped two bagels into the toaster, one for him and one for Alyssa. "Will you be home for dinner tonight?"

He considered it as he filled two mugs with Trader Joe's Dark. "Um . . . no. I've got a fundraiser."

"For who?"

"The governor of Virginia." He slid a mug in front of her.

"Well, bully for you. I've got a fundraiser tomorrow—I'm selling brownies at Alyssa's soccer game."

"Trade you."

"Not a chance, Major. You picked the game, you play it."

Bryce cut his coffee with milk and took a long steamy sip. When the cup came down his face was set in a wide smile. *The* smile. The one that hadn't changed in seventeen years, since she'd first seen it outside the freshman dorms at Princeton. Easy and natural, Hollywood-level charisma. The smile that, as alluded to by exit polling, had won eighty-six percent of the college-educated female vote in Virginia's affluent exburbs.

Sarah smiled back. "What's on the agenda this morning?"

He checked the calendar on his phone. "Looks like a breakfast reception downtown, then a Veterans Day event at a hotel. After that, committee meetings and a strategy session with Mandy before lunch." Mandy Treanor was his campaign manager, a lithe, auburn-haired knockout five years younger than either of them, and a Georgetown Law grad to boot. She was paying her dues in a cutthroat profession, which for now meant babysitting a freshman congressman. Given Bryce's smashingly successful first campaign, Sarah had no doubt Mandy would be moving up the Beltway ladder soon.

The toaster popped out two perfectly browned bagels. Bryce fingered one clear and began slathering it with butter. When he turned toward the fridge, Sarah noticed his leg.

"You're bleeding," she said.

"What?" He looked at her, then followed her gaze to his right calf. A crescent-shaped cut, three inches long, smiled up at him. "Oh, that. There was some construction on the path and I had to climb over a fence to get around it. Must've gotten nicked. It's just a scratch."

"Want me to clean it up?"

"I can handle it. I'm highly trained in battlefield medicine."

"And I'm highly trained in overconfident husbands. I could at least—"

"Mom!" Their conversational thread snapped as if cut by a machete. Alyssa's voice, terse and demanding. They looked up the wooden staircase in unison, knights staring into a dragon's lair. Only a teenage girl could suffuse one word with such peril.

"Guess she's awake," Bryce said. "I gotta go shower."

"Coward."

"Don't tell anyone. It would ruin my well-honed warrior image." He started up the stairs, coffee in one hand, warm everything in the other.

Sarah found herself distracted by the scrape on his leg. It didn't look bad, yet she kept staring.

"I can't find my brush!"

The thought misted away. "I'll be right there, baby . . ."

2

WHITE MARBLE TESTAMENTS

The rooftop terrace of the Watergate Hotel was one of D.C.'s up-and-coming hot spots. Situated in the shadow of the infamous office complex, the hotel's recent renovations had hit a sweet spot with local influencers. There was a brass-and-mirror bar and a casual dining area, all under cover of a mainsail awning. The rest of the establishment was open air, sprawling across an expansive terrace. Outdoor furniture sat clustered in tiny islands: thick-cushioned chairs, intimate settees, knee-high tables, all of it sprayed with sealant to withstand rain and spilled mojitos. It was a place where good times were had and business consummated. A place for the old and the young, for the rich and the imminently so. Legendary bachelorette parties raged in the spring, while summer featured Nats games on the bar's big-screens. Autumn veered toward business, everyone back to work at the turn of the federal fiscal year, deals struck and commissions made.

On the cusp of winter, however, the rooftop took on a different vibe. Space heaters replaced umbrellas, and the daiquiri dispenser behind the bar gave way to an espresso machine. Like the greenbelt along the Potomac, brown and leafless in the distance, the rooftop of the Watergate Hotel was a biome of its own, conforming to the seasons. On offer this morning: hot chocolate and promises.

Mandy Treanor checked her watch. Senator Bob Morales, long-tenured Floridian and intermittent front-runner in a clogged cast of Republican presidential aspirants, was due to arrive in ten minutes. She still saw no sign of Bryce.

Working for a freshman congressman, Mandy wore twin hats. She was both his campaign manager and chief of staff—if one receptionist, two part-timers, and an intern could be classified as a workforce. She didn't really mind. Unlike many of her counterparts, she believed in her man: Bryce was a stand-up act in a cutthroat town. Still, she fretted over her congressman's schedule like any good manager, and in that moment her irritation was amplified. For the last five minutes she'd been fending off come-ons from the less than honorable Benjamin Edelman, four-term senator from New Jersey and serial philanderer. The man's eyes had been undressing her from the moment she'd reached the rooftop, and she had already turned down one offer of a drink—this before ten in the morning. Mandy was dressed in a perfectly professional manner, yet men like Edelman seemed to imagine that no modest blouse-and-skirt ensemble was complete until accessorized with a stripper pole.

Having retreated to the far end of the bar, she surveyed the elevator lobby from behind a shivering potted palm. Still no Bryce. A sharp gust of wind snapped across the terrace, more mid-December than early November. Mandy considered the rooftop a risky venue for a Veterans Day ceremony. She could understand the general appeal—there was no better backdrop in Foggy Bottom for sweeping views of the White House, Capitol building, and National Mall. Unfortunately, on a dreary Monday in November, with swirling winds and threatening skies, it seemed a protocol disaster in the making. She picked out Senator Morales's chief of staff near the dais, saw him looking up worriedly at the ragged pewter overcast. *Probably praying for a bit of global warming*, she mused.

Today's gathering was a standard midrank affair. There would be a smattering of Senate leaders, along with staffers, lobbyists, and invited guests. Seated in front were two dozen veterans representing every campaign going back to World War II. This was how Bryce had scored his invitation—only a half dozen House members had been included, all with military backgrounds. Bryce had been typically reluctant, but Mandy turned the screws, presenting it as a chance to mingle with deep-pocketed donors.

Finally, she spotted him in the elevator lobby, sweeping past a table full of coffee decanters and sweet rolls. Six minutes to spare. He surveyed the terrace, spotted her right away, and began shouldering through a forest of Brooks Brothers and VFW hats.

"Hey, Mandy," he said.

"Morning, boss." This was how she addressed him when she was peeved. Bryce didn't seem to notice, and she added, "If you'd been here ten minutes ago, I could have introduced you to the CEO of Boeing."

"Sorry, traffic was bad."

"It's D.C. Traffic is *always* bad." She caught sight of Edelman ambling their way. "Christ," she muttered, "here he comes again."

"Who?"

"Senator Edelman. He told me he might have 'A position opening up on my staff.'"

"Did he ask for your resume?"

"He was ogling my resumes."

Bryce might have smiled.

"Bryce, my boy! Good to see you!" said Edelman. He was a big meaty man, the typical linebacker from a minor college who'd let himself go. When he thrust out his right hand it looked like some crude martial arts move—which, in D.C., it effectively was. The tumbler in Edelman's other hand remained rock-steady.

Bryce endured a predictably bone-crushing grip. "Good to see you, Senator."

"I was just talking to your lovely campaign manager. She tells me your reelection bid is right on track."

"She tells me the same thing."

"Good, good. Your father would be proud. How is he?"

"No change," Bryce said. Walter Ridgeway had suffered a stroke three years earlier, a debilitating event that had decimated his body, robbed him of his mental faculties, and forced him into full-time care at a nursing home. It was a devastating turn for a man who had twice served as ambassador to Austria, and before that Czechoslovakia. A power broker in D.C. politics for a generation, he'd fallen to little more than a memory inside the Capitol's marble-lined halls.

"He and I go way back," Edelman said. "Walter was a man who knew how to get things done."

Mandy gave Bryce a cautious look, hoping he wouldn't react to the use of past tense.

Edelman rambled on with well-feigned sobriety, "I

always thought he should have run for Congress himself instead of wasting so much time at the State Department." He tipped back his drink—based on the scent, Mandy concluded, a gin and tonic.

"Dad went where he thought he could do the most good," Bryce said.

Mandy piped in, "At least he convinced Bryce to carry on the fight." She maneuvered to keep Bryce between herself and the senator.

"Yes, indeed," Edelman seconded. "You've got a long career ahead of you, young man. Although I'm not sure it was wise to spend so much time in the Army. You could have filled that square," he paused to snap his fingers, "then moved on. But I'll never argue against a man serving his country."

Mandy went still, a bomb squad tech who'd just watched the wrong wire get clipped. Bryce didn't take kindly to fools—particularly those who denigrated military service but had never served themselves.

"Excuse me, Senator," Bryce said.

He put a hand to the small of Mandy's back and steered her away. She looked at him with surprise, and once they were clear she said in a low voice, "That was good. I thought you were about to coldcock the guy."

"Nah, that's the old Bryce. It might have felt good in the moment, but it wouldn't be a career enhancer."

"Your campaign manager approves. Anyway, thanks for rescuing me."

Bryce ushered her to the far side of the terrace, cutting through the crowd like a bouncer through a nightclub. Mandy had always viewed him as something of an enigma. Bryce had been born to privilege—the best East Coast prep schools and a BA from Princeton—yet he'd cast aside the life plan designed by his father to join the Army. Law school was replaced by officer candidate school. While his Ivy League classmates were summering in the Hamptons, Bryce had been excelling at Ranger training. Instead of six-figure bonuses from Goldman Sachs, he'd gotten combat pay for deployments to faraway and dusty hellholes. Then, three years ago, everything had changed in one terrible moment. Bryce had been in the passenger seat of a Land Rover, on a dusty road in Mali, when a bomb hidden beneath a culvert had detonated. He'd been seriously injured, forced to take a medical discharge.

It was an abrupt end to a promising military career. Bryce's father, however, viewed the tragedy as more a beginning than an end. He saw a dream resume for a neophyte politician, and while it had taken time to get Bryce on board, in the end his father prevailed. The successful congressional campaign, launched with the blessings of the retiring Republican incumbent in a deeply red district, had been a slam dunk. Mandy had her eye squarely on a second term.

Bryce led to a standing-room-only section behind the main seating area, and soon Mandy caught a flourish of activity near the elevator. Senator Morales was arriving. Tall and angular, Morales had entered national politics as a smooth-faced lawyer. Thirty-six years later he'd become something else. The burdens of Washington seemed etched into every line on his craggy face. His posture was stooped, his gaze rheumy, and twin wings of white hair swept back from his temples like unmolted plumage. Framed by younger aides and two robust D.C. police officers, he stalked across the terrace like an arthritic heron.

"Looks like we're about to start," Bryce said.

Mandy looked across the terrace at a brimming crowd. She'd heard that two hundred invitations had been sent out, and it appeared every one had shown. The senator was taking his time, glad-handing his way to the front, special attention given to a man she recognized as an Exxon lobbyist. Bryce took a long look at his watch.

"Got an appointment I don't know about?" asked the woman who micromanaged his every minute.

"No . . . I'd just love to see one of these things start on time for a change."

"Since I have your undivided attention, maybe we could have a congressman to chief of staff conference."

"Sure."

"I've heard there may be an opening next year on the judiciary committee."

"The what?"

"*Judiciary* . . . I have it on good authority two members will be leaving. Assuming we get you a second term, it's time to start pressing for a worthwhile committee assignment."

"Yesterday at the office we were talking about Veteran's Affairs."

"It's an option. But I mentioned Judiciary too."

"Did you?"

"As you were leaving, getting into the cab."

"Oh, right. I guess either one is good."

"No, Bryce, they're not in the same league. Look, I know you miss the Army, but you have a new professional ladder now. Judiciary would be a promotion, like making colonel."

"I barely pinned on major."

"Which is my point. In this world, play your cards right and you can jump ahead a few ranks. It's a much more important committee, one notch below Ways and Means. If you have bigger aspirations, that's the way to go."

He glanced at her, a reply brewing. In the end, he only said, "Okay, Mandy. Let's talk about it later."

Morales was nearly in place, shaking hands and pointing all the way to the makeshift stage—as if he knew every face in the crowd. He was momentarily lost amid a cluster of bodies around the podium. Situated to face that focal point were a dozen neat rows of chairs, all occupied. Old soldiers wore ballcaps scripted with unit emblems and campaigns. A pair of World War II vets sat in wheelchairs in front, while the next three rows were a mix: Korea, Vietnam, the Gulf War. The remaining seats were taken by spouses, congressmen, dignitaries, and VA officials. The balance of the terrace was relegated to standing room for staffers.

Mandy recognized two lesser Republican presidential candidates seated near the back—the senior senator from Colorado, and the governor of Ohio. Both were polling in low single digits, mired in a massive primary field of nineteen hopefuls. *What a silly way to choose the most powerful person on earth*, she mused.

She looked out over the rail across the National Mall. The hotel's fifteenth floor—its height was limited so as not to overshadow the Lincoln Memorial—offered a reaching panorama of the nation's power centers. The Capitol building, White House, Washington Monument, and Pentagon, a veritable gallery of white marble testaments. In the sullen morning light, they all looked gray and exhausted, as if dreading the next national calamity.

A voice brought Mandy's attention back to the rooftop soiree. Senator Morales was being introduced.

IRREFUTABLE MOMENTUM

Good morning, and thank you all for coming," Morales began, his hollow voice creaking like an old door. "We have gathered this morning for the worthiest of reasons, to honor those among us who have served our great country . . ."

Mandy actually listened to his remarks, viewing it as part and parcel to her job to decipher the message within. There was always a message, and it usually had to do with money: either promoting pet spending projects or soliciting contributions to one's own campaign. She had to admit, whatever wonk had written this morning's speech was good. It touched on problems at the VA, yet never lost the spirit of the day—a fine line to hew—and left no doubt that veterans care would be at the top of the senator's agenda in the run-up to next year's election. Mandy leaned toward Bryce and was about to share these thoughts when she realized he was neither watching, nor apparently listening to, the droning figure behind the lectern. His eyes were riveted on a point across the broad terrace.

Until that moment, Mandy thought she had seen the full range of Bryce's character. She'd seen him circulate like a pro at cocktail parties, seen him distracted after tiffs with Sarah. Seen him stiff-arm lobbyists with the elusiveness of a running back. Regardless of the challenge, never once had he lost his calm, easy-going demeanor. Now that relaxed visage had gone to stone, his gaze cold and expressionless. Mandy swore she could see muscles tensing beneath his felted wool jacket.

"Bryce . . . what is it?"

No response.

"*Bryce?*"

"That guy over there," he said in a dead voice. "Twentyish, thin, dark blue jacket."

Mandy looked into a sea of people standing casually with lattes and orange juice and sweet rolls. Then she spotted him: a slightly-built young man in a blue jacket. He was moving across the terrace thirty feet from where they stood, slow and methodical, slaloming between bodies along the far railing. He *did* seem different, Mandy thought, although she couldn't pinpoint how.

"What about him?" she asked.

"His right hand."

She looked more closely, saw his right hand in the pocket of his jacket. It didn't seem unusual on such a chilly morning. His attention was mostly fixed on the stage, yet Mandy noticed his eyes flicking nervously. "Bryce, I think we should—"

Before she could finish the thought, Bryce grabbed two flutes of orange juice from a tray on a table and started across the terrace. With a glass in each hand, he cut through the crowd like a practiced waiter. His head was canted toward the lectern, yet Mandy knew his attention was elsewhere—she was watching nothing less than a trained soldier launching a full-frontal assault.

When the gap reached twenty feet, the young man glanced in Bryce's direction. They were the only two people on the terrace moving, the rest of the crowd absorbed in the senator's remarks. Mandy felt a terrible foreboding.

Fifteen feet.

Mandy checked left and right. She'd seen policemen when she arrived, at least a half dozen uniformed cops near the stage and in the inner lobby. *Where had they all gone?*

She looked again at Bryce. Ten feet.

What happened next seemed like a sequence of jagged images. Bryce rushed the man, his arms outstretched, flutes of orange juice flying outward. The man reacted, his eyes wide. The intruder pulled his hand from his jacket, and it was holding . . . something. Bryce lunged for whatever it was.

He wrapped up the much smaller man, battered him into the outer wall. Mandy watched as they careened toward the rail. A pair of men in thousand-dollar suits jumped back like they were avoiding a splash from a passing taxi. Bryce pinned the man momentarily against a waist-high concrete wall that was topped by a bronze handrail.

A woman screamed.

Senator Morales fell silent.

Everything seemed to freeze for an instant as Bryce and the man locked in a stalemate, two grappling bodies wedged against the wall. Their interlocked arms were outstretched, but then Bryce's left hand twisted free. There was a sudden shift of limbs, and she watched in horror as Bryce hooked his free hand under the man's crotch and lifted him completely off the ground. With one great twist he heaved him over the fifteenth-floor rail.

That trajectory ended abruptly when the man seized Bryce's jacket, both hands locked in a death grip. The maelstrom of physical forces conspired: the smaller man's irrefutable momentum, Bryce being off balance, multiple points of contact. Mandy watched helplessly as Bryce lurched, his body folding over the top of the wall. That image hovered for an instant, balanced on a knife's edge. Then, in one final snarl of flailing limbs, both men plunged over the wall and disappeared.

"*Bryce!*" Mandy screamed. She began running across the terrace, but before her second stride a massive explosion rocked the morning.

The shock wave threw her to the tile deck. She lay stunned for a moment, her ears ringing like cymbals. When she looked up people everywhere had gone to ground—either pummeled by the blast or in the instinct of self-preservation. Mandy struggled to her feet and lurched across the terrace.

Echoes from the explosion reverberated between buildings. Car alarms wailed all around. A cloud of smoke rose beyond the outer wall. One of the thousand-dollar-suits bolted to his feet and reached for something. Mandy saw a lone hand gripping the iron rail—little more than a row of white knuckles, one with a wedding ring. The suit locked down on the hand, then seized an attached sleeve.

Two other men rushed to help.

A second hand appeared, followed by another sleeve.

Inch by inch, Congressman Bryce Ridgeway was hauled back to safety.

4

NEWTONIAN PRINCIPLES

Sarah dropped two bags of groceries on the kitchen counter, and three oranges rolled out and tumbled across the granite like tiny bowling balls. She caught two near the edge, then blocked a third from falling with her knee. She'd no sooner gotten the situation under control when her phone buzzed. With a muted smile, she thought, *Life in the burbs.*

She checked her phone and saw a text message from Bryce: I'm safe.

Her smile flattened instantly. "Safe?" she whispered. She typed out a quick response: What happened?

She waited. No reply.

Sarah called Bryce, but it went straight to voice mail. "Hey, is everything okay?" she said after the rigid congressman's greeting she loved to rib him about. She ended the call, and immediately her phone lit up with another text.

Not Bryce this time, but her best friend Claire: Is Bryce okay?

Before Sarah could type, What the hell are you talking about? two more messages arrived.

Mrs. Marden from the school office: I saw what happened to Bryce. Can we help?

Then Valerie Hempstead, a neighbor: Was that Bryce I just saw on TV? OMG!

Sarah dropped her phone on the counter and rushed to the living room. She turned on the TV but struggled to find a news network—Bryce was the only one who watched them. When she finally found the right channel, a breaking news banner was scrolling across the bottom. TERROSIST ATTACK IN CAPITOL—SENATOR ROBERT MORALES TARGETED.

She clicked up the volume in time to catch a few words: "warning" and "graphic nature." Sarah stood mesmerized as a video clip began to play. It had a distinctly jarring, cell-phone quality, the camera canted up toward the roof of a large building. Out of nowhere the figure of a man flew out into space, but then suddenly jerked back. The image resolved into two intertwined human shapes. Moments later, one fell in accordance with Newtonian principles while the other dangled from the rooftop by a single handhold.

The figure in free fall flashed past three stories of plate-glass windows, its reflection captured like a horrid sequence of snapshots. Then, less than halfway to the ground, the flailing set of arms and legs simply . . . exploded. In a flare of fire and mist, the human form disappeared, a few bits and pieces spinning outward at odd angles.

Sarah's thoughts ran rampant, the texts replaying in her head. *I saw what happened to Bryce. Is Bryce okay?* Her heart was racing, and she steadied herself by sitting on the cushioned arm of the couch.

The face of a somber news anchor replaced the video. Sarah notched up the volume further and the woman's sonorous voice came clear. "*Congressman Bryce Ridgeway was pulled to safety and later treated for minor injuries. A Metro Police spokesperson is scheduled to provide a briefing soon, yet FBI sources have confirmed that they are treating the event as an act of terrorism . . ."* The anchor began setting up the video again, more lurid cautions about viewer discretion. Shock-porn media at its finest.

Sarah shrank back from the screen. Her phone was trembling nonstop on the kitchen counter. No doubt, as it would all day. *Bryce says he's safe.* In that she would trust. It wasn't the first time he'd sent her such a message—she'd gotten three similar notifications during Army deployments. Those texts hadn't been a reaction to breaking network news, but rather a hedge against the only communications grid on earth that was faster and more ruthless: the military wives' network. In each of those events, Bryce's unit had taken casualties, and he'd sent a message to put her at ease. Conversely, there had been one tragedy after which she *hadn't* gotten his assurance—the time he'd been severely injured.

Sarah drew a slow, deep breath, the scent of oranges on the air.

He says he's safe, so he is, she told herself again. Her thoughts reacquired order, and she knew what she had to do. Her phone blowing up would only be the tip of the iceberg. A forewarning of what was to come. Instagram, Facebook, Twitter.

Alyssa. I have to take care of Alyssa.

She went to the kitchen, retrieved her phone, and called her daughter's school.

5

THE HAPPIEST PLACE ON EARTH

Where's the high-wire act?" asked Troy Burke.

The desk clerk looked up. He was a beefy sergeant in blues, no doubt close to retirement. Sitting behind a bulletproof window, he was the gatekeeper of the first floor holding area of the D.C. Metropolitan Police's 2nd District Headquarters.

The sergeant flicked through a short stack of papers, settled on one and scanned it before looking up. "You Burke?" he asked.

Burke looked down. The lanyard holding his credentials had drifted under his lapel. He straightened it out and the guy with a shoulder full of stripes compared the picture on the ID to the face before him. Thick features, alert brown eyes, month-old chop-shop haircut, north side of fifty. Beneath the picture, the FBI caption: Troy Burke, Special Agent in Charge of Counterterrorism, Washington Field Office.

"Okay, you're good to go," the sergeant said.

"This is my partner, Nina Alves." Burke nodded toward a petite woman behind him whose broad face and jet-black hair reflected her New Mexican heritage.

Another ID check, another nod.

They were buzzed into the inner sanctum without the usual interagency banter. Burke, of course, knew why. D.C. Metro had been in charge of security on top of the hotel, and what happened on top of the hotel was a fail. An attack had gone down on their watch. To their credit, after getting the VIPs safe, they'd locked the place down hard. Now, because it was clearly a terrorist attack, the FBI was taking over. Burke had already spent an hour on the rooftop, going over the terrace where a bomber had gotten within thirty feet of a leading presidential candidate. From here on out, D.C. Metro would be little more than an observer in the inquiry.

As head of the nearest Joint Terrorism Task Force counterterrorism branch, the D.C. Field Office, Burke had drawn the assignment. He wasn't particularly happy about it. This was going to be a high-profile investigation. Lots of congressmen and department heads asking questions, demanding updates and briefings. Burke knew how consuming that could be, and he suspected the investigation would take up a good chunk of the two years he had left until retirement.

"Down the hall," the sergeant said once they were inside, "room four."

"Is he alone?" Burke asked.

"He is now."

"Now?"

"A crisis counselor came to see him."

"Christ," Burke muttered. "Is she still in the building?"

"It's a *he* . . . and no, I think he left."

Burke and Alves pressed down the hall.

"Nailed you there," Alves said. She loved to prod him about being a Neanderthal.

He gave her a sullen look, which these days was pretty much a default setting. Fifty-three years old, Burke was forty pounds heavier and probably an inch shorter than when he'd started at the bureau twenty-eight years ago. A grumpy vet who'd been through the wars.

"Any word on the Anchorage transfer?" Alves asked.

"I decided against it."

"Would have been a promotion—nice bump to the retirement check."

"I never saw myself as management."

"Me neither."

That got a smile. "After six field offices, I'm happy to finish here. Anyway, Vicky hates the cold."

They reached the interview room with a black-stenciled 4 on the door. A corn-blond crew cut was standing outside. He was young, the creases in his uniform blade-sharp. His cheeks were actually rosy. A new guy, planted here by his supervisor like a three-gallon geranium.

Burke addressed him without preamble. "Did they bring him straight here?"

"No sir, the congressman had some minor injuries. They took him to the hospital first to X-ray his arm."

"Okay."

"You need me anymore?" asked the crew cut, whose ID said Smithers.

"Nah, we got it."

The young man saw his chance and made a dash down the hall.

"You want me inside?" Alves asked.

Burke thought about it. "No, I'd rather you watched from the theater." All D.C. Metro interrogation rooms were wired—cameras from three different angles and good quality audio. Every move could be watched in real time from a viewing room down the hall. With two rows of chairs, it was referred to as the "home theater." "But I will need that," Burke added, gesturing to the laptop under Alves's arm.

She handed it over.

Burke entered a generic interrogation room, three metal chairs and a cheap table, everything gray and cold and utilitarian. It was warmer than it should have been, either a bad thermostat or an ongoing strategy. The air was laced in the sour scent of nervous humans.

He recognized the congressman instantly—his face had been backdropping every newscast for the last six hours. That image, his official photo backdropped by an American flag, seemed stuck in Burke's head: Bryce Ridgeway smiling broadly, as if Capitol Hill and not Disneyland was the Happiest Place on Earth. His haircut was perfect, his suit squared like a military service dress. Burke doubted he'd ever seen the congressman's picture before today, but he *had* heard the name. Ridgeway was making waves during his first year in office, and as far as Burke could remember, not for anything scandalous.

Now the Boy Scout gone-large was sitting behind an institutional table. Even after a rough day, he looked like a soldier, confident and composed, everything regulation. Burke walked over and the congressman stood to greet him.

"Congressman Ridgeway, good to meet you. I'm FBI Special Agent Troy Burke."

Having reached the point where they would normally shake hands, Burke gestured to Ridgeway's right arm which was hanging in a sling. "Hopefully no damage done, sir?"

"No, I'm good. They did a scan, but it's just a sprain. And please, call me Bryce."

Burke found the request unusual. The few congressmen he'd interviewed in the past had not been so inclined, their superiority complexes well in place.

"Okay, Bryce. First of all, I'm sorry about this." He gestured to the room like a minor league coach lamenting a smelly away locker room. "I'd really like to get a statement while things are fresh in your mind, and this was the most secure place to do it. As you can imagine, this will be a high-profile investigation. Somebody just tried to kill a senior senator, and we need to get to the bottom of it."

"I understand," Ridgeway said, taking his seat again. Burke grabbed one of the two opposing chairs, spun it backward, and sat with his arms folded on the back. To the uninitiated it might have appeared casual, but the truth was more self-serving: Burke was intimately familiar with Metro interrogation rooms, and he knew how uncomfortable the chairs were.

"I have to say, after seeing the video of what happened . . . you really saved the day."

The congressman shrugged. "I did what the Army trained me to do."

"Maybe so, but this attack would have had a very different outcome if you hadn't taken the initiative."

"Do you know who he was?"

"Not yet, but I think we'll figure it out—his DNA is all over Rock Creek Parkway." Burke admonished himself internally. As much as it seemed to fit, he wasn't talking to another cop. "Hopefully there will be a match in our database."

"And if there isn't?"

Burke hit the pause button. "Look, Bryce . . . it's very early on. I'm guessing you'd like to get home. That'll happen a lot faster if I ask the questions."

"Right, sorry."

"Had this morning's event been on your calendar long?"

"My campaign manager, Mandy, arranges my schedule, but I think the invitation came in a few weeks ago."

"What time did you arrive?"

"I was running a little late, traffic like usual. I walked onto the terrace . . . I don't know, maybe ten minutes before the scheduled start."

"Did you see much in the way of security when you arrived?"

"I remember seeing some uniforms near the door. I think a couple of plainclothes as well."

Burke raised an eyebrow. "You look for that?"

"No. It's just that I go to a lot of events like this, and having been in the military—I sort of recognize the type."

"Okay, yeah. Makes sense you'd be more security-conscious than most congressmen." Burke straightened in his chair. "Bottom line, there was coverage on the place, but somehow an attacker slipped through."

"It happens."

"Tell me, what drew your attention to this individual?"

The congressman shrugged the shoulder that wasn't in a sling. "He seemed out of place. I noticed he was moving toward the podium while everyone else was standing still. And he was wearing a bulky jacket."

"A lot of people were wearing heavy clothes, weren't they? I mean, it was a chilly morning."

"True, but most people were dressed more formally. Jackets and ties, overcoats. I also noticed the guy's hands—his right hand was rigid in his jacket pocket, while the left was free."

Burke looked at Ridgeway curiously.

"It's a little unusual if you think about it," Ridgeway expanded. "People generally move with both hands in or both out."

"Yeah, I guess that would be a little odd."

"Altogether, I spent something like six years downrange. Iraq, Afghanistan, Mali. You never let your guard down in places like that, even when you're inside the wire. Little things can stand out."

Burke opened the laptop on the table between them. "We've got some footage of what happened. Are you up for taking a look, maybe walking me through events from your perspective?"

"Sure," said the congressman, adding a half smile.

Burke booted up the laptop and found the file he wanted. While it loaded, he said idly, "What I'm going to show you is from a hotel security camera on the roof. I'm guessing you haven't been watching the news?"

"Haven't had a minute. I sent my wife a text to say I was okay, then turned off my phone. It was blowing up big time—reporters mostly, trying to get a statement. By the way, will I get my phone back when I leave? They took it when I came inside."

"Yes, absolutely. It's just an internal security thing." Burke half stood, shifted his chair to the end of the table, and angled the screen so they both could see it. "There are at least two other videos making the rounds online."

"Online?" Ridgeway repeated.

"You know how it is—everybody's an amateur videographer these days. A staffer was making a video of the speech and caught part of the confrontation. Somebody else posted footage online that was taken from ground level—we think a nearby parking garage." Burke had already studied that one at length, including the aftermath as people poured out of the building—it looked more like a prison break than an evacuation.

Burke hit play and the video filled the screen. It was a decent angle, a camera near the bar that looked out across the terrace. He said nothing through the first playback, simply letting the video run and watching the congressman's reaction. Ridgeway seemed engrossed, and Burke was convinced he hadn't seen the footage before. He paused at the point where Ridgeway was being pulled back to safety by three men in suits.

The congressman tipped back his chair. "Wow," he said in a barely audible voice. "That was a close call."

Burke weighed the reaction. "It was," he agreed. "But then, this probably wasn't your first near-death experience."

Ridgeway collected himself. "No . . . no, of course not. It's just that in the Army you don't usually have video to prove how close you came to dying."

Burke cued the video backward and paused where the two men first made contact—a blurry rugby tackle by Ridgeway. "I see you went for his hand."

"I assumed he was wearing an explosive vest. The best chance to intervene seemed to be locking down the trigger. My plan was to clamp down tight on his hand, then hope for help. Problem was, once I saw the switch and got a good grip, he really started fighting. I could feel myself losing control of his hand."

"And that's when you decided to launch him over the side?"

"I admit, it wasn't exactly a well-thought-out plan. I was just reacting. In the milliseconds I had to think about . . . it seemed like the best shot. If nothing else, getting him over the wall would protect the people on the roof."

Burke regarded the congressman for a long moment, then nodded thoughtfully. "I've watched this clip a few times, start to finish. I only saw one other option . . . one that I'm glad you didn't take."

"What's that?"

"You could have dived behind the bar to begin with. That's what most people would have done."

Bryce said nothing.

Burke ran through the video a second time, stopping and starting, asking a number of questions. Ridgeway answered them all. At that point he folded the computer shut. "Look, I know you've had a rough day. I'll need to talk to you again soon, put together a formal statement."

"No problem. I'll do whatever I can to help."

Burke stood to suggest they were done. He said, "I know there were mistakes made today, particularly with regard to security. But in the end, things worked out as well as they could have."

The congressman went silent for moment, then grinned and shook his head. "I was just thinking . . . after everything I went through on so many damned deployments. It would have been a hell of a thing to be taken out by a jihadi on a rooftop bar in Washington."

Burke chuckled.

Ridgeway handed over a business card, and said, "Call me anytime, Agent Burke. If I don't answer this number directly, you'll get forwarded to the office. Ask for Mandy—she runs my schedule and I'll make sure she has your name."

Burke took the card. "Thanks."

He led the congressman to the door and found the crew cut down the hall. Burke asked him to escort the congressman outside and reminded him to retrieve Ridgeway's phone.

Moments after they were gone, Alves appeared from an adjacent room.

"So, what did you think?" she asked.

Burke hooked his thumbs into his pockets. "Honestly, if I lived in his district . . . I'd vote for the guy."

6

TRUE FAITH AND ALLEGIANCE

arah looked out the front window, curtains framing the view between perfectly coiffed tiebacks. She saw at least ten people on the sidewalk in front of the house, including a man standing in the dormant flower bed, a microphone in his hand as he talked to a camera. Two news vans were parked across the street, their roof-mounted antennas telescoping into the sky.

"Mom!" Alyssa called excitedly from upstairs. She came quick-stepping down the staircase. "It's Dad!" She held out her iPhone. "He said he couldn't get through on yours. I talked to him and he's good. He said he'll be home soon."

"Thank God!" She swept up the phone. "Bryce?"

"Hey, sweetheart. I'm sorry I couldn't call sooner, but it's been chaos. I hope you got the text I sent."

"Yeah, I did. You're really okay? CNN said you had some minor injuries."

"I'm fine. I'll explain everything when I get home."

Alyssa plopped on the couch, watching and listening. Brimming with excitement.

"I can't imagine what you must be going through," Sarah said.

"It's been a hell of a day."

Sarah moved away from the window. "I should warn you, our front yard is full of news crews."

"Great, just what I need."

Sarah smiled for the first time in seven hours. "No such thing as bad publicity."

Bryce didn't reply.

"Do you want me to play the pissed-off Army wife and send them packing?"

"No, no. You don't have to get involved."

"Maybe you should park at the Smiths' and hop the fence." The Smiths were close friends and lived directly behind. There was a fence between the backyards, but their young son had a ladder permanently wedged near a tree for retrieving errantly punted footballs. "If you go that route, Rex might have at you."

"Who?"

"Rex . . . the retriever that knocks you on your ass with love every time you go over there."

"Oh, right. Actually, about the reporters. I think the best thing would be for me to deal with them. Maybe if I offer up a decent sound bite, they'll have their pound of flesh and move on."

"You know best."

"Okay, see you soon." The call ended. Before she could give the phone back to Alyssa, it began vibrating with multiple inbound texts from friends—her daughter was going to have a busy night. Alyssa snatched her phone back and rushed upstairs.

Sarah diverted to the kitchen, ending up at the stove behind an empty six-quart pot. She felt wary, off-kilter, yet decided it was only natural. The flood of phone calls and messages, a platoon of reporters on their front lawn. *Who wouldn't be on edge?*

She went to the pantry and tried to concentrate on dinner.

The reporters were waiting when Bryce pulled into the driveway. They swirled around his Tesla like remoras around a shark, and were popping off questions before he'd even opened the door.

He stepped out and, with his right arm still in a sling, held up his left palm in a *stop right there* gesture. "Listen, guys, I'll be happy to give you a short statement." He looked around briefly, an artist in search of a landscape. "Let's do it over here."

Bryce led the pack to the sidewalk, drew an imaginary line on the lawn with a finger, then continued a few steps farther. He did an about-face that belonged on a parade ground, took up a perfectly framed position between well-trimmed evergreen hedges. Behind him the gray-paver path showed the way to his modest home, stalwart and enduring in the fading evening. Warm light shone from the windows like embers from a hearth. His wife and daughter, who'd appeared moments after his arrival, stood patiently, expectantly, on the front door's elevated landing. One of the reporters would later remark to her cameraman that she could not have envisioned a more perfect setting.

Bryce waited a moment for all the cameras to be focused, for microphones to be sound-checked. Around the perimeter, clutches of neighbors stood gawking at the scene, and Bryce gave them, collectively, a friendly wave.

When everyone seemed ready, he began.

"This morning we witnessed an attack against the

heart of America. It targeted our government, our institutions, and our people with wanton disregard for human life. I must begin by expressing my thanks. The Metro police in Washington D.C. responded quickly and professionally to this cowardly assault. They secured the scene and took every measure to ensure an organized response. The fire crews and EMTs of Fire Station 1 were on the scene within minutes. By grace of God, there were few injuries to deal with. None of us can say what might come tomorrow, but we can always trust the dedication of our first responders."

Bryce paused, then gestured to his right arm, the sling still in place. "As you can see, I've suffered a minor injury, but I can tell you that Army Rangers bounce back quickly. At this time, I've been instructed by investigators to provide no specific details about the events of this morning. I have given my account of what occurred to FBI special agents and, going forward, I stand ready to support them in every way. The men and women undertaking this inquiry are exceedingly competent, and I have no doubt they will discover who is behind today's reprehensible attack."

A measured pause. "If nothing else, the events of this morning have proved yet again that we, as Americans, can never let our guard down. Many years ago, I took an oath of commission in the United States Army. I swore to uphold the constitution against all enemies, foreign and domestic, and to bear true faith and allegiance to the same. In my view, that promise was permanent. The fact that I no longer wear the uniform each day does not relieve me of that duty. My actions this morning have generated considerable attention, but I assure you that any of my Army brothers or sisters would have acted precisely as I did. This, in essence, is the kind of commitment that sets America apart. Indeed, it is what makes us the greatest nation on earth. Thank you."

The reporters began shouting questions, but Bryce's left palm came up again. "I won't be taking questions tonight, but I promise to make myself available tomorrow. My office will arrange the details. If you'll excuse me, it's been a trying day and I very much want to see my family."

Every camera was still rolling when Congressman Bryce Ridgeway turned up the path and took the final steps toward his family. He greeted them with one arm open wide and was embraced simultaneously by his wife and teenage daughter. The group hug went on for a full thirty seconds. No one could hear the muted words flowing between them, yet even from fifty feet away the daughter's tears were evident. The three of them finally walked inside, still arm-in-arm, and when the front door closed it did so with the finality of a theater curtain dropping.

In a gesture one reporter thought generous, the coach light next to the front door was left on. In fact, it would remain shining that entire night, bright and true like an eternal flame of hope.

7

BELOW THE WATERLINE

Almost without delay, the new three-minute clip of Bryce Ridgeway on the sidewalk in front of his house began beaming across the nation. So too, the world. Having already seen grainy video of his heroics, people who'd never heard of the freshman representative from Virginia were moved to tears by his words. By the end of that night, his congressional Facebook page would have four hundred thousand new likes. His campaign website crashed. In certain quarters of the capital, however, Bryce's performance stirred far more consequential interest.

Not surprisingly, Mandy Treanor was among the first to recognize the significance of what she'd just seen. She had talked to Bryce briefly after he was pulled back over the railing at the Watergate, but at that point the police had swarmed the rooftop and put it on lockdown. Bryce had injured his arm, and while the damage seemed minor, the half dozen EMTs who'd responded deemed him to be one of the few casualties, notwithstanding the bomber himself whose remains were splattered over half a city block. For the rest of the day Bryce hadn't answered his phone.

Now Mandy sat mesmerized watching a newscast from the highboy counter in her apartment, a half-eaten microwaved burrito in front of her. The setting, the story, the delivery—everything had been pitch-perfect.

Bryce's jaw had never been more square, his focus more resolute. His blond hair was slightly tousled, as if he was moments removed from having been pulled back from the precipice. The easy smile was gone, but how could it have been there? Not given what he'd been through. Not with his arm in a sling. After hearing the third replay of Bryce's speech—there was no other word for it—she realized she was witnessing something special. Lightning in a bottle. The core elements had long been in place. The tried and true decency she knew to be in Bryce. His battle-forged martial skills. The nascent political acumen. All of it had fused before her very eyes. Forged into something far, far stronger. The rest of her burrito went cold.

At the FBI field office, Troy Burke was pouring a cup of coffee in the break room when Alves came in and turned up the volume on the TV. They both watched and listened in silence as the man Burke had been questioning a few hours ago spoke from his front lawn. Burke was struck by the congressman's composure and earnestness, both qualities he'd sensed in person. Ridgeway had nearly fallen fifteen floors to his death, yet here he was talking to reporters with all the ease of a winning ball coach, no trace of anything posttraumatic in his mood or demeanor. During the interview Burke had written it off as a soldier's steel, or at the very least, a soldier's compartmentalization. What he saw now only reinforced that opinion. When the clip ended, he and Alves watched the talking heads dissect one exhaustively documented act of bravery. Among the anchor's three guests, all of whom were experts on terrorism, there seemed a rare consensus. Words like "hero" and "selfless" rained like confetti, along with laudatory phrases such as "put his life on the line." The only negative comments were reserved for the Metro Police who, by all appearances, had let a suicide bomber get within twenty paces of a leading presidential candidate.

Alves turned down the volume, and said, "Your boy looked good."

Burke glanced down at her—Alves was eight inches shorter. "You think he's hot?"

"Damn right, I do."

"If we interview him again, you want to do the honors?"

"Better not. I think he's married," said Alves.

"So are you."

Her lips pressed into a grin as she walked away.

Burke looked back at the TV. A photo of Ridgeway dominated the screen. He said, "Huh," then crushed his Styrofoam cup, threw it in the trash, and headed back to the logjam of emails on his computer.

Eighteen blocks from the FBI field office, a very different kind of institution lays reservedly between M and L streets. The Mayflower Hotel is conveniently situated five blocks north of the White House, slightly farther from Capitol Hill, and, perhaps most fittingly, ten blocks south of the D.C. Department of Corrections.

Steeped in a hundred years of Washington history, every president has, by varied means and intentions, roamed The Mayflower's chandelier-encrusted halls. Most have stayed the night, although not always as a matter of record. Charles Lindberg was bestowed the Hubbard Medal at a breakfast attended by a thousand, and some years later Churchill committed a rare faux pas, unaware that his off-color joke at a state dinner would be amplified by the dining room's acoustically perfect muraled domes. It was here that J. Edgar Hoover dined at his private table on virtually every work day for twenty years, the wood floors beneath polished smooth by his heavy black Oxfords. The Mayflower has hosted royalty and spies, movie stars and prostitutes. Her wainscoted walls have backdropped a thousand society weddings and certainly more scandals. Over the years, its lounges and salons have come to be regarded as the inverse of the nearby Capitol building—The Mayflower was a place where little was said, most of it quietly, and where things got done.

On the lee side of happy hour, a great floridfaced man sat in the company of a very dry martini. His name was Henry Arbogast, and he was camped at his customary table near the bar. Having arrived early for a meeting with a farm lobbyist, ostensibly to discuss swine export legislation, he too found himself mesmerized by the scene unfolding on television. The big screen, mounted over the bar and framed by a formidable array of top-shelf liquor, was tuned to Fox News—like most hotels in town, The Mayflower wore its allegiance openly. Moments earlier, someone had prompted the bartender to turn up the volume. This in itself Arbogast thought notable. The hotel's clientele didn't come to be bombarded by today's headlines, but rather to make tomorrow's, and so it was as a grievous breach of etiquette to make such a request. That the bartender had complied was even more extraordinary, although to his credit he kept the volume low.

Arbogast settled back in his club chair—that was how he thought of it, *his* chair—and the sturdy frame groaned in protest. He was to the human species what dreadnoughts were to navies—an imposing and thickly armored variant, built for the most formidable of missions. At six-foot-three and a charitable two-ninety, his pie-plate face was dominated by sagging jowls, and his bulbous nose was flecked with burst capillaries. A longtime political operative, Arbogast had twice been the lieutenant governor of South Dakota. His second term had been abbreviated when he was appointed to half a term in the U.S. Senate, taking the place of the poor incumbent who'd fallen off Mount Rushmore—or so the press release had said. Arbogast was one of the few privy to the truth—the man had actually fallen from a precipice on a South Dakota riding trail, barely within sight of the monument, after suffering a heart attack while trying to keep up with his much younger mistress on a mountain bike. Arbogast had personally engineered the cover-up, seeing no reason to distress the senator's grieving family, or stain his mostly good name. Never one to squander opportunity, he and the governor had made a simple bargain: *keep the party out of trouble, and the seat is yours.*

Arbogast likely would have held the seat in re-election, yet he despised campaigning, and three years in D.C. had opened his restless eyes. He'd identified a number of opportunities that seemed far more inspiring—and, played correctly, far more lucrative. Which was how, nearly eight years ago to the day, Henry Arbogast had become chairman of the Republican National Committee.

It was an organization he'd long viewed as something akin to an iceberg. While the mission on the surface was always in plain sight—the promotion of the conservative agenda—what lay below the waterline carried far greater weight: the linking of lobbyists and deep-pocketed donors to the politicians they yearned to control. Over the years, Arbogast had come to view his job in increasingly transactional terms—he was a broker, a political matchmaker who, regardless of issues or agendas, was due a cut from one side or the other. Whenever possible, both. By that mindset, there were few men in Washington who were better at recognizing opportunity.

Idly caressing his lowball glass with blunt-sausage fingers, Arbogast couldn't take his eyes off the television. One heel tapped the wooden floor as he sat transfixed by the looping images. He suspected tens of millions of Americans were no less enraptured as they watched from dinner tables and on iPhones.

The idea brewing in his head was not completely of his own making. Arbogast had taken a call some weeks ago from a potential new donor who professed very deep pockets—and he thought it might be true. After so many years at the helm of the RNC, his olfactory sense for wealth was acutely tuned. The donor had expressed reservations about where the party was headed. He also offered a vague vision of how to fix it, and a promise of support should Arbogast devise a plan. A promise so specific it had included account numbers and a fee with eight digits to the left of the decimal. Maddeningly, Arbogast had not yet conjured a viable path for fulfilling the donor's vision. Now, however, in the pixelated drama playing out before his eyes, he was beginning to see a solution.

He pulled out a phone with rock-solid encryption—an absolute requirement for a man in his position—and placed a call. It was answered on the second ring by a familiar voice. Male, baritone, Israeli accent.

"I have a special assignment for you," Arbogast said.

"How special?" asked the man, whose name was Kovalsky.

"Top priority. Drop everything you're doing."

"Who's the target?"

"Congressman Bryce Ridgeway."

A pause. "Very well. Is there a deadline?"

"Forty-eight hours."

"You don't ask much."

"And you ask far too much. Earn it." Arbogast ended the call.

8

PLANS AND ACQUISITIONS

The sun cut a gap through the curtains of the eastern window. Sarah blinked awake and checked the bedside clock. 7:10 a.m. Alyssa had to be at school in an hour, yet it felt like a Sunday. That was typically the only day Bryce took off from his workouts, the only day they both slept in. Feeling him stir, she rolled closer and draped an arm over his bare chest.

They'd stayed up late last night, Bryce recounting his tumultuous day to her and Alyssa. His first version of his intervention in the attack was short on details—for Alyssa's benefit, she was sure. Only later, after Alyssa had gone to bed, did he tell Sarah the rest. He recounted how, as he'd lifted the bomber over the railing, the man had reached out and, with surprising strength, dragged him over the edge. He confessed how surprised he'd been, how he'd lunged to get a hand on the rail at the last instant. No sooner had he arrested his fall than the bomb went off. It was far enough away that he was spared any shrapnel, yet the shock wave of the blast had been massive, hammering him against the wall. Somehow, he'd held on.

It all hit Sarah hard. Over the years he'd glossed over a handful of firefights from his deployments, invariably redacted for spousal sensibilities. Never, before last night, had she heard such emotion in Bryce's voice. Her husband, the most rock-solid person she'd ever known, was shaking as he recounted nearly losing his grip and falling to his death. Afterward, Sarah felt like a new threshold had been set in their relationship: a revision of the need-to-know standard.

Of greater concern was his confession after they'd gone to bed: ever since the blast, he'd had a headache. *That explosion . . . it rocked me pretty good.* For months after his Army discharge, Bryce had suffered recurring headaches, likely the result of trauma from the blast that had ended his career. Thankfully, those had dissipated in time. Sarah couldn't say what caused the one yesterday, but she knew it was the real deal—Bryce had taken two Advil. This from a man who viewed medication as a sign of weakness.

After he'd fallen asleep, Sarah had lain awake, telling herself it would all pass. Bryce had had a close call, been in the wrong place at the wrong time. But he'd survived, and soon their lives would get back to normal.

She glanced guardedly at the window. The reporters had left after his comments on the sidewalk last night. Had they returned? Was her husband still a "Breaking News" headline? She pushed the thought away. No phones, no TV, no email—at least for a few more minutes.

Sarah had slept fitfully, but now the rise and fall of Bryce's breathing, slow and easy, had a calming effect. She looked at his face, striking in its stillness. A face that a hundred million people had come to know in the last day. Her eyes fell to his shoulder, the familiar scar. Ragged, four inches long, shaped like a letter V. This was the injury that had ended his Army career—a piece of shrapnel had torn through the connective tissue, damaged the joint. The doctors had done their best, but the end result was inescapable. Bryce would forever have limited use of that arm, no more than half strength. And Army Rangers didn't fight at half strength.

Sarah had seen him deal with a lot during fifteen years of service, but she knew the hardest thing he'd ever done was to take himself out of the fight. His logic reflected the credo of his Ranger badge. *If I can't pull my weight, I'll be a drag on the unit. The one thing I'll never do is put my brothers at risk.* With that realization, his decision was made. He could have taken a staff job. Sat behind a desk in the Pentagon working plans and acquisitions. Six years until retirement. That, of course, had never been an option.

She brushed the scar gently with her fingertips. *The world might know your face, but some parts of you will always be mine.*

He half-rolled closer. Sarah began stroking his chest and his eyes flickered open, squinting against the light. A hazy grin. Her hand was moving toward his stomach when the moment was ruined.

A crash from downstairs.

"Dammit!" Alyssa's voice, jagged, shooting up the stairwell.

Sarah eased out of bed, put on her robe, and went downstairs. She found her daughter in the kitchen wiping a dish towel across the counter. Glass shards carpeted the floor. "What happened?"

"Sorry!" she huffed. "The *stupid* tea maker overflowed, and when I tried to pull the carafe out I dropped it."

"Okay, I can help." She got the broom and dustpan from the closet and began sweeping up glass.

"How's Dad?" Alyssa asked.

"He's fine. Sleeping soundly."

"My phone is melting from so many texts."

"I can imagine. Do you want to go to school today?"

"Why *wouldn't* I? What Dad did was lit and everybody saw it."

"It might be a distraction in class." Sarah immediately sensed a mistake, and added, "But I'm sure it'll blow over soon. I'll take you in."

"Could Dad do it?"

Sarah looked at her daughter blankly. Never before had Alyssa expressed a preference as to who drove her to school. "If he doesn't have appointments, I'm sure he will."

"Talking about me?" Bryce said. He came down the stairs yawning.

"Morning, Dad!" Alyssa said, sunshine in her voice.

Sarah eyed her suspiciously, then went to meet Bryce at the bottom of the stairs. She moved in for a hug, but hesitated. "Where's the sling?"

He moved his arm in small circles, a pitcher warming up. "It's better this morning."

"And your head?"

"I'm good," he said, initiating an in-front-of-the-daughter embrace. When they broke, Bryce went for his phone on the counter. "Damn," he remarked. "Good thing I silenced it last night."

Sarah looked over his shoulder. Seventy-four emails, ninety-eight texts.

"Maybe you better call Mandy," she said.

"Guess so."

He made the call and stepped into the living room.

By the time he came back the mess was cleaned up and Sarah was scrambling eggs.

"So what's going on?" she asked.

"Mandy says videos of the incident are going viral online. Apparently my 'overnight trend' is skyrocketing—whatever the hell that means. She set me up for a press conference this afternoon."

Sarah frowned.

"What's wrong?" he asked.

She gave the eggs a final stir. "I don't know. What you did yesterday was noble. It scared the hell out of me to see it, but you did the right thing. Now . . . I'm afraid people around you are going to use it. They'll want to spin this to boost your career, not to mention their own."

It was a conversation they'd had before. When Bryce was in the Army his missions had been dangerous and demanding, but there was always clarity of purpose within the unit. Politics was altogether different, a quagmire of cross-purposes and self-dealing that seemed to suck the life out of everyone.

Bryce said what he always said. "I can't make the game better unless I play. Mandy's only doing her job."

She looked at him long and hard. They'd been together so long it seemed their thoughts sometimes interweaved. Right then, however, Sarah was drawing a blank.

"Can you take me in this morning?" Alyssa asked while she set the table.

"Sorry, baby, I wish I could but my schedule is packed."

Alyssa's phone buzzed with a message. She glanced at it and rushed upstairs.

Sarah and Bryce exchanged a look. "Boy?" she wondered aloud.

"Probably." He edged closer and wrapped an arm around her, his hand ending on her bottom. "Too bad we can't finish what you were starting up there."

She leaned into him for a moment, then pushed back until their eyes met. "Will you promise me something?"

He responded with an inquisitive look.

"Don't ever be so valiant again."

He grinned and shook his head. "It shouldn't have been a close call. I had a big size advantage over the guy—should have been able to launch him over the rail no problem. He surprised the hell out of me when he nearly dragged me along. That wasn't part of my hastily-drawn plan."

Sarah studied him. Back in the day she'd overheard Bryce make mea culpas to buddies in his unit, generally humorous confessions at beer bashes after a deployment. Yet there had been an unwritten rule that families got a different story: one about warriors who couldn't be beat.

Recognizing perhaps a misstep, Bryce changed course—he smiled The Smile. "You have my word," he assured her. "My days of valor are behind me."

9

BETWEEN JFK AND GOD

Sarah didn't check her phone until she returned home after delivering Alyssa to school. There were over a dozen missed calls—mostly unknown numbers, reporters she assumed. The few contacts she recognized were acquaintances, book club friends and soccer moms who no doubt wanted the scoop. She saw one call that seemed unrelated to Bryce's newfound fame, an editor she'd been playing phone tag with for weeks. There was only one call she wanted to return: Claire Hall, her best friend since college. They typically met once a week, and Sarah could really use a caffeine confessional. She took a seat at the kitchen counter and tapped the screen.

"Hey, girl," Claire said. "How you holding up?"

"So you've seen it."

"Are you kidding? The whole world has seen it. Bryce is a freakin' hero."

"We had a wagon train of reporters circled on our front lawn last night."

"Yeah, I caught his little speech. He sounded good, quite the patriot."

"For better or worse. I guess that's his specialty. Hey, are you free to get together this morning?"

"Ah, sorry. Wish I could but I've got a really important meeting at work." Claire was a research scientist for the Department of Defense. "Could we make it to-morrow morning?"

"Sure. I'm behind on some work myself." It was a stretch but seemed like the gracious exit. She had two short pieces to edit, and the deadline wasn't until next week.

"The Grind at nine?" Claire said, referring to their favorite coffee shop.

"See you then."

Sarah set down her phone, making sure the ringer was off. She looked at the TV but decided it would only be showing reruns of her husband's near-death experience.

She went upstairs and retrieved her work from the nightstand—a printout of two magazine articles and a red pen. On the way out of the bedroom her eye snagged on something on top of Bryce's highboy: his Ranger Battalion challenge coin. Even now, two years removed from the service, he typically took it to work. A handful of congressmen and staffers on the Hill were former Rangers, and they never seemed to tire of challenging Bryce to produce his coin. Sarah had always thought it a peculiar tradition, yet Bryce played along unfailingly, claiming he didn't want to be on the hook for a round of drinks. She decided it was understandable that he'd forgotten the coin today—the distractions of the last twenty-four hours had been monumental.

Or maybe he's finally outgrowing the Army.

She traipsed downstairs toward the coffeepot.

Troy Burke was at the office by eight that morning. It wasn't particularly early by agency standards, but in his own view commendable—he hadn't gotten home until one last night. As the lead investigator on the "Watergate bombing," as it had become known, he didn't expect a regular schedule for weeks.

The third floor was a muddle of sensory confusion, the bright lights inside contrasting to a dour morning in the windows. The aroma of coffee battled that of print toner and whatever caustic disinfectant the cleaners used overnight. He found a sleepy Alves waiting in the cubicle they shared—her apartment was only ten minutes from the office.

"Morning, Nina."

"Is that what it is?"

"Yeah, I know. The next couple of weeks are going to be like that. Anything new?"

"Quite a bit. We've got some new footage. The hotel's security cameras captured our bomber entering a service door and using the staff elevator. The best clip of the attack is still the one that popped up online. It shows pretty much everything: our congressman hanging on for dear life, the bomber falling, and the gory moment when he went to his seventy-one virgins."

"Seventy-two."

A *Christ Almighty* roll of the eyes. "Only a guy would know that. And at that point—who's gonna still be counting?"

"Not going there—it's a me-too world. Any luck sourcing that video?"

"It showed up on YouTube and Twitter at pretty much the same time, but no luck yet tracking down who posted it."

"Think we'll be able to?"

"There's a fair chance. Whoever shot it might want to get famous, maybe cash out on the rights. Does it matter where it came from?"

Burke shrugged. "I guess not."

"It's still the preferred clip on news networks—sanitized, of course, for viewer sensitivities."

"Meaning they cut it off one frame before the bomber becomes a cloud of red vapor?"

"Something like that."

He looked up, saw the wobbling ceiling fan that had been spinning for years—nobody had ever been able to find the switch, and rumors persisted it was actually some kind of listening device installed by either the Chinese or the Russians.

"What about an ID on our attacker?" Burke asked. The forensics team had easily recovered partial remains yesterday.

"The DNA profile came back—we're getting faster. We ran it through CODIS but didn't get a match." She was referring to the Combined DNA Index System, the FBI's inhouse database that contained over twenty million DNA profiles. "We're trying to access a few others—Great Britain, France, the usual overseas allies. That'll take a day or two."

"What about ethnicity?" This was a new channel of pursuit, a genealogical test like those available commercially for determining ethnicity. Burke had never seen great value in knowing what corner of the planet a suspect's ancestors came from, but it was at least quick and reasonably accurate.

"He's Middle Eastern, probably Syrian or Iraqi."

"Claims of responsibility?"

"So far, just the usual cast of crackpots. Manifestos put up on social media, anonymous calls to diplomatic stations. Nothing that sounds legitimate."

"But we're chasing them all down."

"Absolutely. Manpower is not an issue on this one."

Burke thought, *Funny how it never is when politicians are targeted.* What he said was, "Okay, my turn. I talked to the command post on my way in. The scene is big and getting bigger—apparently that's what happens when a bomber detonates a hundred feet in the air. Two windows on the hotel were blown out—or actually in—and we cordoned off the rooms. We have fragments of the bomber's clothing, including a big swathe of his jacket. There was nothing useful in the pockets—no ID or bus tickets.

"The mobile command post is in place outside the hotel. We've got twenty-six people on the ground right now, more inbound. Oh, and we have the guest list from the event—together with the hotel staff and self-identified bystanders, the potential witness list is already over a hundred. I'm organizing a team here at the field office to chase down interviews. We've been promised support from across the spectrum—CIA, NSA, DOD."

Alves blew out a long sigh. "This is gonna take some time."

"Tell me about it. You good to head out to the scene?"

"Let's do it."

They made their way to the elevator, marching down a corridor lined with the official photos of every director since J. Edgar Hoover.

Alves said, "I did notice something in the footage from the service entrance."

"What's that?"

"It struck me that when the bomber came in from

the street, his jacket didn't look as bulky as it did on the roof. Security at that entrance was loose, but there *was* a bomb dog posted near the door. He never alerted."

"You think the bomb was prepositioned in the building?" Burke asked.

"Must've been."

"Which might imply our man had help."

"I'd bet on it."

Burke sank the elevator call button and a car arrived instantly.

"Oh," Alves added, "the director himself wants a video conference this afternoon."

"Of course he does," Burke said, wondering how he would fit that into his day.

Mandy was waiting in Bryce's office at the Rayburn House Office Building. The room was standard-issue, partly a stage for photo ops, but also used for small meetings. The decor was purely subliminal. Enough wood to imbue gravitas, bookshelves of federal code to suggest scholarship, and a nest of folders on a blotter to imply industriousness. The requisite American flag hung from a pole behind the desk—lacking the breeze for which flags were designed, it drooped like a wet towel in a locker room.

When Bryce walked through the door twenty minutes late, she said, "Ready for a big day, Major?"

"Do I have a choice?" He tossed his jacket carelessly on the club chair in the corner.

"Your heroics yesterday have been a breath of fresh air for the networks. For the last few months they've been slogging through the run-up to the presidential primaries. The debates have been a complete snooze."

"Nineteen candidates with . . . what . . . about five hundred years of Washington experience among them?"

"Something like that."

Bryce dropped into his executive chair, while Mandy settled a hip on the desk's well-polished mahogany corner. She hesitated before saying what came next—even if it *was* her job to say it. "Bryce, we need to get some mileage out of what happened yesterday."

He looked at her with surprising interest. "You want to convert my derring-do into votes?"

"Bluntly put, yes." Mandy braced for a counterattack. Bryce was no fan of the Washington playbook, having been brainwashed years ago, apparently, by the Army's God-family-country doctrine.

"Well," he pondered aloud, "I guess that's what I pay you for."

She took a moment to recover, then pressed her advantage. "This is a big opportunity. Your overnight likability ratings are somewhere between JFK and God."

"God has a likability rating?"

"I'm being facetious."

"Right."

"I'm working out a trend analysis to see how long this will last. Oh, and before I forget, I've got an addition to your schedule tomorrow."

"Mandy—"

"No, Bryce, this one you can't miss. Henry Arbogast, the RNC chairman, wants a private meeting, three o'clock at The Mayflower Hotel."

Bryce was silent for a time. "What's it about?"

"I assume he wants to thank you for saving the life of one of his leading presidential candidates."

"Wives included?"

"No, and I'm not going either. You're on your own, although he implied there might be a couple of other heavy hitters."

His eyes narrowed. "Are you saying Arbogast called you directly to schedule this?"

"He did."

"And by doing it that way, you could hardly say no."

"Bryce, there's no downside here. I postponed a speech to the Virginia teacher's union and gave your regrets for the foreign correspondents' dinner. Everyone was very understanding—they know what you've been through."

He spun a one-eighty in his chair and looked out the window. It was the worst view in the Rayburn building, an overlook of the inner courtyard that was completely blocked by a tree. "Okay," he said with measured reluctance. "I'll be there."

10

A HOLOGRAPH OF HERSELF

Three miles outside Rockville, Maryland, a modest four-story office building lays bedded at the end of a curving and canopied road. To those who lived nearby, and there were few by design, the question of who owned the place, and for what purpose, had long been a matter of speculation.

Since its construction four years earlier, the facility had remained both nameless and faceless. The outer façade was a study in earth tones, and the dearth of architectural flourishes befitted a warehouse. The perimeter was ringed by a twelve-foot, razor wire–topped fence. Next to the brick guardhouse was a handsome marquee—the kind that typically trumpeted a Fortune 500 name—that offered nothing beyond a street address, and even this was presented in curiously subdued lettering. The best hint to the building's ownership was found at the lone entry point where a crack squad of Army MPs stood watch 24/7/365.

Taken together, the implication was clear. Anyone with reason to be here knew what was inside. All others could stay damn well away. Yet there was another subtle clue regarding the building's mission, the kind of inference often made by trained intelligence analysts. The building outside Rockville was perfectly equidistant between the headquarters of two vast government agencies: the CIA and the NSA.

"Good morning, Eric." A smiling Claire Hall flashed her creds to the MP at the gate. The young corporal knew her well, but he checked her ID all the same—less a matter of security, she supposed, than for the array of cameras that recorded every entry and exit. What the surveillance captured was a woman in her midthirties, attractive in a corporate way, with wedge-cut hair and an indoor complexion.

"Have a nice day, Dr. Hall." The MP waved her through, and the sturdy barrier opened.

Claire endured a secondary security check at the main entrance, where she deposited her personal phone in a safekeeping area. From there she normally would have taken the elevator to her third-floor lab, but this morning she had an appointment on the ground level. She walked into the anteroom of the facility commander's office.

She'd been prepping for this meeting for weeks, ever since the latest cache of test results had come in. The Technology Applications Research Center, or TARC, was overseen by Air Force Brigadier General Karl Fosse. Fosse was one of three active duty officers assigned to the lab, and while he was a decent sort, with a B.S. in mechanical engineering, his grasp of technology was rooted in the 1990s. To Claire's thinking, the general was far less interested in cutting-edge breakthroughs than climbing his career ladder.

The general was taking a call, and his stiff-mannered receptionist said it might be a few minutes. She offered tea from a Keurig, which Claire politely declined. She was wired enough as it was.

Claire had been lured to TARC from academia. After earning a Ph.D. from Georgia Tech in software engineering, she'd received dozens of job offers from private industry. Her particular area of expertise, however, was inextricably tied to the government. Claire specialized in data fusion—in effect, funneling vast amounts of information into a product that was both usable and timely. When explaining what she did to the uninitiated, she often compared it to the way the human brain integrated various sensory inputs. Sight, sound, hearing, touch, smell—all of it had to be merged into one great picture of the world. In Claire's version, however, the sensory inputs came from thousands of different sources: intelligence agencies, defense networks, law enforcement, private companies. Her project, code-named EPIC, had taken nearly three years to build, and with the yeoman's work complete, her dream was nearing reality.

She was reviewing a printout of the latest test results when the receptionist said, "The general will see you now."

Claire tucked her papers into a portfolio, and in a moment of panic she wondered if she should have stopped in the lady's room for a look in the mirror. She had a workaholic's tendency toward neglect. Skewed hair, rumpled clothes. Gloss hadn't touched her lips in years. Thankfully, a full-length mirror was tacked to one wall, probably for the general's self-inspection of ribbons and insignia. She caught a glance and was relieved to see nothing amiss.

She walked into a standard-issue Army commander's office. One wall held generic family photos, another plaques of appreciation from units departed. Behind the desk were a few conversation pieces, the usual trinkets from overseas postings. A dagger from Korea, a beer stein from Bavaria, and a paddle from Hawaii that had certainly never been used. Claire tried to envision the balding man behind the desk, whose edges had been profoundly softened by middle age, surfing an outrigger canoe down the face of a wave. It didn't float now, and probably never had.

"Good morning, Claire," Fosse said.

"Good morning, General."

"I'm sorry to keep you waiting."

"No problem. How was Colorado?" she asked, desperate to get through the preliminaries. Fosse had recently traveled to Peterson Space Force Base for a cyber conference.

"Oh, the usual. Saw some old friends, drank a beer or two." He gestured for Claire to take one of the two seats facing his desk. "It looks like consolidation of cyber among the services might finally happen."

"I think it's the right move. And it would make EPIC even more relevant." She pulled a sheaf of the latest data from her portfolio. "I have the results from—"

"Claire," the general interrupted. "I'm afraid I have some bad news. I got a call from General Lewis yesterday."

"Who?"

"Major General Lewis at the Pentagon. He works for the assistant Secretary of the Army, Financial Management and Comptroller."

Claire went still, something in the general's tone.

"This year's budget is being slashed. It's not just our group, but R&D across the board. As you know, the president has upped our commitments abroad. We're standing up major new bases in Europe, and a surge is inevitable in the South China Sea. And of course, operational accounts always have priority."

"So . . . I'll have to cut my staff?" she ventured.

Fosse looked at her gravely, a doctor giving bad news. "No . . . I'm afraid it's worse than that. EPIC is being shut down."

Claire opened her mouth to speak but nothing came. Then, "Sir, the latest results are just what we hoped for. EPIC can revolutionize intelligence analysis, give us an advantage over our adversaries."

Fosse held up two hands. The doctor again. Telling her not to give up hope. Telling her how long she had to live. "I understand, Claire, truly I do. You've done extraordinary work, and it won't be lost. Budgetary constraints run in cycles. In two years, maybe four, funding for work like yours will surely be reinstated. But for now . . . the decision has been made."

She stared at him blankly.

"You'll have to give your staff two weeks' notice."

"Two weeks?"

"I can authorize you and one other team member to stay on for a time. You'll need to wind things down. The interfaces and comm links, remove the primary code from the mainframes for secure storage."

Claire looked at him numbly. EPIC was her crowning achievement. She'd created it from scratch, built a working group for its implementation. "How long do I have?" she asked.

"Funding will be zeroed by the end of January."

It hit like a haymaker. *January. Less than three months.*

Fosse kept talking, but his words barely registered. Five minutes later, as Claire zombied toward the door, his parting words came as little more than background noise. Something about being "so sorry."

Claire didn't go to her office. Her team would be there and she couldn't face them. Not yet. She made her way back to the entrance, stepped outside, and was greeted by a brittle November morning. A gusty wind swept leaves across the parking lot, trees shivering in its wake. She stood motionless, not feeling the cold, not feeling anything. Like a holograph of herself.

Never in her life had she felt so defeated.

11

GOING ALL PTSD

For Mandy the day was frenzied. She'd expected that the initial maelstrom, fueled by footage of Bryce's heroics, would ease off by noon. Quite the opposite happened. She tried to keep her congressman on schedule but it was entirely hopeless. Congress was in session, meaning everyone was in town, and there wasn't a congressman, lobbyist, or staffer on the Hill who didn't want a picture with the hero of the day—no doubt for instant posting to their social media pages.

To his credit, Bryce held up well. He gave sound bites Mandy couldn't have scripted better herself. Patriotic, humble, strong. The arm sling was gone, implying a man who either healed quickly or endured pain well. Either way, a win. In seemingly every hall of the Rayburn building, Bryce was buttonholed for photos and sound bites. Without fail, he looked good and sounded good. Mandy couldn't keep up with the messages on her phone, and by three that afternoon she was ignoring any contact below cabinet level. It was four thirty when they finally reached his office, closed the door, and instructed Janet, his receptionist, to pull up the drawbridge.

If Bryce's office had any charm, it came from the stately writing desk along the back wall. The desk had been gifted him by his retiring predecessor, and from a hidden cabinet Bryce extracted a bottle of Barrell bourbon and two tumblers. He set them both up—a steward had supplied a bucket of ice—and handed Mandy a bracer.

"To the Unsub of the Watergate Hotel," he said, lifting his glass with mock ceremony. "May all terrorists be such amateurs."

Mandy clinked her tumbler to his but didn't reply.

Bryce sank into a year-old chair behind his desk, its freshman leather crinkling like bubble wrap. He loosened his tie, leaned back, and crossed his legs indifferently on the desk. His sleeves were already rolled up, as they'd been all afternoon. Put a Budweiser and a remote in his hands, Mandy thought, and he could be settling in for a playoff game.

"How are you holding up?" she asked.

"Just great."

"You and I have been through a lot, but never anything like this."

"No politician in town has gone through anything like this."

Her campaign manager lobe took over. "We can still get mileage out of it. I was thinking you could introduce a bill, maybe something about combating terrorism. You'd get a lot of cosponsors right now."

"I could make it the price of a photo op," he said flippantly, swiveling his chair toward the terrible view.

"Bryce, this is an opportunity to make some headway."

"Headway?" he shot back. "You mean I should

capitalize on some poor Muslim kid blowing himself up in the name of Allah?"

"That's not what I meant. And how do you even know he was Muslim?"

"He looked like a raghead."

She double-checked the door—thankfully it was closed tight. "I'll thank you to keep such observations to yourself, congressman."

He turned back to face her, his expression oddly distant. It was a look she'd never seen before. Mandy knew Dad Bryce and Photo Op Bryce and Town Hall Bryce. Right then it was . . . Stone Cold Bryce.

"Do you know how many men like that I've killed?" he asked in a dead tone.

Mandy set her drink silently on the desk. She was rarely speechless but had no idea how to respond. An uncomfortable silence settled. Bryce suddenly broke into a grin and began laughing.

"Had you going, didn't I?"

She smiled back thinly.

"Don't worry, I'm not going all PTSD on you."

He got up and came around the desk, eased toward her. For the second time in a minute she was put off—this time not by his stare, but by his closeness. She looked up at his expressionless face, caught traces of a musky scent—this morning's cologne on top of a hectic workday.

After a long moment, he snapped back the last of his drink and set the tumbler on the writing desk. "I gotta get home, Mandy. I'll see you tomorrow."

She stared at the door after he was gone. They'd been working together for two years now, and in all that time she'd never felt uncomfortable around Bryce. She wasn't sure if she felt that way now.

"Well . . ." she murmured, tipping back the last of her own drink, "that was awkward."

Sarah heard the front door open at the usual time, Alyssa arriving home from school after clubs. Two months ago, she'd been picking her up at the parent loop, but now friends were driving her home. Soon all bets would be off—she'd gotten her learner's permit three months ago. Her daughter was growing up fast.

"Hi, Mom," she called out, her voice cracked and brittle. On the verge of . . . something.

Sarah was ready with an apple and some leftover mac and cheese—Alyssa was always famished when she got home from school. "I'm in the kitchen."

Her daughter came in and dropped her backpack on a chair as if punishing it.

"How was your day?" Sarah asked, sliding the snack warily across the counter.

Alyssa settled behind it with a glowering expression. "Okay."

Sarah was familiar with her daughter's moods— they'd been on clear display in recent years—yet this seemed beyond hormones. She moved to the opposite side of the counter.

"Want to talk about it?"

A heavy sigh. "The kids at school were insane today. Everywhere I went people were huddled around phones watching the videos of Dad. I even saw Mr. Guerlich doing it during our chemistry quiz."

"I take it you've seen these videos?"

"Some of them. There are like five different ones now."

"Are the kids teasing you about it?"

"No, it's not that. I've gotten really popular all the

sudden. It's just that . . . they act like they're watching trailers from some Hollywood movie. They laugh and joke about it. But to me . . ." her voice broke, "it's my *dad*, and he almost died!"

Sarah walked around the counter and gave her daughter a hug. Tears began to flow.

She waited as a day's worth of pent-up emotions subsided. The food helped, and they talked all the way to an empty plate. That was followed by a cup of half-caf. By the time Alyssa went upstairs to do homework, she was back on level ground.

Sarah felt herself tipping the other way.

She was cleaning up afterward, trying to predict what might arise at school tomorrow, when her phone buzzed. She saw a text from Bryce: Home late tonight. Sorry. Work is crazy. Love, B.

Sarah typed out the only viable reply: No problem. Will wait up for you. Love, S.

12

WORLD'S WORST WINE STEWARD

Alyssa was much improved at dinner. Sarah made beef tacos, one her favorites, and after helping with the dishes her daughter retreated to her room. Supposedly to do homework, but doubtless with some messaging built in. By ten o'clock the light in her room was out.

Sarah settled on the couch in the company of a lighthearted novel—not work, but a pure pleasure read. She had trouble focusing and soon drifted off.

She was stirred awake by the rattle of the front door opening.

Bryce walked in, his tie hanging around his neck like a withered scarf. His shirt looked like he'd slept in it. Sarah got up and gave him a heartfelt hug. When she pulled away he removed a dishrag from her shoulder—she hadn't realized it was there.

"I've been gone too long."

She smiled wearily.

"Sorry I'm so late." He leaned in and kissed her on the cheek, then headed for the kitchen. She snapped the dishcloth on his receding ass. Forgiveness complete.

"Have you eaten?" she asked. "I saved a couple of tacos."

"No, thanks. I just need a drink. Mandy and I ordered takeout—we were at the office all night."

"Tough day, huh?" She moved behind him and started massaging his shoulders.

"Yeah, nonstop. I must have looked at fifty cameras today."

"What about tomorrow?"

"More of the same, I guess. In the afternoon I've got a meeting with the RNC chairman, Henry Arbogast."

Sarah kept her hands on his back, but leaned around to catch his eye. "Really? That's unusual. What's it about?"

"Don't know, but if I were to guess—he probably wants to thank me for keeping one of his candidates from being blown to bits."

Sarah sighed. "Naturally. Well . . . sounds like some good face time. I doubt many freshmen in the House have had a private meeting with him."

"Mandy said there might be a couple of others coming. But yeah, it should be good." He performed a playful reversal and pressed his hip into her backside. "What do you think? Bottle of red?"

"Sounds great."

He perused the rack near the dining room table and plucked out a Merlot. "Ahh . . . where's the corkscrew?"

"Right where it always is."

She went to get two glasses from the kitchen. Bryce followed, and soon he was standing with the bottle, looking lost, his eyes alternating between kitchen drawers. Sarah returned to the dining room, and from a shelf near the wine rack she pulled the corkscrew out of a pinch-pot—an ancient preschool treasure of Alyssa's. She handed it over to the world's worst wine steward.

"Right," he said. "Meet you in the living room? I'll get a fire going."

"Done."

He disappeared through the connector. Sarah stood still for a moment, but her distraction was broken when she heard the *plop* of the cork being pulled from the bottle.

Eighty yards away, in front of the Schreibman's house two doors down, the *plop* was picked up loud and clear by a highly sensitive directional microphone. The microphone was concealed artfully in the sidewall of a work van, right behind the logo of a notional plumbing company. Were anyone to call the phone number beneath the logo, they would hear a short message followed by a request to leave a number for a callback. To the best of the owner's knowledge, no one had ever done so.

Kovalsky sat behind a computer in the van's concealed cabin—the only windows were those in front, and he'd installed dual curtains to shield the darkened work area. He'd parked as far away as he could, and on a slight angle to the curb to give the antenna a better look angle. Last night he hadn't been able to get near the place until very late, the residence having been surrounded by news vans and gawkers.

He was wearing a noise cancelling headset, and though he'd heard the wine bottle open—few sounds were so easily recognizable—it hardly seemed notable. Kovalsky remained focused on his primary mission, which was so far going well. It had taken only twenty minutes to hack the home's Wi-Fi router. The password had been reasonably good, twelve random characters and numbers, but his brute force cracking software was better. It was top-of-the-line code, acquired from Mossad—something he'd awarded himself on leaving as a kind of retirement gift.

Once he was in, the chore became to penetrate individual devices. He'd so far identified two cell phones—those of the wife and daughter—the wife's laptop, and an iPad owned by the congressman himself. This last device became his focus. For the most part, he downloaded files and histories for later study, yet he also took the time to insert a tracking app that would give him updates over the next twenty-four hours. After that, the software would scramble itself, leaving no trace of its existence or purpose.

Kovalsky checked his watch. 10:15. It was time to wrap things up. Plumbers rarely worked this late, no matter the premium, and the van hadn't moved in nearly two hours. More to the point, he was quite sure he had what he needed. With his research phase complete, it was time to move on.

Tomorrow, on schedule, he would fulfill the final act of a very lucrative contract.

13

A DAMNED
GOOD-LOOKING MAN

Because Henry Arbogast's political party was the lifeblood of The Mayflower, he had no trouble securing a private room for the meeting. The East Room was selected, and furnished with a large round table and four chairs that blended with the decor: dark blue carpet, inlaid with rose petals and fleur-de-lis, and walls accented by pillars and gold trim. Portraits of presidents, all with conservative leanings, observed from the surrounding walls. There was a deepness to the room Arbogast had always appreciated, as if its designers had fully anticipated meetings like the one about to convene.

He sat at the table with three others. Carlson Watts was the Senate majority leader, and Elizabeth Carr, his minority counterpart in the House. The third person was Arbogast's researcher, Kovalsky, who was waiting patiently as everyone digested his three-page executive summary.

The fact that it was a mere three pages was a positive sign. Arbogast had commissioned Kovalsky to undertake many such investigations, and most reports were far longer. This job had been rushed, yet Kovalsky was extremely thorough, and the fact that he'd dug up no hidden darkness on their subject was a good thing.

A very good thing.

Carr was the last to finish reading, and when she looked up Arbogast regarded Washington's two most important Republicans in turn.

"Do either of you have questions for Mr. Kovalsky?" he asked.

Senator Watts, ever cautious, addressed the researcher. "How far back did you go?"

Kovalsky said, "As far as anyone can, aside from tracking down friends and family and former employers for interviews. When you get back into the nineties, digital records become less reliable. Fortunately, the age of our subject is in our favor—that takes us back to his middle school years, which is generally adequate."

Watts nodded, asked for a few clarifications, which Kovalsky handled ably. He then said he had nothing more.

Everyone looked at Elizabeth Carr. "No," she said, "I'm satisfied. I think, given the current climate, this is definitely the right move."

With that settled, Kovalsky was dismissed, and the three most powerful Republicans in the nation were alone. It was a rare event for them to meet—and a reflection of the party's grave trajectory. Arbogast hoped this would not be lost on the man about to join them: the junior congressman from Virginia's Tenth.

He picked up his phone and sent a one-word text.

As they waited, Watts began a telling joke about a certain liberal news anchor. He never reached the punch line. Everyone shifted their attention when the door opened.

Bryce Ridgeway walked in, escorted by a security man. The usher quickly disappeared, closing the door behind him, and Ridgeway paused to take in the scene. He then set out across the royal blue carpet.

Arbogast was not unhappy with what he saw. The congressman had a way about him, a natural aura of youth and vibrancy. He was slightly on the tall side, trim and athletic, and if there were any effects from his injuries—either those of recent days or his service in the Army—Arbogast didn't see them. He was wearing a well-fitted suit and double-Windsored tie, and the sum image caused the RNC chair to recall a comment from yesterday's online Washington Post article, which had included a photo of Ridgeway—in the words of the female contributor, he was "a damned good-looking man."

In that moment, Ridgeway appeared guarded. Arbogast expected nothing less. Everyone at the table stood. In any public setting the legislators would have taken the lead, yet here the RNC chair was out front. "Bryce, good to see you. Henry Arbogast. We met briefly at the freshman swearing-in ceremony."

Bryce paused behind the lone empty chair. "Yes, I remember."

"And of course, you know Senator Watts, the majority leader."

Bryce shook his hand, and said, "Certainly by reputation, although I don't think I've ever had the pleasure."

"Actually, we did meet once," Watts said. "It was only briefly, at a swearing-in bash."

"Did we? Sorry, but my first few months on the Hill were a blur."

Watts smiled, his teeth an ivory keyboard. The same smile he likely gave a hundred times a day to lobbyists and contributors. Almost genuine.

Elizabeth Carr stepped forward—as House leader, she was the most familiar of the three. "Bryce, I can't thank you enough for what you did. You literally saved Senator Morales's life."

"I meant what I said on camera afterward. I was only doing my duty."

The three hosts beamed.

On Arbogast's cue, everyone sank into their soft leather chairs. He took the lead, asking about the media whirlwind Bryce had been enduring in recent days. Bryce played along for a time, but it didn't take long for him to air his suspicion.

"Forgive me," he said, "but I don't think you've brought me here for a pat on the back."

Arbogast smiled. And truly he was pleased. He liked directness.

"To begin, Bryce, what we're about to discuss must remain in strictest confidence." He waited for a nod and got one. "Honestly, what brings us here today is our concern for the party." Arbogast paused for good measure. "I have been in politics for a very long time, and if there's one thing I've learned it's that change is more often the offspring of opportunity than planning. There are singular events, things that unexpectedly shift the playing field. Iraq's invasion of Kuwait, the 9/11 attacks, the economic collapse of 2008, COVID-19. One rarely sees such upheavals coming. My duty, in managing the party, is to respond to them. And, of course, benefit wherever possible.

"As I'm sure you're aware, Bryce, you've become a household name overnight. The closest parallel to the attention you're getting might be Lindberg crossing the Atlantic—although that *was* a bit before my time."

Ridgeway smiled politely. He was wondering where this was going.

"As you know, our party is strong. We currently control the Senate, and are closing in on the House. Unfortunately, the Democrats have the White House. President Connolly has proven adept at obstructing our agenda, using the veto and executive orders to block conservative policy on every front."

Arbogast joined his fingertips beneath his chin, almost as if in prayer. "You've captured the nation's imagination, and in a way we haven't seen in a very long time. On top of that, your record of service, both in the Army and during your brief time in Congress, has been nothing short of exemplary. Bryce, our party is on the verge of great things, but to succeed we *must* win the White House. At present, there are nineteen contenders for the Republican nomination, and no clear front-runner. Of the seven with a realistic chance, the youngest is sixty-four years old—men and women, I dare say, from an era that's drifting into the past. Polling tells us enthusiasm among prospective voters is critically low."

He paused, wanting to emphasize what came next. Ridgeway filled the gap with, "And let me guess . . . you want me to do my part. An endorsement to put your preferred candidate over the top?"

Arbogast exchanged a look with the others. All of them smiled softly. "No, Bryce, it's quite more than that. America is polarized as never before. The electorate is disengaged. President Connolly has fumbled the economy and he's facing scandals in virtually every cabinet agency. His big government ideas are exploding the national debt. It was almost painful to watch his press conference yesterday—the man can no longer hide his incompetency. As one editorial put it this morning, he's the political equivalent of a bad carpenter—a man who cuts twice before measuring once."

Carr picked up, "The problem, Bryce, is that our own party's candidates are . . . shall we say, less than inspiring. Those leading the pack are exclusively creatures of this city."

Carr continued for a time, and then Watts took his turn. As they spoke, Arbogast studied Ridgeway, probing the handsome face for a reaction. Curiously, he saw nothing. The RNC chair, who considered himself a decent poker player, vowed to never engage the congressman on that front.

When Watts was finished, Arbogast decided it was time for the sharks to stop circling. "By now I think you see what we have in mind, Bryce. The GOP desperately needs a fresh face, someone who can engage the next generation. We would very much like *you* to be that person."

Ridgeway's gaze stepped between the power brokers. "Me . . . run for president."

"How does it sound? President Bryce Ridgeway."

The words hung in the air like some unseen gravitational force.

"You can't be completely surprised," Arbogast prodded. "You've led an extraordinary life, Bryce, and worked hard to get where you are. Everyone in this town dreams of a day like this, and while yours has appeared out of nowhere, you've earned it. I can also tell you that your father and I have been friends for a long time—he's always had the highest hopes for you."

"How is he, by the way?" Carr asked.

"No different," Ridgeway managed. "His memory isn't what it used to be, but he's hanging on."

"Please give him my best when you see him."

Ridgeway promised that he would, yet gave no response to the greater question.

Arbogast said, "Understand, our offer comes with certain advantages. You would be getting into the race late, but I've had a few exploratory, off-the-record discussions with certain megadonors. If you were to run, I think you could expect strong financial backing. The RNC can facilitate that, and also help you get a staff up to speed, people who know the ground and digital games on a national level."

Ridgeway's gaze narrowed. "What about Mandy, my current manager?"

Senator Watts said, "By all accounts she's done a wonderful job, Bryce. But understand, this elevates things to a whole new level."

"If you like," Arbogast said, "I'm sure we can find a spot for her. But we have to put experienced people at the top."

Ridgeway didn't reply.

Arbogast said, "Look, I know this is a lot to take in. Unfortunately, time *is* critical—certain primary filing deadlines are only days away. That said, we can't expect you to make such a decision without consulting your family. Talk to them tonight, sleep on it. But we must have an answer tomorrow."

Ridgeway nodded slowly. "All right."

Arbogast looked at him very directly. "I must also tell you that our support is conditional."

"Conditional?"

"When a man runs for president, he can expect

his background to be investigated thoroughly. I will tell you up front that we've done our due diligence. I've had a man going over your history in recent days. So far, he's uncovered nothing . . . untoward. That said, we've supported candidates in the past who have tried to conceal indiscretions. Marital infidelity, financial impropriety, campaign abuses. Make no mistake—others will spare no effort or expense in sifting through your past. We can give you an excellent shot at winning the presidency, Bryce. But if there is anything in your history we should know about—anything *at all*—now is the time to make it known."

As three sets of eyes drilled him in the silence, Bryce Ridgeway held an even gaze, and said, "My life is an open book. I've got nothing to hide."

14

THE MOTHER OF ALL BOMBS

S arah took the call from Bryce as she was picking up Alyssa from soccer practice—he wanted to meet for dinner at Demetrio's, their favorite hole-in-the-wall Italian joint. She didn't argue, happy to not have to rush home and cook. Even more, she was ready for a little normalcy after the mayhem of recent days.

The restaurant had an authentic feel, a disjointed warren of rooms in a hundred-year-old building beside a cobblestone street. Neon beer signs hovered over tables with red-and-white checked tablecloths, and red-leather booths lined the walls, each with its own unique stained-glass lamp. The smells were straight from Italy, oven-baked dough and roasting garlic.

Sarah didn't see Bryce in the first two rooms, so she kept moving toward the back. Alyssa was right behind, her cleats clacking over the waxed tile floor. She found Bryce sitting at an isolated corner table—over the years, probably the only one they'd never occupied. The parents kissed while their daughter went to the restroom, ostensibly to clean up after miring around for ninety minutes on a muddy field.

"Never sat here before," Sarah said, sliding into the booth across from him.

"I thought a little privacy might be nice."

She looked around, saw an elderly woman in a

green jacket staring. Bryce, an anonymous congress-man two days ago, was suddenly one of the most rec-ognized faces in the country. "I feel like we should be wearing baseball caps and sunglasses."

"I know. I've got interviews scheduled a month out. If Mandy had her way I'd be—"

"Bryce," she said, cutting him off. "While it's just you and I . . . I had a talk with Alyssa."

"What about?"

Sarah felt the green jacket watching. She tried to tune it out. "I didn't mention it last night, but she's up-set. Your heroics have been getting a lot of attention at school."

"Can't say that I'm surprised."

"The thing is, she's having trouble dealing with it."

"In what way?"

"Those videos that went viral. To the other kids, it's like a clip from an action movie or something. But to her . . . she's watching her father nearly get killed."

He nodded understandingly.

"When you were in the Army, we did our best to be honest with her. She understood you were in dan-ger during deployments. But she was young then, so it was all kind of academic."

"And this is more real."

"Right there on YouTube from five different an-gles."

He cast a glance toward the restroom. "How do you want to handle it?"

"I don't know. I just wanted you to know she's struggling with this."

"Okay, noted." Then a hesitation.

"What?"

"We need to talk about something, the three of us."

"That sounds ominous."

"No, it's all good. But—" He gave her a sideways nod. Alyssa came bounding to the table and slid onto the bench seat next to Sarah. A familiar waitress buzzed up right behind her, delivered their usual drinks, then hovered like a hummingbird in front of a flower.

"Same as always?" Alyssa asked.

"Sure," replied Bryce.

Sarah placed the order. "Large pizza, half cheese for the girls, half sausage and anchovies for the cavemen."

The waitress scrawled the order on her pad and was gone. They bantered for a time about school and soccer, no mention of recent events. Sarah suspected it was intentional on everyone's part—concentrating on the sunshine while storm clouds were brewing. She felt more relaxed than she had in days. The woman in the green jacket had even gone back to her calzone.

Finally, after Alyssa's account of a goal scored in today's scrimmage, Bryce took on a more serious tone. "I had a meeting today." He paused there, adding weight to what was coming—congressmen had meetings every day. "It was with the top Republican in the House and the Senate majority leader."

"Wow," said Alyssa. "Even I know who they are."

Sarah glanced at her daughter curiously—Alyssa had never shown a whit of interest in politics.

"There was one other person," Bryce continued. "Henry Arbogast, head of the Republican National Committee." Another hesitation.

It felt like a held breath, and Sarah sensed a twinge of something foreign.

"They want me to run for president."

The twinge went to full-on numbness.

Alyssa, who'd been sucking Coke through a straw, coughed and sputtered, caramel liquid dripping from her nose. She looked at him as she recovered, then shot a glance at her mother. "Are you *serious*?"

"It seems they are. I said I wouldn't commit until I'd discussed it with my family."

"Oh my God!" Alyssa gushed. *"President?"*

Bryce made a calming motion: both hands, palms-down. "Not so loud. They're asking me to *run*, but that's a long way from the White House."

"Everyone I know would vote for you!" Alyssa said in a barely lower voice.

"Everyone you know is too young to vote," he countered.

"No, I know some seniors. This is *so* cool! I'd be like instantly popular."

Sarah could almost see the grandiose visions spinning in her daughter's head.

Alyssa asked, "Would we actually live in the White House?"

"Baby, there's a lot to this decision. We need to think about it rationally. It would change our lives, even if I don't win."

"But if you did . . . would I like have Secret Service guys following me everywhere?"

"If I got elected, yes, that's part of the bargain."

And with good reason, Sarah thought, but didn't say. Indeed, she hadn't said a word since Bryce had dropped the mother of all bombs. He looked at her tentatively. "Your thoughts?"

"I . . . I don't know what to say." And truly she didn't.

Sarah had always considered herself a supportive

wife. In the Army she'd gone to the wives' club meetings, the baby showers—at least, when she hadn't been up against a deadline. She might not have been a standard-issue Army spouse, but she'd done her part for Bryce. When he turned to politics the landscape shifted, high-end dinners and fundraisers, yet still she'd done her bit. But *this* . . . this had never been on her radar.

"You're right," she finally said. "It would definitely change our lives."

He said, "Look, I know how you feel. This took me by surprise too. But let me explain my thinking. This country is in trouble—I know better than most because I've had an inside view for the last year. It's run by professional politicians, most of them millionaires going in, all of them millionaires going out."

"And you can fix that?" Sarah asked.

"I don't know. But to find out, I have to get my foot in the door."

"Of 1600 Pennsylvania Avenue."

"That would be such a *lit* address!" Alyssa beamed.

Sarah's focus on Bryce never wavered. "I've heard a lot of men and women start out with platforms like that. 'Time for a change. A better America.' I've never seen one that didn't become part of the problem. The backroom dealing, the lobbyists. Do you really think you'd be different?" Her gaze was level, strong. Demanding an answer.

"What do you think?" he countered.

Sarah knew there could be only one response. But still she hesitated. "Yes . . . I think you might have a chance."

Bryce smiled.

Sarah said, "It's too bad your father can't be here. This was his dream."

"He told me as much once—as I remember it, he was trying to talk me out of joining the Army." Bryce went on to explain things much as Arbogast had: the weak field of candidates, the RNC's desire to find a younger, fresher face to lead the new generation. He told them how his recent heroics had vaulted him into consideration by the party.

"We don't have to decide immediately, but there is some urgency. The filing deadlines are getting close for a number of state primaries. I'd need to work fast to get a ground game in place. Let's sleep on it and talk again in the morning. Until then, not a word to anyone." He looked squarely at Alyssa. She was positively giddy but nodded to say she understood.

Sarah felt as if she were on top of a mountain, only one she hadn't climbed herself. More like she'd been dropped by a helicopter, left scrambling for purchase on loose stones. *Primary deadlines, ground game.* She knew Bryce better than anyone, and so she knew *his* decision had been made.

"You'd be such an awesome First Lady!" Alyssa said.

Sarah looked at her daughter, thunderstruck by the transformation.

The pizza came five minutes later. Alyssa was first in line, famished from either two hours of soccer or the prospect of being First Daughter. Bryce slid a cheesy triangle onto Sarah's plate, using a fork to spin away the connecting strands of cheese. He then took a slice of the other half and began picking off anchovies.

Sarah watched him distractedly. "What are you doing? You've always loved those."

He shrugged it off. "Guess I'm losing my taste for them. But the sausage is great."

15

8.1 SECONDS

The coffeemaker in the field office break room was not of this millennium. Nor was it for the faint of heart. Nicknamed La Brea, its spewings resembled tar from the famous Pleistocene pits of California. Which was why, when Special Agent Burke arrived for his first meeting of the day, he had a Starbucks Venti in hand.

It was not yet seven in the morning, but Alves had called an hour ago, causing him to wonder if she ever slept. They converged in the third-floor lobby.

"Forensics has something they want to show us in The Lab," Alves said. They began walking in that direction. "We got an ID on our bomber," she added, waving a printout at him.

Burke was mildly surprised. "That was quick. What's the degree of confidence?"

"As close to a hundred percent it as gets in our business." She read from the paper. "Mohammed al-Qusami, Saudi national, twenty-one years old. Former ISIS fighter, captured in northern Syria four years ago. The Kurds had him in lockup for over a year, then he escaped when Turkish forces came across the border and everything went to hell. Fortunately, during his captivity the Brits paid a visit and took pictures of all the detainees for their rogues' gallery. While they were at it, they took DNA samples. Al-Qusami's is a perfect match to the bits and pieces we're collecting outside the Watergate."

"Good on the Brits for taking the initiative. Any idea where al-Qusami went after his jailbreak?"

"Once we nailed down the name, we found a file in our own archives. Unfortunately, combined with what the Brits had . . ." She held up a single page. "There was a report that some of the group he escaped with went south. The question of who they eventually fell in with is anybody's guess. That was Assad's territory then, and mostly still is. Syria, of course, is swarming with Russians and Iranians, and then you've got about twenty or so different militias. Odds are, al-Qusami and his buddies either joined one of the militias, or went to ground waiting for ISIS to make its comeback."

"Lovely. If we had some credible claim of responsibility for this attack we might know where to start."

"We're still watching, but nothing passes the sniff test yet. On a more positive note, the night shift began comparing the picture the Brits provided to recent arrivals at our big east coast airports—Dulles, Atlanta, JFK. Our software is getting really good at matching surveillance footage with known faces, and it didn't take long. Al-Qusami flew into Dulles five days ago, a nonstop from Cairo. After clearing immigration, he took a taxi to a very unclean hotel twenty minutes from the Watergate—the place has all the ambiance of a Turkish prison. We've had a team going over the room for a couple of hours, but so far it's a dry hole."

"Was this guy on the terrorist watch list?"

"Mohammed al-Qusami was, but all we had was the name when he arrived—we hadn't tied in the photo yet."

"Meaning he entered under a false ID," Burke surmised.

"Yep, and a pretty good one. We haven't found any trace of the passport, so he must have ditched it at some point. But between immigration and the airline, we were able to find the name he was traveling under. That's what led us to the hotel room. It's a Saudi identity. Not legitimate, but backstopped pretty professionally—a real passport was issued six months ago. Valid address, employment records, travel history, the works. Somebody went to a lot of trouble to make Mo's entry seamless."

Reaching the door of the forensics room—fondly referred to as The Lab—Burke drew to a stop. "So we've got a twenty-one-year-old kid who probably started fighting for ISIS when he was, what . . . seventeen?"

"Probably less."

"Which means the chances are good he's not highly educated. Probably never had any training beyond which end of a Kalashnikov to point downrange."

"That'd be my take. He was a low-level recruit— the usual jihadi cannon fodder."

Burke stood pondering. "That all fits the profile of a suicide bomber, I guess. Young radicalized male, early exit to Paradise. Still . . . something about it feels wrong."

"In what way?"

Burke pondered, then shook his head. "I dunno."

"Oh, we also had a couple of dogs work the hotel. They hit on an equipment room near the service elevator, some kind of control closet for the fire sprinkler system. Traces tested out positive for Semtex."

Burke eyed his partner. "What do you think? Any chance he's a lone wolf?"

"It's conceivable he could have put it there himself the day before, but given the timeline of his arrival—it seems really tight. To begin, he would have had to acquire the explosives. I can't imagine him driving out to West Virginia and busting into the explosives shed of some mining operation."

"Agreed," Burke said. "One way or another, the kid had help. Was he traveling alone?"

"As far as we know, yes. No apparent associations on the flight in, and the desk clerk at the hotel where he stayed remembered him checking in alone and never saw any visitors."

"Let's track back on that camera footage from the hotel service entrance, at least a week. I'm thinking somebody probably delivered a package before our bomber was even in the country."

"I'll work on it."

Burke eyed the door to The Lab. He didn't fantasize that every answer was inside. But one or two would be nice. "All right, let's see what the OTD guys have."

OTD was the agency's Operational Technology Division. Burke and Alves walked into an expansive room bristling with equipment. Hardware and monitors topped every table, and cables ran across the floor like the root system of some vast computational forest. The trash can overflowed with takeout food containers, and a whiteboard on the far wall displayed lines of code that looked like dry-erase hieroglyphics.

Burke immediately recognized Tom Waters, the local office's leading expert on bombs and explosives.

He'd worked with Waters before, and in every case had been impressed by his depth of knowledge. Seated next to him was a younger man—wrestler's build, mil-spec haircut, two-day growth of beard.

Waters rose and shook hands with Burke and Alves, then introduced the younger man. "This is Cody Aarons. I called him in special for this one." More handshakes as Waters continued, "I know my stuff domestically, but Cody here is fresh from downrange. He was Army EOD, spent most of the last six years in the Middle East. The bombmakers there, the ones who build the vests and IEDs that kill so many of our guys, improvise constantly. Since we don't know the provenance of this device, I wanted every opinion I could get, and Cody knows the latest trends overseas."

"Sounds like a good idea," said Burke. "What's the consensus?"

Waters deferred to Aarons, who picked up, "We've narrowed things down, but we don't have the whole picture yet. The guys on scene are still finding bits and pieces of the device, and we haven't identified every fragment of what's in the evidence room. It's going to take some time to put together. I can tell you the explosive material was definitely Semtex."

"Can it be sourced?"

Waters said, "The factory adds chemical taggants to identify batches, but postexplosion—it gets more complicated. There are tons of Semtex floating around the world, getting sold and resold, smuggled across borders. It's notoriously difficult to track. This vest was rigged from two nylon backpacks, the kind you can buy at any big box store in the world. They packed it with commercial grade hardware, which is equally useless for determining origin. The nuts, bolts, and nails you see in the Middle East are the same ones you buy at Home Depot in Alexandria. All of it comes from factories in China, just takes a different boat."

"So far it sounds pretty generic," Alves said.

"Mostly," Aarons agreed. "But there is one element we're looking at more closely. As I'm sure you know, all explosive devices have four main components."

"Power source, explosives, initiator, and switch," Burke replied.

"Exactly. We found what was left of the battery— that kind of dense, soft metal gets banged up but generally stays intact. We actually found two, a primary and a backup, both common six-volt DC battery packs. We also recovered bits of wiring we've tied to the initiator. It was an electric detonator, Russian manufacture. Again, pretty common for military use and mining across the world."

"And you already covered the explosives," said Burke. "Which leaves the switch."

"That's what we're focusing on," Aarons said. "There are a lot of creative ways to do it, so the design can be a telltale."

"It was a handheld, right?" said Alves. "The congressman said he saw something in the guy's hand."

"Yeah, we're certain about that. We identified parts scattered in the street below. In my experience, the standard configuration is a dead man's switch. You press the button to arm the device, then releasing it sends the triggering impulse. That way if the bomber is incapacitated, success is guaranteed."

"Incapacitated, or say . . . tackled," Burke ventured.

"Exactly. From an attacker's point of view, it's a bit of insurance. But there's something unusual about this one—I first noticed it looking at the videos. Put in simple terms, I think the switch might have had a built-in delay."

Burke straightened. "A time delay? Of how long?"

"We're trying to nail that down. If you watch the video, Ridgeway grabs the bomber's right hand. It was the right move, pretty much his only option. He had to keep al-Qusami from releasing the trigger."

"He told me as much during his interview," Burke agreed. "He said he knew a little about vests, so he tried to clamp down on the guy's hand."

"Which probably kept him from releasing the trigger while they wrestled," Aarons said. "That lasted about ten seconds. But right before he lifted the bomber toward the rail, their hands came apart. From that moment to the initiation of the explosion was another 8.1 seconds."

"Isn't it possible the bomber was holding the switch down all that time?" Burke ventured. "I mean, he was fighting for his life—in the heat of the moment he might have subconsciously kept his hand clenched."

"Possible," said Waters. "None of the videos are of high enough quality to tell. Either way, Cody's observations got us thinking. Our electrical guys are piecing together what we think is debris from the switch—so far, thirty-five bits of circuit board and plastic. They don't have enough yet to prove or disprove what we're suggesting, but there is some evidence to support the idea."

"Such as?" Burke prodded.

"The switch itself is unusual, not something you'd

buy at a hardware store or online. It looks like a custom job—some real engineering, precision circuitry."

"Who could make something like that?"

"I've never seen anything like it," Cody admitted. "But then, jihadi bombmakers are good at adapting—they try to stay one step ahead."

"We've still got a lot to figure out," Waters cautioned. "If there *was* a delay, it could have been anywhere from the 8.1 seconds—the moment the congressman lost his grip on the bomber's hand—to as much as thirty-four seconds. That's the interval from when al-Qusami's hand came out of his pocket."

"Will your guys be able to figure that out?" Alves asked.

"Probably. But again, it'll take some time. Most of the pieces we're putting together are smaller than a grain of rice."

Burke considered it. "Tactically, it might make sense. If a bomber is rushing a target and security intervenes, maybe wounds him in the final moments, there's a good chance he'll let go of the switch. But if he has an extra few seconds, he might get a little closer."

"True," said Aarons. "Like I said, the guys who design these things are ingenious, albeit in a sick way."

Burke stared at Alves, who shrugged.

Minutes later the two were walking away down the hall.

"What's wrong?" she asked.

"What makes you think something's wrong?"

She stared at him like a longtime partner would, even if they'd only been teamed together for a year.

"I don't know. I keep thinking about that video, the one from ground level."

"What about it?"

"To begin, we still don't know where it came from. And the person who took it—what were they doing? You couldn't see the ceremony from ground level. Who films the side of a building? It's like . . ." His voice trailed off.

"Like they knew what was about to happen?"

Burke shrugged.

"Maybe it's a deep fake."

"A what?"

"You know, a deep fake. One of those clips that are doctored professionally—they show people doing and saying things that are pure fiction."

"Oh, right," he said. "Well, that's not an issue here. We've got footage from five different angles, five different sources, not to mention about a hundred eyewitnesses."

"True. Crazy as it seems, this all really happened."

After a long pause, he said, "That footage taken from the rooftop—the view that showed al-Qusami closing in."

"What about it?"

"Tell me what struck you about him."

Alves considered it. "I guess the fact that he was moving. Everyone else was static—standing and listening to the senator."

"No, I mean al-Qusami himself—what was unique about him?"

"Well . . . I guess he was pretty small."

Burke nodded. "That's what I thought too."

Alves pulled the printout she'd referenced earlier from her pocket. She searched out the vitals, and said, "When he was a guest of the state in northern Iraq, he clocked in at five-foot-four, ninety-nine pounds."

"Huh."

"That was probably after a few months of Kurdish prison food. He might have gained a few since then."

"True," Burke allowed. "But either way, he was not a big individual."

"Is that relevant?"

"I don't know. At the very least it's . . . notable."

"What now?" Alves asked.

"It'll be a few days before OTD gives us any answers. In the meantime . . . I think I'd like to have another word with Congressman Ridgeway."

16

OUT OF NOWHERE

Alyssa appeared early for breakfast that morning. Bryce was the straggler—he'd gone for a run but cut it short, claiming a sore Achilles tendon. Sarah knew it had to be bad—he wasn't the sort to complain—yet he didn't seem to be limping when he came down the stairs after showering.

Breakfast was hot cereal and coffee, Sarah wanting to keep it simple. She'd slept poorly last night—the idea of Bryce running for president was rocket fuel for insomnia. If he carried through, and won, their lives would change forever. Alyssa would have to change schools. She'd also likely be accepted to any university in the country. For Sarah there would be state dinners, a staff to manage her day. She'd have to come up with a worthy cause. Wounded veterans? School safety? Pre-K reading? She imagined every prospective first lady harbored similar thoughts, yet most, being the wives of governors and career Washington politicians, had probably been plotting it out for decades. She'd had but one night of tossing and turning to decide how to make the world a better place.

"I *so* think you should do it!" Alyssa blurted out as Bryce sat down behind a bowl of oatmeal.

"I take it you're referring to our big decision?"

"You'd be awesome. So much better than the old farts who are running."

Bryce couldn't contain a laugh. "Maybe that could be my campaign slogan. 'Better than the old farts.'"

Alyssa giggled.

Sarah remained impassive.

Bryce looked at her inquiringly. "Well?"

She met his gaze squarely, confidently. Supportively. Or as best as she could manage—something she might be doing a lot in the coming year. There could be only one answer, and her response was as honest as it was measured. "I think you'd be a great president."

The telegenic smile. "Okay . . . I guess it's settled then!"

Alyssa beamed.

For five minutes Bryce went over what they could expect. Campaign events, travel, the microscope they would find themselves under. Sarah listened reticently. Alyssa with unchained enthusiasm. At the end Alyssa cleaned up her dishes and bolted upstairs.

Sarah was peeling an orange when Bryce asked, "Did you really mean it?"

"What?"

"That I'd make a great president."

She took a moment to consider it. "I'm concerned how your running would affect our family. Even more so if you win. But on the simple question of your being president . . ." she went behind him, leaned down, and draped her arms across his chest. "Yes, I think you'd be terrific."

The Daily Grind was as ever, fifteen hundred square feet of espresso machines and high-top tables set in an ancient brown-brick building. The place strove to be cute and, in Sarah's view, largely succeeded.

The muffins of the day were listed on a chalkboard in loopy writing, and rough-plastered walls were inscribed with happy messages, drawn with child-thin fingers, that promoted world peace and contagious kindness. The playlist on the sound system was from the sixties, soft rock chords and drug-inspired lyrics, all piped in at a sedate volume that would have affronted the original artists. In any corporate chain it would all have come off as manipulative, but here it worked.

Sarah found Claire waiting on a stool in back. She'd already procured two lattes, the pumpkin spice seasonal special. They exchanged a hug, and despite the mental fog induced by recent events, Sarah immediately noticed the downcast set in her friend's face. They'd been besties since freshman year at Princeton. It was Claire who'd been waiting in the dorm for a report after her first date with Bryce, and she was the first to suggest that he was "The One." Sarah had been there for Claire as well, most importantly during a rough semester when her father had been diagnosed with terminal cancer. Their paths had since diverged geographically, yet the bond remained, and they'd stayed in close touch until two years ago when their lives intersected again in Virginia.

"Okay, what's wrong?" Sarah asked, feeling a curious urge to hear someone else's problems.

"It's not good," Claire said, pausing a beat. "EPIC is being canned."

"*What?* But why?" Claire had never gone into detail about the project—it was, after all, classified DOD work—yet Sarah knew it had to do with data analysis. On a more personal level, she knew that Claire viewed it as her crowning achievement.

"The usual kiss of death—funding cuts."

"I thought it was going well."

"Success has nothing to do with it," Claire lamented. "We were getting great results. That's what makes it hard . . . we were only a few months away from validating every plan objective."

"I'm so sorry."

"Yeah, me too."

"Will you be able to continue the work somewhere else? Maybe a university or a tech company?"

Claire shook her head. "Not really. I'll find a job, I'm not worried about that. But I could never duplicate EPIC in the private sector. For a year now I've had access to government databases that are unique—there's no way it works without the DOD on board." She twisted her mug distractedly.

"There's no chance it could be reinstated?"

"I doubt it. Decisions like this are made at a high level."

Sarah looked forlornly at her friend. She hadn't seen Claire so gloomy since the news about her father in college. "It doesn't seem right—you worked so hard for this."

"It's basically an offshoot of my Ph.D. dissertation. So yeah . . . it's what I've been trying to put together my whole adult life. I have to let most of my team go before the new year. Atticus and I will keep things going until the end of January, but only to shut EPIC down and make a record of what we accomplished." Atticus was her assistant, whom Sarah had met once.

The thought that sprang into Sarah's mind surprised her. "All Defense Department money is appropriated, right? Maybe I could talk to Bryce and—"

Claire's eyes shot up from her coffee. "No, Sarah! I would *never* ask you to do something like that."

"You didn't ask, I'm offering. I don't know if he can do anything, but it's worth a try."

"No," she insisted, "it wouldn't be right. Anyway, without being on the right committee, I doubt even he has enough clout."

Clout? Sarah thought inwardly. *Something else that might change soon.* She opened her mouth to say it, but then held back. She'd had one day to come to grips with the idea of Bryce becoming president. *And here I am thinking about abusing it.*

Claire said, "Look, enough about my sorry life. How the hell are you? Every time I turn around I see Bryce on TV."

Sarah struggled to shift gears. "Yeah, the last few days have been crazy. Reporters camping out on our lawn, Bryce in meetings with every bigwig on the Hill."

"He's quite the hero."

Sarah noticed someone reading the *Washington Post* two tables away, the actual paper version, and there it was again, the very same word on a midpage headline: HERO CONGRESSMAN LAUDED BY PRESIDENT CONNOLLY.

"I'm glad he saved so many lives," she said. "But honestly, I wish someone else had played Superman."

"Why?"

Sarah blew out a long breath. "I don't know. I guess I liked our life the way it was. This has been hard on Alyssa." She told Claire about her daughter's breakdown after school. "She's getting a lot of attention, but that's a two-way street."

"Yeah, I suppose it would be."

Sarah took a long pull from her mug, a big wide-brimmed thing with a quote about the faithfulness of dogs—every mug in the place had different words of inspiration. Caffeine cured a lot of the world's shortcomings, but right then she wished her coffee was seasoned with something stronger than pumpkin.

"There's something else bothering you," said Claire.

Sarah wasn't surprised—Claire knew her better than anyone. Maybe even Bryce. Maybe better than she knew herself. She'd been depressed all morning, and only now did the reason click into place. "It's Bryce. I'm worried about him."

"In what way?"

"Monday night, after the attack . . . he had some issues."

"I saw his little speech on the lawn—he was wearing a sling on one arm."

"No, it's not that," Sarah said. "Bryce . . ." she tried to say it while pushing away the image, "he was hanging over the edge of that building when the bomb went off. He was exposed to the blast, and I'm afraid it might have aggravated an old injury."

"What injury?"

Sarah paused a beat. If it was anyone but Claire she would never broach such a sensitive subject. Sarah herself had only been made aware because Bryce wanted it that way, waiving the doctor-patient privilege with his physician. In the end, she rationalized that she could tell Claire because she had Bryce's best interest at heart. "He's having headaches again."

"What do you mean, 'again?'"

"After Bryce got out of the Army, he had some sessions with a psychiatrist. He was having headaches, and the doctor said they might be an aftereffect of the explosion that hit his vehicle. The doctor explained that blasts like that create a sudden overpressure that can damage the brain. He said each case was different, but at the time he thought the chances were excellent that the headaches would simply go away. And they did . . . until now. He had a bad headache after this recent explosion."

Claire considered it. "It's been a few days now. Is he still having them?"

"No . . . at least, not that he'll admit to."

"Well, there you are. I'm sure Bryce had a crazy day on Monday. I'll bet he didn't eat or drink anything until he got home. Hell, I'd have had a headache too. Look, the problem went away so it's probably nothing."

Sarah was unmoved. "There's more," she said. "It's a small thing, but last night we decided to have some wine. Bryce went to open the bottle, but he couldn't find the corkscrew."

"And this is a big deal? Maybe it ended up in the wrong drawer."

Sarah studied her mug. "No, it's been in the same place for ten years. He's used it a hundred times. It was just . . . weird. And there have been a couple of other things lately. He had to ask me for a password yesterday, one that he knew last week. And when I asked him to drop off some dry cleaning, he didn't remember where the place was."

Claire took on a soothing tone. "Sars, we all have those moments. You've both been under a lot of pressure in the last few days. Roll with it. Things will smooth out."

Sarah couldn't hold back a humorless laugh.

"What?"

"Oh . . . it's just that there is one more tidbit of family news."

Claire cocked her head inquisitively.

Sarah looked around guardedly. A man and a woman at the next table, both wearing business casual, were the only ones within earshot. The woman was going over a spreadsheet on a laptop, the man watching intently. Even so, Sarah leaned closer. "I have to tell you something, but you've *got* to promise to keep it secret."

Claire looked at her incredulously. "You have to say that? To *me*?"

"When you hear what it is, you'll understand."

"Okaaay."

Another perimeter check, then in a low voice, "Bryce is going to run for president."

Claire stared at her expectantly, as if waiting for Sarah to break out laughing. When it didn't happen, she said, "No. You are not serious."

Sarah gave her the same *I sure as hell am* look she'd been using since college.

Claire straightened on her stool, speechless. Sarah could see her mind processing, not unlike the mainframes she operated. "President," she repeated, as if trying to make it stick. "Of the United States."

Sarah only stared.

"Well . . . that's great! I mean, isn't it? Why do you look like somebody just kicked your dog?"

"I'm still trying to wrap my head around it."

"What brought this on? The hero thing? All the publicity?"

"In part." She went over Bryce's meeting with the

Republican kingmakers, their search for a fresh candidate, a new image for the party.

While she talked Claire's face broke into a smile, slow like a sunrise. "Sarah, this is righteous! Your husband is running for president of the United States. Not only that, I'd say he has a good shot at winning. How can you not be happy about that?"

"Part of me is, I guess. I know Bryce could do a lot of good. He's smart and decent. But the whole thing is so sudden, so . . . overwhelming. It came out of nowhere."

"Didn't you once tell me this was what Bryce's father always wanted?"

Sarah nodded.

"Well . . . at least someone's dream is coming true."

Sarah was in her car twenty minutes later. The key fob was in the ignition, but her hand was nowhere near it. It had been cathartic to talk to Claire, and she realized she had to do something about the doubts building in her head. Fingers tapping the wheel, she could think of only one option.

She picked up her phone, swiped through her contacts, and found a number she hadn't dialed in two years. Sarah placed the call, tapped through a phone tree, and was greeted by a receptionist.

"Dr. Chalmers's office."

"Yes, I'd like to make an appointment."

"Are you a patient of Dr. Chalmers?"

Sarah hesitated. "Not exactly. My husband is—or was. The doctor included me in their sessions. He told me I was welcome to come see him if I ever had concerns."

"Ma'am, if your husband wants to see the doctor he should call himself and—"

"Please," Sarah said, cutting the woman off. "Would you do me one favor—just give the doctor my husband's name."

"That's really not how we—"

"My husband is Congressman Bryce Ridgeway."

A pause, then, "Let me put you on hold."

It took no more than thirty seconds.

"Yes, the doctor said he'd be happy to see you. What time would be convenient?"

Sarah smiled an empty smile. *At least it's all good for something.*

17

CHUCK NORRIS HAVING TEA

From the street view, the Rayburn House Office Building was as imposing an edifice as any on Capitol Hill. Presiding at the main entrance were dual twelve-foot statues, The Spirit of Justice and The Majesty of Law, both gazing down in everlasting wisdom. More subliminally, the workplace of the nation's leaders was surrounded by vibrant parks, including the United States Botanical Garden, the designers likely seeking counterweights for a legislative body where so many high-minded principles withered and died.

Burke had come alone, Alves staying behind at the field office. He'd been to the Rayburn building twice before. In the first instance, five years ago, he'd interviewed a congressional staffer who had been propagating terrorism-related conspiracy theories on social media—as it turned out, a web-based smear campaign against a primary rival. In the second instance, Burke had raided the office of a congressman accused of bribery, a man who'd ended up in federal prison. His visit today, he expected, would be far more routine.

He breezed through security, and had no trouble finding the office of the junior congressman from Virginia. In the anteroom Burke spoke to a college-aged woman with a cheery demeanor and high-pitched voice—an intern, he guessed. After introducing himself and showing his credentials, he was shown straight into the main office. If nothing else, Ridgeway was making good on his promise of being accessible.

The congressman was on the phone, and he raised an index finger to say *just a minute*. Burke's eyes drifted and he saw what he would have expected. Weighty furniture, a few plaques, bookcases suffering under volumes of federal statutes. Ridgeway was as he remembered, if somewhat more subdued. After seeing him in action at least a hundred times—the same thirty seconds viewed repeatedly from various angles—watching him talk on a phone from behind his desk seemed oddly anticlimactic. Like watching Chuck Norris having tea.

Ridgeway ended the call and came around the desk with an extended hand. "Special Agent Burke, good to see you again."

Burke took a firm handshake. "Thanks for seeing me on short notice."

"No problem. If you were a reporter it would never have happened, but I meant what I said. If I can help you get to the bottom of this—I'm always available."

Burke nodded obligingly.

The congressman backed up and took a seat on the front of his desk, his arms crossed casually. It was a pose few on the Hill could have pulled off, but for Ridgeway it worked. He was young and energetic, his gaze fixed singularly on Burke. During their first encounter in the interview room, the congressman had been seated behind a table. Now, seeing him in full measure, Burke's first impression was magnified—the carriage and bearing of a soldier.

"How goes the investigation?" Ridgeway asked.

"I've been pretty busy since we last talked, but I'd like to hear the latest."

Burke tipped his head to one side. "As I'm sure you know, we're always careful about divulging the details of investigations. But given your involvement, not to mention your security clearance, I suppose I can share a few things. We identified the bomber, and we'll be releasing his name later today—Mohammed al-Qusami. He's a Saudi national, twenty-one years old, and a former ISIS fighter. He was captured in northern Syria four years ago, then escaped." Burke watched closely for a reaction, and he did see something, a flicker of recognition in Ridgeway's eyes. What it meant Burke had no idea. Was the congressman flashing back to his Army days? Had it struck him that the enemy he'd fought for so long, the one that had ended his career with a bomb on some godforsaken desert road, was now here, launching attacks against America's leadership? Whatever the connection, it dissipated as quickly as it came.

"Was he part of a cell or acting alone?"

"We're not sure yet," Burke said. "Both possibilities are being considered and we've got a few leads to track. You might be able to help with one of them."

"Shoot."

"On the roof of the hotel, when you tackled al-Qusami. You told me you went for his hand."

"That's right. I figured if he was wearing a vest, that's where the switch would be."

"Do you remember actually seeing the switch?"

Ridgeway's eyes went distant in thought. He shook his head. "I saw something . . . at some point. Things were happening really fast."

"So, you tried to clamp your hand over his."

"Exactly. I wanted to keep it locked down."

"Why?"

"Like I said the other day, I've had some training. Vests often use a dead man's switch. It's a mechanical thing—you squeeze to arm the circuit, but the bomb only goes off when the trigger is released. It's a fail-safe—insurance in case the bomber is taken out right before the endgame."

Burke said nothing.

"I guess I thought if I could keep his hand closed, I might be able to keep the bomb from going off."

Burke nodded as if this made perfect sense, quietly imagining the nerve it would take to reach such a conclusion and act on it—all in a matter of seconds, and in the heat of a life-and-death struggle. "Let's move forward a few beats. You've got your hand over his, and he's fighting back. It doesn't look like plan A is going to work, so you decide to heave him over the rail."

Bryce held out his hands, a *What's a guy to do?* gesture. "You give me more credit that I deserve. I'd like to say there was a plan, but the truth is, I was just reacting. Tossing him off the roof . . . that was probably survival instinct kicking in."

"Okay. Next you get him up over the rail, but at that point he surprises you, tries to take you with him."

"No telling what was in *his* mind. I suppose my jacket was the only thing he could reach. I was off balance, and he got a good grip. I went over with him but somehow got one hand on the rail. I was lucky. *Really* lucky."

"I guess so," Burke agreed. "Then al-Qusami lost his grip and fell."

"That's right."

"Now, somewhere in that sequence you let go of his hand."

"Like I said, it all happened fast. I can't tell you exactly when I let go, but I'm sure it's on the video." The congressman regarded him for a moment, then said, "But then the bomb didn't go off . . . at least not right away."

Burke remained silent.

Ridgeway straightened his arms on his desk. He looked like he was doing a dip at the gym. "Actually, I did wonder about that. Do you think he held the switch for a few more seconds?"

"Why would he do that?" Burke asked.

"I don't know. He had to be scared shitless, amped up. One second he's fighting me, the next he's falling off the roof of a building. Who knows what goes through a jihadi's mind in a situation like that. I guess he froze, lost track of what he was doing."

Burke pursed his lips ponderingly. "Maybe so."

"Whatever the reason, Agent Burke, I'm glad it worked out the way it did."

"Yeah," Burke said, allowing a grin. "I'll bet you are."

18

RIGHT PLACE AT THE RIGHT TIME

As Arbogast sat waiting for Bryce Ridgeway in the Mayflower's Edgar Dining Room, he did so with a deep sense of satisfaction. He never doubted what Ridgeway's answer would be to his proposition, and, aside from the professional gratification of another deal made, that guaranteed his incentive fee.

In his years heading the RNC he'd made a great many pitches to prospective candidates, although most of them involved senatorial or congressional seats. On only one occasion had anyone turned him down. That individual, an Alabaman with a strong evangelical base, had confessed to Arbogast a decades-old scandal involving a very young boy, an indiscretion that had unfortunately been videoed in an attempted blackmail scheme. Sordid as it was, Arbogast had thanked the man for confessing his "crisis of conscience," knowing full well the pervert would have buried the transgression had there been any prayer of doing so successfully. Inwardly, he'd cursed his own carelessness for not performing due diligence. The next day he'd hired Kovalsky.

The Israeli hadn't disappointed him yet.

Sitting alone at a table for two, if one didn't count the martini, Arbogast waited patiently at the height of the lunch rush. The table was one of the few in the cloistered Edgar with an all-around view—there *were* times when one wanted to be seen. He spotted his man at the maîtred's stand.

Henri gave directions, and Bryce began slaloming between tables and high-backed chairs. Again, Arbogast weighed him visually. Handsome and magnetic, he exuded a cowboy masculinity without seeming to try. Arbogast himself had never been so endowed, which was why, when it came to seeking female companionship, he'd long ago reverted to the usual fallback allures—money and power.

He diverted from his candidate to watch the reaction of the room. Virtually overnight, Bryce's face had become one of the most well-known in the nation. Most people simply smiled as he passed; a few called out, "Hello" or, "Way to go, Bryce!" Arbogast's favorite reaction came three tables away, a defense lobbyist he recognized who went for a fist-bump. With ceaseless good grace, the congressman accommodated them all. Arbogast knew perfectly well what his polls were telling him, but none of that was as persuasive as the ten seconds it took for Bryce Ridgeway to cross the Mayflower's cloistered dining room.

He stood and they shook hands.

"So, we meet in public today," Bryce remarked.

"And why not?"

A waiter appeared instantly to take their drink order. Bryce asked for iced tea, Arbogast a provisional second martini.

Arbogast asked, "How did your family take the news?"

"My daughter is delighted. My wife is . . . on board."

"Some hesitation is natural, especially given your

brief tenure in Washington. It must have come as a surprise."

"Like it did to me."

Arbogast smiled inwardly. There wasn't a legislator on Capitol Hill who hadn't at some point fantasized about the White House. Stay in congress, and you might someday get a bill passed into law. The executive branch—*that* was the stage of legends. "Suffice to say, my decision to back you wasn't taken lightly. Your path is irregular, but it hasn't been easy. You've taken risks, gotten a few good breaks."

"I'm not sure if getting dragged off a rooftop by a suicide bomber qualifies as a good break."

A wry smile. "All a matter of perspective. If there's one thing I've learned in politics, Bryce, it's that the route to high office is never predictable. Would Kennedy have risen had he not written a memoir of his trials in World War Two? What if Reagan hadn't gotten the right film roles in Hollywood? There's a talent for being in the right place at the right time, for striking notes that resonate with voters, with the mood of the country. Three days ago, you weren't on anyone's radar, at least not outside your district. You can call what happened fate, an accident, an act of God—but here you are." Arbogast gestured across the dining area. "Walking across a room to adulation."

Bryce scooped a handful of trail mix from a bowl, flicked a few nuggets into his mouth.

"So? Are you in?"

A nicely theatrical pause. "I think you know the answer. I think you knew it yesterday."

Arbogast smiled. "Your father would be proud. It's too bad he can't grasp it."

"You're right—I wish he could be here."

"Where exactly is he?"

"A facility over in Winchester. They specialize in memory care, although at this point it seems moot. He hasn't recognized any family in months."

"I'm sorry to hear it," said Arbogast. Of course, he already knew more about Walter Ridgeway's condition than any one of his doctors. The man had descended into a fog years ago and there was no going back. It was all in Kovalsky's report. "Have you discussed your decision with Mandy?"

"Not yet."

"As I said, we'll find a spot for her on the team. You and I have a meeting this afternoon with Jack Mahoney."

Bryce's gaze narrowed. "*The* Jack Mahoney?"

"Best in the business. He's run two successful presidential campaigns. So far, he's kept his powder dry this cycle, but when I told him you were considering a run, he jumped at the chance. He knows a winner every bit as much as I do. He'll have good ideas—listen to him. You've got a lot of work ahead, but the next few weeks are critical. We'll file where deadlines are tight to start a buzz, but hold off on the official announcement. Maybe put out word of an exploratory committee."

Bryce pushed back in his chair and laced his hands behind his neck, a baseball fan in the seventh-inning stretch. "You really *were* sure I'd say yes."

"They all do, Bryce. They all do." Arbogast sipped his martini before saying, "There is something I'd like to clear up now."

"What's that?"

"Your wife—will she want to get involved in the campaign?"

"Honestly? I don't see it. Sarah is solid, and she'll play the game . . . at least as far as I ask her to. But her heart is at home with our daughter."

Arbogast thought about that at length, then nodded understandingly. "All right. Then that's exactly how we'll present it. It'll play well with the evangelicals."

Bryce pulled his buzzing phone from a jacket pocket. He glanced at the screen, and said, "Sorry, I have to take this. It's my daughter."

Arbogast motioned for him to go ahead, then listened to half of a father-daughter conversation.

Bryce ended the call in less than a minute. "Alyssa plays soccer on a club team. She wants me to pick her up after practice today."

"Of course she does. Your newfound fame will do wonders for her popularity. This is going to have an effect on your family. You should spend as much time with them as possible in the next few days."

"Yeah, I know. I won't be watching soccer games on Super Tuesday."

"Precisely. Mahoney will meet us at two o'clock—I reserved a conference room in the Old Post Office."

"Is that wise? Won't word get out if people see the two of us meeting with a campaign manager of his stature?"

"Let's hope. Rumors are good at this point. By the time we schedule the official announcement, you'll be getting more coverage on FOX than all the other candidates combined."

"Okay," Bryce said. "I guess you know what you're doing."

"Oh, I do," Arbogast said assuredly. "I most certainly do."

19

FEELING A LOT OF TENSION

At the same moment Bryce Ridgeway was committing to run for president of the United States, his wife was walking into his psychiatrist's office. Dr. Chalmers greeted Sarah enthusiastically.

"Thank you for seeing me on such short notice," she said.

"It's my pleasure, Sarah. I have to admit, Bryce has been on my mind in recent days."

"You and everyone else in the country."

Chalmers's office was in a medical annex near Walter Reed Army Medical Center. The decor was Freudian contemporary: a desk on one side, and in the adjoining sitting area an arrangement of soft chairs to replace the traditional couch. All of it was plotted with the care that might go into a prayer garden. The walls were draped not with diplomas and certificates of professional achievement, but two abstract cubist paintings, presumably to put minds and souls at ease. Notably, there were no family photos or career trinkets, nothing at all to distract from the off-loading of mental freight.

A VA psychiatrist, Chalmers specialized in PTSD and traumatic brain injuries—an in-demand specialty, Sarah presumed, in the era of asymmetrical warfare. Since the injuries that ended Bryce's service were the result of an IED blast, he'd been required to attend a half dozen sessions with Chalmers in conjunction with physical therapy. Sarah had been included in the last two meetings.

Chalmers led to the sitting area, and Sarah sank into a great marshmallowy love seat—the same one she'd occupied previously with Bryce.

"So, what brings you in?" he asked.

"In our final meeting you said that if Bryce or I ever had any concerns we should call."

"Yes."

"Well . . . recently, I've had some concerns."

"I see. And you think it relates to the injuries he suffered in the line of duty?"

"I'm not sure. I wanted to get your opinion on some . . . behaviors."

Chalmers steepled his hands beneath his chin. His bony, white-collar fingers seemed improbably straight. "How long has it been since we last met? Two years?"

"Roughly, yes."

"To begin, I should remind you that we're on delicate ground. I'm happy to see you regarding Bryce's well-being, but you understand there are limitations to what we can discuss."

"Yes, I know. I'm not here to ask about his history. I only want to explain some things I've noticed lately, get your opinion as to whether they might be significant. I'm sure you saw the video of what transpired Monday."

"Of course. I also saw the interview he gave that night—he came off as quite the patriot."

She smiled. "Yeah, that's always come naturally for Bryce."

"I noticed his arm was in a sling."

"Oh, his arm is fine. There were a few dings and scrapes from the scuffle on the roof, but nothing serious. I'm more concerned about what happened immediately after that."

Chalmers sat straighter in his chair, seeing where she was headed. "Are you referring to the explosion?"

Sarah nodded, glad to have the doctor on the same wavelength. "He was exposed to the blast. Thankfully, he wasn't hit by any shrapnel, but the bomb was close when it went off." She told Chalmers about the headaches Bryce had confessed to having afterward, and also his bouts of forgetfulness.

When she was done, Chalmers struck a thoughtful pose he'd probably learned in residency: two of the long fingers now pressed to one cheek, his eyes on the distant wall. As if he were mentally sorting through volumes of medical literature and case studies.

"Is he suffering any balance issues?"

"No, none that I've noticed."

"Dizziness, nausea, motor dysfunction?"

"No."

A professorial pause. "I understand your concern, Sarah. But understand, the symptoms you describe could be attributable to a great many things. First and foremost, one would have to consider stress. Bryce has clearly been dealing with a lot lately. There are also any number of illnesses that could present the indications you've mentioned."

"I understand that, and yes, he's been under a good deal of stress. In our sessions, though, you said that the brain trauma Bryce suffered in the original blast made him susceptible to follow-on injuries."

"It's true that brain trauma can be thought of

as cumulative. Yet it's also maddeningly difficult to attribute specific symptoms to particular events. The memory loss you're suggesting would be retrograde amnesia, the loss of old memories. If he's truly had a regression, and I'm not convinced he has based on what you've told me, it could be due to any number of triggers. The original blast, this recent incident, or something else altogether—something you may not even be aware of."

Sarah weighed it all, debating whether to tell Chalmers the kicker—that Bryce would soon be announcing a run for president. Not sure how this might affect his thinking, she resolved to wait. She felt like she was going behind Bryce's back as it was, and didn't want to compound the mistrust any further.

Chalmers clearly saw her internal wrestling match. "Trust your instincts, Sarah. The fact that you've reached out tells me something has changed. But it might only be temporary."

"Really?"

"Time has a way of healing. Clearly, what happened the other day pushed Bryce into a very bright spotlight. I imagine you're both feeling considerable strain."

"To say the least."

"I take it you haven't discussed these concerns with Bryce?"

"No, not really. I wanted your opinion first."

"All right then, here it is: give this a few weeks. If you see anything unusual in Bryce's behavior, try to discuss it with him. And I'd advise you to not look too hard for failings. We all forget things now and again: misplace our car keys, forget appointments. I suspect that when all this hype has blown past and

Bryce is out of the pressure cooker, your lives will get back to normal."

Sarah forged the best smile she could, thinking, *Our lives back to normal? What are the chances of that?*

Chalmers stood, a gentle reminder that he had other patients. Sarah followed him to the door.

On reaching it, the doctor paused with his hand on the handle, and said in a palliative tone, "If anything more happens, if you find yourself worried about Bryce's welfare in any way, please call. We'll get him in for a full workup."

Sarah promised she would.

"I'm glad you came to see me," Chalmers said. "If you call again, use the code word 'coffee.'"

"Code word?"

He said in a stage whisper, "It gives you a bit of priority with my staff. They'll forward any message right away."

Sarah thanked him and shook his hand. As she walked away down the hall it struck her that she had acquired yet another new privilege. It was comforting in a way: the ability to cut to the front of the line at the psychiatrist's office. She hoped like hell she'd never have to.

Mandy stopped by the office to drop off paperwork and found Bryce behind his desk balancing a pencil on his nose. She did a brief double take, never having seem him in pure slacker mode.

"Hey, Major. Glad to see you're back and working hard. How'd it go at the legislators' education summit?"

"It was mind-numbing, but shorter than usual. The moment it was over I made a beeline for the door."

"Good move. I'm glad I caught you. Your brush with fame still hasn't worn off. I've had three requests today for—"

"Mandy," he said, cutting her off, "we need to talk."

She looked at him more closely. Having worked with Bryce for nearly two years, she was adept at reading his moods. Right then she was drawing a blank. "Sure . . . what's up?"

He wagged a finger for her to close the door.

Mandy complied.

Standing behind his desk, he put his hands on his hips. He looked like a coach about to give a halftime pep talk to a team that was way behind.

"It has to do with that meeting you set up for me yesterday with Henry Arbogast."

"Oh, right. Any follow-up? Is he going to push your name for a committee slot?"

A clipped laugh. "Actually, a lot more than that."

She cocked her head, bewildered.

"When I walked in it wasn't only Arbogast," he said. "Carlson Watts and Elizabeth Carr were there as well."

Mandy's radar notched upward. "You met with the Senate majority leader and the House minority leader . . . in *addition* to the head of the RNC?"

"For nearly an hour."

Her tone went to caution. "Can I ask what you discussed?"

"It's not so much what we discussed as what was . . . offered."

She looked at him critically. Rarely had she seen

Bryce hedge, but that's exactly what he was doing now—talking circles around something uncomfortable. He moved to the side of his desk, but stopped there.

"Mandy, they want me to run for president."

She let that replay once in her head, as if she'd misheard. "President."

Bryce covered what they'd told him: President Connolly was vulnerable, but the cast of characters hoping to take him on were feeble. He explained how the attack at the Watergate had vaulted him into the public eye. And more critically, how quiet polling had quantified his popularity.

"What did you tell them?" she asked.

"I said I wanted to discuss it with my family."

"And did you?"

"Yes, last night. Alyssa thought it was a great idea, although I'm not sure she really grasps how it would change our lives. Sarah was more cautious, but she'll back me if that's what I want."

Mandy waited for the rest.

"I spoke to Arbogast earlier today. I accepted."

For Mandy a dozen thoughts seemed to crash in all at once, a green flag raised in some mental demolition derby. Then it dawned on her, the strange mood she'd been sensing, and reality hit home. "You'll need a bigger staff," she said cautiously.

"I'll need a lot of help. Arbogast and I met with Jack Mahoney, and he's agreed to come on board."

Things were beginning to make sense. "Jack Mahoney. He's going to take over as campaign manager."

"I—"

"No, I get it," she said. "I don't have any background at that level. It's the right move, totally."

"Mandy—that's the thing. Arbogast says I have to make a clean break. He wants to bring in an entirely new team. I went to bat for you, really I did, but Arbogast was insistent. He said he could find a spot for you in D.C., maybe polling or research with the RNC, but you won't be on the campaign travel team."

Mandy fought to remain calm. She had been with Bryce since day one, always his biggest cheerleader. She'd bucked him up when he needed it, coached him through debates and policy papers. She'd been his manager and even a friend—or so she thought. Never in her life had she felt more betrayed. "*Research?* A cubicle out in Maryland?"

"Look, I know that isn't what you—"

"Go to hell, Bryce!" She threw the papers she was carrying at him and stormed out the door, making sure to slam it on her way out.

In her wake, Bryce stood silently. Papers drifted to the floor around him, oscillating like leaves in an autumn breeze. He took a half step back, waiting, watching the door as if expecting her to return. When the coast seemed clear, he gave a slight shake of his head. He circled the room and ended at the back wall. On a row of shelves were a few keepsakes reflecting his short time in office, among them a plaque commemorating an official visit to the Russian embassy.

He pulled out his mobile phone—a secure model issued to all congressmen—and placed a call. It was answered by a woman. Sultry voice, thick accent.

"Is now a good time?" he asked.

She said it was ideal.

"All right, I'm on my way."

20

CONFETTI AND BANNERS

A lyssa stood with one cleat on her soccer ball. She was staring at her phone, which was completely dead. The days at school after her father's sudden fame had been draining in more ways than one.

It was nearly dark, and all her teammates had left the park.

"Alyssa, you got a ride?"

She turned to see Coach Rick walking in from the practice field, a mesh bag full of balls and plastic cones over his shoulder.

"My Dad was supposed to pick me up."

"He probably got caught in traffic leaving town." Like everyone on the planet, Rick knew who her father was. "Want to use my phone?" he offered, holding it out.

"Thanks, that'd be great." She dialed her father's number but it went straight to voice mail. She ended the call without leaving a message and handed the phone back. "It's pretty hopeless. His phone had been melting down for the last couple of days. He's not going to pick up an unknown number. Same with my Mom."

Rick pocketed his phone. "Tell you what, I remember where you live—I took you home after that game when your mom had car trouble. I'll drop you."

"Isn't it out of your way?"

"Nah, not at all. Hop in."

Bryce looked pleadingly across the dinner table. "Guys, I'm really sorry. Have I ever been late before?"

"It's okay," Alyssa said through a mouth full of fried rice.

Sarah didn't respond. Bryce had gotten home twenty minutes ago, oblivious to his forgetfulness until he walked in and saw Alyssa wearing her soccer gear.

"Things got crazy and I lost track of time. It won't happen again."

"Next time, call me," Sarah said flatly. "I'll cover for you."

"I know, but I feel like I put so much on you already. I'm going to be on the road a lot soon and I want to pull my share while I'm still around."

Sarah softened slightly. He was saying all the right things. "Okay, forget it. Thankfully, Rick is great. He never leaves the field until everyone's ride shows up."

"He's a nice guy," Alyssa said, chasing clumps of rice around her plate. "But I wish he knew more about soccer."

"I thought he was good," said Sarah.

"He's okay. But Klaus last year was awesome. He used to play professionally in Germany."

"For who?" asked Bryce.

"You wouldn't know the team."

"Try me."

"Eintracht Frankfurt."

"Pretty good—first division."

An incredulous stare. "You're a total American football guy."

"True. But I can take an interest in my daughter's extracurriculars, can't I?"

On a spectacular Tuesday in mid-November, under clear skies and a crisp wind, Congressman Bryce Ridgeway announced his intention to seek the Republican presidential nomination. He did so from a temporary stage in West Potomac Park. The site was well-considered, a tiered backdrop with low hills behind the stage for sign-waving supporters. Beyond that, the Washington Monument spired into a sapphire sky.

Just out of sight, although near enough to be pointed out by the candidate, were the hallowed grounds of Arlington National Cemetery where a number of his close comrades had found their final resting place. Arbogast had pushed for a military angle, although his preference leaned more toward the "present tense"—he'd suggested an event at the front gate of Fort Bragg, surrounded by Bryce's former comrades-in-arms. For reasons the RNC chair couldn't fathom, Bryce had shot that idea down. Arbogast had seen such willfulness before, candidates testing their new empowerment. In the end, he decided there would be worthier battles ahead.

It hardly mattered.

Bryce's reception by America, which would be quantified by polls soon after, displayed an undeniable fervor. Or as Jack Mahoney, his new campaign manager, put it, "He could have declared his candidacy from a lift pit at Jiffy Lube."

Arbogast's instincts were proving dead-on. Owing to his intervention in the Watergate bombing, the candidate's name recognition was off the charts. His single-word associations, as noted in subsequent surveys, drew two consensus replies: "relief" and "inspiring." A certified American hero had arrived to rescue the party from the associations of its other candidates: "tired" and "scandal." Bryce would inevitably be attacked for his youth and inexperience, but those were the kind of problems Arbogast did not fear—they were predictable, which meant his candidate would be prepared to tamp them down.

All in all, the campaign launch was a model event. The climactic scene on stage was captured from a dozen different angles, and carried live by every media outlet in the country: Bryce Ridgeway smiling broadly, bookended by his attractive wife and daughter, a carnival of confetti and banners whirling around them.

It was an image that resonated around the world.

21

STEAMROLLING

It was the next three weeks for which the word "blur" had been created. Bryce was on the campaign trail continuously, a regular in Iowa and New Hampshire, with swings through South Carolina and Alabama. He passed through home like a train through an outstation, stopping briefly to exchange dirty laundry for clean, kiss cheeks, and promise a better stream of phone calls next week.

For Sarah it felt like another deployment, which in a sense it was. Only instead of fighting rifle-toting jihadis, Bryce was engaging reporters with microphones and opponents wielding bare-knuckle criticisms. The field of battle wasn't the high desert, but church picnics with red-checked tablecloths and fusty VFW halls. The refrigerator calendar looked like a party favor, the coming months speckled in colored pencil—Sharpies had been outlawed the first week.

Also like a deployment, Bryce was missing Alyssa's milestones. In the Army it had been birthdays and Thanksgivings, the first day of grade school. Now the highlights had shifted, but they were no less notable. A boy had shown up at the front door to take Alyssa to a school dance. Her team won its first tournament the week before Christmas, and after celebrating with pizza, she and Sarah had bought a six-foot Douglas fir, tied it to the roof of the car, and decorated it by themselves.

The only recompense, if it could be so considered, was that Bryce's campaign was on a roll: by the second week of December, he'd officially cemented his status as the GOP front-runner. The man who'd formerly had that target on his back, a senator from Utah with a penchant for gaffes, had twice in the last week forgotten where he was campaigning, referring to Greensboro as Charlotte, and telling a crowd in a Des Moines retirement home that he was happy to be in Michigan. Allowances might have been made for a younger man, particularly one enduring the travel gauntlet of a presidential campaign, yet for a seventy-four-year-old who'd spent forty years in Washington, no mercy was shown. His nearest opponents referenced his missteps obliquely, but brought them up all the same, while those languishing on the bottom of the polls all but diagnosed him with dementia.

Against the advice of his strategists, Bryce took a higher road. He refused to address the matter at first, and when pressed by the media he allowed that all candidates made mistakes, himself included, and reminded everyone of the senator's "many decades of honorable service."

From the comfort of her living room, Sarah watched it all unfold with surreal detachment. She couldn't help but take pride in Bryce's performances, and noted how he was growing into the campaign. A tentative public speaker two years ago, he was finding his stride, and increasingly Bryce reminded her of the best commanders in the Army. Straight-shooters who told you the good news and the bad, and who never lost sight of the mission. His speeches were buoyant and patriotic, a salve for a divided America. By mid-December Bryce was steamrolling his opponents, with the pundits all but giving him the nomination.

Sarah followed it all from a distance, Alyssa by her side most evenings. They watched the first debates with a bowl of popcorn, and listened as the talking heads gave their considered opinions, most of which fell in Bryce's favor. Seemingly every segment of news was led by the graphic, "The Race for the White House," with the iconic building in the background. The most high-profile address on earth. A place once occupied by the likes of Lincoln, Kennedy, and Reagan. *All of whom had been shot*, Sarah thought lamentably.

As she listened to jabbering reporters, waxing anchors, and one endearingly animated daughter, Sarah found herself hardening into an opinion on her husband's run that would have surprised them all.

The candidate's wife hoped very much that he would lose.

22

DARK THOUGHTS

B ryce was given leave—that was how Sarah viewed it, some distant remnant of Army life—for five days over Christmas. There were fundraisers in D.C., but no travel beyond the drive into town. The first day was completely free, and Bryce spent Christmas reconnecting with his family. Two days later, he attended one of Alyssa's soccer games and seemed more interested than usual, even if halftime was spent shaking hands and hearing, *Good luck, you can count on my vote, Bryce!*

That night Sarah and Bryce went out for dinner, a long overdue date night. She had a dress in the closet waiting for the occasion, and as she put it on, Sarah saw him watching in the mirror. She smiled lasciviously, watching him watch. Sarah was quite attractive, but tended toward simplicity—something Bryce had once told her he admired. She herself was of the opinion that women who tried too hard, those who primped and spackled and bleached, were taken less seriously for it. In any event, she was comfortable in what she was.

And so too was Bryce.

They took the Tesla to their favorite upscale restaurant, The Capital Grille in Tysons Corner. The wine list was like a book, and white tablecloths and crys-

alline chandeliers cast the room in a pleasantly soft
ambiance. The menu was packed with words like
demi-glace and free range, and the fish selections were
"line-caught." Probably by hand, maybe by Heming-
way's old man himself. The scents of seared grain-
ied beef and simmering butter drifted in from the
kitchen. Calories embraced and presented without
shame. They'd dined here a half dozen times, anniver-
saries mostly, the odd Valentine's Day. The difference
tonight was the attention they were getting. Everyone
seemed to be looking at them, some discreetly, others
gawking as if they were A-list Hollywood celebs. A
woman near the wainscoted wall was taking not-so-
discreet pictures with her phone.

Sarah reflected on her life's progression. She'd gone
from Mrs. Lieutenant to Mrs. Major to The Honorable Mrs. Congressman. And now? Now she was on
track to receive the spousal promotion of the highest
order. Jackie O for a new millennium. It should have
made her head swim. Should have made her fantasize
about ordering new White House china or First Lady
stationery, about attending every elite gala on the
planet. All she could think about was how it would
affect Alyssa.

"I like your new dress," he said, snapping her out
of her distraction.

"You noticed. I bought it for a special night out."

He smiled approvingly. "I think this qualifies."

The sommelier arrived with a bottle of Montepul-
iano. When she pulled the cork and offered a sample,
Bryce gestured to Sarah. "She knows more about it
than I do."

The young woman gave the glass to Sarah, who

sipped and nodded approvingly. Before leaving, the sommelier said, "That was a nice thing to say. You have my vote, Mr. Ridgeway."

Bryce smiled dutifully, and the woman was gone.

"I feel like we're living in a fish bowl," she said.

"That's part of the deal." He sipped the wine, nodded approvingly. "Yeah, that'll work."

The waiter appeared and took their order.

When he was gone, Bryce asked, "Salmon again?"

"Omega three fatty acids are good for you."

"Compared to what I've been eating on the campaign trail, this filet mignon will be health food. If I see another plate of fried chicken and baked beans I'm going to puke."

"I wouldn't put that in your stump speech."

"And what *would* you put in?"

She gave it some thought. "How about, 'I love my wife, my daughter, and America.' That should about cover it."

"I'll run it by Jack."

Sarah gave him a circumspect look. "Have you heard from Mandy?"

"No, not directly. I heard she got picked up by Morrison's campaign—he's getting desperate, probably hoping she has some dirt on me."

"Does she?"

"No." He tipped back his wineglass. "Don't feel sorry for her, Sarah. She and I had a good run, but this is another level. I offered her a top job at headquarters, but that wasn't what she wanted. Mandy's a big girl—she'll get over it."

He was about to say something else when a voice interrupted.

"Bryce!"

Sarah turned to see a familiar face—Lieutenant Colonel Brad Martin, one of Bryce's last commanders in the Army.

"I just wanted to say hi," Martin said, pausing beside their table. "How are you guys?"

"I'm great, Brad, good to see you!" Sarah replied.

Bryce stood, and when the two men shook hands Sarah saw a distinct guardedness in her husband's manner.

"So, what have you been up to?" Bryce asked.

"Still on active duty, hoping to make O-6 on the next promotion board."

"Good luck with that," Bryce said.

"I don't have to ask what you've been up to—congrats!"

"Thanks. Life has gotten really busy."

Martin went over his postings since they'd parted ways. At the end, he said, "If you make it to the White House, I'll ask you to sign my next performance report."

"Yeah, will do," Bryce said.

"Look, sorry to interrupt. You guys have a great evening."

Bryce smiled.

"Good to see you, Brad," Sarah said as Martin backed away. "And say hello to Becky."

"Thanks, I will," he called out over his shoulder.

Sarah looked at Bryce, who was watching Martin retreat.

"It's funny how often—" Bryce cut his thought short, noticing her expression. "What?"

Her eyes narrowed. "You had no idea who he was."

"That's silly—of course I recognized him. It's just

that his name escaped me for a moment." He shrugged and took a sip of wine.

Sarah kept staring.

"Do you know how many people I've met in the last month?" he said.

"He was your commander. You deployed with him to Africa for a year."

"Actually, only part of a year. Max Gavin rotated in to replace him halfway through."

Sarah hesitated, then said, "Anyway, he looked good. I hope he gets his eagles—he's one of the good ones."

"I don't know. I liked him, but he struck me as one of those guys who always seems to be going places but never quite arrives."

"That's a little harsh."

"That's the Army," he said, attacking the bread basket.

Sarah was mildly surprised. Bryce was a lot of things, but never callous. She wondered if something had happened between them during the deployment. Then the thought she'd been pushing away returned. Could the explosion have affected Bryce's memory? Could it be affecting his moods? *Am I being paranoid?*

She remembered years ago having coffee with a group of wives during a deployment. One woman's husband hadn't called on their anniversary, and she'd jested it was due to his brain trauma. The joke went over like an iron blimp. Yet it opened the floodgates, and three other wives, all of whom had husbands who'd suffered blast injuries, admitted to having similar dark thoughts. Every time their husband forgot to take out the garbage or lost his favorite wrench, a stab of worry set in. In the end, humor had reigned, everyone sharing anecdotes about their addled spouses—because what else could you do?

Not wanting to put a damper on dinner, Sarah let it go. The food was good, the wine outstanding. When Bryce ordered a second bottle, she protested on the grounds that one of them had to drive ten miles to get home.

"I've got that covered," Bryce said. "It's one of the perks of my new status." He sent a text right then, and when they walked outside thirty minutes later a Town Car was waiting.

"This doesn't look like an UBER," she said, trying not to sound tipsy.

"Jack's orders—it's on the campaign."

"Is that a valid expense?"

"I shook a few hands in the restaurant, so yeah, I was campaigning. More to the point, Jack doesn't want me to screw things up by getting a DUI."

"Probably just as well," she said. "Maybe it's my imagination, but you seem to be driving faster lately."

"Am I? Probably just high expectations."

"What?"

"If I win, I might not get behind the wheel of a car again for another eight years."

She giggled and they bundled into the Town Car's backseat like teenagers into a graduation limo.

"Home, sir?" the driver inquired.

"Home," Bryce said, an earl to his chauffeur.

"I've been wondering," Sarah said, "at what point do you get Secret Service protection?"

"It's not a big agency, so they try to hold off as long as possible—a manpower thing. Once I win the nomination, it's a done deal."

"*If* you win the nomination."

"Superstitious?"

"Maybe."

"There is one exception when it comes to protection."

"What's that?"

"If a viable threat is made against a candidate, then they cover him or her."

A flutter of dread drifted into Sarah's light head.

"Don't worry. Last guy who messed with me, I threw him off the top of a fifteen-story building."

"Bryce—"

He interrupted with a deep kiss. When it finally broke, he said in a low voice, "Did you say Alyssa is spending the night at Julia's?"

"She is."

"Good." He kissed her again and his hands began to wander. Sarah's head was swimming from the second bottle of wine—they never found the bottom, but had made a valiant effort. When his hand cupped her breast she whispered, "Can it wait 'til we get home?"

In the scant light of the backseat he met her eyes, and Sarah saw something she didn't quite recognize. "Sure," he said, pulling away. "Waiting always makes it better."

23

THE PRICE WE PAY

Sarah felt stirring beneath the warmth of the blanket. She opened her eyes, saw a gloomy daybreak faltering at the window. The suspect pane was as crooked as ever, yet there was no draft. As if the morning outside was holding its breath.

She half-rolled to her right. Bryce was next to her, a rare occasion these days. Her head hurt from the wine, but only a little. His eyes fluttered, began to pry open. Nothing was said, and they lay together for a time in silence. Letting the world come into focus. Keeping the sharp edges at bay a bit longer.

Finally, Bryce rolled away and checked his phone.

She said, "You were enthusiastic last night."

"Was I?" He set his phone down and pushed back the sheet. "I guess it's been a few weeks."

He got out of bed naked and she watched him walk to the bathroom. He looked the same as ever. Strong, lean body, knotted muscles wearing his battle scars like so many medals. He disappeared and she heard the shower come on.

"What time are we picking up Alyssa?" he called out.

"Noon, last I heard."

"I told her I'd get her. I'd like to see how her driving is coming along."

"She's doing all right, just lacking in confidence. I don't see her going solo anytime soon."

"She'll be fine. Peer pressure will do the trick."

She recalled him saying the same thing months earlier, on the day Alyssa had gotten her restricted. "Maybe, but I don't want to push. She doesn't have to do it on the earliest possible day."

Bryce's phone, still on the nightstand, buzzed. Sarah saw a text message flash to the unlocked screen. She picked it up, thinking it might be from Alyssa. It turned out to be from a contact labeled AR: Come to our place this morning. Have something special for you.

Her stomach lurched. Sarah read it again, trying to force the words into a context other than what first came to mind. She failed mightily. Sitting up in bed, she threw a glance at the open bathroom door. She actually wished Bryce would come back. She wanted to hand him the phone, watch him check the screen. Wait for a harmless explanation that would make her think, *Oh, of course. How silly of me.*

He didn't come out.

Sarah kept thinking.

And not for the first time.

She'd been sensing it for the last month, a change between them. Something subtle and ill-defined, yet undeniably persistent. She'd tried to write it off to the stress, a reaction to the heady events that had been thrust upon them. The attack at the Watergate, Bryce's sudden fame. Running for president and a frenzied travel schedule. Taken together, it would strain any relationship.

The phone's screen went to sleep. Sarah bit her bottom lip. The shower was still on and she heard intermittent splashing. Steam wafted through the half-closed door like fog rolling in from the sea.

Deep in a bed that smelled like him, she studied his phone. In years past they'd always managed security features to allow access to each other's phones. Bryce, unfortunately, had been given a new phone by his campaign, and they'd never gotten around to setting it up that way. Sarah saw no button for a thumbprint, and when she tried to open the screen there was no keypad prompting a code. She guessed it used facial recognition, which meant getting in was hopeless.

Feeling a twist in her gut, she put the phone back where it had been.

Naked under the sheets, she picked up her robe—discarded on the floor at some point last night—and shrugged it on. She stood and glanced out the window, saw a tiny tornado of leaves spinning a gyre on the driveway. Her thoughts were no less aswirl. With a clunk from the plumbing the shower went silent. Sarah went to the walk-in closet and put on a pair of pajamas. When she came out, Bryce was emerging from the bathroom, one towel wrapped around his waist, another drying his hair.

"I'm famished," he said. "How about eggs and pancakes? I'll cook, you're in charge of coffee."

"Sure," she managed.

He picked up his phone, unlocked the screen—definitely facial recognition—and checked his messages. Oddly, while the phone might have read his face, Sarah couldn't. Bryce turned away and walked into the closet. He disappeared for a time, and while she made the bed she heard him pulling clothes off hangers. The towels came flying out into the room.

Then, "Damn!"

"What's wrong?" she asked.

Silence for a time. He emerged wearing sharply creased chinos and a blue button-down shirt still open in front. "Something's come up," he said, buttoning his cuffs. "A minor crisis, but I have to go meet Jack. It should only take a couple of hours. I can still pick up Alyssa."

"Okay." She forced a smile. "Downtown?"

"Yeah. Sorry about breakfast. We'll do lunch with Alyssa."

"Sure."

He pulled up behind her as she fluffed a pillow. Wrapped his arms around her waist and planted a kiss on her cheek. "I'm sure JFK and Jackie had the same problems. It's the price we pay, right?"

"Yeah. The price we pay."

If Bryce sensed her suspicion over the next days, Sarah saw little evidence of it. The holiday season flew past for the three of them, sharing home-cooked meals and exchanging gifts. Bryce held his promise to keep work to a minimum. They called Sarah's parents in Florida, her sister in Seattle, and Bryce even found time to straighten the doorbell. The drafty window remained untouched.

If there were more suspicious texts, Sarah never saw them. Not that she tried—his phone went off like a spastic pinball machine, and she was determined not to be consumed by his reaction to every incoming call and text. Still, that one suspect message stuck like a burr, nagging and constant. *Come to our place this morning. Have something special for you.* Any number of explanations could render it harmless. The text could have been from Jack, its context misconstrued.

Or one of Bryce's staffers—there were more every day, most of whom she'd never met. There had to be *one* with the initials AR. Sarah didn't want to be blind, but in the end she decided to do what she'd always done—she would trust her husband.

The only thing she noticed out of character during the holidays was when Bryce didn't want to go see his father—they'd never missed a Christmas. His reasoning, that "Dad doesn't even recognize us anymore," seemed peculiarly harsh. When she pressed, he promised they'd make the two-hour drive to Winchester sometime in the new year.

Bryce hit the trail again three days before New Year's Eve. In his absence, Sarah tried to keep busy, and by extension, keep her suspicions at bay. She was thankful to have Alyssa home from school—she'd taken an interest in cooking, and they spent hours together in the kitchen. Snicker doodles and muffins, mac and cheese from scratch. A holiday soccer tournament came and went. Still, Sarah found herself slumping into a peculiar weariness. She hadn't been sleeping well, yet it was more than that. Something deeper and more disquieting. As much as she tried to deny it, she knew what it was: the weight of lingering doubts.

On New Year's Eve morning, she went to Alyssa's room and found her daughter sitting on the bed, back to the headboard, knees pulled to her chest. Sarah had seen her share of teen angst, but this looked different.

"Everything okay?" she asked, a lion tamer entering a cage.

"Dad is being weird."

"What do you mean?"

Her eyes scrunched closed, tears welling. "He didn't want to go see Grandpa for Christmas!"

Sarah sat down at the foot of the bed, offering both comfort and distance. "I know, honey. But try to understand. Your father has got a lot on his plate right now. He promised we'd go soon. Anyway, Grandpa's memory is pretty bad."

"He was alone for Christmas."

Sarah weighed arguing that he hadn't been alone, that the nursing home staff always tried to celebrate and prepare a special meal. It might have worked five years ago, but her daughter was far closer to an adult than a child. "Well," she finally said, "maybe you and I should go see him today."

24

CAPRICIOUS MOODS

The drive to Winchester took roughly two hours. Because Alyssa wasn't ready to negotiate winding hills, Sarah took the wheel. They cranked up the music, sang along with Tom Petty, and for the first time in weeks the strain seemed to ease. Alyssa confessed a minor crush on a boy on the high school soccer team, and this gave Sarah pause. She recalled, when she was not much older, having a crush herself on a certain star lacrosse player.

The entrance road to Autumn Living was soothing by design. Even now, on high winter, the brown lawn and dormant shrubs presented a neatly trimmed appearance, ready to be reborn in spring. A more jaded eye than Sarah's might have viewed it as contrived, a symbol of the cycle of life's continuance, playing out subliminally, at a place whose mission was inescapably more finite.

Walter Ridgeway had suffered a stroke three weeks after Bryce was elected to Congress. That the cerebral event had ruined his body was a given—the seventy-six-year-old scion, who days earlier had been playing tennis and hiking, and who was a longtime fixture in D.C. power circles, was forced into a wheelchair.

Even more devastating were the effects on his mind.

In the first month there had been hope, his primary

care doctor assuring everyone that, given the best therapies and tended to by the right caregivers, recovery at home might be possible. There were tests and specialists, yet each successive result only hardened the damning truth. The Walter Ridgeway of Washington D.C., a fierce Russia hawk who for a generation had set the course of Eastern European diplomacy, would never be the same.

In the weeks after Bryce's swearing in, his father's mental state deteriorated. He became forgetful, combative, and a string of battle-weary home health nurses quit after only days on the job. On three occasions, Sarah had been forced to fill the gap until a replacement could be found, awkward nights spent in Walter's sprawling Shenandoah Valley mansion handling an increasingly obstinate father-in-law who was more a stranger every day.

After three months, the doctor recommended placing Walter in a memory care facility. Sarah and Bryce had weighed taking him into their home, but Walter's doctor dissuaded them. He said Bryce's father was failing rapidly, and that full-time professional care would soon be a necessity. Autumn Living seemed the best of the bad choices.

"It's never the same people," Alyssa said quietly as they signed in at the front desk.

Sarah looked around and could only agree. She saw only one familiar face—the facility's director was on the phone in her office. "I guess there's a lot of turnover at a place like this. I'm sure Lucy will be here."

Lucy was a nurse's assistant who seemed omnipresent. She was petite and cheerful, with adorable nose-freckles, and seemed impervious to Walter's capricious moods.

They were buzzed through a locked door into the living area. The halls were still decorated for Christmas, cheap paper snowmen and Santas dangling by fishing line from the ceiling lattice. Sarah spotted Lucy almost immediately, and she came over with her ever-present smile. "He's in the sunroom," she said, after exchanging New Years greetings.

Lucy led the way.

"How's he been?" Sarah asked.

"Oh, the same. There are some great pictures from Christmas on the website."

"Sorry we didn't make it," Alyssa said. "Dad was really busy."

"So I gather," Lucy said.

The comment put Sarah off, even if it made sense—the chaos of Bryce's schedule would be evident to everyone in America. Even so, Autumn Living had always felt like a kind of refuge. A place where the distractions of D.C. could be left behind to focus on family.

They cornered into the sunroom and Walter was there, sitting by a window with a Tartan blanket in his lap. He stared out the window blankly. His gray hair looked mussed and was getting a bit long.

Alyssa rushed up and put an arm around his shoulder, gave him a kiss on the cheek. "Hi, Grandad!" She leaned into his field of view and Walter stared at her. His expression never changed, Alyssa getting the same blank stare as the window.

"Hello, Walter!" Sarah said cheerily.

His eyes went back outside. Someone had put a

string of plastic beads around his neck, a silvery *Happy New Year!* charm at the front.

Alyssa began talking, an endearing one-way narrative of school and soccer and girlfriend mischief.

Sarah took a few steps back. Alyssa was Walter's only grandchild, and he'd been smitten since day one. It was a rare event these days, but Alyssa *did* make the occasional connection, evoking traces of familiarity in his typically rheumy gaze. Alyssa had always touched Walter like no one else, Bryce included.

Lucy leaned in and said in a soft voice, "He's been eating really well, keeping a good schedule. Always in bed by eight."

Like the other residents, Walter had a private room decorated with a handful of furnishings from his twelve-thousand square foot mansion—a downsizing of monumental proportions. The walls were decorated with family photos, and a few shelves held keepsakes from his days with the State Department. The hope, ostensibly, was that some of it might cue memories. Sarah hadn't seen any sign of it in nearly a year.

"What does he do when he's in his room? Watch TV?"

"No, not any more. That's pretty common—they can't keep track of what's going on, so they lose interest. Same with books and newspapers. He gets up on his walker now and again, moves around the room chattering."

"Chattering?"

"Yeah, I've heard it through the door a few times when I pass his room, and the night staff have mentioned it. They say he stays up late, shuffling around and talking to himself."

"Is that common?"

"It is. You hear conversations with spouses and friends, even parents who've been gone for years."

"Walter would talk to his wife, I think. Or maybe Bryce."

"Could be. All in all, he seems comfortable."

A nurse came into the room, buttonholed Sarah, and they went over Walter's meds—a monthly requirement at the facility. For a man of his age and condition, Walter was on surprisingly few.

They stayed for another hour.

When they left Walter was staring out the window again, the same glazed look as when they'd arrived. Yet if he seemed unmoved by their visit, it had a buoyant effect on Alyssa. This, in turn, raised Sarah's spirits.

The ride home brought more music and some blissfully off-key singing. They stopped for a Frappuccino halfway home. By the time they reached the house, however, the sugar had worn off. Alyssa's mood sank precipitously.

Sarah bit the bullet as they pulled into the driveway. "What's wrong, Baby?"

"I don't know . . . I guess I still don't get it. Why Dad didn't want to go see Grandpa over Christmas."

"Honey, he's under a lot of pressure. People are calling him at all hours, he's traveling constantly. Give him a pass. Grandpa is doing well, and your father promised to go see him soon."

A frown like a sad emoji: hollow eyes and a mouth like an upside-down U. Without another word, Alyssa got out and disappeared into the house.

Sarah didn't move, her hands rigid on the wheel. A getaway driver outside a bank. The truth was, she couldn't shake the same thought. Why hadn't Bryce gone? Even if his father didn't realize what was happening, you did it for Alyssa. Did it for the family. Because that was the right thing to do.

And Bryce always *does the right thing.*

Every marriage has its sixth sense, and right then Sarah's was going off like a klaxon. She supposed it was the reason the text had hit a nerve. She'd tried desperately to discard the notion that Bryce had been unfaithful, yet something was wrong between them. Small gestures gone missing, a lack of touching when they were together. Glances that seemed out of synch, guarded phone conversations. Any one disconnect, alone, would be nothing more than an outlier. Taken together, however, it seemed a harbinger of . . . *what?*

Sarah pushed the question away and went inside.

25

A TERRIBLE NO-MAN'S-LAND

The investigation into the Watergate Hotel bombing had been going sideways for weeks. After discovering the attacker's identity, there was virtually no progress on who had helped Mohammed al-Qusami carry out the strike. FBI technicians scoured the scene, but came up with few useful leads. Their best hope, the custom-made switch with a built-in delay, had been reconstructed in painstaking detail. Unfortunately, the hardware could not be sourced.

Special agents immersed themselves in social media, searched for money trails, and performed exhaustive overseas interviews. All proved to be dead ends. The sum of evidence on week seven was little different from the first week: one disaffected young Saudi had botched a thoroughly planned attack. No group ever claimed credit, and the only casualty had been the attacker himself.

Yet as Burke's frustration mounted, it was tempered by one positive development: he was getting little pressure from above for results. He'd originally thought that such a high-profile inquiry would generate constant requests for updates from his superiors, who in turn would be getting congressional pressure. What happened was quite the opposite. After releasing the name of the attacker, along with the photo from his forged passport, interest in the bombing quickly dissipated. Conspiracy theories, of course, ran rampant on the internet—plots pushed by the fringe left, alt-right, and Russian trolls being the front-runners—investigative albatrosses, one and all, that were easily shot down. By early December, Burke's email inbox had begun to thin. By the end of the year he suspected it had gone off-line.

The disinterest cascaded down through the chain of command, to the point that he and Alves had been given two new cases in the last week. They'd discussed it all over beers a few nights earlier, and come up with only one answer: the multiple high-res videos of the attack, which had dominated the news cycle for weeks, had affected a sense of closure. The attacker was dead, no harm done but to himself, and a new American hero had been born. A hero who was today running for president. That twist seemed to have crushed any remaining interest in the original event. The questions of whether the bomber had help, or if other strikes might be in the works, were no longer of concern to Americans.

To Troy Burke, however, they were very much a concern.

"Still nothing," he said, sending the latest update from the CIA spinning onto the desk he shared with Alves.

She looked at him above the frame of her readers, an iPad in hand as she sat with her feet propped on the desk. Without comment, she traded the iPad for the printout. The classified reports had been coming in daily, each seemingly shorter than the last. When it came to tracking down foreign nationals, CIA was the go-to agency, yet there seemed to be precious little regarding one Mohammed al-Qusami: he was a former ISIS fighter who'd been captured, imprisoned, and then vanished into the abyss of souls that was Syria.

After reading it, Alves summed up the latest report. "CIA tracked down two guys who knew al-Qusami in prison. One was repatriated to Belgium and is still locked up there. The other made his way back to Jordan and is living with his parents. Both say al-Qusami was a hard-core jihadi, and consensus opinion is that he wasn't the sharpest knife in the drawer. These associates gave up a few names, guys he hung with in prison, but so far there's no bead on any of them. They could be kicking around in Syria or Afghanistan, could be dead, or maybe they just took their AKs and went home. Chances are, the names listed are likely noms de guerre which have been either dropped or changed."

"More dead ends," Burke said, a verbal shrug. "All the blame for the attack stays on one kid who blew himself up. I'm still not convinced it's so simple."

"Thousands like him out there," she argued. "Disaffected, no education, no prospects. Maybe al-Qusami lost a father or a brother in battle. Maybe his sister was killed by a stray bomb and he held America responsible."

"I get all that," said Burke.

"Then what's bugging you?"

"To begin, why no claim of responsibility? This attack took some planning, had backing. Why would somebody go to all that trouble, then keep it secret? And why *this* event? A senator running for president is a viable target, but I might have expected whoever's responsible to aim a little higher."

"Like who . . . the president? That's a whole different level of security."

Burke drew up a spare roller chair and sat. "True. But something still feels off. He *must* have had help."

"Trouble is, we can't prove it. We know the vest was stashed in the equipment closet, probably the day before the attack. Unfortunately, the only camera that could have captured it went on the fritz two days earlier." This had been established in the first week of the investigation.

Burke leveled a finger at his partner like a lawyer in a courtroom. "Does that not strike you as a terrible coincidence?"

"Of course," Alves agreed. "But our cyber team has been all over that camera. It crashed from a power surge—it happens."

Burke tapped his fingers on the arms of his chair. "Did you read OTD's final report on the trigger?"

"Saw it last night. They nailed down the delay circuit in the switch. It's about what we figured, an eight-second interval from activation to initiation."

Burke was staring blankly at a muted television on the far wall when a familiar face came into view. The set was tuned to CNN, and a segment on New Year's Eve preparations in Times Square yielded to an ad for the next Republican primary debate. Seven candidates had made the cut. One of them Burke had spoken to twice in recent weeks.

Alves saw him staring. "You think our boy's gonna get the nomination?"

Burke chuckled. "Given who he's running against? I don't see how he couldn't."

The news anchor came back on, a blond with over-managed hair and impossibly white teeth. Burke saw a few words in closed caption, something about "Bryce Ridgeway's meteoric rise . . ."

He turned away from the TV to address his computer. As he logged in, an old memory surfaced. It was the observation of a former partner who'd put away a big-time Hollywood producer for money laundering. *"Ever think about that saying, Troy? Meteors don't rise. They go the other way . . . and it always ends badly."*

The soft 60s rock at The Daily Grind had yielded to Christmas classics. It was Sarah's turn to buy, Peppermint Spice lattes now the seasonal special. The place was packed on New Year's Day: students home from school, families gathered for the holidays, everyone loud and animated. The entire D.C. metroplex seemed to have taken the week off work.

Everyone, that is, except for Bryce. He was midway on a swing through the southern primary states, and after that bound for New Hampshire where he was polling in a dead heat for the lead. Sarah had muddled through the holidays, but now, with Bryce set to be gone for the next ten days, too many empty nights were wreaking havoc on her psyche. After waking this morning, she'd found herself staring at the nightstand where his phone had been. She knew she could never confront him about it—the evidence was too slim, the lack of trust too clear—yet that put her in a terrible no-man's-land. To the positive, there had been nothing else to fuel her suspicions. Bryce had always been the model husband, and now he was the model presidential candidate.

She and Claire hawked for a table, swooping in when one opened a few steps away.

After they settled, the first thing Claire said was, "All right, what's wrong?"

"Is it that obvious?"

"To me it is. Is it Bryce? He's not having headaches again, is he?"

"No, I don't think so. But it does have to do with him." Sarah drew in deeply on the espresso-laced air. "Since that day at the Watergate, he's been acting strangely."

"In what way? Is he still forgetting things?"

"Maybe, here and there. But it's more than that. He seems . . . distant or something. Even when he's home, he's always on his phone or sending emails. Alyssa has noticed a difference too. Bryce took her driving, and she told me later he seemed impatient."

"I don't mean to take sides, but Bryce is dealing with a lot right now. What he's doing, running for president, has got to be crazy busy. The travel, the handshaking, staff constantly throwing speeches and policy papers at you. Every word he says in public gets recorded by the opposition, and any slip of the tongue goes viral. Granted, these are self-imposed problems—goes with the territory. Still . . . it's a hell of a lot of stress."

"I know, I get that."

"What then?"

"A few weeks ago he forgot to pick up Alyssa from soccer practice."

After an extended silence, Claire shook her head. "What else, Sars?"

They were nearing sacrosanct ground, yet Sarah had to unload what was building inside her. "It's possible Bryce is having an affair."

The busy sounds around them—the conversational chatter, the call-outs of names on cups, the whir of blenders—all seemed to disappear. Sarah was almost surprised she'd said it, but now that she had it seemed more real. More frightening.

Claire's face collapsed, something between shock and disbelief. She was silent for a time, then said, "You need to give me the deets, sister."

Sarah took a long moment to compose herself. Then she did precisely that.

26

AN IMPENDING MOMENT
OF BRILLIANCE

Claire listened patiently, supportively. Sarah knew her friend to be eminently analytical—the reason she so valued her opinion—and right now she needed a cross-check on her own newly suspect judgement. Once she finished, Claire fell silent for a time. Sarah steeled herself for a rebuke, a heavy dose of, *One text and you no longer trust your husband?*

What Claire said was, "I admit, it doesn't sound good."

Sarah remained still and quiet. Resignation in its human form.

"It's possible the text was innocent. What concerns me more is that you and Alyssa are *both* getting bad vibes . . . that tells me something's wrong."

Sarah's heart lurched. She hadn't planned on confiding in Claire. Or had she? Either way, she'd gone ahead expecting to be told her worries were baseless. *No, Bryce would never do that! He's totally committed to you!* Instead, her fear was being validated, and by a source she unfailingly trusted.

"I don't know what to do about it," Sarah said.

"What you *can't* do is let it fester—you have to get to the bottom of what's going on."

"How? Confront him? Accuse him of seeing someone else?" She went silent for a time, trying to imagine it. "I couldn't even if I wanted to. It would take time to work through and he's never home for more than a day. It'll be that way for months, probably until the convention this summer. Even longer if he wins the nomination. Look, maybe I shouldn't have mentioned it. It was just one suspect message, a few odd feelings."

A rigid stare. "You need more information."

"I'm not going to spy on him."

Claire's gaze went distant, calculations being made. "You don't have to," she finally said. "I can do it for you."

"What?"

Claire explained what she had in mind, if only in vague strokes.

When she was done, Sarah sat stunned. "Is that even *possible*?"

"Unfortunately, in today's world . . . yes, it is. Give me a day or two."

Sarah looked across the table uncertainly. Then she surprised herself by saying, "Okay, go ahead."

For the first time in weeks, Claire walked into her lab at the TARC building with a mission beyond sealing her project's crypt. She rounded a stack of empty cardboard boxes at the entrance. Even on the best of days the place wasn't pretty. The tables and chairs were institutional, and a dozen monitors provided eerie illumination, their flickering screens strobing the walls in patternless confusion. Wiring ran scattershot between tables, heavy-gauge bundles wrapped by cable ties snaking along the baseboards.

Claire loved all of it.

This was the place where her dream had nearly become reality.

She saw her assistant, Atticus, working at a standing desk, twin monitors in front of him streaming digital life. He was his usual overcaffeinated self, bouncing on his heels like a kid on a pogo stick. The rest of the team was gone, let go right before Christmas. Claire's pathetic attempt at a going away party had all the aura of a wake. Since then, with EPIC's shutdown imminent, Claire and Atticus had been running every imaginable test scenario. It had taken three years to get the system up and running, and they committed to analyzing as many functions as possible before disconnecting from the ultrasecure DOD network. Her reasoning was simple: she might never again be able to leverage so many highly sensitive networks.

"I ran scenario sixteen-five last night," Atticus said.

"Which was that? Overseas, Eastern Europe?"

"Yeah. Special Ops product, classified military and civilian combined. Telecoms, financial, municipal—all the compromised databases. High speed analysis, priority two."

"How'd it come out?"

"In two words . . . holy shit! I just started making crap up. I tried to locate the Bulgarian foreign minister. Turns out he was at his mistress's place. Nailed his location from a supposedly secure phone—NSA had a bead on it. Then I found a video loop from the hallway of her apartment that showed him going inside fifteen minutes earlier. Facial recog put the confidence at ninety-nine point five. In real time I got moaning noises from her Alexa audio. If I was a perv, I could have accessed video from the camera on the Smart-TV in her bedroom."

"How long did all that take?"

Atticus looked at the notepad where he jotted down results—some things were just easier the old-fashioned way. "One minute, twenty-eight seconds."

"Seriously?"

"Just for fun, I put in a call to his phone from his wife's number. He didn't pick up, but the moaning stopped and I heard his mistress start bitching."

"You're a bad person, Atticus."

"Yeah, I know. But this is like . . . addictive."

"Do no harm, my friend. We're here to learn, not to create an international incident."

"Sorry, guess I got carried away. But it was all in good fun."

"Not for the foreign minister."

"Claire, this has got *so* much potential."

"I'm the choir, Atticus."

She paused at a workstation worthy of a jumbo jet.

"How long until we actually have to cut the cord?" he asked.

Claire tapped the keyboard to wake her screen. "It's executed from our end, so no official deadlines. The general wants us out by the end of the month, so as far as I'm concerned, we run as many scenarios as we can until then. The actual shutdown sequence won't take more than a day or two. After that, you and I can go through the hard storage. It'll take at least a month to figure out what worked and what didn't."

"Will we still be getting paid at that point?"

"Doubtful. But the more data we gather, the more likely we can get EPIC resurrected at some point."

"And who's going to grant that funding? We already got chopped."

Claire's first thought was speculative, and she checked it to say, "I don't know . . . but if we can prove the concept, there's hope."

Her only remaining supporter went silent.

"Listen, Atticus. We've been working together a long time, but I'd understand if you don't want to hang around. Alphabet, Amazon, Apple—you could get a job anywhere with one phone call, and at five times what I'm paying you with stock options to boot."

He sighed. "Don't worry, I'll sell out one day. But you and I put a lot into this—I'd like to see how it turns out."

"So would I . . . and thanks." Claire began logging into the system.

"What scenario are you going to input?" he asked, pulling his coat from atop a disconnected monitor.

"I've been thinking up a new one, domestic. I want to challenge the internal restrictions."

"We have restrictions?"

"I'm not talking about tech constraints—it's more about our mission guardrails. EPIC would never have been approved without guarantees that we wouldn't violate surveillance laws."

"But this is pure research. We're not actually *using* any of the data we get—we're just documenting what can be done."

"You and I know that, but the bean counters who signed off on our funding insisted on legal protections."

"Well, that won't be a problem anymore," Atticus said sourly. He shrugged on his jacket. "I'm going to Chipotle. You want anything?"

"No, I'm good."

"Back in an hour." He pulled out his ID lanyard, carded through the heavy door, and disappeared.

Claire navigated to the main system menu. She knew an hour was optimistic: Atticus drove a hoverboard, meaning Chipotle was fifteen-minutes each way, not counting the time it took to run the building's security gauntlet. He was a good friend, and a big-picture guy, but right then she'd rather he didn't see the search she was about to input. Even under their loose operating rules, it would be strictly out-of-bounds. She found herself not caring, the frustration of recent weeks peaking. She and Atticus had been working long hours, challenging the software from every possible angle. EPIC was hurtling toward its climax like a star collapsing on itself: one impending moment of brilliance before it disappeared forever.

Claire reached the screen she wanted, blank fields for dozens of variables. Facial profiles and voiceprints could be uploaded. Documents, videos, IP addresses.

Claire selected the most basic of them all.

She typed in a name, then added a title: Bryce James Ridgeway, United States Congressman.

27

A THIMBLE OF ANTACID AND A STOUT NIGHTCAP

At 8:15 that same evening, as Claire was programming EPIC for its newest mission, and as Congressman Bryce Ridgeway was delivering a carefully tailored speech on race relations in a Birmingham church, Henry Arbogast left a steak house in the Golden Triangle district, a few blocks north of the White House.

He had reached his culinary limit, which for Arbogast was saying something. The porterhouse had been exquisite, and he'd downed more Pappy Van Winkle than any sensible man should. But then, when lobbyists were footing the bill, his proclivity to excess was always at its worst.

These indulgences came at a price. His stomach was churning, and it was a damning statement on Arbogast's condition that the most alluring image he could conjure at that moment was the bottle of Pepto Bismol in his bathroom cabinet. He set out on the sidewalk along K Street, lacing ponderously through the evening crowd. An inelegant man on the best of days, Arbogast walked slowly, deliberately, the bourbon having had its effect. The disorientation he felt, thankfully, was allayed at the first cross street. He looked right, up the length of 16th Street, and in the distance saw a vision from a dream. Beyond the geometric paths of Lafayette Square, the White House stood in all its uplit glory.

Arbogast paused to appreciate the scene, if only for a moment.

Soon, he thought. *Soon I'll have the opposite view.*

The excuse for the dinner had been business. Two back-slapping, Midland-based, oil lobbyists had been pushing for an easing of fracking regulations, although they seemed far more enthusiastic about a post-dinner rendezvous with a flock of three blondes from an expensive and, they'd been assured, highly discreet escort agency. Expense accounts were cyclic by nature, but right now, with the price of crude back to nearly a hundred dollars a barrel, the good times were rolling across the Permian Basin with no less authority than the subterranean tremors that made it all possible.

The lobbyists had implored Arbogast to join them for what they promised would be an epic night in their hotel suite. He'd been tempted, but in the end he explained that as head of the Republican National Committee he had to maintain a certain measure of decorum—or barring that, plausible deniability. His job, he confessed, put a target squarely on his back, and these days Democrats everywhere—to include bellmen, housekeepers, and, yes, even highly discreet escorts—had phones with cameras.

It was true, at least in part. Despite having divorced ten years ago, Arbogast tried to avoid compromising situations. That practical reasoning, however, was perhaps window dressing for the unhappy truth. Arbogast was fifty-eight years old, morbidly obese, and after a four-thousand-calorie dinner he felt like a stranded whale. In that moment, he wanted nothing more than to go home, pour a thimble of antacid and a stout nightcap, and go to bed.

He lowered his head and set sail eastbound. The air was cold, winter taking a hard grip. The wind stung his cheeks. All around him were buildings dressed for Christmas, lights and holiday displays in every window, wreaths adorning light posts. The crowds were heavy, thick-jacketed bodies bounding like frozen marbles over the sidewalks. He vaguely recalled something about a holiday concert tonight on the National Mall.

He searched for a taxi, and not seeing one right away, he decided to move to the next block. In his experience, there was no better quarter mile in town to find a cab than along the lobbyists' lairs of K Street. He pinballed left and right, spotted the familiar curb ahead.

Arbogast was nearly there when he had the distinct impression of an express train crashing into his back. He went down hard, expelling a grunt as his rotund body smacked the sidewalk. Arbogast turtled onto one side, feeling pain in his right hip. He'd taken worse hits—probably a thousand when he'd played football at Duquesne. In those days he'd simply gotten up and jogged back into the game. Now he lay stunned and still on the sidewalk, taking stock of what might be broken. Happily, aside from the soreness in his hip, he seemed largely unscathed. People moved around him like water rounding a boulder in a stream. Then a thick pair of legs appeared next to him.

"You are all right?"

"Yes, I think so," Arbogast croaked. Fortunately, he'd been wearing gloves—otherwise his palms would have been scraped raw. He tried to rise onto a knee, and was halfway there when two strong hands came to his aid, one under each armpit.

"Thank you, I—" before Arbogast could finish the words, he felt a sharp prick under his left armpit. It felt like a bee sting, but whatever it was, it dissipated quickly.

Still dazed, he tried to steady himself. He turned to face his benefactor, a big amorphous man in an overcoat and baseball cap, who said in accented English, "You are okay. Good night." The man melded into the crowd and was gone.

Breathing in gasps, Arbogast began to get his bearings. He couldn't say if the man who helped him up was the one who'd knocked him down, but he decided the point was moot. Gingerly, he moved toward the curb and, as hoped, quickly found a cab.

The drive to his Chevy Chase condo took fifteen minutes. He used the time to continue his self-assessment. Any lingering thoughts of dinner faded, and the prospect of blond escorts had fallen completely off his radar. His hip seemed better, yet he did feel a certain generalized discomfort. By the time the cab pulled in front of his building, he was strangely anxious. His chest felt tight and he was sweating beneath his jacket.

His building was a six-story affair, each floor containing four luxury apartments. Owing to its limited size, a coded entryway took the place of a doorman. He made his way to the elevator, sank the call button, and immediately faced more bad news. It appeared to be out of order.

Arbogast cursed under his breath and headed for the stairs. Because he lived on the top floor, and because he abhorred all forms of exercise, he'd only used the stairs twice before. He took his time, yet was sweating profusely when he reached the third-floor landing. By the time he reached the sixth, he was breathing in ragged gasps. His front door lay thirty feet away. It seemed like a mile. He put a hand on the wall, trying to steady himself as he moved, but was soon overcome by a rush of dizziness. That was when the real pain stuck.

Arbogast clutched his chest, his hand clawing at his overcoat, and collapsed in a great heap in the middle of the hall.

Arbogast was found twenty minutes later by a woman returning with her dog from "last call." Seeing her neighbor collapsed and unresponsive, a shaken Mira Rosenbaum set down her Maltipoo, Prince, and dialed 911. The EMTs arrived twelve minutes later—it would have been sooner had they not been forced to take the stairs—and registered no signs of life in the immense body on the hallway floor. They went through the motions all the same, removing Arbogast's coat and shirt, and made an honest effort to resuscitate him before yielding to the protocols of death on the scene.

At that point it was a matter of removing the body, which presented no small challenge—lifting three-hundred rolling pounds onto a transport gurney. To their relief, a policeman showed up and offered to help. Better yet, by the time Arbogast was loaded and secured, the elevator was again working.

The ambulance made its way to George Washington University Hospital with flashing lights, a few burps of the siren, but little sense of urgency. The same could be said for the emergency room doctor who certified Arbogast to be dead from what appeared to be a massive heart attack.

It would be another forty-eight hours before the cause of death was finalized by the city's last responder, the D.C. medical examiner. The ME reviewed an incident report that could not have been more telling: one white male, fifty-eight years old, who weighed twice what he should have, and who, in the minutes before his death, had climbed five flights of stairs while deeply intoxicated. The death certificate that bookended the life of Henry Arbogast was little different from a hundred others the ME had signed that year.

IMMEDIATE CAUSE OF DEATH: Myocardial infarction
UNDERLYING CAUSES: Coronary artery disease, morbid obesity

Straightforward as it all seemed, there were three points of interest that might have given the medical examiner pause had he known of them. The first involved a tiny puncture wound deep in a fatty fold of Arbogast's left armpit. As a rule, it was his duty to seek out such evidences, but in this case the obesity of the victim, perhaps combined with the ME's predisposed thought process and an impending dinner date, left the needle mark undetected.

The examiner could never had been held responsible for the second missed detail—a malware, inserted into the building elevator's control software, that had disabled the lift for precisely thirty-two minutes after Arbogast arrived.

The third discrepancy, too, would have necessitated an investigation far beyond any ordinary postmortem.

It involved the existence of an account in a Bahamian bank into which an eight-figure deposit had recently been stuffed. As it turned out, this final clue was perishable: by means that not even the bank's executives understood, the account was zeroed out in an electronic transfer the day after Arbogast's passing. The bankers were justifiably alarmed, but relief came some months later when they learned that Arbogast's estate made no mention of the transfer, or for that matter, the very existence of the account. Very quietly, the account was closed and expunged from the bank's records. No further questions would ever be asked.

28

TRAPPED IN THE BELLY

The room was silent save for the hum of cooling fans venting heat from rows of computers. The air was stagnant, sterile. All hints of the outdoors—pollen, evergreen, pollutants—had been scrubbed away by a high-volume, hospital-certified HEPA filtration system. Glare-free, indirect lighting gave the workspace a clinical aura, even if the effect was ruined by a surfing poster taped to one wall, a lone rider tubed in a near-perfect wave—Atticus's contribution to the decor.

After spending the previous afternoon logging parameters for the new search, Claire had gone home to let EPIC work overnight. Certain results would come quickly, yet others were more nuanced, requiring the system to manipulate multiple databases and, at times, wait for access authorizations from humans at the host agencies. More critically for Claire, it gave her a shot at a decent night's sleep.

She returned at nine in the morning to find the lab empty. Atticus, she knew, had been here much of the night programming his own work—he was a classic backside-of-the-clock geek. He'd be home sleeping now, and if he returned before noon Claire would be surprised. Not by chance, this gave her the morning to work alone. In truth, she wished Atticus was here. Alone in the great room, surrounded by banks of soulless hardware, she felt like Jonah trapped in the belly of some great technological whale.

When the results began filling her monitor, Claire immediately saw a problem: having set broad parameters, she was faced with prioritizing nearly six hundred files EPIC had unearthed overnight. Fortunately, this, in microcosm, was the feat for which the system had been designed—to parse oceans of data into something manageable. Or as Atticus carelessly termed it, to cut through the "byte noise."

She set to her task, narrowing search fields and building new constraints. Bryce's college transcripts and military records were set aside, along with bank accounts and financial information. Any of that could prove relevant, but for the moment it was little more than clutter that diverted from the central question. Was Bryce seeing another woman?

It occurred to Claire that the search she was performing had recently been echoed by two other D.C. establishments. The Democratic Party would be mining in earnest, exhuming all the dirt they could on a rising Republican star. For two reasons she doubted they would find much. First was that the Republicans would have done their own search prior to backing Bryce. The second was even more persuasive and, uncharacteristically for Claire, completely unanalytical: she had known Bryce Ridgeway half her life, and knew him to be beyond reproach.

The trouble was, she knew Sarah even more intimately than Bryce. If her friend had doubts, there was something behind them. She found herself navigating an awkward crosscurrent of loyalties, and not for the first time, Claire wondered if she was doing the right thing by leveraging the colossus that was EPIC.

The media, of course, would also be scrutinizing Bryce, yet a search using EPIC would make any other pale. She and her team had built a metadata research engine that was without parallel on Earth. The greatest challenge to its inception had not been software design, but rather gaining pathways to an array of highly classified government networks. It necessitated a nightmarish web of legal authorizations, disclaimers, and consent agreements. Through sheer force of will Claire had pushed it all through.

The project was backed by the DOD in the name of cyber research. The principal boundary, which she'd always maintained to a fault, was that no product of EPIC could leave the building. So restricted, Claire and her team had been granted unprecedented freedoms. Privacy laws that had long hampered the military and intelligence agencies, in an increasingly net-centric world, were sidestepped for one carefully crafted experiment.

Without warrants, EPIC could initiate wiretaps and track mobile phones. It could co-opt public and private CCTV networks to monitor cameras, and even recover backdated video. It could monitor banking transactions and trace offshore accounts, at least to the limits of the abilities of the NSA, CIA, and FBI—which was to say, virtually without bounds. The system could command the nation's intelligence agencies to initiate electronic searches, perform targeted intrusions, and in certain test cases, even insert manipulated data or take control of hardware.

It was cutting-edge work that, if successful, could revolutionize cyber warfare, bringing an information arsenal to the fingertips of a select few: the president, spymasters, or conceivably unique cyber-enabled

Special Forces operators. To the nation's leadership, EPIC was the proving ground for the future of intelligence gathering and warfare. To Claire, however, it was something else altogether. It was a matter of pushing science to the limit.

That is, until today.

Alves was on the phone when Burke came into the office. He assumed she was working one of their new cases, a money laundering operation tied to an Atlantic City casino.

As he pulled up a chair and waited, he noticed a copy of the *Washington Post* on their shared desk. Alves read the *Post* most days—not because she cared about politics, but because, in her words, "No self-respecting FBI agent can work D.C. without keeping an eye on the circus."

She finally ended her call. Burke looked at her, expecting an update on Atlantic City. It didn't come.

"What?" he asked.

She nudged the newspaper toward him. "Short article, bottom right."

He read the headline. "Henry Arbogast? Head of the RNC?"

"That's the one."

"He died yesterday."

Alves waited.

"And this is important because . . . ?"

"A few weeks ago, it was Arbogast who decided to put Congressman Bryce Ridgeway on a rocket to the stars."

The two looked at each other blankly, an out-of-synch comedy team. "Really? He's the one who convinced Ridgeway to run?"

"If you read the *Post* you would understand. Nobody but Arbogast could have punched his ticket. I figure he looked at the cast of duds already in the race and saw trouble. Then he saw the video from the Watergate, like we all did, and recognized a star in the making. Guys like Arbogast, that's what they do. They spot talent, and when they find it, they act. He probably bundled everything together for a turnkey campaign—manager, pollsters, strategies. Arbogast was a kingmaker."

Burke thought about it. "How did he die?"

"According to the article, natural causes."

This time Burke waited.

"I know, it's pretty vague, so I looked into it."

"That's the call you were on? Just now?"

"I have a friend who has a friend at the medical examiner's office. Apparently Arbogast had a heart attack. He'd just gotten home from a big dinner with some lobbyists. The elevator in his building was broken, so he had to use the stairs. He was a big guy . . . really big. Made it to the sixth-floor hallway and keeled over. A neighbor walking her dog found him pancaked in the hall. He was already in first stages of rigor by the time the EMTs arrived."

He shot her a skeptical look. "So why are we talking about this?"

Alves frowned.

Burke couldn't deny it—he felt the scratch as well. Another nagging coincidence. "Bad luck," he said, more to himself than to Alves. "Sounds like the guy was a heart explosion waiting to happen."

Alves said nothing.

He leaned back in his squeaky roller chair and put his hands on the armrests. Burke twisted side to side a few times before asking, "Where's our boy now?"

"Congressman Ridgeway?"

He gave her a pained look.

"Louisiana, maybe? I think South Carolina later today. It'll be that way pretty much until November. He's a hard man to get hold of."

"Even if I could reach him, I'm not sure what I'd say."

"Me neither," Alves admitted. "It just seems . . . I dunno . . . weird how fast things happened for him."

Burke looked at the *Washington Post* sitting on the desk. Then he looked at his partner. "Huh."

29

THE FIRST HINT OF A PROBLEM

Claire began with what she knew. Sarah had provided the time and date of the suspicious text she'd seen, and harvesting phone records was EPIC's version of child's play. Claire quickly found the text in question: Come to our place this morning. Have something special for you.

Then Bryce's reply: Will try.

Claire recovered every available message with that contact, and found threads going back seven months. She noted there were no voice dials to the same number which, if it had indeed been a mistress, would have been expected. The other texts were no less insipid than the original.

Thursday at 2.

New furniture arrived.

Back in one week.

On its face the string sounded more administrative than romantic—to the point that it seemed even more suspicious. The contact on Bryce's phone, designated only as AR, showed no identifying information beyond the phone number. More damningly, when EPIC performed a search on the number it hit roadblocks. Owing to encryption and some unusual security protocols, the owner could not easily be identified or located. Even the world's best cyber trackers could be stymied by solid encryption, or at the very least delayed. As if thinking along the same lines, the overseeing agency that had supplied the phone information—NSA, Claire imagined—conveniently offered a 53.6% probability that, if tasked and given enough time, it could defeat the encryption to locate the phone and identify its user.

A better than even chance, Claire thought, *but not much. And who knows how long it would take.*

Having hit a cul-de-sac with the phone number, she switched to tracking Bryce himself. His phone was the primary reference, but that could be augmented by other discrete sources. The most glaringly simple was his car—the Tesla Model 3 was wired to the hilt with connectivity. Aside from a record of its continuously transmitted GPS position, Bryce's arrivals to and departures from the Rayburn House Office Building were confirmed by security cameras at the House Members parking garage. His car's license plate had been captured on hundreds of municipal traffic cameras, and passes through toll stations were also recorded.

Car and phone data were only the beginning. Systems accessible to EPIC included nearly half the world's public and private CCTV networks. By combining facial recognition software with the CIA's latest application—a somatic-based software that classified individuals through body shape and movement—EPIC identified Bryce at no fewer than three hundred locations, everywhere from the National Air and Space Museum to a Target checkout counter in Fairfax. There were inevitably blanks and gaps in the trail, along with three outlier hits that the system purged via quality assurance filtering. The end result, however, was rock-solid: over a thousand verifiable location plots for Congressman Bryce Ridgeway.

The next phase was where EPIC truly shined. Data from these disparate sources were fused, and in a matter of minutes Claire was looking at a nearly faultless log of Bryce's movements for the last sixty days. The tapestry could be displayed in any number of ways. Her first instinct was to go with a map, yet because he'd been traveling extensively in the last month, the entire United States was presented. Claire adjusted the timeline, limiting the window of movement to the days before he'd hit the campaign trail.

She saw the expected clusters converge, the most prominent being his home and his office in the Rayburn building. Secondary were a few regular lunchtime haunts, and the Capitol building itself. Finally came the outliers. She saw a visit to a Virginia VFW post, another to the George Washington University conference center. On Veterans Day, the fateful half hour at the Watergate Hotel was recorded, followed by George Washington University Hospital and the Metropolitan Police's 2nd District Headquarters. Later that week, she noticed two visits to the downtown Mayflower Hotel. This gave Claire pause, but she pressed onward.

The next step was to put it all in motion. Claire wheeled her roller chair sideways in the U-shaped workstation to address a different monitor. She reconfigured the output, arranging things chronologically, and watched Bryce's computed position move across a map. The days progressed at a rate of ten seconds per hour. She watched him go for a run, an Apple Watch tracking his progress faithfully. After getting home, he took a shower, EPIC registering an uptick in the web-enabled water meter, and shortly thereafter a rise in gas use that correlated to a recharging hot water heater. These were only inferences on EPIC's part, but delivered with a high level of confidence based on millions of data points taken from regional utility usage—a new feature created by Atticus. After the shower, a Wi-Fi-enabled Keurig brewed two cups of something—technology had its limits—before Bryce left for work. His car and phone were tracked faithfully to a morning meeting at the Longworth House Office Building, and there his face and stride were captured by no fewer than six cameras.

And so it went.

Claire watched Bryce, virtually, through an entire two-week window. She knew the log wasn't perfect— any system was only as good as its data—and she was assuming Bryce hadn't engaged in countermeasures, things like letting someone else drive his car or carry his phone. Any gaps EPIC filled as best it could. It notified Claire anytime the raw data fell below a preset degree of confidence, and when that flag appeared, an AI algorithm projected his movements to the next known location using historical data. On a drive to western Virginia, where coverage was spotty, presumably to visit his father, EPIC estimated his average speed with respect to known traffic, including a quotient for driving aggressiveness—the congressman was a modest lead-foot, particularly in the morning. For Claire it all played out in a God's-eye view.

It was on day five that she saw the first hint of a problem. On days seven, eight, and ten she saw it again. Her concern mounting, Claire stopped the playback and recast the entire search, going back one year with a new focus—a particular address in Georgetown.

The implications of what she was seeing caused her heart to sink, and while the new search ran, Claire diverted to the far side of the room. She pulled a bottle of iced tea from the minifridge, wrenched off the cap. Stretching her sore back—the unavoidable consequence of too many hours, too many years, spent rooted to a workstation—she took a sip, then held the bottle to her cheek. The touch of the cold glass was a shock, a thermal awakening.

She was facing a classic programmer's paradox. Her system had performed exactly as designed, yet the outcome was taking her into personally rocky terrain. It wasn't the first time she'd felt conflicted. The core mission of the system was to pry into people's lives: websites visited, financial transactions made, messages sent to lovers. The ethical conundrum could not have been clearer. Owing to the top-secret nature of her sources, EPIC's raw results were restricted to this room. This was the principle Claire had used to sell the project, an inviolate rule that she, and she was quite sure her staff, had never violated. Now, however, EPIC was providing information that affected her dearest friend.

Should she stop before she went deeper?

Or was it already too late?

Claire sipped from the bottle, then whispered to no one, "Be careful what you ask for."

30

A VOICE OF REASON

Sarah was in the kitchen dicing peppers when the doorbell rang. She set down the knife, wiped her hands on her apron, and on the way to the door used a wrist to flick back a few loose strands of hair. Had she even brushed it this morning? The little things were starting to slide.

She opened the door to find a middle-aged man holding out credentials.

"Mrs. Ridgeway?"

She nodded.

"FBI Special Agent Troy Burke—I'm with the Washington Field Office."

Sarah stared at a photograph that looked more or less like the man behind it. Plain features, bad haircut, a bit faded with age.

"Did I get you at a bad time?" he asked cordially.

"Oh, no . . . I'm sorry. You just caught me by surprise. I was expecting a produce delivery. What can I do for you?"

"Actually, it's more what I can do for you. My partner and I are the lead agents investigating the terrorist attack at the Watergate Hotel. I spoke with your husband afterward, and I promised to give him an update on things. Unfortunately, he's a tough man to track down these days."

"Tell me about it," she said.

"I was in the area, so I thought I'd stop by and introduce myself. And I thought if I gave you the latest, you could pass it on to him."

"Well . . . sure. Come in."

She led Burke through the living room and into the kitchen. Sarah removed her apron, set it on the counter next to a cutting board full of peppers.

"I hope I didn't interrupt," he said.

"Oh, I was only prepping for dinner. Our daughter is babysitting so she won't be home for a couple of hours. I still have half a pot of coffee—can I get you a cup?"

"Actually, yeah, that would be great."

While Sarah pulled mugs from the cupboard, Burke wandered the attached dining area. He paused to study a clutch of family pictures that had taken over one wall. "You just have the one daughter?" he asked.

"Yes, Alyssa. She's a sophomore in high school. Do you have kids, Agent Burke?"

"I do, a boy and a girl, both in college."

Sarah delivered two full mugs to the dining room table. The dregs of the morning's pot were thick, but Burke declined cream and sugar. They sat down facing one another.

"So, about the Watergate," she said. "You want me to pass the latest on to Bryce?"

"If that's all right. I know it must have been a difficult time for you."

"Yes, it was."

"Funny how things work out. Your husband was in the right place at the right time, and his military training kicked in. He ends up a hero, and the next thing you know . . . here he is, running for president."

"Yeah, I never saw that one coming."

"I'm sure you didn't. I've worked in the D.C. office for years, long enough to know that politics is a strange business. I was wondering, did Bryce ever mention Henry Arbogast?"

"Arbogast? Yes, the head of the RNC. According to Bryce, he was the one who floated the idea of a presidential run. It's a shame . . . I talked to Bryce this morning and he told me Arbogast passed away yesterday."

"He did."

Sarah played her fingers over the warm mug. She was getting an odd vibe. "I heard it was his heart. According to Bryce, he wasn't a very fit person."

Burke shrugged. "I couldn't say—never met the man."

"So . . . you said you had information about the attack."

He took a long pull. "In truth, not a lot has changed since the last time I spoke to your husband. The thing is, I promised to keep him updated." Burke mentioned a few things Sarah had already read online. His manner was that of a judge, a voice of reason, innately trustworthy. He explained that while the attacker had been identified early on, there was little progress in determining whether he had support. "So far, he appears to be a lone wolf. Mind you, we're not giving up. A lot of agencies are working on this, both here and abroad. Unfortunately, these things take time."

"I'm sure they do. I'd like to think it was just one deranged individual."

"That may turn out to be the case. The conflict in Syria has been going on a for long time. When people suffer loss, their hatred can get out of control. What's unusual is for a solo attacker to reach us here Stateside.

Fortunately, the last line of defense turned out to be your husband. How is he handling it, by the way?"

"I'm not sure what you mean," Sarah said cautiously.

"Well, what happened on the rooftop—a lot of people would have found it pretty traumatic. But then, given his background, I'm sure he's seen worse."

Sarah had a fleeting thought that Burke had learned about her visit to Dr. Chalmers. She pushed it away. "Yes, Bryce saw a lot during his service. But to answer your question, he doesn't really talk about things like that. Never has. I think I lost more sleep over the Watergate attack than he did."

Burke nodded thoughtfully. "I served a short stint in the Army myself, right out of high school. Nothing like what your husband did, but enough to get the idea. I'm glad to hear he's gotten past it."

"Like you say, Bryce has been there, done that."

"I should probably ask . . . are *you* okay? We have professionals on staff who are trained to help victims and their families deal with traumatic events. I could get you in touch with someone."

"No, I'm good. But thanks all the same."

"No problem." Burke downed the last of his coffee. He went to the sink and started to rinse his mug.

"Don't worry about that."

He set the mug on the counter. "I should let you get back to dinner."

"I'll tell Bryce you came by and relay what you told me."

"Please do." At the front door Burke smiled and held out a business card. "If you have any questions, feel free to give me a call. Anytime—I mean that."

Sarah thanked him and took the card. Burke

walked away and she watched him all the way to his car, a dark blue sedan that had government written all over it. She retreated inside, put her back to the door, and murmured under her breath, "What the hell was *that* all about?"

31

ARM-DEEP

The image on Claire's monitor couldn't have been more banal: a modest two-story row house on a quiet street in Georgetown. Not tidy, not gone to ruin. The eastern unit in a covey of four, brunt brick frontage, two windows on the second floor and one by the front door. A short set of steps led to a tabletop landing. There was nothing distinguishing about the place. No flower boxes in the windows, no flag bracket waiting for the Fourth of July. The flat eastern wall had a few scars, all touched up with slightly mismatched paint. Altogether, it was an unremarkable residence on a street full of the same.

Except for one thing.

Bryce Ridgeway, prospective president and her best friend's husband, had been a regular visitor. Twelve times in the month of November alone.

Claire's first instinct was to call Sarah, ask her if she knew why her husband would be making regular stops at a private residence in town. *Yeah, right,* she thought. *What are the chances of that going down in flames?*

Her second thought prevailed—back to the analytics.

She widened the period of look-back, going back a full six months. EPIC uncovered six more visits in

December, nearly every day Bryce was briefly in town. Before mid-November, however, there was nothing. Eighteen stops altogether, with the average length of visit being two hours. The longest stay was six hours, the shortest five minutes. All were during daylight hours.

Claire leaned forward in her chair, a fist under her chin. Rodin's Thinker. Every answer only seemed to raise more questions.

What are you up to, Bryce?

She decided to widen the net.

Claire tasked EPIC to find out who owned the row house. The results took longer than usual, and were maddeningly opaque. The property was titled in the name of a limited liability corporation, which in turn was controlled by a Katjusha-doll series of shell companies. The thread of ownership took her from Panama to Kazakhstan to the Cook Islands. From that point, nothing more could be learned without presenting oneself in person at a Cook Islands courthouse—by no small coincidence, one of the most remote places on earth, deep in the southern Pacific. A blue-water cul-de-sac at the bottom of the world.

The circuitous scheme was an answer in itself. Whoever owned the place, they didn't want it known. It was a partial victory, and dumped half a bucket of cold water on the theory that Bryce was seeing another woman—no doe-eyed congressional staffer or hot yoga instructor would go to such lengths.

Tapping the nub of a pencil on her desk, Claire chose a different path—she tried to determine if the place had a security system. EPIC quickly determined that if the condo had security, it was an internal system, nothing web-based or linked to one of the usual commercial providers. EPIC then mapped out video surveillance for the surrounding block. The most promising network turned out to be across the street, an auto parts store with a web-enabled, high-resolution system. In no time Claire had access, and she concentrated on a camera that sat overwatch on the parking lot—a hundred feet beyond which, across the street, was the front door of the condo in question.

She accessed historical footage from the camera, and while it loaded she pulled up the timeline on another screen. Soon the two were side by side, giving the correlation Claire wanted—on November 17th, 3:18 p.m., she watched Bryce arrive at the condo. He took the designated parking spot, his distinctive blue Tesla pulling into the slot marked 4. Bryce got out, walked straight to the front door, and without knocking opened it with a key. Claire watched closely as he shouldered inside, yet saw no sign of a greeting. He left the door momentarily ajar, as one might to disable an alarm, then after a few seconds kicked it shut with his heel.

Claire kept watching, but soon grew weary of staring at the door. She increased the playback speed, keeping her eyes on the stoic, unmoving door for three hours and fifty-two minutes, at which point Bryce emerged, sank a dead bolt with his key, and walked calmly to his car and drove away. In that time, no one else came or went.

She watched another sequence three days later, saw the same drill. Two hours and six minutes. No visitors. Claire let this video run, increasing the speed and watching all the way through to the next morning. Nobody else in, nobody out.

She backtracked the video to capture the best shot

of Bryce, froze it, and let EPIC run digital enhancements. The image resolved before her, sharpening pixel by pixel. The final photo was somewhat grainy, but sufficient for Claire to recognize a man she'd known since college. Square-jawed and handsome, undeniably photogenic. Yet something seemed missing. The affable smile? His ease of movement? Then it hit her. Not something missing. Something new. There was an alertness in his gaze, in his bearing, that she'd never seen before. It might have fit if he'd been in uniform. In a place like Mali or Afghanistan.

She pinched the bridge of her nose, heaved a sigh, and pushed back from the desk. When she refocused on the main monitor, her attention went past Bryce to what was behind him. The door of the condo.

Claire recalled an application Atticus had unearthed some months ago—an AI filter called Redeye, designed by the CIA, designed for tailored surveillance. Facing a world drowning in raw data, Langley was automating its yeoman's work. The concept was simplicity itself: set your parameters, then let AI software watch endless hours of video or listen to thousands of phone calls. The system could monitor a traffic camera for a specific license plate, listen to phone calls for key words or names, sweep airport arrival corridors for a specific face. What Claire wanted was more basic than any of that: she wanted to know how many times one door had opened in the previous year. Or at least, as far back as the video record went.

It took ten minutes to program Redeye. Then she clicked EXECUTE and headed for the Keurig.

Sarah was at the grocery store, arm-deep in a frozen food cooler, when her phone trilled. She pulled out three pot pies, dropped them in her cart, and picked up when she saw who it was.

"Hey."

"Hey," Bryce said, "I saw you called. Everything okay?"

"Yeah, all good. Where are you?"

"South Carolina . . . at least, I think. It all kind of runs together. Two states today, three tomorrow. How's Alyssa?"

"She's great. Got an A on her chem midterm. The only glitch was yesterday—she almost ran a red light on the way to soccer."

"Not good."

"That's why they call it a learner's permit. She'll be fine. Listen, the reason I called was because I got a visit at home today from an FBI agent, a guy named Burke."

After a pause, Bryce said, "Oh, right—the one who interviewed me after the thing at the Watergate."

"That's him. He said he promised to keep you updated on the investigation."

"So he came to our house and talked to you?"

"Apparently you're hard to get ahold of." Sarah recounted what Burke had told her.

"Seems a little strange," he said. "Doesn't sound like much we don't already know."

"That's what I thought."

Bryce seemed to weigh it. "Well, I wouldn't worry about it. Honestly, it's something I've been seeing a lot of lately. When you run for president, people find excuses for face time. I've been getting messages from Army buddies, and college friends are coming out of the woodwork. Some woman called and said we dated back in the seventh grade."

Sarah held steady. "Before my time. Should I be jealous?"

"Desperately."

She tried to put a smile in her voice. "I guess it's understandable. In a year you might be the most powerful man in the world."

An awkward silence.

"Bryce?"

"Yeah, I'm here, but I need to get going—Jack is waving me over to a bunch of guys in suits. Gotta keep the dollars flowing into the campaign."

"Okay. Are you still going to be home two days next week?"

"That's the plan. And Sarah . . . I don't want that guy Burke bothering you. If he shows up again, let me know. I'll put a stop to it."

"It's not a big deal. He seemed like a decent guy."

"Just tell me if he gets in touch again. Gotta go."

"Bye, love you!" she said.

"Yeah, you too."

The call ended.

Sarah stood staring at her phone, her hand rigid. When she finally lowered it, the motion caused a light in a freezer two doors down to flicker on. Her mind flew back sixteen years, searching and sifting. At least a hundred phone calls during deployments, training assignments, and congressional travel. She couldn't remember it happening before when Bryce was out of town.

For the first time ever, he hadn't ended with ". . . *and give Aly a kiss.*"

32

WHEN EVERYTHING
FELL APART

The Redeye program, playing high-tech doorman, took eighteen minutes to run its scan—an eternity by EPIC's lightning standards. The final tally was definitive. The condo had been accessed sixty-one times in the last nine months—the point at which the surprisingly lengthy video record ended. All the hits were since July, and on fifty-nine occasions, as verified by facial and somatic recognition, Bryce was identified as the visitor. Claire bull's-eyed in on the other two.

On July 18th she saw a man arrive. He parked a late-model Ford van in the reserved spot like he owned the place—which he might have. He was thickset, dressed in loose summer clothes. A horseshoe of dark hair ringed his gleaming bald crown. He opened the condo's door using an app on his phone, then blocked it open. For fifteen minutes he transferred boxes of office supplies and light furniture from the van to the condo. He then closed the door and remained inside. For forty-six hours and ten minutes. In that time, the camera recorded no other visitors, no food delivery. The only activity: a knock on the door from what looked like two weary Jehovah's Witnesses that went unanswered. Finally, after two days, the man emerged wearing the same clothes he'd arrived in. With thick stubble on his cheeks. He locked up and drove away.

On October 2nd the same man appeared, driving

a similar but slightly different van. He was dressed for autumn, light jacket and a Nats baseball cap. This time he carried in a few office supplies: printer paper, light bulbs, a few boxes. He stayed inside three hours, then locked up and left.

Claire was relieved on at least one point: whatever was going on inside, it seemed more business than pleasure. Was it a secondary congressional office? Something to do with Bryce's campaign? Either would be a happy ending. Neither felt right.

She tried to identify the man, again using EPIC. Unfortunately, even under the best digital filtering and enhancement, the image was not of sufficient quality to attempt a match. She shifted to the two delivery vans, but they proved equally problematic. Not surprisingly, both were rentals. Claire was no detective—not in any conventional sense—yet her instincts told her that tracking down who'd rented the van would be no less a tail-chase than tracing the condo's ownership.

Try as she might, she could think of no good explanation for what she was seeing. Even the bad ones were few. EPIC chimed a notification, and she saw the results from another search she'd ordered: the system had hacked into Bryce's office calendar without so much as breaking a cyber-sweat. She cross-referenced its entries to her map from November and December. It was as she feared: the hours Bryce spent at the condo had been blocked out by ill-defined meetings and conferences. None included staff, nor was there any mention of who he was meeting or where. Whatever Bryce was up to, he was being secretive.

Claire went back further, to the summer, matching Bryce's location data to known visits. And that was when everything fell apart. For the earlier dates, his EPIC-computed location mismatched every appearance at the condo. She stared at the screen, dumbstruck, not knowing what to make of it. Once again, a progress on one front only muddied the greater picture.

When her thoughts finally righted, Claire had a revelation. For all the technology at her fingertips, sometimes there was no substitute for firsthand knowledge. For eyes on a target.

It was time to take a drive.

She was just pushing back from her workstation when she heard the *access granted* chime at the entrance. Atticus came in riding a knee scooter. He'd texted earlier with the sad story: he had cracked an ankle bone playing ultimate Frisbee that morning, and now his lower right leg was clammed in an orthopedic boot.

"Who gets injured playing Frisbee?" she asked.

"Don't want to talk about it." He wheeled toward a workstation, his hopeless beard and dead-leaf-brown bangs framed by a Cal Tech hoodie. Standing one-legged, he circled his gaming chair like a dog about to lay down, then lowered himself gingerly into the seat. "Sorry I'm late," he said.

Claire checked the only clock in the room that wasn't on a monitor—an analog Disney item from Frozen mounted over the door. Olaf's stick-fingers pointed to the two and the twelve. "I'm kidding, Atticus. How's the ankle?"

"It's fine—just a little sore. What are you working on?"

Claire kept mostly to the truth. "I'm testing a few of the apps on a particular condo in Georgetown."

"Everything working as advertised?"

"Mostly, yeah." She went to the rack by the door and pulled her jacket off a peg. "I'm heading out, but I'll be back later."

"Okay."

Claire swiped her ID and palm-smacked a green mushroom button to unlock the door. She paused at the threshold. "You going to be here for a while?"

"Yeah, I'm seeing a friend for dinner, but not until seven. Need me to do something?"

"Probably not . . . but if anything does come up, I'll call the landline."

Burke was tidying his desk when his phone went off. It showed an unknown number. He picked up all the same. Robocalls were as much a bane to the FBI as anyone, but woe be the special agent who let a hot tip go cold on voice mail.

"Agent Burke."

"Hello, Agent Burke. Bryce Ridgeway."

Burke's attention notched upward. He heard heavy background noise on the line, almost as if Ridgeway was sitting in a call center. "Good to hear from you, Congressman." He waited, remembering the drill: *call me Bryce.* It didn't come this time.

"Glad I was able to reach you. My wife told me you stopped by this afternoon. She forwarded the latest on the case, but it sounds like not much has changed. One Saudi jihadi with no clear links to any organization."

"Yeah, that's basically it." Burke weighed which way to steer things, and after a moment added, "Our techs did nail down one detail."

"What's that?"

"When we last spoke, you mentioned how you

held your hand over the bomber's—you thought it might keep the switch depressed."

"Right. And you wondered why he didn't release it right away when I sent him over the rail."

"Exactly. As it turns out, we believe he did release it the moment you let go of his hand."

"How could that be?"

"Our techs put together some fragments of circuitry and discovered that the trigger had a built-in delay. That's why the bomb didn't go off immediately."

"How long of a delay?"

"Almost ten seconds. Or from your point of view, just enough."

"Well . . . lucky me."

"Guess you picked the right day to intervene."

Burke heard someone call Ridgeway's name, and the congressman put him on hold for nearly a minute. When he came back on, Burke said, "Sounds like you're busy."

"You can't imagine. I'm in Charleston, on my way to another event. I just wanted to give you a call so you'd have this number. The card I gave you previously has my official number, but this is my personal line. Please keep it to yourself, and if anything comes up regarding the investigation, call me direct—no need to involve Sarah as a go-between."

"Understood. I've got the number now and I'll make sure it stays private."

More commotion on the South Carolina end.

"Sorry," Ridgeway said, "gotta run."

"Good luck with the campaigning."

Burke had no sooner put his phone down when Alves walked up with a file in her hand. "Who was that?" she asked.

"Bryce Ridgeway."

Her face flared with surprise. "Really? What did he want?"

Burke looked blankly at his phone, then at Alves. "I'm not really sure."

The drive to Georgetown went quickly in light holiday traffic. Claire crossed the Arlington Bridge, then passed the city's most famous riverside monument: Lincoln, seated in his great marble chair, looking forlornly across the seats of power. Claire wasn't political by nature, but she imagined what he might think if he could see the current state of affairs. *No, no, you've got it all wrong . . .*

Her next thought came as a natural extension. Could Bryce fix what ailed America? Could one man make things better? She hoped the answer was yes.

Before he got the chance, however, there were questions to be answered.

She veered north toward the K Street exit, skirting Foggy Bottom and bypassing the Watergate complex. The infamous office building loomed with its cruise ship curves, oblivious to the role it had played in bringing down a president. Adjacent to that was its sister building, the wrap-around, C-shaped hotel that might soon be linked with the rise of another president.

Two more turns took her into the heart of Georgetown.

Claire had always thought the borough seemed out of place in the District, as if a piece of suburban Pangea somewhere in Virginia had cracked off and migrated into town. It didn't have the rough edges of the surrounding neighborhoods, the aura of managed decay.

Things soon began to look familiar—the result of hours spent studying the condo and its surroundings. In the distance she saw Georgetown's namesake university, its spire towering into a gray-shaded sky. Classic Federal-style homes on one corner gave way to new-build luxury complexes on the next. Cobblestone paths curved through alleys, and trendy bistros and artisanal coffee shops were shoehorned into every gap.

Claire had no trouble finding P Street, and she immediately recognized the auto parts store. It looked frail and dated, a business that had probably gotten its start selling points and plugs for '58 Chevys, but that now found itself struggling in an age of online parts sales and microchip-managed engines.

The street was quiet and there was virtually no traffic, only a single car a hundred yards back. Soon the angles changed and Claire spotted the condo. The unit in question was the rightmost in a group of four. All were painted different colors, and there were minor architectural distinctions between them. A wrought-iron rail sided one set of steps, while shutters accented the windows next door. The unit marked 4 was the least notable of the bunch, and looked much as it had on her monitor.

Claire brought the car to a crawl as she neared the building. Only the leftmost parking spot was occupied, the space marked 4 being empty—as it had been for most of the last year. One section of the front sidewalk was quaking up, an elm spreading shamelessly. Claire studied the three front windows, all of which were covered by heavy blinds. Windows in the other units popped with light in the sullen afternoon.

As hoped, she saw a few things that hadn't registered in her cyber-stalking. She noticed a bus stop across the street. An old woman was sweeping leaves from the sidewalk of number 1, a blue-faced unit with Cape Cod trim. Behind, on an acute angle, were the fourplex's shared dumpster and a stack of mailboxes. She wondered if Bryce had ever used any of them.

She swept past the condo, through an intersection, and looped around the block to make a pass from the opposite direction. On her second approach, Claire was forced to stop, trapped behind a working garbage truck. With the car idling, she checked the rearview mirror. To her surprise, she saw the same car she'd noticed earlier.

Or was it?

Dark blue sedans were common enough.

Claire had been so focused on driving and navigating, she'd paid little attention to what was behind her. The car was well back, paused at the previous side street. Curiously, it sat motionless at the stop sign, despite no oncoming traffic. An eddy of gray vapor coughed from the tailpipe. On the first surveillance mission of her life, Claire wondered if paranoia was getting the better of her.

The garbage truck began moving, turned right at the corner. Claire accelerated and turned left, bypassing the condo a second time. Her eyes flicked between the road and the mirror. The blue sedan made two quick turns and was soon back behind her.

Her heart skittered a beat. Her hands tightened on the wheel. Claire no longer had any doubts.

She was being followed.

33

THE SOUND OF FAST KEYSTROKES

Claire had no idea what to do.

Visions of Hollywood car chases flashed to mind, then atomized just as quickly. She knew nothing about tactical driving, about shaking tails. Keeping a steady speed, she made a series of turns. The car followed her through the first two, then she lost sight of it. She accelerated as much as she dared, her comfort level redlining at ten miles-an-hour over the speed limit. She thought she was clear, but then the blue car reappeared. It was closer than ever, as if tethered by an unseen wire.

Panic began to rise. Should she drive faster? Make a series of quick turns? Or was it better to simply ignore her shadow? If she could reach the office, the gate guards would turn away whoever was behind her. Only one thing seemed certain: she was out of her league, facing a problem outside her programmer's wheelhouse.

Or was it?

The answer came like lines of code on a screen.

She picked up her phone and fumbled to make a call.

"What's up?" Atticus said, answering the lab's landline on the second ring.

Claire tried to force calm into her voice. Surely, she

failed. "I need to test a couple of the upgrades we added last week."

"Sure, which ones?"

"The traffic light function, to begin."

Atticus laughed. "You mean like, for real?"

"It's our job to validate. Are you picking up my phone?"

"Your mobile? Hang on . . ."

Ten seconds felt like ten hours. The blue sedan never wavered.

"Okay, got you. M Street east of Wisconsin."

"Right. I'm looking at a car behind me, a blue sedan. I'd like to try and lose them at an intersection."

"Whoa . . . *lose* them? How does that—"

"Atticus, please! Would you do this for me?"

A hesitation. Atticus had every right to be suspicious. "Boss, is everything okay?"

"Actually, no. But I can't explain right now. I just need you to *do* this!"

"Okay, okay . . . I've got your back."

"Thank you. I'll explain when I get back to the office. I'd also like to add something else. See if you can grab that plate when it goes past a camera."

"It'll take some time to set up . . . hang on."

Some time turned out to be ninety seconds. Two more intersections. Claire slowed, kept a straight line. The blue car crept closer in the traffic on M and was fifty yards back now.

"I've got the next three intersections captured, both signals and cameras."

"Good," she said. "Next light. As soon as I'm through, stop him."

"If you say so."

Claire was just short of the intersection when the

light turned yellow. She made it through, and the blue car ended up stuck behind a utility van. Claire felt a wave of relief. Her plan had worked perfectly. Then brake lights blinked ahead. Bloodred warnings.

Forced to stop, she craned her head left. A car ahead was parallel parking, traffic stalled behind it. A municipal truck blocked the opposite side of the street, a work crew beavering away at a storm drain behind orange barriers. "Dammit!"

Momentarily stuck, she checked the mirror. The blue car remained trapped but was edging left. She could make out the dark blob of the driver's head straining to see ahead—keeping eyes on, ready to catch up as soon as the light changed.

"New plan!" she said. Claire explained precisely what she wanted.

"What?" Atticus replied. "No—no way!"

"We talked about this," she said. "You know it's doable."

"I know I can *do* it! I can also be thrown in jail for—"

"Atticus, you know I wouldn't ask unless . . . unless I was in trouble! Please, nobody will get hurt!"

A sigh. The sound of fast keystrokes.

At the intersection behind, the light turned green. The van turned right and the blue car shot ahead to catch up. What the driver couldn't know was that the lights had gone green in every direction. A city bus turned left in front of him. The blue car swerved left and the driver slammed on the brakes. Its nose bobbed down for an instant before the right front quarter-panel smacked into an accelerating yellow cab. Claire heard horns blaring behind her. Soon hazard lights were flashing, doors opening. Angry fingers pointing.

The road ahead cleared. Claire swerved around a jaywalker, turned left onto the Key Bridge, and quickly blended in with traffic. Her nerves were raw, her hands sweaty.

All the same, she couldn't contain just the slightest of smiles.

34

IN SWASHBUCKLING FASHION

hanks for getting here so quickly," Claire said.

"You sounded upset," Sarah replied.

They'd arrived at The Daily Grind simultaneously, and neither had gotten around to ordering. Looking at the ten-deep line, Claire said, "Could we just sit outside?"

"Sure."

They single-filed to the door, and as soon as they went through the coffee-shop sounds disappeared. The gloom was thickening and a light rain had begun to fall. The patio was vacant, but a naked metal table sat cold beneath an awning. They crossed the glistening tile terrace and took opposing seats in chain-mail chairs. Sarah's yoga pants were helpless against the frigid metal but thankfully she'd worn a heavy jacket. Water dripped from the awning in rhythmless percussion.

"I'm sorry about this," Claire said, wiping dew from her cheek with the back of a sleeve. "I'm a little off my game. I've never done fieldwork before."

"Fieldwork?"

"I did what we talked about."

Sarah stared at her. "You spied on Bryce?"

"Nobody uses that word any more. I surveilled him."

"How?"

Claire drew the kind of breath people used to compose themselves, long and deep. She explained how she'd tracked Bryce's whereabouts in recent months, tens of thousands of hits from dozens of sources to build a pattern of his behavior.

Sarah sat stunned. "This system you've built . . . it can do all that?"

"And a lot more. Most of what I saw looked innocuous, but there was one thing that didn't have an easy explanation." She told Sarah about the condo.

"I see," she replied guardedly. "Do you know who lives there?"

"I tasked EPIC to find out who owned the property, but no luck. That's suspicious in itself. The place was purchased last year through a series of shell companies; the kind of smoke and mirrors people use to conceal ownership."

"So . . . what does that mean? Are you saying Bryce bought this place secretly?"

"Honestly, I don't know what to make of it. But I can tell you one thing for certain—aside from Bryce, only one other person has been there in the last six months."

Sarah's hands gripped the chair's cold steel arms. A death-row inmate waiting for the jolt.

"A man visited twice."

"A man," Sarah said repeated.

"I got a look at him on some video. He looked like a delivery guy, hauling boxes of office supplies and some light furniture into the place."

"Well, that's good . . . maybe Bryce is only using it as an office."

"He already has an office."

The rain turned steady, its broken rhythm going to static. The wind began rising. As the awning became saturated, its natural jade hue went to a dark evergreen.

"All right," Sarah said, in a tone that added *Miss Know-it-all*. "What do *you* think he's doing there?"

Claire stared into the gloom. She was obviously rattled.

"What's got you so flustered?" Sarah asked.

"I went to take a look this afternoon."

"You went to this place? Why?"

"I wanted to see it firsthand, maybe find some detail I was missing online. Like a camera that wasn't showing up on EPIC, or a home security system I could hack."

"Okay. So what did you find?"

"It wasn't so much what I found as . . . as what found me. A car started following me."

Sarah's tone turned cautious. "How do you know that?"

"Look, I'm not trained in this kind of thing, but it was obvious." She explained how she'd spotted the car, how it had shadowed her. Then she explained how Atticus had intervened.

For the first time ever, Sarah found herself doubting Claire. "You're saying this EPIC thing can control traffic lights? Even cause accidents?"

"It's not exactly our crowning achievement, but yes. The hack is actually simple. Certain traffic lights are Wi-Fi enabled, a way for the city to manage traffic flows. Some of them don't even require passwords to gain access."

"You *caused* this car to crash."

"Atticus . . . or actually EPIC . . . look, it was like bumper cars. Not a big deal. A dent to a couple of fenders, maybe one city bus involved."

"*A city bus?*" Sarah repeated, dumbfounded. "And here I thought you were some plodding government researcher, all soft chairs and cubicles."

"It worked, okay? It got the guy off my ass. Atticus is trying to identify the car and driver."

"I probably shouldn't ask, but how?"

"He'll start with traffic camera footage, get the license plate. With any luck, a preliminary accident report will get filed soon by the Metro Police."

"You can see that?"

"I told you, EPIC has access to virtually every government database. Chances are, there'll be an insurance claim as well."

Sarah considered that. "Insurance company files aren't government databases. Are you saying EPIC can penetrate private companies too?"

"I'm saying that given enough time, we'll know who was tailing me."

Sarah shook her head, as if everything Claire was telling her was clogging her brain. She checked her watch. "Look, I've got to get going. I'm supposed to take Alyssa to a friend's house for a sleepover."

"That's perfect."

"Perfect? Why?"

"Sarah, something strange is going on here."

Sarah's lips parted briefly, but no argument came.

"Whatever it is, we need to get to the bottom of it."

The editor in Sarah noted the first-person plural

usage. Realizing no red pen would save her, she asked, "How?"

Claire told her.

"No."

"Yes, Sarah. There's no other way. And it's got to be now!"

The first Monmouth national poll declaring Bryce Ridgeway to be the overwhelming Republican front-runner came out shortly after three that afternoon. It registered instantaneously in Charleston, where Bryce had just finished a speech on health care.

In a back room of the Charleston Convention Center a spontaneous party broke out. Bryce's travel team nibbled canapés and tipped back light drinks. Backs were slapped and fists bumped. Through it all, the candidate kept an admirably even keel. Dressed in khaki pants, and with the sleeves of his oxford shirt rolled up in swashbuckling fashion, he gave an impromptu speech to his staff. He began with thanks, shifted to caution, and ended with a stirring demand for everyone to work harder in the pursuit of their mission. That was increasingly how he hued the campaign, both internally and on stage—a military operation with hard objectives, threats to be engaged. By the time everyone boarded the bus, headed for the airport and a flight to New Hampshire, the mood was nothing short of ebullient.

The Monmouth poll also registered on the third floor of the FBI's Washington Field Office. Burke saw a scrolling banner on the TV in the break room as he was heating a vending machine pocket sandwich in the microwave. Back at his desk he mentioned it to

Alves, who gave him a disapproving look. He wasn't sure if she was reacting to the news or his dinner.

"Stop!"

Sarah's head snapped forward as Alyssa slammed on the brakes. The little Toyota Camry stopped on a dime, its nose rocking down a few feet short of the intersection.

"What did I do?" Alyssa asked.

Under the racket of the wipers beating back and forth, Sarah pointed to a stop sign through the side window.

"Oh, crap! I never saw it."

"It's okay," Sarah said. "The rain makes it harder."

After an extended look in every direction, Alyssa set back out at a snail's pace.

She'd been driving for a few months, but still lacked confidence. They'd been keeping to less busy streets, daytime only.

"When is Dad coming home again?" Alyssa asked

Sarah hesitated to distract her daughter with conversation. On the other hand, she supposed it was part of the learning process. "He said he might get back for a day or two later in the week."

"It seems like he's never home anymore."

"I know, honey, but that's part of running for president. Honestly, it won't get better anytime soon. Certainly not if he wins."

Silence from the driver's seat.

"Are you still okay with that?" Sarah asked. "Your dad being president?"

"I guess. Are you?"

It was a perfectly simple question, but for Sarah one that generated a host of others. All of which were far more complex. *What was Bryce doing at that condo? Why am I plotting with Claire to find out? And most damning of all: Can I still trust my husband?*

"Mom?"

Sarah returned to the here and now. "It's tough, Aly," she said. "But I support your father, no matter what."

Minutes later Alyssa pulled to a cautious stop in front of Ruby's house—her bestie since middle school.

Sarah said, "I'll pick you up at ten tomorrow. Text me if it changes."

"Okay. What are you doing tonight?"

"Oh, I'll probably dive into some editing."

"Don't get boring just because Dad isn't here."

Sarah actually smiled. "Boring is highly underrated." She gave her daughter a kiss on the cheek. "Bye, baby."

Alyssa bustled out of the car and dashed through the rain to the front door.

35

WHAT . . . THE . . . HELL

Sarah had always been a rule follower. In elementary school she unfailingly raised her hand before speaking in class. During college, working a summer stint as a waitress, she reported every penny of tip income to the IRS. When the Fort Bragg base housing office overpaid a deposit reimbursement by twenty dollars, she'd straightened it out that day. She liked order, craved predictability. Which was why the idea of breaking into someone's home didn't sit well.

"We don't even know who owns it," she groused from the passenger seat of Claire's Mazda roadster. They were crossing the Francis Scott Key Bridge, the rain-swollen Potomac a blackwater whirl below. The storm was working into a lather, a slow-moving cold front flogging the Eastern Seaboard.

"Whoever *does* own it is trying to hide the fact," Claire argued.

"It's not Bryce—he wouldn't buy a place like that without telling me."

"Maybe his campaign set it up."

"No. This started before his presidential run, and first-term congressmen have shoestring budgets."

"Well, whoever the landlord is, they gave Bryce the key."

Sarah felt overwhelmed. The condo, the presidential run, Mandy being fired. So much had changed in the last two months. "Speaking of keys, how are we going to get in? Don't tell me this EPIC creation can cut a key to fit any dead bolt."

"Not in the usual way."

She gawked at Claire incomprehensibly. She felt like a middle schooler seeing her first bag of weed.

"Turns out, the front door has a remote access lock."

"What, like one of those home monitoring systems with cameras and everything?"

"Essentially, although it's not tied to any home security company. It's a web-enabled system—the manufacturer calls it 'Smart Lock.' It registers each time the door physically opens and closes, and lets you lock and unlock remotely using a phone."

"And let me guess—your system can defeat that?"

"We interrupt with proxy software to unlock the door, disable the access sensors, and loop old video footage to show an empty doorstep while we're inside."

Sarah pushed deeper into the bucket seat and closed her eyes.

Claire glanced over. "I know it's a lot to fathom. But that's the world we live in, Sarah."

"You put a lot of faith in your technology."

"I designed it from the ground up. It works."

"So now the government can open anybody's front door?"

"No. That would be illegal."

Sarah stared harshly.

"EPIC is only an experiment. It exists to see if these things *can* be done."

"Can it break us out of jail if we're arrested?"

"Depends on the jail." Claire grinned.

Sarah didn't.

"Anyway, we're not gonna get arrested. Even if the system fails and an alarm goes out, the police will get sent to a different address."

"I hate to ask, but how?"

"Atticus was able to map the security network. He altered some administrative data, including the condo's street address. Until today, two phones controlled that front door. Now there's a third. She pointed to her own which was mounted on the console."

"Did he identify the other two?"

Claire paused a beat. "Yeah, he did. Both numbers are new, changed out a couple of weeks ago. They're pretty much anonymous as far as ownership goes. We could track them if they were turned on, but neither one has been—at least, not in the short time we've been watching."

Sarah was disturbed by the first thought that came to mind: that one of those phones was on its way to New Hampshire right now.

The car hit a pothole, water slapping against the undercarriage. Claire negotiated the final turns into Georgetown.

"You make it sound easy," Sarah said.

"Let's hope."

Claire parked along the curb a block away from their target. When she shut the engine down the only sound was rain tapping on the roof.

"You can see it from here," she said, pointing to a quad of two-story row houses on the corner ahead. A leafless elm stood guard in front, its skeleton bending in the wind.

"This still feels wrong," Sarah said.

"We'll be in and out in no time."

"It's not that. Just coming here, doing this . . . it proves that I don't trust Bryce."

"No, what's *wrong* is that he's been spending time here and you knew nothing about it."

Sarah studied her for a long moment. "Claire . . . what about you? Have you lost faith in him?"

Claire ratcheted the parking brake on the gentle hill. "I don't know what to think. I've known you both for a long time, and Bryce has always been on my A-list. Based on what you're telling me, though, and what I've seen in the last day . . . there's been a change."

Sarah felt something capsize inside her. She'd felt it as well . . . Bryce *was* acting differently. "Could it be that he's running for president? All the adulation, the attention?"

Claire didn't respond.

"What?"

She pulled her phone off the dash mount and shoved it in her jacket pocket. "It's a small thing, but . . . I told you that I tracked Bryce's movements for the last couple of months."

"Sure, that's how you found this place."

"And I mentioned there was video footage from that auto parts store." She pointed up the street, and Sarah saw a dated storefront with dim lights inside. "One of the cameras looks out across the street. By referencing the location track on Bryce, I actually saw him going inside. Eighteen times in November and December, I watched your husband walk through that door. Then I got curious, I went further back. Turns out, the video system had a huge external hard drive. There was half a year's worth of footage. Using EPIC,

I saw Bryce go through the door forty-one more times since early last summer."

"You're sure it was Bryce?"

"Ninety-nine-point-nine percent—that's the highest level of confidence EPIC allows. But then things got weird. I cross-checked the location data: car, phone, cameras. They showed basically the same patterns as the last two months—with one glaring exception. Prior to mid-November, Bryce never came to this place."

"But you said you saw him here in the videos."

"I did, no question. But his tracking data showed him to be nowhere near the place."

"How could that be?"

"The most obvious answer is that he was using countersurveillance. Going to the condo without his phone, maybe taking a bus."

"Why would he do that?"

"Honestly, I can't think of any *good* reason. But then something changed two months ago."

"When he intervened in that attack."

"Essentially, yeah."

A silence ran, until Claire pointed up the street, and said, "This is our best chance, Sarah. If we can get inside, we might figure out what's going on."

She nodded listlessly, knowing Claire was right: what was inside could explain everything. She zipped up her jacket, bracing for a cold and rainy evening.

With a final nod, Claire got out in a flurry of waterproofed nylon and jangling keys. Sarah steeled herself, then followed. They half walked, half trotted to the condo entrance. The rain was coming sideways, slapping their upwind cheeks. The deluge subdued the scents of the city, moisture from the Appalachians bucketing down in a righteous cleansing.

They splashed through puddles sure to delight the neighbohood's kids, Sarah's sensible flats soaking through instantly. As they neared the building, Claire slowed. They stopped side by side twenty feet short of the condo's front step. Two kids at the gate of a haunted house.

"You okay?" Claire asked.

"Yeah. You?"

"Let's do this."

With curtains of rain sweeping under the streetlights, Claire took one final look up and down the street. There wasn't a soul in sight.

Claire was first to reach the short set of stairs. Stripes of black mold, swollen by the cold rain, lined the joints between steps. At the top landing Claire hesitated, half turned, and gave a *fingers crossed* look. She hunched over her phone to keep it dry and tapped a few commands. Sarah heard a muffled *clunk*, and Claire reached for the handle. It turned freely, and she pushed the door open with spread fingertips.

Both of them hesitated like burglars waiting for an alarm. Nothing happened.

Claire ducked inside, Sarah right behind. The only light came through the open door, the interior a tapestry of shadows. They paused at the entryway, muddy and wet. Sarah saw a backlit security keypad on the wall next to the door—the status light was steady green. Tranquil and unworried.

"Okay," Claire said, "we're in."

Sarah closed the door and the room went pitch-black. The lone first-floor window seemed impervious to outside light. The only trace of illumination came from the second floor, cascading down a barely visible staircase. Sarah was struck by the staleness of the air—it was dank and still, like a basement that hadn't been visited in years. Yet there *was* something else on the air. A vaguely chemical scent.

Her eyes reached into the room, adapting to the darkness, and she noticed that the blackness was punctuated by a dozen specks of red and green. It looked like a tiny Christmas display in a starless night sky, yet the flecks of color were so small they gave up nothing about their source.

Claire said, "I guess if we were any good at this we would have brought a flashlight."

Sarah pulled off a glove and ran her naked hand across the wall near the door. She felt the door trim, followed by oatmeal-textured drywall, and finally what she was after—a plastic plate with two rocker switches. She snapped them both on.

An explosion of light.

The two women froze like convicts caught in a searchlight. Standing side by side, their eyes began to adjust. Neither said a word as they took in the scene before them.

Sarah inhaled a sharp breath, found herself holding it.

Claire was the first to get her wits about her. Without taking her eyes off the room, she said, "*What . . . the . . . hell?*"

36

WATCHING YOU

Sarah stood stock-still. She blinked twice, as if trying to alter the image before her. Trying to soften the visual overload.

The center of the room was much as expected. They were looking at an office, a series of cheap plastic tables wagon-trained in a circle around a padded gaming chair. Half the tables were occupied by a network of computers and monitors, all connected by the usual tangle of cables and power strips. Three other tables supported rafts of files and printouts and three-ring binders. A printer sat on a cardboard box near the front window, indifferent to the pulsing storm rattling the glass above.

All of that was fine.

What immobilized Sarah were the hundred pairs of eyes on the perimeter. They were illuminated by track lighting, a half dozen fixtures that had been artlessly screw-gunned to the ceiling, connected by extension cords, and angled outward. Every inch of wall in the presumptive dining area was plastered with photographs, hundreds and hundreds taped to the drywall like an explosion of high-gloss confetti. Attached to many of the pictures were handwritten notes on yellow Post-its, informational barnacles Sarah couldn't read from a distance. It was like an art museum on acid. A high school yearbook that had detonated and stuck to the walls.

"We have to make sure there's no one here," Claire said.

Sarah was so distracted, so stunned, she didn't register what Claire had said until she hurried up the narrow staircase. In the next moments she felt horribly alone. Thankfully, Claire reappeared seconds later.

"Nothing upstairs, only two empty bedrooms." Predictably, Claire was drawn to the bank of computers that dominated the room like a starship command post.

Sarah was mesmerized by the rest.

She edged forward to the biggest section of wall, a fifteen-foot-wide semigloss canvas where the dining room buffet should have been. The first twinge of fear hit when she recognized a snapshot of Alyssa. It was a photo she remembered taking, middle school years, her daughter hamming it up before a soccer game. Beneath the picture, a block-print scrawl in a vaguely recognizable hand: *Alexandria Soccer Academy*. The club she'd played for three years ago. Another photo was circled in red pen: she and Alyssa smiling at the head of their favorite hiking trail in the Monongahela National Forest, a high overlook with sweeping views of the neighboring valley.

Sarah felt a slow upwelling of dread as she realized that most of the faces on the wall were familiar. Friends and neighbors had been grouped together, labeled with names. Another section seemed dedicated to people Bryce worked with. Congressman, aides, lobbyists; a virtual family tree of Capitol Hill. Some Sarah recognized, others she'd never met. No matter—in this section each picture had not only a name but a bio of sorts. Who the individual worked for, where they were from, and most curious of all, bullets beneath written in the same handwriting: *Interactions. Met on September 6th, discussed military retirement benefits. Mutual friend with Congressman Todd Wilkins.*

Another section seemed historical. Bryce's Army buddies, old commanders, college and teenage friends. His life reduced to the format of a photo album. Everything was arranged in a timeline that, as far as she could tell, was quite accurate. There was an arrow— red Sharpie directly on the wall—pointing to the photo of Lieutenant Colonel Brad Martin, the former commander they'd run into at dinner. The officer whose name had escaped Bryce. With that cue, Sarah saw the outline of a solution, something that put it all together. Could Bryce be secretly worried about his mental acuity? Had he been having lapses? His father suffered from dementia, albeit the result of a stroke. Had Bryce realized his recent behavior was off-kilter? Could he have created this room as a kind of self-administered therapy center? She wished Dr. Chalmers could see what she was seeing, give her his professional opinion.

Sarah arced her hand over the wall as if waving a magic wand. As if trying to make it all disappear. The burden seemed infinite, like the wall should tumble down under the weight of it all. She couldn't pull her eyes away from the family photos. A group shot at Christmas with two rarely seen cousins. Bryce with Sarah's sister and her kids at the zoo, names written beneath. She studied the handwriting more closely, saw sloppy block lettering with a right-handed cant— editors recognized things like that. The script wasn't Bryce's—not quite—but there was a definite similarity.

Sarah's spell was broken when Claire said, "You need to see this."

She was standing over a table covered in files and binders. Sarah joined her and Claire held up a thick folder labeled in black Sharpie: SARAH.

Claire set it on the table and began paging through photos taken from Sarah's personal albums. They'd likely been lifted from cloud storage, printed in high resolution, and arranged chronologically. Sarah as a toddler on a three-wheeler; class pictures from elementary school; a gap-toothed girl before braces. High school kicked things up a notch, followed by college—including dozens of photos documenting her burgeoning romance with young Bryce Ridgeway. Fifty more pages took them to the present day, many of the recent photos annotated. The cruise they'd taken last winter, a moody Alyssa in tow. A getaway last summer to the Biltmore in Ashville, just her and Bryce.

Sarah saw a binder labeled ALYSSA. Another called FAMILY. She opened Alyssa's volume and saw a recent picture on the first page, a classroom shot labeled "summer science camp." Sarah reached down and touched it with spread fingertips. As if trying to convince herself it was real.

Sarah said at a near whisper, "This feels like . . . like a shrine to Bryce's life. To *our* lives."

"To me it looks more like research."

Sarah bit her lower lip, and said, "Or therapy."

"What?"

She explained her theory to Claire.

"Bryce? Dementia?"

"Wouldn't it make sense? Everything we're looking at here, so much secrecy?"

Claire studied the room anew. A skeptic, but

considering the idea. She hadn't seen Bryce since the beginning of December, a cookout on the Ridgeways' back deck. "The last time I saw him he seemed pretty sharp." Then her thoughts seemed to snag.

"What?" Sarah asked.

"There *was* one time . . . he and I were talking out back and he offered me a beer. I told him I hadn't had a beer since O'Hara's." O'Hara's was their favorite college hangout. "He got this blank look and changed the subject. I didn't think much of it then, but now . . ."

Claire turned away and began working a keyboard at the central monitor.

Sarah scanned the other binders and pulled one free. The name on front: WORK. She saw a few pictures of Mandy, but most of the book was comprised of notes. Policy papers that bore Bryce's signature, a list of donors from his first campaign. News articles covering recent public appearances.

Sarah pushed the book away and sank gently into a swivel chair. She told herself it all made sense. Somehow. Yet something in her theory felt wrong. Everything around her was so . . . extreme. Bryce could be intense at times, but this went light-years beyond any semblance of logic and practicality. Was her husband losing his mind?

Or am I?

The clatter of typing stopped. Claire stared at the screen impatiently. "I can't get in without a password."

It took Sarah back to the task at hand. Away from her bizarre surroundings. "Password? Can you figure it out?"

"On my own? Not likely. But I remembered seeing the guy in the video footage hauling computers inside, so I came prepared." She fished into the deepest pocket of her jacket and pulled out a small device. It was the size of a large mobile phone, a bit thicker, and trailing from one end was a short cable with a USB connector. She plugged it into a port behind the computer.

"One of EPIC's design criteria was that it be able to penetrate remote networks and connect them to the primary."

"So that thing—it can connect this computer to EPIC?"

"It's CIA hardware, DS&T—Directorate of Science and Technology. They call the system HIWAY. Not sure what that stands for, but they gave us a device for validation with the project. It provides a gateway when you have physical access to a machine. If it works as advertised, we'll have the best tools available to break in."

Break in, Sarah thought. *Like we've done to this row house. Like Bryce has done to my life and Alyssa's.*

Claire went back to work.

Sarah couldn't keep her eyes off the wall. So many familiar faces looked back. It seemed straight from a nightmare. Intrusive and creepy. A serial killer's lair. *But the man who created it is my husband.*

She opened another binder, this one labeled ARMY, and saw a copy of Bryce's service records: performance reports, commissioning papers, a letter of commendation from a commander. Another file, MEDICAL scribed on the cover, contained Bryce's service medical records. There were scans and physician reports, lab results and discharge papers. An evaluation by Dr. Chalmers. She saw photographs of his injuries, including the scars on his back and arm. With another turn of the page she stiffened. Certain images of his scars had been enlarged and marked up. There were notes in the margins that bore no resemblance to Bryce's hand, and for the most unfathomable of reasons: the notes were in Cyrillic.

Sarah saw a handwritten comment on a nearby note, this in the more familiar script: *Ask Radanov for rest of medical records.* Sarah had never heard the name. Was he a doctor? A records administrator at the VA? She looked up at Claire, saw her staring at the screen like a fortune-teller studying an orb.

"We're in," she finally said.

More confused than ever, Sarah fixated on the monitor. Status lights on Claire's HIWAY device were flashing green, and soon the screen burst to life. Code began scrolling down, an alphanumeric waterfall. After less than a minute, a standard Windows menu appeared. It seemed innocuously familiar, almost quaint compared to the theater of chaos around them.

Claire began sorting through files. "A lot of this looks the same—old photos, copies of records. But down here . . ." Her voice trailed off as she selected an icon Sarah had never seen.

"What is that?"

"Based on the application, some kind of live feed."

"Like a camera?"

"Apparently. Although not just one—looks like there are at least a dozen sources."

The screen divided into four quadrants, each a streaming view from a different fish-eye lens. Sarah felt a jolt of something primal when she realized what she was looking at. Slowly, precariously, she leaned in to get a better look.

All four black-and-white views were intimately recognizable. A table for six sided by a granite-topped buffet, modernist chandelier above: her dining room. Top right was Alyssa's bedroom, a boy-band poster on the wall and throw blankets on the rumpled bed. Bottom left was her own bedroom, and bottom right showed a wide-angle view of the master bathroom and shower.

Sarah's hands began shaking.

"Sarah . . . is this what I think it is?"

The best she could manage was a nod. Words were impossible.

"He's been watching you . . . and Alyssa."

Sarah said nothing.

Claire stepped to the next page, found four more cameras—two other rooms in the house, the garage, and a view of their back deck. She kept going, and finally, mercifully, something different—two views of Bryce's office, and a pair of what looked like conference rooms. In one of them a meeting was going on at that moment, four people Sarah didn't recognize. Clearly intrigued, Claire brought that feed to full screen and clicked on the speaker symbol in one corner. The deathly silence was broken by two men arguing over a tax break for a gas company. Sarah didn't recognize the faces, but she knew staffers and lobbyists when she heard them.

Claire killed the audio, and said, "HIWAY also has the ability to upload files. I'm going to transfer a few to EPIC." She was about to say something else when her phone rang. She picked up and Sarah heard half a conversation.

"What's up, Atticus?"

A long pause.

"Okay, what about it?"

Claire straightened like a steel rod had been jammed into her spine.

"How close?" she asked. Then, "Shit! Can you do something about it?"

A shrill reply loud enough to be heard. *"Like what?"*

"Do what you did last time!" Claire pleaded. "Anything! Just give us a couple more minutes!" She ended the call and jumped up. "We need to get the hell out of here!"

37

SHATTERED

What's wrong?" Sarah asked.

"Atticus finally identified the car that was following me. He started tracking it and he thinks it's on its way here."

"Atticus knows what we're doing?"

Claire put the computer to sleep and disconnected the HIWAY device. "Don't worry about Atticus. I trust him as much as I trust you or . . ." Her words trailed off. They both realized she was about to say *Bryce*. Claire began straightening the binders. "Is this how these were?"

"Yeah, pretty much." Sarah pushed the chair back where it had been. "How much time do we have?"

"Five minutes—maybe a little more if Atticus can change a traffic light or two." When they reached the door Claire looked around the room. "Is anything else different?"

"Yeah." Sarah pointed to two sets of muddy footprints at the entrance.

"Crap!" Claire said.

"We need a towel or something." Sarah looked at the small kitchen, then through the open door into the first-floor bathroom. No towels in sight.

Claire quickly unzipped her jacket, took it off, and pulled her cream-white cotton shirt over her head. As she began scrubbing the carpet, Sarah did the same. A minute later they had the worst of it cleaned up. "It'll have to do," Claire said.

They both zipped their winter jackets over their bras and headed outside, filthy shirts in their hands. Sarah remembered to turn off the lights.

She started moving toward the car, but Claire said, "No, this way!"

Claire led down a narrow alley that connected to a parallel street. She pulled out her phone and locked the front door. Rain was hammering down. Claire looked repeatedly over her shoulder, and they were nearly to the next street when she grabbed Sarah's arm and yanked her behind a dumpster.

"*What—*"

Claire cut her off with a finger over her lips and pointed back. Sarah saw a sedan with one slightly accordioned front fender pull into the parking spot marked 4. They watched closely.

Nothing happened for a time. Sarah blinked away rain as she peered around the rusted metal sidewall. The dumpster was rancid, wet piles of trash inside topped by a ten-gallon plastic bucket labeled *Asia Yum Soy Sauce*. Next to that, a cardboard box stenciled *Lucky Brand Fortune Cookies* was swarmed by flies. Sarah thought she might never eat takeout Chinese again.

Finally, a light snapped on in the car's interior. Through the driving rain they watched a man get out and walk to the front door. Heavy build and average height. Dark jacket with a baseball cap.

"That's him," Claire said at a whisper even though they were fifty yards away. "It's the guy I saw twice in the video footage."

He paused at the door, then hunched over his

phone to protect it from the rain as he thumbed the access code. Moments later, he disappeared inside. The man was out of sight for no more than thirty seconds. He came back out and stood on the front step. With rain beating the brim of his cap, he looked all around, a lighthouse beam scanning a steady arc.

As the sweep of his gaze neared the dumpster, Sarah and Claire drew back from the corner. There was no chance they could be seen, but it was comforting all the same. When they ventured another look, the car was backing out. Then it was gone.

Claire looked at her, and for a moment Sarah was afraid she was going to suggest going back inside. Instead, she said, "Let's get the hell out of here."

Claire tried to focus on the road—the visibility was awful and rush-hour traffic was bogging down. Night had fallen hard, the oncoming headlights creeping past as blurry paired circles. The rain had reached car wash intensity, her little Mazda's wipers groaning from exhaustion.

They'd driven in silence since leaving Georgetown, and in the darkness Claire caught glimpses of Sarah in passing streetlights. She was pressed deep into the passenger seat, curled against the door with her arms crossed as if she were cold. Claire was no medical professional, but she knew the signs of shock when she saw them. Limbs pulled in protectively as withdrawal took hold. Pale fingers and lips, blood retreating to the more vital parts of the body. She could almost hear Sarah's heart pounding away.

For Claire it was unsettling. She was used to Sarah being Sarah, calm and unflappable. A stalwart military wife who stood by her rock-solid husband, the two of them combining as an unshakable foundation. Now that base had been shattered.

Claire distracted herself by contemplating what mistakes they'd made, a burglar's self-assessment. Had she locked the door properly? Left fingerprints? What might they do differently next time?

Next time.

She couldn't shake the imageries she'd seen on the camera feeds. She'd shown some of it to Sarah, but never gotten around to the rest—what she'd discovered while Sarah was going through the binders. Aside from the live feeds, Claire had uncovered thousands of hours of archived recordings. She'd sampled a few, enough to learn that the videos were matched by high-quality audio. In essence, a record of virtually every moment in every room of Sarah's home going back half a year. Not to mention a feed from at least one congressional office building. Claire had kept it to herself, figuring enough damage was done. But at some point, Sarah had to know.

The silence became unbearable.

"Are you okay?" she asked.

No response.

Claire looked outside and saw a third-tier strip mall ahead. She turned in and pulled into a parking spot between a dive bar and a massage parlor. Both had red neon signs, one offering two-for-one specials, the other happy hour. She put the car in park, and finally Sarah's thousand-yard stare broke.

"Are you okay?" Claire asked again.

"No. But I'll get past it. I have to . . . for Alyssa's sake."

"She's staying at a friend's tonight?"

"She is."

"That's good. Maybe you should do the same. I've got the spare bedroom."

Sarah didn't respond.

"Look," Claire said, "at least we know what we're up against now."

"Do we?"

"Okay . . . maybe not exactly. But we can buy time, figure out how to deal with it."

Sarah's tone turned sarcastic. "Yeah, we're kind of in a bind, aren't we? We found evidence of a crime in the course of committing one ourselves. Then again, I'm not sure if any of what Bryce has done is illegal. He installed a really extensive nanny-cam system in his own home. Then he either bought or rented a condo and put pictures of his family and friends on the wall. Where's the crime in any of that?"

"Sarah, *we* are not in the wrong here! To begin, do you really think Bryce is behind this? Because I don't."

"*You* told me he's the only one who uses this place. Now you're defending him?"

Looking out into the rain, Claire rubbed her temples with two fingers. "I don't know what's going on, and I don't know who's behind it. But we can figure this out."

Sarah blew out a humorless laugh. "Those cameras—they pretty much shot down my theory about Bryce having dementia. The terrible thing is, I don't know if I'm happy or sad about it."

"We can find out more. I'll use—"

"*EPIC? Again?*" Sarah closed her eyes. For a time there were no sounds beyond rain tapping on the hard top, the white noise of cars hissing past. When Sarah spoke again, her tone was softer. "Look . . . I'm sorry. This is a lot to deal with."

"I know."

Sarah straightened in her seat. "There's something we can't lose sight of—the fact that Bryce is running for president. If your system starts running searches, there's no telling who's going to catch wind of it."

"You're right. We have to be careful how we approach this. Honestly, the way I used EPIC to uncover that condo—it violates pretty much every privacy agreement I signed in order to get so much access."

"So it *is* illegal."

"Technically, yes. But EPIC has also been dead-on accurate."

A vehicle pulled abruptly into the space next to them. Claire's hands flew to the wheel and gearshift. She saw a Hyundai crossover—not a blue sedan with a wrinkled front fender. The driver, a tall black man, got out and trotted through the rain toward a nearby pizza place.

Claire eased. Her nerves were shot. "Sarah, there's one very simple way to get to the bottom of all this."

A soft nod. "I know."

"When will he be back?"

"His schedule is pretty fluid, but as it stands . . . in about five days."

Claire hedged, "This isn't something you can discuss over the phone."

"True . . . and for a lot of reasons."

"Okay. Then, we've got some time. I say we sleep on it tonight. Will you please come to my place?"

Sarah considered it, but a hazy thought drew her in the other direction. "No. I'd like to go home."

"Even knowing what we know?"

"*Especially* knowing what we know. I might find something there to help explain what's going on. My house is wired, but knowing that going in—I can deal with it."

Claire saw something new in Sarah's expression. It was a face she'd seen before, when Bryce had gone on deployments. Steely resolve. She backed out of the parking spot. The Mazda splashed through a puddle like a pond and soon they were back on the street.

Claire felt suddenly revitalized. She knew Sarah could be stubborn.

And she was no less so.

38

NOT IF YOUR LIFE DEPENDED ON IT

Sarah sat in the dark, limp-limbed as though she'd been poured into the plush recliner. It was the most comfortable chair in the living room, supple fabric and well-trained cushions. Bryce's favorite chair, molded to the shape of his body.

Strobes of light stabbed through the parted curtains at the front window, jagged lines clawing across the floor. After Claire had dropped her off, Sarah could do nothing more than find the chair. Flipping on a light had never crossed her mind. She might have closed the front door.

Claire had offered to stay, but Sarah didn't want that. With Bryce on the road—New Hampshire?—and Alyssa gone for the night, she longed for time alone to think things through. So she'd jettisoned her wet jacket and shoes, padded across the room, sat in the best chair. With its familiar softness. Its familiar scents.

Thirty minutes later she was still there.

The seminal events of life often emerged slowly. You needed time to absorb things, to wrap your mind around what you were seeing. Unfortunately, what Sarah had seen tonight at the condo . . . that seemed unwrappable.

The pictures, the videos, the notes. All damning in so many ways. Yet also so . . . implausible.

Claire had felt it too. Sarah recalled their parting exchange in the driveway.

We'll figure out what's going on.

Will we?

I don't think you should be alone.

I'm not alone. In the morning, I'll have Alyssa.

I'll call you first thing.

Sarah had simply nodded. Then a dead walk to the front door through driving rain. She'd heard Claire back out, heard the Mazda slosh away down the street.

From the chair she surveyed a room cut in shades of gray. Had she avoided turning the lights on to promote a peaceful aura? Or was it the other?

Bolts of doubt flashed through her gloomy thoughts. Her mind kept resetting, going back to the monitor in the condo, its quad-display of scenes inside her home. She remembered seeing the chair in which she was sitting, and estimated where the camera had to be. In near darkness her eyes lifted. Somewhere above the fireplace. Beside the brick mantel was a portrait of Bryce's grandmother on porcelain, a family heirloom that had been on the wall since they'd moved in. She imagined the eyes moving like a cartoon mystery. *No, the angle would be wrong.* The crooked doorbell Bryce had finally straightened? Next to that was an air vent. *Yes*, she thought, *that's it*. She imagined where the vents were in every room, and those she could remember correlated to the live feeds she'd seen. The garage and the backyard would be different, but the interior cameras were concealed in the air ducts.

When she'd first seen the streaming video, she'd been justifiably shocked. Yet now she felt something different. Acceptance? Resignation?

No, she decided.

Confirmation.

She'd been sensing it for weeks, ever since the morning of the Watergate attack. She remembered Bryce returning from his early run, a bloody scrape on his calf. How did that fit in? Countless discrepancies flickered into her head. Sights and sounds and words from recent months took on new meanings.

It was overwhelming.

An alternate reality.

Sarah sat motionless, refracting her husband through a new lens. Phrases that seemed out of character, the occasional microexpression in his lovely face that seemed . . . different. Yet in so many other ways he *was* Bryce. The movement, the voice. The *scars* for God's sake. She remembered the pictures at the condo. *Why pictures of his damned battlefield scars?*

What was real?

What wasn't?

She looped back to a variant of her earlier thought. Could some kind of mental illness be involved? She'd already reached out to Dr. Chalmers once, but he'd invited her to call if she had further concerns about Bryce, even given her a code word to jump to the front of the queue. Now however, a new dynamic was in play, and would be for the foreseeable future: Bryce was running for president. Which meant talking to his psychiatrist carried serious implications. What could she confess to Chalmers, knowing it might leak out? What would the doctor say if *he* saw the condo? How could her husband be the same, yet so very different?

As she tried to process it all, a fleeting image ran through Sarah's head. Something she'd noticed months ago, but written off at the time. And avoided ever since.

The TV remote control was on the table next to the recliner. It belonged in the wicker basket by the TV, but her normally squared-away housekeeping had gone askew. She turned on the television and navigated to the online menu, selected YouTube. A few key words took her to the clip she was after. It had fifteen million views, one of which was hers in the immediate hours after the attack at the Watergate. She'd vowed then that once was enough. Good for a lifetime. Even on that occasion she found herself averting her eyes, which was only natural. What woman wanted to watch her husband cheat death so narrowly?

Yet now she *did* want to see it, because one detail kept pinging in her head. Perhaps it hadn't struck at the time. Or maybe it had and she'd tuned it out. Sarah hit play and the scene began to run. The video had been captured from ground level across the street, the camera canted slightly upward. On the distant rooftop of the Watergate, Sarah saw people lined along the perimeter rail, many with refreshments in hand. All were facing the lectern where Senator Morales was beginning his remarks. Then a slightly-built, jacketed figure appeared. Moments later, she saw Bryce. He looked competent and self-assured. A swirl of motion commenced at the roof's edge. Two bodies intertwined, engaged in a struggle. She saw Bryce attempt to heave the smaller man out into space, only to be dragged over himself.

Then the critical moment.

Sarah paused the clip, then backtracked. She looped the same five seconds, again and again. Eventually she narrowed it down to two seconds. Bryce hanging from the rail by his left hand, clinging for life. Sarah stepped the video forward frame by frame. She watched carefully as his right arm lifted over his head to get a second handhold, doing so with the ease of a gymnast working a high bar. No hesitation, no impinged motion.

His right arm.

Bryce had not lifted that arm above ninety degrees since the tragic day in Mali three years ago. It was the injury that had forced his medical discharge. The limitation Bryce would have moved heaven and earth to overcome, yet one that doctors had assured him was beyond repair. She'd gone with Bryce to his final consult, and the words of the orthopedic surgeon rang in: *I'm sorry, Bryce, but the mobility of that arm won't ever improve—not if your life depended on it.* Then Bryce's tortured reply as he confronted what it meant: *It's not my life I worry about. It's the guys in my unit.*

The doctor had been right—the injury hadn't improved in the intervening years. How many times had Sarah seen it out of the corner of her eye? Bryce fighting to raise his right arm to paint a wall, to reach a cabinet, every time defeated. He'd suffered through a year of rehab: punishing exercises, endless stretching routines. In the end, none of it had helped. Indeed, only last summer he'd confessed to her that, if anything, the lack of mobility had gotten worse. It didn't affect his day-to-day life, and Bryce had gotten good at masking the limitation. But it was there. And it was permanent.

. . . not if your life depended on it.

Sarah turned off the television.

There could be no more doubt. Taken with what she'd seen earlier, a new clarity emerged. Seemingly impossible. But now indisputable. The man in her life today was not Bryce Ridgeway. Whoever, whatever he was, he was a stranger. An interloper who had studied and mimicked and hijacked her husband's life. Who'd hijacked all their lives. And a man who was today running for president of the United States.

A sudden rattle from the storm door brought her back to the moment.

Sarah rose out of the chair. "Alyssa? I thought you were spending the night at—"

He stood in front of her casually, suitcase in hand. The man who looked very much like her husband, but most certainly was not.

He smiled broadly. "Surprise, surprise."

39

THE KNIFE RACK

When Claire got back to the lab, Atticus was waiting. He was visibly angry—or as visibly angry as a skinny twenty-six-year-old in a hoodie and riding a knee scooter could be.

"So, this new life of yours as a spy," he began, "is it a career change or just a hobby?"

"Maybe both."

He stared her down.

"Look, Atticus, I'm sorry to have dragged you into this. A friend needed help, and it's turned into a big deal—a *very* big deal."

"Maybe if you explained what's going on I could be more useful."

Claire considered it, not surprisingly falling back on digital logic. Did she need Atticus's help? And would he agree to help if he knew the truth? Thinking the answer to both would be yes, she put her results into an AND gate and got the high result—not zero but one.

"Okay," she said, "here's the deal. You've helped Sarah and I a lot. Going forward, we could really use backup. That said, it's not fair to drag you any deeper without a full explanation. If you want to back out, now is the time. You go back to what you were doing yesterday, and we'll pretend today never happened. I wouldn't think any less of you for taking that path, and it won't have any bearing on my recommendation when we close the doors here—no harm, no foul. On the other hand, if you want to keep going, help me leverage EPIC in what could be very delicate circumstances, then I'll tell you what we're up against."

"But if you tell me what this is all about—there's no going back?"

Claire cocked her head to one side. "Yeah . . . that's pretty much it. It's the kind of thing you can't unhear."

"It's important."

A nod.

"And it relates to Sarah, who's married to a guy who might be president next year."

"You're getting warm . . . but no more hints until you tell me you're on board. You've got to be sure."

His irritation faded, a star student who knew he was the teacher's pet. "Do I get a raise?"

"No. But nice try."

Atticus sulked in mock disappointment. "Okay. I'm in anyway."

Claire smiled. Then she began talking . . .

Sarah was kneeling on cold tile, a toilet bowl full of vomit in front of her. Her fingers walked up the ceramic reservoir, found the flimsy steel lever, and pulled. A whoosh of water, a counterclockwise swirl. Then a knock on the door.

"You okay, Sar?"

Sar. The intimate version of her name, heisted via home audio. Was that how it would be? she wondered. Every word, every gesture deconstructed, sourced?

"Sar?"

"I'm fine," she croaked. "A little food poisoning, I think."

Of course, it was nothing of the kind. On seeing Bryce—that was still how she thought of him—her stomach had lurched. Not knowing how to react, afraid of what she might say, she'd bolted to the bathroom and slammed the door. A finger down her throat seemed the next logical move. After all, it had to be convincing. And there, in one vulgar thirty second sequence, was proof of how far her life had sunk.

"Can I come in?" His voice muffled now, a softer knock. The real Bryce wouldn't have asked. He would have come to her aid without question.

Sarah didn't answer.

The door cracked open and he edged in. "What did you have for dinner?"

"Leftover Chinese. Must have gone bad." She got to her feet, convincingly wobbly, and flushed the toilet again. The air was putrid.

"What can I do to help?" he asked.

"I'll be fine." She sidled to the sink with all the steadiness of a drunken sailor. From the faucet she cupped water to her mouth with a hand, rinsed, and spit.

"Where's Alyssa?" he asked.

"Ruby's. A sleepover."

"Ah, damn. Guess I'm gonna miss her. This storm is hitting New England hard—a real Nor'easter. All the flights got cancelled. I'm here until ten tomorrow morning, then off to Texas."

"Oh, good." She took another slurp of water, spit with intent. "Looks like I might not be the best company tonight." Sarah stood straight, looked in the mirror and saw him standing behind her. He held her eyes with an expression she couldn't place.

"I saw your jacket and shoes by the door—they were soaked. You went out in this?"

Sarah edged away, moved into the living room. "Claire and I got together this afternoon."

"Oh, good. How's she doing?"

"Claire is Claire."

"I haven't seen her in a while."

"You could probably say the same for most of our friends. Ever since you became famous our social life has gone south."

"Is that an accusation?"

Sarah wanted to look him in the eye but couldn't bring herself to do it. She saw mud tracked across the runner that led to the front door. He was still wearing his shoes. *How many times do I have to tell you, Bryce Ridgeway . . . wet shoes at the door.*

Her heart thumped in her chest. She diverted to the kitchen, weaving around the island to the corner counter. The lights seemed brighter than usual. She leaned on the counter for support. Mr. Coffee was by her right hand. The knife rack near her left.

When Bryce came in she pretended to look out the window at the peaking storm. Rain splattered against the window, big drops that hit like gravel. In the reflection she watched him reach into his pocket. His hand came out with a few neatly folded papers. "They still give me notes," he said, moving toward the trash can. "I don't need them anymore. I could recite my stump speech in my sleep." He stepped on the foot pedal to raise the lid and dumped the papers in.

Would he notice there was no Chinese takeout container inside?

"I'm really not feeling well," she said.

"Too bad. We don't get many nights alone these days."

She sensed him closing in from behind. His hand touched her shoulder, then drifted beneath her hair to brush her neck. Sarah went rigid. She simply couldn't help it.

"Is something wrong?" he asked.

She exhaled, then turned to face him. "What do you mean?"

"I don't know. You just seem . . . agitated."

She did her best to mirror his gesture, her hand rising to his shoulder—the most intimate contact she could bear. "My stomach is in knots. And honestly . . . I haven't been sleeping well lately."

"Really? Why not?"

"I don't know. I'll be fine."

"Okay. I guess we should put you to bed."

Sarah started toward the staircase. When he fell in behind her, she said, "Actually, a cup of that herbal tea might help settle things. Would you mind making it?"

"Sure. Which cupboard is it in?"

She pointed to the pantry.

"Oh, right."

He set to his task, and while he was distracted Sarah swept her phone off the counter. In the dining room she made a flash-dig into her purse, then hurried upstairs. She heard him putting water in the kettle.

Sarah reached the bedroom and shot an upward glance. The vent concealing the fish-eye lens was directly overhead. Watching, listening. She moved to the bathroom, but faced the same problem. Unable to resist a closer look, she leaned toward the big mirror and looked up in its reflection. Sure enough, between two of the metal louvres, she saw a tiny glass eye protruding on a wire. A high-tech viper. A tangential thought she'd had earlier recurred. Who besides Bryce had access to these feeds? The man they'd seen at the condo, the one who'd been following Claire? *Am I being watched right now?*

There was no time to think about it.

Sarah hurried to the closet, closed the door, and was instantly enveloped in darkness. Was there a vent in the closet? She turned on the light, looked up and saw a louvered grate. Had there been a feed here? She didn't remember seeing one, but paranoia was taking its grip.

"Honey?" he called from downstairs.

Bryce had never in their marriage called her that.

She cracked open the door and called down, "What?"

"Do you want *honey* with your tea?"

"Oh . . . yeah, that'd be great." Score one for the imposter. She often took honey with her tea.

Sarah addressed her phone and referenced what she'd retrieved from her purse. She thumbed out a text message and hit SEND.

40

IN A HOT ZONE

Burke was in the driver's seat of his Ford, the door cracked open and his left leg planted outside. He'd stopped to put gas in his car, but the high roof at Wawa did nothing to keep the rain from sweeping beneath. That being the case, he'd taken shelter in the driver's seat while the pump ran. The smell of gas was strong, countless tiny spills on the ground leaching out with the moisture. Transferring to his shoes. And then to the floor mat.

His detective's brain never stopped working.

He was on his way to dinner with his wife, but running late. Burke picked up his phone to send Vicky an ETA text when a message from an unknown number arrived. He read it once. Then more carefully a second time.

Agent Burke. This is Sarah Ridgeway. I have critically important information. You need to see what's inside a townhouse at 3012 P Street. I'm guessing you will have to get a search warrant, but trust me—it is VITAL that you look into this.

I'll get in touch again in the morning. PLEASE do not call or text back now. Will explain tomorrow. Once you see what's inside this residence, you will understand.

Burke stared at the screen. His first inclination was that Sarah Ridgeway had come unglued. Had she been drinking? Was he getting caught up in some nasty marital spat? He'd been with the FBI a long time, long enough to have a knack for reading people. His initial take on Sarah Ridgeway had been positive. A solid woman with a lot on her plate, but coping well. He was glad he'd taken the time to track her down. Unfortunately, none of that squared with the message he was looking at now.

The pump outside clicked off, breaking his trance.

He typed in the address she'd given him on Google Maps. A seventeen-minute drive into the heart of Georgetown. He checked the time on his phone. He would be severely late for dinner if he diverted there and started poking around. Without a warrant, there was little he could do. Maybe circle the place on foot, look in a window. Possibly manufacture an excuse to knock on the door if he was feeling ambitious.

"Search warrant," he muttered. What were the chances of that at seven o'clock on a Friday night? Close to zero, even if he could show good cause. What he *had* was a vague text from a woman he barely knew. It might be different this time next year—if she became First Lady of the United States. Today, however, Sarah Ridgeway was just like anybody else.

Then there was the other side of the equation: Burke had broken more dinner dates with his wife than he cared to remember, and tonight was their anniversary. He couldn't stand Vicky up. What was it? Twenty-four years? He needed to do the math on the way.

Moments later, he splattered out onto the road headed for Angelino's. He would check out the address in Georgetown first thing in the morning. Maybe call

Sarah Ridgeway before he did and get a little more information.

Whatever she was stirred up about, it would have to wait.

Sarah lay in bed like a swooning Victorian dowager—all that was missing was to put the back of her hand to her forehead.

"I'll be fine," she said as Bryce came out of the bathroom.

He sat next to her on the bed. A terse smile. It reminded her of . . . nothing.

"I thought you might want this," he said, holding out an old bottle of Ambien. She'd been given a prescription during his final deployment. Alyssa had been going through a rough patch, and Bryce was in a hot zone, his unit taking regular casualties. Sarah had been at the end of her tether, not sleeping, and her doctor suggested medicating.

She said, "I haven't used those in a long time."

"I know. But you kept them. There's only a few left, but if you're having trouble sleeping—why not?"

Sarah took the pill bottle, set it on the nightstand next to her tea. "All right . . . maybe."

"I'm going to grab a shower." He got up and walked to the bathroom, stripping off his shirt on the way. She saw the familiar scars on his back—which was probably the point.

The door closed and the shower began running. Sarah picked up the Ambien, saw four pills remaining. Hadn't there been more? She looked at her tea suspiciously, picked up the cup and took a guarded sip. No odd taste. Paranoia was definitely taking hold.

She heard splashing in the shower and steam curled

under the base of the door. It seemed oddly malevolent. Sarah opened the bottle, dumped two pills into her palm. She got up and carried them, along with the mug of tea, to the bathroom down the hall—no camera there, as far as she could remember. She poked both pills down the sink drain, dumped half the tea, then flicked on the water to wash away any traces. She hurried back, returned everything to the nightstand, and rolled onto her side. Sarah drew the covers up to her chin, a portrait of misery.

When he came out of the bathroom minutes later, her eyes were shut tight. She heard him pad across the wood floor, pause nearby. It was all she could do to remain motionless, keep her breathing rhythmic. Then a tiny clatter—the last two pills rattling, followed by a plastic tap as he returned the bottle to the nightstand.

His next stop was the closet, probably for sleeping shorts and a T-shirt. He went downstairs, and soon she heard him talking on the phone. Something about the campaign.

Part of her wished she'd taken the pills. She envisioned him coming to bed in an hour, the sheets pulling back as he slid in behind her. His humid breath on her neck. Sarah was exhausted, yet she doubted she could sleep.

As she lay alone, silent and nerve-racked, her thoughts diverted to a new question. One she'd managed to avoid since grasping the truth.

If the man downstairs was an imposter . . . *then where was the real Bryce?*

The only realistic answer was too dreadful to think about.

41

THE PIPE

There was winter. There was cold. And then there was January on the shores of the Barents Sea.

The tiny building was ninety miles from any city of note, if Murmansk could be so imagined. There had once been a minor fishing village nearby, a place called Zubovka. Generations of depopulation, however, along with a declining crab harvest, had sealed its fate—the last holdouts had given up ten years ago. The structures left behind were little more than corpses, a village of caved-in roofs and hangnail siding. Stacks of crab pots sat rotting, and the hulk of an old ship lay stranded on the distant wash, its reddened hull flaking rust, its rigging snapped like deadwood branches.

Situated on the spine of a cape that resembled a howling dog, Zubovka was the northernmost point in western Russia, a minor appendage to the greater Kola Peninsula. The only road connecting to the mainland was closer to a suggestion, a path of least resistance that meandered loosely through the permafrost and seasonal bogs. As it turned out, the very remoteness that had led to Zubovka's demise was instrumental in its revival, even if it was limited to the hand of one particular government organization: the SVR, Russia's foreign intelligence service.

In its search for an exceptionally remote interrogation site, the agency deemed the shores of the Barents Sea ideal: the area rivaled the Far Eastern District for lack of populace, and matched Northern Siberia's severity of climate. For the SVR, it was a natural choice.

The agency had moved in two years ago with the opposite of fanfare. A minor procession of trucks and work vans had made the crossing in summer—a painfully short season, albeit with endless daylight. The single building they rehabilitated came to be referred to as The Dacha, a callous euphemism given the nature of its mission. On the best of days, the twenty-mile journey to the main road took a full two hours. Now at the height of winter, it could be reached only using four-wheel-drive vehicles, and even then only when the weather was agreeable.

Belying its name, the improvements made to The Dacha were more fitting to a penitentiary than any kind of executive getaway. The construction was uncommonly solid to begin, yet certain concrete walls were shored up further. The one interior door added was all but impenetrable. Curiously, there was a complete lack of perimeter security. Cameras, motion sensors, razor-wire fence—none were necessary. External security was achieved through isolation. The Dacha, in essence, was a cellblock for one, seemingly dropped by a careless God onto a forsaken shoreline.

In the late seventies, the KGB's Chief First Directorate had built a series of such sites. That program had been abandoned during Gorbachev's Perestroika, in the time when Western ideals and openness were all the rage. Then a new man had taken charge, and the Chief First Directorate was replaced by the SVR. It was one of that agency's founding chiefs, a holdover from the "good old days," who'd revived the concept of secret interrogation sites. The program was initially revived in the wilds of Siberia and the mountains of Kamchatka, and served host to a running cast of reprobates: nonconforming politicians, insubordinate oligarchs, the odd investigative journalist. All became guests of the state, handled by rotating teams of interrogators. Yet with the impending arrival of one very special guest, a new locale was needed. One that existed on no maps. Nor in anyone's memory.

Which was how, on that frigid January morning, five people found themselves inside a thick-walled bunker outside the ghost town called Zubovka.

Four of them knew perfectly well all this history.

The one who did not lay on a glacial concrete floor, much as he had for weeks. Or was it months? Bryce Ridgeway really couldn't say. Any notion of time had long ago been stolen. Owing to his training, he knew this was a basic tenant of interrogations. It allowed those who conducted the proceedings to be less concerned with faultless questioning, inflicting overwhelming pain, or using the perfect drug. It was all about the taking. The systematic removal of the foundations of human existence. Time, light, sound, touch. Absent such basics, lacking a world in which to exist, the human spirit invariably weakened. All one needed was patience.

Bryce rolled onto his side, even if, in that moment, there was no compelling reason to do so. Movement only brought pain, yet he did it anyway. Perhaps it was survival instinct. More likely belligerence. At this point, was there a difference?

His right foot, swollen to the size of a football, hurt

like hell. He couldn't say precisely what the damage was, yet it struck him as peculiar that for days now, despite an array of other injuries, the foot had become his focus. Not that there wasn't pain elsewhere. He was sure he'd endured multiple broken bones. His cheek, one eye orbit. Ribs, hands, feet. His face felt like pulp, and he'd given up trying to suppress the swelling using his two good fingers. Because he was wearing a hood, the extent of his visual field was a ten-degree segment straight down. He supposed they allowed it on purpose, better to see the matted blood, the bruises in their rainbow of pain—black, blue, red, purple. He looked through the gap at his right foot. It was of marginal use—the last time he'd tried to stand he collapsed on the concrete floor. More pain. The fact that they were doing it this way, leaving so many indelible marks, did not bode well for his long-term prospects.

But that, of course, was a thought he couldn't dwell on.

When he finally got onto his right hip, he adjusted his leg for the least amount of agony. The icy concrete pulled every trace of warmth from his raw skin. He was of course naked, another deprivation sourced straight from the textbook. He'd undergone considerable training in the Army. SERE, they called it: survival, evasion, resistance, and escape. He had skipped straight past the survival and evasion. Bryce hadn't been captured in a firefight behind enemy lines, but rather while jogging on the Washington and Old Dominion Trail. He had a vague recollection of two men passing him in the opposite direction, then nothing after that. He guessed it had been a blow to the head, coming out of nowhere. After that he had a few hazy

recollections of being on a jet, very likely under seda-
tion.

And so, here he was: straight into resistance.

The voice of a SERE instructor returned. *Control
what you can.*

He found this increasingly a challenge. Bryce was
helpless from a physical standpoint, in constant pain
and shackled at the ankles. All the same, he never
stopped logging information. He knew the door to
his cell opened inward, evidenced by the way his interrogators' feet shuffled back and forth with each
exit, but never on entry. He'd registered eight distinct
voices so far, two teams of four that swapped duty
perhaps twice a week—he didn't have a clock to go
by, or even a reference to daylight, but the schedule was unmistakable. Each team consisted of two
interrogators, with the others acting essentially as
guards. All spoke Russian when they were outside
his cell. The only vehicle he'd ever heard came during shift changes.

The questions they'd been asking him were telling. *Tell us about the new Columbia-class submarine.
What assault tactics did your Ranger unit use?* They
knew he was a congressman, and also a former Army
Ranger. Bryce had held a top secret SCI clearance,
by different authorities, for the last thirteen years.
He'd tried to hold back in the beginning, knowing
there were limits to what any man could endure. He
gave them a few snippets of the truth, along with a
steady diet of lies and misdirection. He'd made this
something of a pastime: inventing a revolutionary so-
nar system, a new training regimen for Rangers that
gave them virtually superhuman strength. His buddies in the unit would have liked that one.

They fact-checked what they could, of course, and knew that at least some of what he was telling them was bullshit. They told him as much when the beatings became more brutal. Gamesmanship all around. Bryce imagined, in some convoluted way, that they respected him for that.

His most closely-held secret they'd not yet uncovered—a glaring failing in their research. Bryce had minored in Russian during college, and while he was rusty, he could make out most of what was being said—both between his interrogators in the cell, and behind the closed door when he was alone. He'd learned that he was being held somewhere outside Murmansk—three hours away by car—and that they were near the Barents Sea. He'd also learned that his interrogators were SVR. They bantered about lousy schedules and loose women, about stupid commanders and promotions. In essence, the same gripes he'd heard every day in the Army.

Of all the intel he'd gathered, the most useful nugget had come six shift-changes ago—which, by his new unit of time, he reckoned to be three weeks. He'd heard two men talking about the camera system in the cell. Since arriving, he knew his every move was being watched—indeed, they'd told him as much during his first interrogation. But apparently the system had malfunctioned. Up to that point, Bryce had been doing little more than enduring his captivity, yet the knowledge that he now had interludes of privacy, a regular window in which he wasn't being watched, fanned an ember of hope. When he was alone, he'd begun trying to move. Nothing near exercise, but small isometric motions. Activating beaten limbs and wasted muscles, testing to see what worked and what didn't. He made progress each day and learned his limitations.

He raised his left foot and began moving it, an exercise he'd been taught by a lacrosse coach back in high school: rotate at the ankle to spell the entire alphabet. He ran through the drill silently, but soon his thoughts were overrun by the most vexing question of all. Why had he been abducted?

Notwithstanding America's support for Ukraine in the war, the idea that Russia had taken to kidnapping and torturing United States congressman seemed completely untenable. Yet here he was, somewhere deep inside Russia and being tortured on a daily basis, all temples of civility and due process abandoned. Try as he might, he could think of no explanation. More frustrated than ever, Bryce turned where he always turned in dark moments. To the two things that kept him going: Sarah and Alyssa.

"Don't give up," he whispered as if they could hear. "Not ever."

He was up to K in his routine when he heard someone talking. The words were indistinguishable, but he recognized the voices—he'd made it a personal challenge to distinguish his captors from one another. His interrogators were coming to the door—the more vicious of the two pairs. One he had privately named Ivan, the other Mengele—after the infamous Nazi doctor renowned for his sadistic tendencies.

What would it be today? Bryce wondered.

If his circumstances could be distilled to one bleak truth, it was that he'd begun to have preferences when it came to beatings. His favorite was the truncheon, not because it wasn't painful, but because there was at least some give to its composite surface, and because it always seemed to hold just a trace of warmth. The mallet was good and bad. Bad because its only purpose was to break bones—hands and face so far. Good because it caused him to pass out quickly, limiting the duration of his agony. The worst, in his new and horrid rating system, was the metal pipe. The damage it inflicted was deep, yet rarely enough to cause him to pass out—he'd tried faking that, but the next blow always made an honest man out of him. The worst part was the material, the cold steel seeming to amplify the pain.

He heard the door open. Someone actually cracked their knuckles. Bryce was lifted to his feet, and his hands were bound over his head—the tendons in his bad right shoulder had long ago failed, rendering the arm all but useless. His good left eye—the right had closed days ago—searched downward through the gap in the hood. He saw the concrete floor, one scuffed boot.

He never knew which would come first, the pain or the questions—a mystery, of course, that was purely by design. One more part of the process.

Out of nowhere, the first blow connected to his naked back.

It was the pipe . . .

42

FAST AND HOT

Sarah woke not knowing what had become of Fake Bryce—that was how she now thought of him. She'd surprisingly fallen asleep last night— had there actually been Ambien in the tea?—and hours later, she'd stirred to find herself alone.

This morning was a mystery, utter silence downstairs.

It finally got the better of her. She sashed herself into her bathrobe and went downstairs, taking the steps soft as a cat. She expected to find him splayed out on the recliner. It was empty. No sign of life in the kitchen. Then she realized his suitcase was gone. Near where it had been, she saw a handwritten note on the dining room table. She lifted it by the edges, as though it might be infectious.

Hope you're feeling better, Sar. Got called out for an earlier flight.
Home next week. Best til then and a hug to Alyssa.
Love, Bryce

Her first thought was derisory. *It's a kiss, you imbecile, not a hug.*

Next came relief. He was gone.

That was followed by an impulse to crumple the

note, burn it, and flush it down the toilet. Nothing accomplished, but eminently satisfying in concept.

With all that out of her system, her thoughts began to organize. She pulled her phone from her robe pocket and called Claire.

She picked up on the third ring, sounding sleepy.

Sarah didn't bother to apologize. "We need to talk."

Burke was up and running early. His anniversary dinner had gone well: good steak, better wine, and all the attendant romance one could expect after twenty-five years of bliss.

Twenty-five. He'd done the math and gotten it right.

They'd turned in by eleven, and Burke slept like a baby until waking at four a.m.—which, as he recalled, was also what babies did. He'd tossed and turned after that, eventually going downstairs to brew a cup of coffee. As he nursed his first cup at the kitchen table, the message from last night played in his head. Then it stuck there.

A distressed Sarah Ridgeway.

An address in Georgetown.

He finally retrieved his phone and woke it up. The screen seemed painfully bright. He tapped on the map and saw the address still dialed in. The red destination flag beckoned like a finish line.

. . . critically important information. You need to see what's inside . . .

"Crap," he muttered.

Washington D.C.'s motto is *Justitia Omnibus*—Justice for All. Burke had always thought Gridlock for All would have been more fitting, but he doubted the ancient Romans had devised such a word.

The drive to Georgetown took twice as long as it should have, even with traffic at its weekend morning best. Burke wasn't scheduled to work, but he knew Sarah Ridgeway's message would haunt him until he followed up. She had promised to explain herself today, so he settled on a drive-by of the address, followed by a stop at the office for an electronic search before getting in touch. He still couldn't fathom why a seemingly balanced woman would send such an acutely unbalanced text.

The rain had ended, a sullen sky taking its place. The wind had picked up considerably, and the forecast was for falling temperatures throughout the day. Burke made the final turn onto P Street, the last straggling sodden leaves of fall spiraling down from above. He referenced his phone and saw that he was two blocks away.

As it turned out, he didn't need the map again.

The first thing he noticed was a glow, pulsing waves of orange reflecting off the gunmetal overcast. That was followed by the telltale reflections of first responder lights—so many, it looked like a red-and-blue disco ball was strobing the neighborhood. Burke's internal radar went to high-rate scan. When the bigger picture appeared, it was sudden and frenzied, a money-shot from a horror movie—everything but the scream.

A fourplex of row houses was engulfed in flames. Fire leaped into the sky, liquid-orange fingers clutching to escape the inferno. The southern end of the complex was getting the worst of it, the front wall having already collapsed. The back and side walls

were partially intact, giving the aura of an overwhelmed barbeque grill. Burke guessed the residence
taking the brunt of the damage had once had a second floor—the three adjoining units did. He checked
the map on his phone, pinching and pulling, if only
to verify what he already knew: the address at the
epicenter of the blaze was the one Sarah Ridgeway
had provided.

Burke counted three fire trucks, their crews working feverishly. An arcing stream of water suggested
another truck in back. The northernmost of the four
residences hadn't yet been touched, and the firemen
were concentrating on the third in line, its southern
wall the battleground.

The police had cordoned off the street a block
short of the blaze. Burke parked as close as he could,
pulling parallel to a Metro Police squad car. He got
out and made his way toward a uniformed cop who
was holding the perimeter.

The officer, a jowly fireplug, held up a hand as
Burke approached. Burke showed his credentials.

"FBI?" the cop said. "Since when do the feds respond to house fires?"

"Since the house burning down is part of an investigation."

The patrolman seemed to think about it.

"Who's in charge?" Burke asked.

The cop pointed to three men huddled near an
SUV behind one of the ladder trucks. Burke bypassed
another squad car, this one parked to blockade the
road, and stepped over a pulsing fire hose connected
to a hydrant. As he got closer he could feel the heat,
and he noticed air being pulled in from behind by
some kind of chimney effect.

The fire chief was obvious enough: a weathered guy with a handheld radio, short iron-gray hair. Burke heard him give orders to two men in full gear, and they dashed off toward the trucks. A crew nearby was attacking the blaze with a standard 2 ½-inch line, and light from the flames dancing mockingly across their hard-set faces. Sensing a pause in the action, Burke was ready with his credentials when the chief turned his way.

"Who the hell are you?"

Burke held out his cred holder. "Special Agent Burke, FBI."

"And you're here because?"

"The unit on the right was a location of interest in an investigation."

"Well, right now, Agent Burke, it's *my* location of interest."

"Yeah, I get it. Looks like maybe that's where the fire originated?"

"Won't know for sure until the forensic guys have a look, but probably, yeah. What kind of investigation you running?"

"Sorry, but I can't get into it."

The chief got a call on his radio and began a back-and-forth with the crew manning the backyard truck. Burke stood watching the fire, flames curling and clawing upward. He heard the firecracker snapping of wood cooking off, and waves of acrid black smoke swirled into the air.

When the chief was done talking, Burke said, "Look, I know you're busy. Could you just tell me one thing—do you know if there was anybody inside?"

"When we got here the end unit was too far gone—we couldn't get in. One of my guys pulled an old woman and her cat out of the next place—got her out just in time. The other two units we evacuated." He pointed to a group of people in bathrobes and slippers on the far side of the street. Burke counted ten, although some were certainly neighbors.

"Okay, thanks. Before I go—a little cross-pollination might do both our departments some good. When you figure out who's going to handle the forensics, can you have them give me a call. I'm really curious as to whether this was arson." Burke held out a business card.

The chief took it, and said, "No way to tell from here, but in my experience—when they go up this fast and hot, there's usually some help. Somebody will get in touch."

"Thanks," Burke said, backing away to let the man work. He was halfway to his car when a section of wall collapsed on the end unit. It sounded like a crack of thunder.

43

A PIN-PULLED GRENADE

Bryce came home last night," Sarah said.

"*What?*"

Claire was across the table in a corner sitting area. They'd met at a Starbucks in Fredericksburg, Sarah insisting they avoid The Daily Grind—right then, she was the more paranoid of the two. The high-top table was discreet, near an all-gender bathroom nobody seemed to use.

"He couldn't fly to New Hampshire because of the storm—or so he said. He walked in with no warning about an hour after you dropped me off."

"That's awkward."

"To say the least." Sarah explained how she'd feigned sickness, gone to bed early, then awoken this morning to find him gone.

After a thoughtful pause, Claire said, "He's back on the trail now?"

"Happily, yes."

Claire sipped a latte made by a barista with a nose ring and Dothrakian eyeliner. She had bought today, although the question of whose turn it was felt increasingly absurd.

"There's something else," Sarah said. "I went back and looked at the video of Bryce at the Watergate. I noticed something I hadn't before . . . or maybe I did, but I refused to believe it."

"What?"

"When Bryce was hanging over the edge, he was dangling by his left arm. Then he raised his right over his head to get a second handhold."

"And that's a big deal?"

"Huge. I probably never told you the specifics, but it's the reason Bryce was forced to take a medical discharge from the Army. Both his right shoulder and elbow had permanent damage—he couldn't raise that arm above ninety degrees. He put himself through hell trying to fix it—physical therapy, surgery, whatever it took. It was hopeless. He knew that if he went back to his unit, he wouldn't be able to pull his weight. He was so afraid of putting his brothers at risk, he took the retirement. I'd never seen Bryce so conflicted, but it was the right thing to do. In that video he lifted his right arm effortlessly."

After a beat, Claire asked, "So how does that fit with the rest?"

"I have a theory. The thing is—"

Sarah's phone trilled with a call. Her newest contact popped to the screen: Special Agent Troy Burke. She nearly picked up, but then let it go to voice mail.

"It's the FBI agent I told you about. I texted him last night and told him he should take a look at the condo."

Claire shot her a guarded look. "*The FBI?* And when were you going to share this nugget with me?"

"When Bryce came home last night, I'd just seen the video. I put it together with what you and I saw at the condo, and . . . I decided someone like Agent Burke needed to see it. He'd left me his card, told me to call if I needed anything."

Claire heaved a sigh. "Okay. I understand why you

called him, with Bryce showing up unexpectedly and all. But you should have told me."

Sarah nodded. "There wasn't much time, but you're right—I should have." Her phone buzzed again. "Looks like he left a message."

Claire made a *Well don't just sit there* gesture.

Sarah listened to Burke's message, a ten-second missive that pushed her already shaky footing off a precipice. Her face went ashen.

"What?" Claire asked, clearly seeing her distress.

Sarah set down her phone like a pin-pulled grenade. "Burke wants to see me right away."

"Why? Did he get inside and see the place?"

"No. The condo burned to the ground this morning."

"This better be good," Alves said. "Saturday is me-day." She rounded the desk where Burke was planted behind their computer.

"I know, sorry." He'd called asking for help on his way to the office from Georgetown. Burke showed her the text he'd gotten the previous night from Sarah Ridgeway. Then he told her about this morning.

"Okay, yeah," Alves agreed. "Very sus. No casualties in the fire?"

"None that they know of. I'm going to head back soon. The fire's out and the investigators ought to be there soon."

"What are you working on now?"

"That's what I need your help with. I'm trying to figure out who lives there, or at least who owns the place. So far, it's nothing but a wall of LLCs. I was hoping you could take over the search—you're better with the online stuff than I am."

"I'm better than you at pretty much everything—except maybe tennis."

Burke shot her a grin, then said, "I just tried to call Ridgeway—went straight to voice mail."

"Which one—the prospective president or the prospective first lady?"

"I'm concentrating on the wife for now. She's the one who highlighted this place, said it was something vital. Now it burns down, and I'm wishing I'd gone last night."

"Why didn't you?"

"Anniversary dinner."

"Oh, right. The big two-five."

Burke looked up from his typing. "How did you know that?"

"Like I said—"

"Never mind. I need to get out to Georgetown."

"Okay. Show me what you've got so far . . ."

The second call from Burke came five minutes later. Sarah ignored him again. Claire reached across and turned her phone off.

"Is that necessary?" Sarah asked.

"I don't know. But it can't hurt."

"It's the *FBI*. I can't just blow him off—I told him to check out that condo."

"I know. But we need some time to think things through."

"Claire . . . this is getting out of hand fast."

"It all makes sense, somehow. We just aren't seeing it yet."

After a long pause, Sarah said, "Actually, I think maybe I am."

Claire stared at her.

"All those files at the condo, Bryce's recent behavior. What finalized it for me was watching that video last night."

Claire didn't reply, yet Sarah knew what she was thinking. "You see it too," she said. "There's only one solution that fits all the facts. No matter how much he looks and sounds like Bryce . . . it's *not* him. The man posing as my husband is an imposter."

"But Sarah, the only way that could be true is if . . ." her voice trailed off to silence.

"I know," she said, finishing the thought. "The only way it could be true is if Bryce has an identical twin."

44

WRECKAGE

Burke's second trip to the condo came with fewer uncertainties. Far greater expectations.

He parked a block away, badged a different uniformed cop to access the site. Small groups of gawkers in housecoats and exercise gear lingered on the nearby sidewalks. Two women in yoga pants, leashed dogs by their sides, stood exchanging gossip. The Lhasa apso and Maltese sniffed the air side by side, probably exchanging their own opinions regarding the neighborhood's new scents.

Burke paused to take in the greater scene.

The fire had been beaten into submission hours ago. Even so, threads of smoke still curled skyward, ethereal demons drifting up, taking their secrets on the wind. The hues and textures were a study in contrast. Wet mud outside the condo's perimeter, a mulch of charred embers within. The unit next door was severely damaged, the shared wall having collapsed. Two perfectly intact rooms looked out over the precipice, complete with frill-curtained windows and a four-poster bed. It looked like a tormented dollhouse, its frippery fluttering in the breeze against walls stained black by smoke. The other two units, farther on, had gone relatively unscathed, the fire department having held its line. In the early light all of it seemed strangely tranquil, at odds with the inferno Burke had witnessed hours ago.

The fire investigator turned out to be a woman. She was wearing the lower half of a protective suit and heavy gloves. When Burke walked up she was near the back of the smoldering eastern unit. In her right hand was a detector of some kind, a box with a handle grip and telescoping sensor.

Burke wasn't going to wade into a probable crime scene without protective gear, so from the remains of the entry landing he called out, "Excuse me!"

The woman turned. She was in her thirties and slender, Saturday hair that was wild and unruly. "Yes?"

"Sorry to bother you, but my name's Burke—I'm with the FBI."

She frowned, flicked a button on her machine, then began slogging toward him through the rubble. When she paused a few steps away, Burke held out his credentials. She seemed to ignore them, and said, "Ashley Cleary, Fire Investigations Branch. The on-scene commander told me you were here this morning—said I might get the pleasure later." Her tone wasn't hostile, but maybe annoyed.

"Are you working this alone?" he asked, wanting to establish the chain of authority.

"I've got some backup at the office, but right now I'm solo."

"Is that typical?"

"For a house fire on a weekend? Pretty much." She tilted her head toward the wreckage. "Rumor is, you had an interest in this place as part of some investigation."

"I had a tip about it. Can't talk specifics right now,

but maybe we could help each other out. My partner is trying to figure out who owns it."

She weighed this for a moment, then said, "Okay. There's an extra pair of boot covers and some gloves in the back of my Tahoe over there. Suit up and I'll show you what we've got."

"A twin," Claire repeated. As if saying it out loud would help.

"It smooths out a lot of things that don't make sense."

"It sounds crazy."

"I know," said Sarah. "Which is why we need better evidence before we go to the FBI."

Claire considered it. "If there's documentation of twins at birth, I could find out using EPIC. Bryce was born in Virginia, right?"

"Yes . . . or at least, that's what he told me."

"Okay. There must be birth records, a DNA profile in his military file. I can approach this from a few angles."

Sarah turned thoughtful. "I might have an angle of my own," she said speculatively.

"What's that?"

"I could talk to his father, Walter. He might remember something."

Claire blew out a humorless laugh. "What—like Bryce had an identical twin brother that they gave up for adoption?"

"I know, it makes no sense. But maybe he can shed some light on it."

"I thought he had Alzheimer's."

"He's got advanced dementia, but there are occasional moments of lucidity. Alyssa is best at drawing him out. Now and again he'll come up with some distant recollection, something really vivid. I'm told it's fairly common. If I can catch him at the right moment, guide him with a few cues, maybe it'll trigger the right memory."

"I guess it's worth a try."

"What time is it?" Sarah asked. Her phone was still shut down.

Claire checked hers. "Ten thirty."

"Okay, I need to pick up Alyssa soon. We'll head up to Winchester this afternoon."

Moments later they were outside, the frigid wind sweeping rotted leaves across the parking lot.

"At some point I need to return Burke's call," Sarah said.

Claire thought about it. "Keep your phone off for now, but ring me before you go to Winchester. I'll tell you what I've found with EPIC. Hopefully you can call Burke back with more than what we've got."

"That would be good. Since what we've got isn't much."

45

SMOLDERING AND OVERCOME

Burke waded through a sea of charred debris. The ashes were wet, and in the synthetic booties he felt like he was walking through quicksand, every raised foot pulling free with a sucking sound. Part of it was the earlier rain, but the hose crews had done their share. Their mission was to put out fires, save lives and property. Preservation of evidence wasn't a priority.

He followed Cleary to what had been the back wall of the building. The tang of burned wood and insulation was thick, something between a campfire and a burning tire. He saw little recognizable remaining: a few chunks of concrete, some wiring, a lump of plastic that had gone molten—probably a computer.

Cleary talked as they moved. "We're bringing in a canine later."

"Canine? You mean for bodies?"

"No. We've already determined there were no casualties. I'm looking for ignitable liquid residues—accelerants." She held up her device. "This thing is good, but the dogs are better."

"What exactly is that?"

"Portable hydrocarbon detector."

"Hydrocarbons? That proves arson?"

"Proof is a strong word, but it's pretty convincing." She turned and faced him. "Maybe you can tell me without giving anything away about your secret investigation . . . *should* I expect to find arson?"

"Honestly, I'm not sure."

She advanced a few more steps and ended at the biggest section of standing wall—eight feet wide, about the same in height. The broken cinder block edges made him think of a half-built Lego house. In the middle of the wall was a half-melted metal box that Burke recognized as a circuit breaker panel.

Cleary waved her wand over the wall, then showed him the gauge—the needle was parked in a red zone. "That's a pretty high reading."

"Meaning this is where it started?"

"Actually, I've been getting numbers like that all over. Let me start at square one. First of all, we didn't have a gas explosion—that would have been obvious in a number of ways. There's not much structure left, but given the readings all around, and the apparent burn pattern, I'd say you've got accelerant—and a *lot* of it."

She held the detector out toward Burke. "Here, hold this for a sec."

He took it, watched Cleary bend down. From a pocket she pulled out what looked like a putty knife and a nylon evidence bag. She took a sample of black residue from a lower section of the wall. After sealing the bag, she took two pictures with her phone—first the label on the bag, then the spot where she'd gotten the sample. After putting it all away, she took the detector back.

"Any idea what kind of accelerant was used?" he asked.

"Hard to say now, but the lab will nail it down. Gasoline and kerosene are pretty common—mostly due to availability. Then you have your exotics. Stuff like Toluene and Xylene."

Burke felt like he was getting a chemistry lesson.

"Whatever they used, they didn't go lightly." She pointed to evidence markers she'd already placed in a half dozen spots. "I've got high readings on five interior walls. Judging by that, and the pour patterns, whoever did this wanted it to go up fast and hot."

As Cleary got back to work, Burke scanned the ashen rubble. He stepped carefully over two-by-fours burned to the width of a finger, exposed metal pipes that had flattened from the heat. In what must have been the kitchen, the remains of a stove sat smoldering and overcome, like a house plant suddenly dropped on Mercury. He noticed a curled edge of paper near his right foot. Burke knelt down, picked it up with a gloved hand. On closer inspection he recognized the corner of a photograph, a thumbnail-sized edge of a gloss print that had survived the inferno. He couldn't make out any image, only shades of black and white. He looked around and saw two similar scraps—thick-bond paper, the remains of memories singed into ether.

He poked around for another ten minutes, found little of note. Standing with his hands on his hips, he called across to Cleary, "I think I'm done here—thanks for your help. I'll leave a card with my number in your truck. Call me later and I'll let you know what we've got on our end."

She waved to say that she would, then went back to probing and marking.

Burke left his card in her SUV, then set out toward his own car. Halfway there he passed the only tree in the area, a leafless elm with roots pushing up the sidewalk around its allotted square of dirt. There, in the elm's tiny sotted biome, he spotted a small strip of paper. It was lying between a crushed beer can and a plastic grocery bag, and could have been part of the usual urban jetsam save for one thing—one edge of the paper was singed. Burke looked around and noticed a few similar bits of black-edged paper on the street and sidewalk. It wasn't hard to imagine how they'd gotten here: fragments carried skyward on a volcano of superheated air, then fluttering to the ground like ashen snow.

He reached down and retrieved the strip of paper. There was writing on one side, an inch-and-a-half remnant from the top of a printed page. Burke knew immediately what it was. After graduating from high school, he'd enlisted in the Army for a four-year stint. The header he was looking at was what every American soldier, from every service, got when they separated from the military. A defense department DD Form 214—the document that served as proof of service for the rest of one's life. The form certified the military branch and dates of service, along with decorations, medals, and campaign ribbons awarded. It noted the type of discharge granted: general, honorable, dishonorable, or bad conduct. None of that was visible on the sliver of paper in his hand. Burke saw only the title, *CERTIFICATE OF RELEASE OR DISCHARGE FROM ACTIVE DUTY*, and on the next line the name and grade of the service member: RIDGEWAY, BRYCE JAMES, Major.

He stood stock-still. The self-reproach that had been building peaked.

Sarah Ridgeway had been right. She'd called for help.

And he had ignored her.

He glanced back at Cleary, saw her waving the wand like a shaman divining for water. Burke reached into his jacket pocket, fished out a plastic Ziploc bag, and dropped the paper inside.

He pulled out his phone and called Sarah again.

Still no answer.

He took a last look around, and found himself wondering how well Georgetown was wired for CCTV. Most commercial districts in the city had video, but in residential areas the coverage was spotty. He checked the nearby intersection—there was no traffic light, only a four-way stop. No cameras in sight. Across the street an old man was unlocking the door of an auto parts store. A possibility. Burke made a mental note to check it later. He'd have to return here as well, see what else he could find after Cleary was done.

He got in his car and headed for the field office, hard questions pinging in his head. How had a copy of Bryce Ridgeway's DD-214 ended up here? Who had torched the condo?

And most troubling of all: Why wasn't Sarah Ridgeway answering her phone?

A KIND OF STEEL

ryce sometimes wondered how he would know if he'd died. There were times he'd seen stars, seen blackness, even perhaps a tunnel of light. It could have been a dream, he supposed, some middling consciousness bridging the pain of this world to whatever lay beyond. Everyone had a date with destiny, yet his seemed maddeningly vague—repeatedly taken to the brink, only to find his fate deferred. Only one thing kept him going: the thought of seeing Sarah and Alyssa again.

He cracked open his good eye, no idea how long he'd been out. Since the light was always on, he never knew the time of day. His best reference came from beyond the door. There were hours of chattering, periods of quiet. These became his sun, his moon, his shaky circadian reference. Right then, he heard nothing but the distant rhythm of snoring. Here—wherever *here* was—it was the middle of the night.

He lay still for a time, his standard procedure. He took careful stock before engaging muscles, before putting battered joints into gear. The smell was as ever, sweat and vomit, the squalid odor of his bucket across the room. He noted the coppery taste of blood in his mouth. One ear had a new pulsing sound, seemingly underwater. Bryce focused on his breathing. From what he could remember—a recollection that certainly had gaps—Mengele had gone after his existing injuries, focusing on his right-sided ribs as he whacked away with the pipe. The pain had been excruciating, and Bryce passed out at least once. He recalled saying something about a field communication network DARPA was building, the details of which might or might not have been true. He'd gotten a briefing last summer. Or was it the summer before? Such details were falling increasingly hazy, which could only be expected. From where he lay, the conference rooms of Capitol Hill seemed light-years away.

The good news, if it could be characterized as such, was that Mengele hadn't inflicted any new damage. At least, none he'd so far registered. In the beginning, Bryce had sulked. Later, he'd felt sorry for himself, the torture of lost hope surpassing what they did to his body. Then he focused on what always brought him back—his wife and daughter. That put him across the bridge to anger.

And more good news. His tormentors had removed his leg shackles. He'd heard them discussing it after lifting him to a standing position for the third time—even in Russian dungeons, apparently, it was dishonorable to hit a man while he was down.

Ivan: *He keeps falling down.*
Mengele: *He can't stand without our help any more.*
Ivan: *We should remove the leg irons—he isn't going anywhere.*

Perfectly on cue, Bryce had crumpled like a pool toy with a pulled plug. A demonstration of hopelessness, even capitulation. As hoped, the key had come out and the steel clamps around his raw ankles were removed.

His anger began cresting. With new options of movement, he separated his legs and worked his way onto his knees. He hadn't tried to stand in at least a week. Two "shift days."

Using the wall for support, he clawed his way upward. Electric pain shot through his ribs. The very act of moving was awkward, dizzying. He reached his feet, swaying like a sailor with sea legs. Slowly things steadied. His ribs felt a bit better. He stood nearly straight, a climber who'd crested a mountain. Which, in a sorry sense, he was.

Distant traces of dinner rode the air, the sizzled-fat aroma of their standard fare—always meat and potatoes. At irregular intervals they slid cold portions into his cell on a dented metal tray—enough to keep him alive, but never enough to satisfy. No one ever removed his hood or tried to place the food in front of him. They simply knew he would find it, like a mole might find a grub. It wasn't half bad, and he was certain he was getting leftovers from whatever the squad's cook whipped up—no one was going to waste time preparing a special gruel for one inmate.

Bryce took a few tentative steps, his good arm guiding him along the wall. He wondered if the camera system was still out of action. *One way to find out.*

He reached up with his good left arm, his two uninjured fingers, and pulled the hood off his head. The light was intense, like he was staring at the sun. He blinked as his eyes adjusted, and for the first time Bryce got a comprehensive look at his surroundings. He'd caught snatches here and there through the gap in his hood, tried to piece it all together in a mental diagram. His model turned out to be reasonably accurate.

Twenty-feet by twenty, ten-foot ceiling. Walls that looked like something from a medieval castle, thick stone and windowless. The floor was solid concrete. The door belonged on a bank vault. No amount of chipping or digging or prying would ever get him out. His slop bucket was in one corner, a simple metal item with a wire handle. He looked up and found the camera above the door, a lens with a tiny LED light beneath. The light was extinguished.

"Let's hope," he whispered.

He took another step, and his right foot screamed in pain. Still, he could put a bit of weight on it— unlike the last time he'd tried. He worked his arms gingerly as he circled the cell, although the right barely moved—he was, in effect, a one-armed man. He stopped and performed something close to deep knee bends. His joints seemed rusted, but after a few repetitions things started to smooth out.

He kept moving and stretching, pushing through jolts of pain. After no more than ten minutes, he was exhausted. Slowly, tentatively, like a nonagenarian getting back in a wheelchair, Bryce sank to the floor. He picked up the hood, but didn't put it on right away, taking a few more moments to analyze a room that defied analysis.

The exertion, along with his miniscule progress, buoyed his mood. Quelled his anger. It also stoked something he'd not felt for a very long time. It wasn't exactly patriotism, but something more primal. Nothing born out of Boy Scout pledges or verses of "God Bless America." He felt a kind of steel, something forged in the Army. The product of fallen comrades and spilled blood. It was a drive he hadn't felt in a very long time, and Bryce suddenly didn't feel alone. He felt a bond, as though he was fighting alongside others, unseen as they might be, on a critical mission that wasn't yet over.

It had been hammered home during survival training that, in dire situations, one thing was vital above all else. Be it floating on a raft at sea, stranded in a jungle, or isolated on a frozen mountaintop, the one thing that set apart those who lived from those who died had been proved beyond a doubt: an unyielding will to survive.

And with that, Bryce was struck by a revelation. As utterly hopeless as his situation seemed, and in spite of his battered physical condition, his thoughts were advancing to the final portion of SERE training.

The second *E*.

Escape.

47

A TRACE OF MELANCHOLY

Claire's initial impulse—to track Bryce's birth records in search of a twin—proved an exercise in frustration. She easily found a birth certificate, copies of which were on file in both the Virginia DMV and Army personnel records. According to that document, he'd been born nearby, at Alexandria Hospital in Alexandria, Virginia.

And there the bog deepened.

EPIC was programmed to verify sources, and an automated crosscheck of the hospital's files found no corresponding record of Bryce's birth. A further search of the Fairfax County Office of Vital Records confirmed the discrepancy. Claire tried to leapfrog the problem, searching the databases of every hospital in Northern Virginia, and adding his mother's maiden name to the field.

Still zeroes.

Sensing a dead end, she expanded her query, focusing not on Bryce but his mother. That turned out to be an eye-opener: on January 28, 1986, the date of Bryce's birth, Marsha Ridgeway had been with her husband in Czechoslovakia. Walter had been appointed ambassador the previous summer, and travel records—diplomatic passport and visa histories taken straight from State Department archives—verified the couple's continuous presence in Prague for more than a year after their arrival. EPIC easily dredged up news articles and State Department press releases documenting their time in country. Claire stepped through a dozen photos taken during the initial eight-month period: Walter shaking hands with various ministers, posing amid groups at embassy soirees. Oddly, despite the fact that the ambassador's wife was verified to be in residence with him, she was nowhere to be seen in the photographs—with, as it turned out, one exception.

Using facial recognition and filtering, EPIC zeroed in on a photograph from *Rudé Parvo*, the now-defunct official newspaper of the Czechoslovakian Communist Party. In early December, 1985, at a state dinner hosted by the country's president, Gustáv Husák, a group of dignitaries—Walter Ridgeway, along with the presidents of Russia and Ukraine—posed with drinks in hand for a wooden photograph. Deep in the background, her image seized and enhanced by EPIC, was an aloof Marsha Ridgeway. She was standing alone at the edge of a dance floor, her level expression concealing perhaps a trace of melancholy. She looked slim and fit in a sequined evening dress—and not the slightest bit pregnant.

Before Claire could react, EPIC spit out its next bombshell. The system had taken the initiative to verify Bryce's birth certificate, and with ninety-eight percent certainty, the document Bryce had used to get a driver's license as a teen, and later to join the Army, showed defects implying that it was a well-crafted forgery.

Claire straightened and pushed back from her computer. At every turn, the enigma that was Bryce Ridgeway seemed to deepen. In trying to determine whether he had a twin, she'd invalidated the very documentation of his birth. Worse yet, she'd discovered that his mother wasn't even pregnant when she should have been.

No steps forward, two steps back.

Claire's index finger tapped on the desk. Behind her she heard Atticus in full mettle, his hands playing his keyboard like a pianist racing through *Flight of the Bumblebee*.

"Do you know where they would have been routed?" he called across the room.

Claire had asked him to locate the files she'd uploaded from the condo. "No, we never got around to validating that function."

The HIWAY device sat on the table next to her—a digital rat with its USB tail. She was thankful she'd remembered to retrieve it in their frantic exit from the condo. It was an excellent piece of hardware, and had breached the computer's security like a bullet through paper. As a condition of obtaining the device, Claire had promised the CIA it would never leave her lab. One more offense for her burgeoning rap sheet.

She wanted to see what HIWAY had stolen from the compromised hard drives. The problem was, they'd left in such a rush, she wasn't even sure there had been time to seal the cyber steal.

"Okay, found them," Atticus said.

Claire went and watched over his shoulder as he scrolled through thousands of digital addresses.

"What exactly are you looking for?" he asked.

Claire didn't know where to begin. Search for copies of Bryce's vital records? Go back to the earliest possible files? *No,* she thought. "Look for unusual files, stuff you don't recognize."

His finger scrolled the mouse, and soon settled on one line. "This one's weird. Compression and encoding to an MPEG file. FTP protocol uses port 21."

Even Claire was lost. "Whatever. Any idea what it is?"

"One way to find out." He double-clicked, and an adjacent monitor showed the results: a split screen with dual playback and time bars. They studied it together in silence.

"Ever seen anything like this?" she asked.

Atticus maneuvered sideways on his scooter to get a better look. "Nope. Looks like some kind of audio analysis app. See the bar graphs at the bottom? Pitch, intonation, loudness. Lemme play the left side."

A two-minute audio began. Claire heard Bryce giving what sounded like his standard stump speech from congressional days. Atticus stopped it, then played the right side, heard the same speech . . . almost.

"I think it's some kind of speech comparison software," said Claire. "Hit the synch icon and play both."

Atticus set it up, and the dual tracks began running simultaneously, minor variations highlighted by the computer. "That's it," she said. "He's practicing, trying to mimic Bryce's delivery, his speech patterns."

Atticus shot her a wary glance. He'd been skeptical of Sarah's "twin" theory. *And who wouldn't be?* Claire thought. He was about to say something when a chime sounded on a different monitor.

"What's that?" Claire asked.

He wheeled left. "I was tinkering with the routing on those live-streams. I think you said they were sourced from cams inside Sarah's house?"

"Yep. Audio and video."

The leftmost monitor showed a quad-split screen of blank images.

"That's weird," he said.

"What?"

"A few hours ago, I had them up and running."

"You were watching the feeds from her house in real time?"

"According to the time-date stamps, yeah. I was working on sourcing the servers."

"So what happened?"

He typed a bit more. "Nothing wrong with the channels or software. I can only think of one thing. Sometime in the last few hours . . . all the cameras dropped off-line."

48

A VISION OF TEENAGE PLEASANTNESS

As a rule, Burke's inclination when hitting a roadblock in any investigation was to revert to the most direct course. In the matter of finding Sarah Ridgeway, he decided Route 1 involved an unannounced visit to her house.

He arrived to find the driveway empty, and immediately felt dispirited. On his last visit he remembered seeing a Japanese sedan at the top of the hammerhead. Burke had already done his homework—or more precisely, Alves had done it for him. Virginia DMV records verified that Bryce and Sarah Ridgeway owned two cars: a Toyota Camry, jointly owned, and a Tesla Model 3 titled in his name only. It suggested the Tesla was the congressman's ride, although owing to his hectic schedule, Burke figured Ridgeway would take a hired car to the airport. Better that than to leave a new Tesla parked outside in the middle of winter. The garage was a single-stall, and he guessed the Tesla was inside right now, probably hooked up to a charging station. Altogether, a lot of conjecture, but the conclusion if it held: Sarah Ridgeway wasn't home.

Walking up the gray-paver path for the second time, he recalled the news conference the congressman had held here the night of the bombing. Bryce Ridgeway had come a long way since then.

Burke rang the doorbell and waited patiently, thinking there was at least a chance that their daughter—Alyssa, was it?—might be home. When no one answered, he sank the button a second time. Burke stood on the landing, his breath going to vapor. The temperature had been dropping since the storm front passed, Arctic air sweeping in.

Nobody came to the door.

He about-faced, walked halfway to the street, and then paused to take a good look at the house. He saw nothing suspicious. The backyard was fenced, but the gate beside the garage was cracked open. Almost like an invitation.

Burke looked left and right down the street. He saw no one.

Sarah pulled to the curb in front of Ruby's house but left the engine running. The drill would normally be to text Alyssa and tell her she was waiting out front. Walking to the front door and knocking had ended years ago—from the teen point of view, nothing good came from moms and dads being forced to chat. A bit of parental social distancing.

The problem today was that Sarah, bound by her newfound paranoia, still had her phone turned off. That being the case, she did what her own mother might have done back in the day—she tapped the horn twice.

A minute later she saw a flutter at the front curtain. Soon after, Alyssa stormed out. She looked peeved. Sarah vacated the driver's seat, walking around to the passenger door so Alyssa could take the wheel.

"Why was your phone off?" Alyssa fussed.

"Sorry . . . long story. You weren't trying to call, were you?"

"Yeah. I wanted to stay longer."

They took their respective seats. A scowling Alyssa adjusted the rear-view mirror as if punishing it.

Sarah said. "I have a lot going on today."

"Like what?"

"I need to go out to Winchester to see Grandpa. They called and said there are some papers I need to sign." Sarah didn't like lying to her daughter, but was surprised how easily it came. "I figured you could come with me."

"I'd like to, but I can't. I've got piles of work to do before school starts Tuesday. Anyway, I just saw Grandpa a few days ago."

Sarah was taken aback. It was a complication she hadn't anticipated, and one that immediately didn't sit well: Alyssa spending the day in a house where every room was wired for video.

Alyssa looked over her shoulder and reached for the shift lever.

"Wait!" Sarah said.

Alyssa froze. "Did I do something wrong?"

Sarah closed her eyes. "No, baby. I was just thinking . . . if you stayed here this afternoon, could you get your work done with Ruby?"

Her daughter's mood bounced like a basketball off concrete. "Sure! We have three classes together—that would be perfect!"

Mom the Educator yielded to Mom the Creeped Out. "Okay. Go back in, make sure it's okay with her mother."

Minutes later Alyssa was thumbs-upping at the

door, a vision of teenage pleasantness. Even a coat hanger smile.

Sarah rolled down the passenger window, and called out, "I'll pick you up before dinner."

Her daughter waved then disappeared.

Before she got under way, Sarah decided to venture a look at her phone. She turned it on and saw the voice mail icon dotted with a red three: Alyssa's call, another from Agent Burke, and a third from Claire.

She tapped on Claire's message and heard two words. "Call me."

Sarah did.

"What's up?" she asked.

"Are you home yet?" Claire asked.

"No, I'm on my way now."

"Okay. When you get there, you need to check something . . ."

49

DON'T TRUST ANYONE

S arah was half a block from her house when she saw the car parked in front. Her foot flew to the brake like she was stomping a roach. She wheeled to the curb and tucked behind a minivan three houses away. She left the engine running while she took in the scene. As far as she could remember, she hadn't left any lights on. In the midday gloom, none seemed illuminated. She wondered if Bryce had returned unexpectedly again, perhaps in a rental car.

She cracked her window slightly, heard Rex the retriever barking. Someone in the backyard? Would Rex be able to distinguish Fake Bryce? As far as she could tell, there was no one in the car, although her view was marginal. Thankfully, it wasn't the sedan she and Claire had seen at the condo last night. Leaving Alyssa at Ruby's for the day suddenly seemed like a brilliant move. Sarah was reaching for her phone, about to call Claire, when movement caught her eye.

A man appeared at the far side of the house. He came from behind the garage, the side yard where a gate accessed the back fence. He was wearing a bulky jacket and gloves, and as he neared his car Sarah got a better look. There was no doubt about it: FBI Special Agent Troy Burke.

She was momentarily relieved, yet found herself wondering why he'd gone around back. Burke turned to look at the house one last time, then got in his car and drove away—fortunately, in the opposite direction. It saved her the degradation of having to duck down like a vaping teenager.

Sarah waited five minutes. As she did, she tried to think methodically. Was there any reason to *not* go inside? The explanation for his coming seemed simple: the condo she'd sent him to check on had burned down. He would have questions, and she hadn't been answering his calls. So he came to look for her, perhaps even make sure she was all right.

All perfectly logical.

Rex stopped barking, but he'd set off at least three other dogs down the street. All were singing in chorus now, the way dogs did. Raising an alarm about another raised alarm, the details of which they knew nothing about. Sarah thought about that.

She bit her bottom lip, put the car in gear, and headed for her driveway.

The call that reached Burke as he headed back to his office wasn't the one he wanted. But it was second place.

"Hello, Agent Burke. This is Ashley Cleary."

"Right, hi. How's the archaeology going?" Burke switched his phone to speaker.

"It's going," said Cleary. "At this point, it's pretty definitive—we're looking at arson. It'll take the lab a couple of days to determine the exact agent, but somebody must have used at least ten gallons of liquid fuel."

"Okay, good to know."

"Have you made any headway on who owns the place?"

"I'm afraid not. The ownership is hidden behind multiple shell companies. It's the kind of setup people use for only one reason—they're trying to keep secrets. We'll probably figure it out in time. Then again, given the apparent level of sophistication, there's a chance we won't."

"I might be able to help you out," she said.

"Really? I'd owe you a bottle of something good."

"To begin, the place didn't have any furniture on either floor. But in the middle of the living room I saw evidence of what looked like a work-station. Plastic tables, a couple of computers. There were also some files and binders. Mind you, most of it is smoke and ash now—this place really went up hot."

Burke looked at the plastic bag on the seat next to him, the top of a DD Form 214. "You don't say."

"We got lucky. One three-ring binder survived with a few legible pages. It was medical stuff mostly, some surgical records and lab results—we think from the VA. Couldn't make out the patient's name on any of them, but there were some curious notes handwritten in the margins on two pages."

"Curious how?"

"I couldn't figure it out, but one of my fellow investigators recognized it right away—the notes were in Russian."

Sarah went inside through the garage connector. She crossed the threshold into the kitchen like she was walking into a Halloween haunted house. Tentative, expecting the unexpected.

She might have simply bypassed the house, gone straight to see Walter, if Claire hadn't been so adamant. The feeds from the cameras had gone blank, and Claire wanted to know why. She said there had to be a transmitter somewhere, probably a wireless hub in the attic or on an upper floor. Claire said the hardware might be traceable, and she'd given Sarah a simple game plan. If she could retrieve one of the cameras or the hub, send a picture of the make and model number, or better yet a serial number, EPIC might be able to track down where it had been purchased and by whom.

Sarah decided to start in the master bathroom. She knew the cameras were concealed in the air vents, and that was the one she'd seen. Before going upstairs, she diverted to the utility closet. She shoved aside a vacuum and a mop to extract a three-step ladder. Once upstairs, she planted the ladder in front of the bathroom sink and climbed up to the vent. She took a good look through the louvred grate but didn't see the lens. She was certain she'd seen it last night—and equally sure it had seen her. Sarah dismounted and went downstairs.

A minute later she was back on the ladder with a screwdriver. Any Army wife worth her salt was handy around the house—compulsory skills when husbands were away for six months at a stretch. Sarah could replace a toilet valve, lubricate the rollers on a garage door. This was second-lieutenant-wife stuff.

She pulled two screws from the vent cover, wriggled it off, and got a clear view inside the duct. What she saw surprised her. She moved to the bedroom and ran the same drill. Same result.

Sarah pulled out her phone and called Claire. "I know why you lost the feeds from the cameras," she said, peering into the empty air shaft. "They're all gone."

"Gone?" Claire asked incredulously.

"I checked two vents, including one where I definitely saw something last night—both are empty. And there's something else. When I got here I spotted a car in front of my house. I parked a few houses away and saw Agent Burke walk out of my backyard."

"Burke? The FBI guy who's been trying to reach you?"

"The very one."

"You think *he* removed the cameras?"

"I have no idea. I didn't see him carrying anything, but he was definitely skulking around."

Claire paused in thought. "This just keeps getting stranger. Your house is being surveilled, possibly by the FBI. And for reasons we don't understand, Bryce may have been monitoring it."

"I know, none of it adds up."

"How long were you gone today?"

"I went to meet you, then I drove over to pick up Alyssa—a couple of hours." She explained that Alyssa had stayed at her friend's house to do schoolwork.

"That's probably just as well."

"Is there any other way to figure out who installed the cameras?"

"I don't know—the model numbers would have helped. I'll put Atticus on it, but it might be a dead end."

Sarah folded the ladder and started downstairs. "I'm going to see Walter now."

"Don't you think it would be more useful to talk to Burke? He's been trying to reach you."

"Twenty minutes ago, I might have. But now . . . I don't know what to think."

"You don't trust him?"

Sarah hit the first floor and put down the ladder. She looked across the room at a pinch-pot holding a corkscrew. "Honestly, aside from you and Alyssa . . . I don't trust anyone right now."

50

HIS PRIVATE PEARL HARBOR

ryce was doing a modified push-up: one arm on a forty-five against the wall was the best he could manage. As he did so, he performed an assessment—the captain of a ship ordering a battle damage report. His right arm was swollen, but feeling had come back to that hand. He could move the fingers, maybe enough to grip a ten-pound weight. His ribs remained extremely sore, restricting certain movements. The most promising development was his right foot—he could almost bear full weight, although walking remained a challenge.

He was fast becoming a student of outside sounds. He heard a pulsing wind rattling a window in the main room, whistling under the weather stripping of a door. He'd heard such sounds before, mostly in recent weeks. The Russian winter announcing its arrival. From where he stood, it changed little. His cell was as cold as ever—the floor had been like ice since he'd arrived, a permafrost rink worthy of a Zamboni.

He was finishing his third set of exercises when he heard voices nearing the door. Ivan and Mengele approaching. Bryce caught a few words: they were discussing what they would do when they returned to Murmansk tomorrow night. *Tomorrow.* A shift change was imminent.

The voices closed in, and Bryce quickly worked the

hood over his head and dropped to the floor. A *clank* as the door unlocked—in the acoustics of the cell it sounded like a dry-fire on the empty chamber of a gun. He sensed them come in, something scraping on the floor behind them. A chair?

Wind moaned in the background.

He was lifted up roughly, pain searing through his ruined right shoulder and ribs. They planted him hard on what felt like a folding metal chair, then drew his legs straight. Just when he was expecting the worst, some new manner of agony, he felt warm cloth being pulled over his ankles, which were still raw from the removed shackles. They lifted him enough to tug what felt like a pair of prison pajamas over his hips, then dropped him back into the chair. His hood was ripped off, and he made a point of averting his eyes. He blinked and squinted like a man who hadn't seen light in months.

Bryce didn't know what to make of it. They'd never before removed the hood for a session. He looked up haltingly.

For the first time, he had faces to go with the two things he'd memorize about each man—their voices and their dented steel-toed boots. Ivan was short and neckless, a soccer hooligan haircut and three-day growth of beard. His hands were hirsute and meaty. Wearing a wrinkled track-suit, he looked like a short-order cook on his day off. Mengele was taller, more angular. He moved like a scarecrow whose frame had come loose, an image accentuated by baggy pants and a long-sleeve shirt with breast pockets. His hair was brown and limp, the bangs cut using a ruler, and his mouth bristled with bad teeth. Beneath all that was a prominent jaw. Bryce took the abstract liberty of over-laying it with a bulls-eye. A rare feel-good moment.

He kept his eyes on Mengele, who was clearly in charge of the four-man detail, and had acted as the primary interrogator. His eyes gave nothing away—they were hard and impenetrable, a sclerotic bulkhead separating whatever lay behind. A corollary to Bryce's earlier thought came to mind: not only were his captors leaving indelible marks, they were now letting him see their faces. Further damnation of his prospects going forward.

Surprisingly, Bryce saw none of the usual implements. Was this the beginning of some new phase? Mengele held what looked like an iPad in one hand. Bryce had no idea what to make of it.

The Russian came closer, hovered over him for a moment. Probably expecting him to waver. Bryce kept a level gaze—or as best he could with one good eye. He caught a slight whiff of citrus, dish soap he supposed—neither man seemed like the body lotion type.

Mengele's lips twisted into something near a smile, although without the usual supporting tics—no creases beside his mouth, no crinkles outside his eyes. Nor did the smile match his gaze, a separation of body and soul that was probably a lifetime in the making.

He said in his usual decent English, "First, I should compliment you, Congressman. You have proved unusually stubborn." His voice had the resonance of a belt sander. "Of course, you have given us most of what we wanted. Still, I think there might be more. I'm sure you imagine it your duty to be obstinate, to insert misinformation, but we will get everything in the end."

Bryce lowered his eyes to the man's midsection, as if to avoid eye contact. Mengele was wearing a wristwatch, a cheap Timex with a plastic band. It was 9:02 p.m. The date was January 3rd. He wore a belt, a military item with a brass clasp. No jewelry. He shifted to Ivan. No watch, simple leather belt, wedding ring on the appropriate hairy knuckle. *Now there's a lucky woman.*

"Still," Mengele continued, "there is something you should be aware of. To begin, have you deduced where you are right now?"

Bryce hesitated. Never before had the sessions been conducted in a conversational tone. The shift in tactics made him wary. All the same, he decided to play along. "No idea," he lied, the map in his head narrowed to a thirty-by-thirty-mile box.

"You are in Russia. The precise location is immaterial, but suffice to say you are extremely isolated. As you will remain."

"Russia is now in the business of kidnapping American politicians?" The accusation was dimmed by his delivery—his jaw was severely swollen, causing the words to slur.

Again, the secluded smile. A secret soon to be shared. "Business? No, that would not be sustainable. You, however, are a unique case. I'm sure this will surprise you, but your absence has not been noted."

Bryce didn't know what to make of that.

Finally, the iPad was brought to bear. Mengele called up a video, hit play, and turned the screen toward Bryce.

He saw footage of himself arriving on an elevated stage in front of a crowd, climbing the stairs on a trot and waving like he was in a parade. The crowd noise was dense, echoing around the venue—and now echoing in a prison cell thousands of miles away. Bryce recognized the signature enthusiasm of a campaign rally, everything fervent and choreographed. It appeared to be a large event, yet, oddly, he didn't recall it. Did that imply he was having memory lapses? Had too many blows to the head fogged his brain?

"Note the date in the corner," Ivan chipped in, a toady eager to twist a broken arm.

Bryce looked, saw December 18th. Little more than two weeks ago, if Mengele's watch was to be believed. *They're screwing with you*, he told himself.

"I'm not impressed," Bryce said. And truly he wasn't. He'd had more than his share of intelligence briefings, so he knew videos could be expertly doctored. "Deep fakes" that looked legitimate to the untrained eye.

"Let me show you another, then," said Mengele.

A second video came to the screen, similar to the first, yet with a better view of the crowd. He saw thousands of people—what would be a fair percentage of his entire congressional district. Many were holding up signs, a blue background with bold red-and-white lettering: Ridgeway for President.

Bryce felt the first tug in his chest—one that had nothing to do with cracked ribs.

Then, tauntingly from the Russian, "And perhaps this one."

This time what Bryce saw sent bile rising in his throat. He was looking at himself in a close-up shot. His right arm was in a sling as he stood in an intimately familiar setting: the path leading to the front door of his house. Behind him on the front step were Sarah and Alyssa, arms around each other's shoulders. It was all Bryce could do to hold back tears. As the video ran, he began speaking to the camera. Except it wasn't *him*.

"This morning we witnessed an attack against the heart of America . . ."

Bryce listened to words that made no sense whatsoever. A delicately nuanced speech he'd never given. *Attack against America?* He noted the date stamp: November 11th last year, Veterans Day. The very day, in the early morning hours, that his world had imploded. His private Pearl Harbor, when he'd been abducted from the W&OD Trail. All suspicions of digital trickery washed away like a failed levee, swept into oblivion by the flood of unassailable images. His family. His home. He himself. All of it, somehow, fitted into a story that was pure fiction, yet one that was playing out before his eyes.

When the video ended, Mengele lowered the screen and looked at him triumphantly. In the way a victor regards the vanquished.

"Yes, of course," he said. "You are wondering how this could be . . . how you are seeing yourself do and say things that never happened."

Bryce didn't respond. But then, how did one react to an alternate reality?

"America's great weakness," Mengele philosophized, "is the structure of your political system. With your constant elections, such a high turnover in governance, your leaders never think . . . what is the phrase? . . . *long term*. We Russians hold an advantage in that respect. Our leaders, whatever you might think of them, remain in power for extended periods. This strategy, as it relates to you, goes back a very long time." He handed the blanked tablet to Ivan who tucked it under an arm. Mengele continued, "I will tell you how this all came to be. What you have just seen, indeed what you are so intimately a part of, is an operation that began nearly forty years ago . . ."

51

A BROKEN SOUL

The drive to Winchester was oddly quiet—Sarah couldn't remember the last time she'd made it alone, without Alyssa or Bryce to help pass the time. The heater was blowing like a geothermal vent, trying to keep up with an outside temperature in the twenties. Gusting winds flogged the gentle hills, and the car buffeted like a ship on high seas.

Sarah didn't like the quiet. Didn't like being alone, today of all days. The dreadful question she'd been pushing away kept filling the void. If the man running for president wasn't her husband, then what had happened to Bryce?

She was reasonably sure *when* the switch had occurred: the day of the Watergate Hotel bombing. That morning her husband had woken up and gone for a run like any other day. Yet someone else had come back. A man identical to Bryce in nearly every way. *Nearly.* She recalled the cut on his calf. Weeks later, after it healed, she remembered thinking the injury had left an outsized mark. Now she knew why: it had been a preexisting scar, a singular difference that could not be erased or explained away. Something to be accounted for. The man had cut himself with precision, drawn a scalpel or knife across the old injury. Or perhaps someone had done it for him. Either way, the ruthlessness was manifest.

She remembered the binders in the condo containing Bryce's medical records—they included photos of his combat injuries. Sarah recalled lying in bed next to him weeks earlier, studying the scars on his back as he slept. They'd seemed familiar at the time, almost comforting. Sufficient to allay any nascent doubts. Now she understood that those scars, too, had been manufactured, a bit of surgical camouflage. Who could conceive of such a ploy? Who would have the expertise, the wherewithal to carry it out?

This imposter, whoever he was, must have had help. The man they'd seen at the condo? Without a doubt. Yet there had to be others.

Troublingly, her thoughts took a darker turn. What was the reason for it all? There seemed but one answer: the man now impersonating her husband was running for president of the United States. And he had an excellent chance of winning. An imposter aiming to become the most powerful man on earth. Whoever was backing the scheme would protect that deception. Protect it without mercy. And right now, only two people on earth understood what was happening: she and Claire.

The road began winding through hills, yet Sarah didn't slow. Beneath a pewter January sky, she gripped the wheel hard, steering toward the one man who might have an answer. Walter *had* to understand at least part of the mystery—yet what were the chances of him remembering?

Helplessly, her sinking thoughts returned to Bryce. The *real* Bryce.

"Where are you . . . ?"

* * *

Sitting on the cold metal chair, Bryce felt more help-less than he ever had. Not when he'd been sprawled on a dirt road in Mali, broken and bleeding. Not here, suffering so much physical pain: broken bones, snapped tendons, violated nerve bundles. Any of that he would have welcomed compared to what Mengele was now inflicting.

The story he recounted was as bizarre as it was grotesque. A tale so utterly surreal it could only be true. For all the disparate facts, the incalculable odds, what the Russian told him connected everything with mind-bending precision—a jigsaw puzzle thrown into the air, all the pieces landing in place. An impossible means to a perfect end.

The videos had been damning in their own right—Bryce had seen deep fakes, but nothing of such scope and precision. Yet one moment had persuaded him above all others. He'd noticed it at the end of the video taken on his lawn, when the camera zoomed in briefly on the hero's wife and daughter. Sarah's beau-tiful face had transfixed him. Only afterward did he understand why.

It was extraordinarily subtle, something no one else would recognize. The slightest microexpression. He saw Sarah watching the man before her with vague discomfort. Saw her clutching Alyssa protec-tively. It was a look Bryce himself had never seen. A reaction he would never have instilled in his wife. This told him something vital.

Sarah knew the man on her lawn wasn't her hus-band. She herself likely didn't realize it in that mo-ment. And who would under such circumstances? Yet to Bryce her response, her suspicion, was as clear as a summer day.

Sarah had sensed the imposter right away.

Which made everything they were telling him true.

All of it.

"Sir!"

A new voice snapped Bryce from his despondency. He recognized it as that of Pavel—one of two names he'd caught in the muffled conversations behind the door. He was one of the two minions. An SVR man who'd reached his top rung, which turned his life into something of a palindrome—the same forward or backward.

Pavel came down the hall, then paused at the open door to look at Bryce. Pavel had likely never seen Bryce's face, and he stared for a moment. With one good eye Bryce stared back. He saw a thin man, roughly his own six-foot-one, with hooded eyebrows that loitered over his eyes like twin awnings. He was wearing mismatched camo clothing and Velcro-tie tennis shoes.

He began an exchange with Mengele in Russian. They were only a few feet away, and with no door between them and two months' practice under his belt, Bryce easily interpreted every word.

"Dmitri has made contact on the radio," Pavel said. "The road to the mainland is impassable due to the storm."

"For how long?"

"At least until tomorrow evening."

"We were supposed to be relieved first thing in the morning," Ivan complained. "After four days we are due our time off." The fog that had enveloped Bryce disappeared. This was good information. One shift equated to four days. It verified his earlier approximation.

"There is nothing to be done," Mengele said. "They will get here when they get here. Make sure Mikhail has transmitted the list of supplies."

Mikhail had to be the last man in residence—the one Bryce had not yet seen. Late tomorrow the B-team would arrive, four different voices Bryce had also catalogued—including two interrogators almost as vicious as these.

Pavel acknowledged the order and disappeared down the hall. Bryce remained limp in the chair, shoulders sagging. Mengele regarded him wearily. He, too, was tired.

"I have given you a great deal to think about. Tomorrow morning, when we resume our usual discussions, perhaps you will have a less obstinate outlook."

He flicked a finger toward Ivan. The shorter man handed the iPad back to Mengele and edged behind Bryce.

Bryce turned his head subtly, trying to protect his good eye. What actually happened surprised him. He felt two meaty hands on his shoulders. Ivan straightened him in the chair until he was nearly upright and ordered him to remain still.

Mengele used the iPad to take three pictures of Bryce, its faux shutter sound echoing in the otherwise silent cell. Mengele picked up the hood and motioned for Ivan to leave. He lifted the hood, putrid with months of sweat and blood and vomit, and sank it over Bryce's head.

As the world went back to black, Bryce let his head droop sideways. A broken bobblehead.

"There is something else you should know," Mengele said, his voice laced in anticipation. He leaned close to Bryce's ear and whispered, as if not wanting Ivan to hear. "Your replacement tells us he is enjoying your wife very much."

They were trying to drive him mad, of course. And perhaps they would.

Bryce lunged toward Mengele, more falling than attacking. He clutched blindly, feebly at his tormentor's chest. He mumbled in English, something about killing him, which drew derisive laughter. The Russian brushed him aside like a bothersome insect, sending Bryce to his knees. The former Ranger wavered for a moment before his collapse finalized, the warrior-cum-congressman puddling onto the concrete. He ended up facing away, his body racked by sobs. The pitiful embodiment of a broken soul.

The session had reached its end.

Crumpled in a pathetic heap, Bryce heard the arrival sequence in reverse. The dragged chair, footsteps toward the door, a dry fire on an empty chamber as the door's bolt sank home. Banter in Russian as Ivan and Mengele walked away: musings on how well the interrogation had gone, followed by more discussion of plans for their days off.

Once the silence returned, Bryce's sobbing stopped abruptly. His fists, clutching and curled in agony, quickly loosened. He peered down through the visual gap near his chin. Ever so slowly, he unfurled his left hand to reveal what he'd taken from Mengele's breast pocket.

A high-quality ballpoint pen.

52

MISTS OF A RAVAGED MIND

Burke was at his desk when his cell rang. His wife's picture bloomed to the screen, a smiling vacation shot taken on a beach in Jamaica. "Hey, Hon. What's up?"

"Hello, Agent Burke."

He stiffened. The voice was definitely not Vicky's. His first thought was that his phone had glitched and displayed her incoming number by mistake. He was wrong.

"I spoofed your wife's phone to be sure you answered. Don't worry, she's fine."

"Who is this?"

"I'll tell you that soon. But first I need to convince you of the imperative nature of what I'm about to ask."

Not sure what else to say, Burke went with, "Okay, convince me."

"I know you stopped at Starbucks this morning, then got gas at a convenience store outside Arlington. You watched *Bosch* on Amazon Prime last night— Season 4, Episode 5. I also know you spent time at Sarah Ridgeway's house today."

Burke went quiet. He finally said, "You know, I've gotten a lot of strange contacts over the years, but this is the first time anyone's ever called to tell me they have me under surveillance."

"I'm only trying to get your attention."

Burke stood and began gesturing frantically to the only other agent in sight, a new woman named Preston across the room. He pointed frantically to his phone and spun a finger, implying he had an important call he wanted to trace.

The woman on the line said, "Tell her not to bother. If you'd known I was calling ten minutes ago you could have set something up, but even that wouldn't work—not with the cutouts I have in place."

Now Burke was creeped out. He looked up at the security camera in the corner of the room. Then at the cameras on the computer monitor in front of him and a tablet computer on his desk. The phone in his hand had two cameras.

"Yes, I'm watching you right now, Agent Burke. Please wave her off."

Preston was crossing the room. Realizing his disadvantage, Burke waved her away and mouthed, *Never mind*.

"Okay," he said. "You wanted my attention, you've got it. What's this about?"

"Bryce Ridgeway. A certain condo in Georgetown."

Burke couldn't even feign surprise—not given how far off-rail he'd been regarding Sarah Ridgeway's tip.

The woman said, "The good news is, you and I are on the same side. I'd like to tell you where I am right now. Come see me, and I'll show you how all this is done. I think we'd find mutual benefit in some data-sharing on Bryce Ridgeway."

"You want me to come meet you . . . now."

"Yes. And alone."

Burke half smiled. "And if I'm *not* alone . . . you'll know that too."

She ignored the question and gave an address in Maryland. "I'll be at the front gate in thirty minutes."

"There's a gate?" he replied, scribbling the numbers on a notepad.

"One that you'll need either a tank or an act of congress to breach if anyone's with you. We have some very unforgiving guards, heavily armed. And don't bother trying to research the place. Whatever Google Maps tells you is inside this building—it's only what I made up."

Sarah turned up the driveway of Autumn Living. Two rows of skeletal chestnut trees lined the road, somber and sagging with the weight of winter. The low sun was fading, and the shadow of a telephone pole fell across the road like a giant sundial.

She parked in a nearly empty lot, her bumper nosing up to shrubs that fluttered in the sharp wind. She killed the engine and sat for a time, weighing how to best approach Walter. His dementia was excruciatingly advanced. On a good day he would show a glimmer of recognition on seeing her, Alyssa, or Bryce. On most he confused them with people long dead, or worse yet, simply stared off into space. Today she had to persuade him to reach back more than thirty years. Not only that, she needed him to confide things about his son that had obviously been a secret to everyone but his late wife.

Sarah tried to temper her expectations. A few years ago, Walter had been a fountain of knowledge, a peerless Washington insider with a memory like a vise. Today, in all likelihood, he would look at her blankly, and she would leave empty-handed. All the same, the answer she and Claire needed *might* still be there—somewhere in the mists of a ravaged mind.

She signed the visitor log at the front desk and then paused near the locked entrance. The facility director passed by, too busy to notice her. So, too, the receptionist, a podgy woman who was sorting mail with the solemnity of an archaeologist classifying sacred scrolls. Sarah had seen mail call before, a clumsy mix of doctors' bills, sales pitches for Medicare supplement plans, and Hallmark cards from relatives—the latter ranging from loving to distant to guilt-ridden. After clearing her throat to no effect, Sarah left the receptionist to her task and piggybacked through the door with a nurse.

She didn't find Walter in his usual spot in the sun-room.

Lucy, however, found her. "Mrs. Ridgeway, how are you?"

Sarah managed a smile. "Hello, Lucy. Good to see you. And Happy New Year!"

"You too!"

"I didn't see Walter in his usual place."

"He's in his room today."

"Is he all right?"

"He seems a little under the weather—been waking up later than usual. But his appetite is fine."

"Oh, good."

Lucy led down the main hall. The door to Walter's room was closed, and she knocked before opening it with her passkey. "I'll be around," she said, turning away. "Call if you need anything."

"I will, and thanks."

Sarah went inside and found Walter in his wheel-chair. He was facing the window, which gave a mid-dling view of the dormant gardens: empty annual beds, freezing topiary, barren trellises. A spitting-cherub fountain dribbled into an algae-green basin.

"Hello, Walter," she called out.

No reaction.

She hooked around the wheelchair to make eye contact. His eyes were closed, his breathing rhythmic, ten gnarled fingers clasped in his lap. Normally she wouldn't wake him. *But these aren't normal times.* She put a hand on his knobby shoulder, which was pad-ded by a plush cashmere sweater, and gave a gentle squeeze.

His eyes fluttered open. Sarah pulled up a wooden chair and put herself squarely in his field of view. "Hi, Walter. It's so good to see you."

A hollow stare. His voice was a tremor, raspy as he said, "Is it time for supper?"

"Not yet," she said with a smile. "It's Sarah—I just came to visit."

No response. But at least she had his attention. "I have something to ask you, Walter. It's very impor-tant. It's about Bryce, your son." She paused, hoping for a glimmer, but saw nothing. Sarah pressed ahead. "I wonder if you remember where Bryce was born. Was it in Virginia . . . or maybe somewhere else?"

His eyes diverted to the window. Outside a flock of sparrows rushed past in a blur, oblivious to the swirling winds.

"Walter . . . did Bryce have a brother when he was born?"

The old man only stared. Sarah saw a bottle of juice and an empty waxed-paper cup on the nightstand. She filled the cup and handed it to him. He downed it obediently, like he did with Lucy, and handed back the empty cup.

Sarah diverted to other topics: She talked about Alyssa for a time, then dropped a few important names from the old days in D.C. She talked about his wife, Marsha, pulling down a wedding picture from the dresser as backup. She kept at it for thirty minutes, and even though there was no sign of progress, Sarah dutifully circled back a number of times to the same question. *"Does Bryce have a brother?"*

On what she decided would be her last attempt, she sensed perhaps a change. Walter looked at her directly as something cued to his lips. Sarah nodded expectantly, willing him onward.

He said, "Are you my mother?"

Crestfallen, she put on her kindest smile. "No, Walter, I'm not."

He looked back out the window.

Sarah heaved a sigh, placed her hands over his. She leaned in and planted a kiss on his cheek.

"I'm tired," he croaked.

"All right. You get some rest. I'll come back to see you soon. And I'll bring Bryce and Alyssa."

His eyes—as blue as the sky but surrounded by amber, an image of stained glass—drifted back shut.

Sarah sat dejectedly, watching the steady rise and fall of his chest. She got up to leave more bedeviled than ever by the unanswerable question: *Where is the real Bryce?*

She closed the door on her way out, and encountered Lucy in the hall—she was pushing a bundled resident in a wheelchair, headed for the door to the garden.

"How'd it go?" Lucy asked.

"Not so great. He says he's tired—I think it's nap time."

"Yeah, that's how it's been. I'll make sure he gets out for dinner."

Sarah edged ahead and opened the door to the garden for Lucy. She wheeled her charge through, and after exchanging goodbyes, Sarah headed for the exit.

Lucy turned right into the garden. She pushed Mrs. Trimble toward the fountain, which was always a favorite among the residents, even at the height of winter. She paused when she got there, her charge captivated by the water trickling from the cherub's mouth into the filmy green pond. Lucy glanced at Walter's window and saw that the blinds were closed. She reasoned that Sarah must have drawn them shut for his nap.

In fact, that was not the case. Indeed, had the blinds been open, Lucy would have been stunned by the most implausible of sights: Walter Ridgeway pacing the tiny room and talking animatedly on a cell phone.

53

ROAD TO CAMELOT

t took forty minutes for Burke to arrive at the address he'd been given. The road curved gently through hills, and high trees blotted out the ashen sky. When the blue line on his phone neared its terminus, the first thing he noticed was a brick guardhouse sided by high concertina-topped walls. Behind all that was a four-story office building so square and bland and artless, it would have brought Frank Lloyd Wright to tears.

He slowed as he neared the gate and, as promised, two smart-looking U.S. Army MPs appeared. They were the perfect accessories to the nearby fortress with their broad belts, sidearms, and camouflage. Burke noticed a painted cinder block sign next to the guardhouse displaying nothing more than a street number. *And how fitting is that?* he thought.

The lead guard held up a palm. Burke pulled to a stop and rolled down the window.

"FBI?" the man asked through a right-angle jaw that didn't seem to move.

Burke showed his credentials. The guard looked at them far closer than most people did, then nodded and pointed past the gate. "Park to the right. Your escort is waiting."

A heavy barrier rolled open, and as soon as he was through Burke saw where to go: a row of empty "visitor" parking spots. Next to them, a woman was waiting on the curb. She wasn't tall or short, heavy or thin. Short brown hair framed a plain face. So perfectly ordinary, Burke thought, she would make a good spy. He wondered if that's what she was.

He got out of the car, and said, "You already know my name."

She held out a hand. "Claire Hall. Thanks for coming."

He regarded the building. "So tell me, Miss Hall . . . what exactly is this place?"

"You can just call me Claire. As for the building, I don't think it actually has a name. Been here about four years, or so they tell me. Basically, it's is a cyber research facility—home to whatever tech projects DOD has on its digital front burner."

"And that's what you do? Front burner research?"

"Yes . . . or at least, I did. Why don't you come inside, it would be easier to show you."

She led him to the main entrance, past an internal security station every bit as intimidating as the one outside: cameras, scanners, an electronic fingerprint reader. A corporal took Burke's phone, but let him keep his weapon and credentials—a curious statement on the new world order. After that came a hamster-maze of elevators and hallways. Claire talked the entire time, giving him a thumbnail sketch of her research program, including the sorry fact that it was going to be shut down soon. She detailed her long friendship with Sarah Ridgeway, and explained how her research had led to the condo. Hall then detailed what they'd found when they broke in. And that was just how she said it: "we broke in." Burke wasn't used to people confessing crimes right up front, and he found it refreshing. Claire Hall didn't strike him as someone who would be held back by procedures or legalese: this was a woman on a mission.

A final keypad put them through to a computer lab. There was one other person inside, a young man in a furry gray hoodie and riding a knee scooter— bouncing awkwardly back and forth between work- stations, he looked like a koala falling out of a tree. The kid waved when Claire introduced them, then went back to whatever he was doing.

Claire seemed to finish her in-briefing.

"So, all this you're telling me about Bryce Ridge- way and the condo," Burke surmised, "you can back it up with evidence?"

"I can."

She addressed a central computer and began show- ing him what she'd uncovered. Historical records, data points, videos, maps. She also went over the basics of how, and from where, EPIC got its information. Burke struggled to keep up.

Even so, within five minutes he was glad he'd come.

After thirty, when Claire hit the punchline, he wished he'd taken the transfer to Anchorage after all.

Bryce kept moving around the cell. Wall to wall, cor- ner to corner. His movements weren't free, weren't fluid, but he was determined to challenge his battered joints, bring his wasted muscles back to life.

He was still reeling from Mengele's cruelest blow: the unveiling of a twin brother he'd never known ex- isted, then showing him how the man had comman- deered his life. Bryce's thoughts lurched from one question to another, much as his feet staggered across the frozen floor.

Had his parents known about it? He couldn't conceive otherwise.

Why hadn't they told him? Because he wasn't meant to know.

Was this the plan all along, switching out the two sons? A hesitation.

With every shuffling step, every awkward about-face, one thing seemed increasingly clear: the dire circumstances he found himself in today—and inversely, the road to Camelot his doppelgänger was enjoying—was anything but a coincidence. It had been *someone's* plan all along.

But who?

Bryce decided to work the problem backward, remove who *couldn't* be responsible. His mother was an angel, gentleness and love personified. He missed her dearly, yet for all her affection she was not an ambitious person. His father was quite the opposite, a man who'd spent his life in the hard-knocks arena of politics and diplomacy. A man who'd groomed his only son for high office since birth.

Could he really have been involved in such a scheme? Bryce wondered.

Yes, he allowed, his father might have had *some* hand in it. Yet he would have needed help, and the answer to that seemed self-evident. Bryce had always believed he'd been born in Virginia, and that his mother had returned from the embassy in Prague to give birth on American soil. His father, at the time the U.S. Ambassador to Czechoslovakia, had remained behind.

Czechoslovakia, he thought. In those days, an Eastern Bloc country, a reliable satellite of Russia. Bryce looked around his cell. *And here I am, captive in a prison on Russian soil. With the imprints of Russian truncheons and pipes on my body. SVR captors taunting me.*

With each passing moment, his discordant thoughts narrowed, an outline emerging. Yet there were inevitably gaps. Details that were simply undiscoverable—at least, undiscoverable from where he now crookedly stood.

Bryce began pacing back and forth, no longer needing the wall for support. His captors had expected the news to break him: the realization that his wife and daughter, his entire life, had been stolen by a stranger. In fact, the effect was quite the opposite. It was a vision that energized him, restored him—and to a degree they could never imagine.

Bryce could not control what was happening on the campaign trail in America. Had no idea what his replacement might be doing at that moment. The *real* Bryce Ridgeway existed in a far narrower world. One that measured twenty feet by twenty. One that was cold and dark and saturated in pain.

Those divergent circumstances combined to bring focus. Combined to instill in him one simple mission.

He was going to leave this place.

Today.

Or he was going to die trying.

54

GETTING A BEAD

A twin," Burke repeated.

No reply from Claire.

"You're saying the guy who's campaigning for president as Bryce Ridgeway ... *isn't* Bryce Ridgeway?"

"It gives everything a new perspective, doesn't it?"

Burke only stared at her. This woman was clearly smart and capable. She had the kind of instinct for digging he always appreciated in his peers. She also had resources at her command unlike anything he'd ever seen. Still, it was hard to wrap his mind around her conclusion.

"Look," he said, "a lot of what you showed me—what you uploaded from that computer in the condo, the way you tracked him, the live camera feeds, the speech comparison software—I agree, it's suspicious. Highly suspicious. He's up to something. But to suggest ..." his voice trailed off, and he suddenly had the impression he was talking more to himself than to Claire Hall.

"There might be a way to prove it," she said.

"Or disprove it?"

"Take your pick."

"A DNA comparison," he ventured.

"I'm no expert on the similarity of DNA between

identical twins. But I'm guessing it would narrow things down."

Burke got up from a roller chair, shoved his hands deep into his pockets. "Actually, I know a little about that—it came up in a murder case down in Alabama a few years ago. Identical twins start out with identical DNA, but that changes the moment the embryos split in the womb. After that you get mutations, and as the siblings age the number of variations increases."

"Meaning the samples would have very minor differences."

"It takes an advanced test to spot them, but yes. You could expect to see slight variations."

"The army has a sample of Bryce's DNA. All we need is one from the imposter to compare—if that's what he is."

Burke considered it. He looked guardedly around the room with its mainframes and monitors and wiring. "This monster you've built—can it dig into pretty much anything digital?"

"Like no other system on earth."

"Then there might be an easier way to get proof. One that wouldn't involve getting a DNA sample from your so-called imposter."

"What's that?"

"Well, it's little old school . . ." Burke explained what they needed. "Can EPIC do that?"

Claire smiled. She was turning toward her keyboard when Atticus interrupted.

"Hey, boss, I've got some new D-points for you," he said.

"Okay, shoot."

"First involves that car we forced into a wreck."

Burke shot Claire a look, and she said in a hushed voice, "I'll explain later. It's the car I told you about, the one that followed me from the condo."

Burke said nothing, but wondered how deep a hole these two had dug for themselves.

Atticus picked up, "I was able to track it pretty easily—it's still driving around with a damaged front fender. We've got an AI program that works through traffic cams to ID body damage—it's very distinguishing, and easier to spot than license plates. I also nailed the driver from footage at the accident scene."

"And?"

"It all fits, and it isn't good. The car's a rental. Payment came from an account that our good friends at the FBI have linked to Russia's SVR. The driver's name is Gregor Popov, also SVR, although apparently he's using an alias—the FBI has him watchlisted, but there's no record of him being in country."

Claire gave Burke a knowing look.

"Russia," he said disbelievingly.

"One other thing," Atticus added, as if the rest wasn't enough. "That phone you wanted me to track down—I'm starting to get hits."

"Phone?" Burke asked warily.

"Our candidate. The campaign issued him a new phone with some high-end security features. We had trouble getting a bead on it."

"You're trying to track him again?"

"Seemed like a good idea at the time. What have you got, Atticus?"

He called out a list of technical terms, routings, and encryption protocols, all of which meant nothing to Burke. Then he said, "I've got a trail that goes back almost three weeks—that's when the phone went active."

"Has he been to the condo recently?"

A pause while Atticus worked it out, then, "Nope, no dots there. All the hits I'm seeing dovetail with where he's been campaigning. But I also got a call log."

"Anything notable?" Claire asked.

"Hard to say without cross-tracking the numbers. Mostly repeats, and the ones I've identified so far look like they're registered to the campaign."

Burke frowned, sensing a dead end. It seemed strangely disappointing. *Am I really buying into this half-baked theory?* he asked himself.

"There was one call today that seemed off-pattern. About an hour ago, a twenty-minute connect to someone in Winchester, Virginia."

"Is it Sarah's number?" Claire asked. "She went to visit Bryce's father."

More typing. "Nope, not Sarah. Looks like a burner phone. I'm trying to ping it now, but apparently it's been turned off. At the time of the call the triangulated location was . . . a nursing home in Winchester. A place called Autumn Living."

Despite Alyssa's promise, not much homework got done. She and Ruby were in the bedroom, Facetiming another friend and talking about boys, when the doorbell rang and the dog started barking. The girls ignored it.

Moments later, Ruby's mom poked her head in the doorway. "Alyssa, time to go home."

Alyssa checked her phone. It was 3:30. There were no messages from her mother, and she'd been expecting a later pickup. "Crap, sorry."

She said "Bye" to both Ruby and the schoolmate on the screen, then gathered up an unopened folder of chemistry notes. Alyssa reached the front door with her backpack on her shoulder, then drew to an abrupt stop when she saw who was waiting. "Oh . . . hey, Dad."

55

THEY HAVE NO IDEA

Bryce's only tactical advantage, he knew, was the element of surprise. The four men outside the door would never expect him to be capable of physically resisting, let alone going on offense. He wasn't sure if he believed it himself. Either way, it was going to happen.

Control what you can.

His only realistic chance was to divide and conquer. As far he could tell from beneath his hood, his captors always entered the cell in pairs, a two-man interrogation team. No more, no less. Even earlier today, when Pavel had come to deliver his message about the delay in their replacements arriving, he hadn't entered the cell. Clearly this was some kind of protocol, and it gave Bryce a measure of predictability. If he could take out the two men who came, do so without alerting the others, then there might be a shard of hope.

Of the four men on this team, he'd set eyes on three. For the last man he had only a voice to go by, a baritone named Mikhail. In the end, it hardly mattered. They were all going to feel whatever wrath he could muster.

He'd settled on a simple plan, dictated by his lack of resources and physical limitations. From the silence of his cell, he always heard Ivan and Mengele as they approached: boots on concrete, bantering freely, the key turning in the lock. There was no viewing port on the door, a mistake on the designer's part. Presumably the camera system was meant to take its place, yet that had gone inoperative. He prayed it was still the case. If so, his captors would be opening the door blind. Also in his favor: his minders appeared increasingly comfortable. Their prisoner was beaten down, and they were looking forward to time off. This was a lesson Bryce had learned the hard way in the Army: people tended to let their guard down at the end of a deployment.

His plan was to flatten himself against the wall near the door, the side away from the hinges. This committed him to attacking the first man through. He would rely on two improvised weapons. Whoever was in front would get a pen to the throat. The second would have his head smashed into a brick wall. Delivered properly, perfectly, two strikes that would prove lethal. Or at the very least, incapacitating.

Bryce weighed every conceivable iteration of how the men might be presented—stationary or moving, various angles between them and distances apart. He allowed for the difference in height between the two men. He rehearsed his stance, contemplated how they might respond. Bryce worked through every contingency he could imagine. What if he was off target with the pen, missing the carotid? What if the pen broke? The floor of his cell was damp and slick—would it be the same on the other side of the door?

One of the most critical questions was unanswerable: How far was it to the other rooms? He guessed the building was small. Aside from his own cell, probably three other rooms: one main area, a separate room for bunks, and some manner of kitchen. Every word he'd heard and dissected over the last two months supported this theory. But a theory it remained.

The question of whether they might have weapons he discarded for the moment. He'd never seen anything other than the implements they beat him with, yet a handgun was possible. If so, he would deal with it. Find a way to make it his.

It was all no more than guesswork, yet Bryce had gone into missions in the Army with far less planning. Far less intel on hand. And never had he undertaken an op with more at stake.

He stood near the wall and kept moving. A football player wired for the biggest game of his life, waiting for the tunnel to open. His silence was absolute, his senses on high alert. Absurdly, he felt a rush of confidence, much as he had on other operations. In other hellholes. The element of surprise was critical, yet he had one advantage that was even greater.

Bryce had spent time learning about Russia. He'd studied its literature and language, its politics and people. Because of it, he recognized the inherent weakness in the modern Russian psyche, honed by a hundred years of subjugation and suspicion: Russians took orders, not initiative.

Based on their questioning, it was clear his interrogators had been given limited information about him. They were issued questions to ask, and dutifully forwarded his answers to some higher authority. They knew he was a former soldier who'd been forced out of the service for medical reasons. They probably surmised he'd gone soft from years of congressional privilege and two-martini lunches. They themselves would see a prisoner ground down by months of beatings and duress.

Yet Mengele and Ivan didn't know the rest. That prior to his incarceration, the former Ranger had been running ten miles a day with thirty pounds of sand on his back. That he punished his body mercilessly with modified CrossFit routines. They didn't know he spoke Russian and had studied their culture. Didn't know he'd once been an instructor in close quarters combat. Most critical of all: they could never comprehend what such a man might do to reach the wife and daughter he loved.

No, Bryce thought with rising certainty. *They have no idea what's waiting for them behind this door.*

"I thought you were back on the road," Alyssa said.

Her father averted his eyes from the road to glance at her. "Change of plans. I've got a couple of days off."

"Great. I guess you told Mom—she was going to pick me up."

"Yeah, she told me you were at Ruby's."

Her father had asked to drive, and Alyssa looked outside trying to follow where they were going—prior to getting her restricted, she'd never paid much attention to navigation. The residential street looked vaguely familiar, homes along either side. Then came a cross-street whose name she recognized.

"Shouldn't we have turned left there?" she asked.

He was about to answer when her phone rang from her back pocket. She pulled it out, and said, "It's Mom." Alyssa was about to tap the green button when he jerked the phone out of her hand.

"Dad!"

He pulled to the curb and turned her phone off. Alyssa looked at her father, confused, and saw a face she'd never seen. Something shadowed and unfamiliar.

"Dad," she said, her voice sounding five years younger, "what's going on?"

56

SOMETHING MORE DECISIVE

Bryce remained patient, silent, and alert.

Finally, the tone of the muted banter from the main room changed. He could make out few words, yet there was no mistaking the shift in pitch and volume. Then Mengele and Ivan were coming, boots on the hard hallway floor. As they neared, Bryce began to translate.

They were talking about him. Wondering how much he'd softened after the shock of the last session.

A perfect mindset, Bryce thought.

He pressed his naked shoulders to the cold wall. Set his stance carefully and prepared to push off with his good left foot, pivot on the weakened right. The pen was ready in his left hand—he'd experimented with a number of different grips, settling on one that leveraged his strongest fingers and gave a three-inch depth of puncture. He mentally rehearsed his moves for the last time. The initial strike had to be perfect—sink the metal point into the carotid of the first man through, then rake inward for maximum damage.

The footsteps came near, paused outside the door.

The bolt slid free.

The door opened on its inward arc.

The first thing he saw was a hand pushing the door. Ivan's hairy knuckles. *Aim point lower.* A momentary freeze, as expected—Ivan didn't see the prisoner.

Bryce lunged toward the passage, his hand arcing, his eyes seeking the target. He saw Ivan's face, eyes going wide. Saw his exposed neck. Bryce sank the pen deep, just below the jawline, and ripped it on an angle. An explosion of warm blood bathed his hand. He released the pen and used the wall to redirect his momentum. A stunned Mengele was raising his hands—not any kind of attack, but a protective instinct.

In a flash Bryce ran option D: Mengele was very close, shouldered to the near wall. Bryce wrapped his good left arm around his neck, then shifted all his weight to bend Mengele ninety degrees at the hips. The move locked his head at Bryce's side. The Russian gave a grunt, but before he could shout Bryce planted his left leg on the wall and pushed with all his strength. Mengele was completely off balance, and they launched in unison toward the opposing wall. The first thing to make contact was the crown of Mengele's head. It met the concrete with an audible crunch, his neck snapping to an impossible angle. Bryce let go and watched him crumple to the floor, his eyes bulging in a forever stare.

Ivan had ended up in a sitting position, leaning against the opposite wall. Two bright red hands clutched his throat, a hopeless attempt to cover the pulsing wound. The pen still protruded from his neck. He stared at Bryce with something between fear and horror, and seemed to be trying to say something, his lips pursing like a fish out of water. The only emanation was a gurgle of bubbling blood. His eyes rolled back and he sagged lower. Bryce weighed a finishing blow, but decided the risk of more noise outweighed the threat.

He quickly moved up the short hallway. So far, he was confident he'd been silent, no alarms raised. He approached an open door on his left carefully, and inside saw familiar darkened shapes: a toilet and a pedestal sink.

He kept moving.

Little of the connecting room was visible. Straight ahead he saw an empty bookcase and a metal chair—no doubt the one he'd been put on for interrogation earlier. The rest of the room spread to the left. He heard a distant female voice, which confused him for a moment. Then he realized it was coming from a television, a news report of which he caught a few random words. Then a creaking noise, like the springs of an old chair.

Bryce edged closer to the corner, listened for a moment before venturing a look.

He saw Pavel on a couch, the back of his head still as he sat watching television. The room was like a hooch anywhere. Sloppy housekeeping, utilitarian furniture, papers nailed to the wall. At the far side he saw the predicted kitchen, a wood-burning stove and some groceries on the counter. A nearly empty bottle of vodka. To the left of that an interior door led to what he imagined was the bunk room—the light inside was on. One heavy exterior door dominated the right-hand wall, and next to that a double-paned window squinted into the gloomy twilight. It was the first natural light Bryce had seen in months.

Where is the fourth man? he wondered. *In the bedroom?*

That had to be it—it was the only room in the place he hadn't cleared. A stopwatch ran in his head. Within minutes, if not seconds, the two remaining men would realize something was wrong. Too much stillness from the hall. They wouldn't hear the expected interrogation.

Bryce needed a weapon. Mengele was still wearing the belt he'd noticed earlier. That might work for the man on the couch. Take him from behind, choke him out. But strangling took time, made noise. And it would be useless against the other man. It could also prove a challenge—Bryce's right shoulder was on fire, damaged further in the brief melee.

He needed something else. Something more decisive.

Another creak from the couch. Wind moaned against the windows.

Bryce chanced a second glance around the corner, and instantly he saw what he needed. On the floor near the junction of the room and the hall, almost within grasp. An old milk crate. And inside, the answer to his prayers.

A truncheon, a mallet, sections of rope, zip-cuffs, sets of work gloves.

And best of all: a two-foot section of galvanized metal pipe.

Still reluctant to use her phone, Sarah didn't message Alyssa—she went straight to the door at Lucy's house and rang the bell. Her mother, Kristen, answered.

"Oh, hi, Sarah."

"Hey, Kristen. How'd the girls do?"

"Good, I guess, but . . . Alyssa isn't here anymore."

Sarah stiffened. "Where did she go?"

"Bryce came to get her half an hour ago."

"Bryce?" There was no hiding the panic in her expression. The brittleness in her voice.

"Is something wrong?"

"Oh . . . no. We must have gotten our signals crossed. I better go home and start dinner." Sarah turned away sharply and headed for her car.

Kristen called out, "Okay, call me sometime. We should catch up. I'd love to hear about everything that's going on with you two."

"Yeah, will do," Sarah called out, picking up speed. As soon as she reached the car she lunged for her phone.

57

THE USE OF BLADED WEAPONS

There was still no sign of Mikhail.

Unfortunately, waiting wasn't an option.

Bryce rounded the corner silently. He reached down with his left hand and grabbed the pipe. The main room smelled a lot like his cell, a stale blend of mold and sweat, the only thing missing being the stench of the bucket. He had only ten feet to traverse over easy ground—a concrete floor topped by a threadbare rug. No creaking floorboards, no slick surfaces. He moved slowly and deliberately, barefoot in cloth-pajama bottoms. The soft sounds of his movement were covered by the Rossiya 1 newscast. *In America today, the leading candidates for the Republican presidential nomination are preparing for the next debate, including upstart congressman Bryce Ridgeway . . .*

The real Bryce Ridgeway tuned it out. He ventured a glance to the other room, saw no immediate threat through the open door.

Four steps away.

Pavel lifted a Styrofoam cup to his lips. Slurped what look like coffee.

Three.

Just as with Mengele and Ivan, there was no thought of mercy. Not given what these people had done to him. Done to his family. What they wanted to do to America. He swung the pipe hard, his arm locked to translate every ounce of body weight—a tennis forehand going for a kill shot. Pavel probably heard something in the last instant of his life, evidenced by a sudden tensing in his neck. It was the last hardwired move he ever made. The galvanized pipe struck just above his ear, a crunching blow that sent him tumbling sideways onto the couch. Coffee splattered the armrest in what seemed like slow motion.

If he wasn't dead instantly, he would be in a minute or two. The time it took for his brain to bleed, for intracranial pressure to build and shut things down permanently. Without hesitation, Bryce rushed toward the last room. There was no more plan, only speed and fury. He burst through the open door, the pipe cocked and ready.

He saw mostly what he expected. A bunk room. Two pairs of stacked beds, clothing and toothbrushes and food wrappers strewn about loosely. There was no fourth man.

Bryce eased, the pipe dropping to his side. Had he been mistaken?

No. There were four men here. *Always* four.

He wanted to think the problem through, but there simply wasn't time. He needed to get out, find some form of transportation. A bicycle or an ATV. Anything to speed his escape.

Bryce hobbled to the front door, threw it open, and was immediately greeted by two things. First was the incapacitating cold of a full-on Russian winter, gale-force winds flogging the landscape into a violent white-out. Second was the figure of a giant man appearing out of the gloom.

It could only be Mikhail.

Bryce saw power in his chest and arms, a softer belly. He was wearing tactical pants and a moth-eaten sweater. One hand cradled a bundle of firewood. The other gripped a hand ax.

For an instant both men stood frozen, five paces apart. Perfectly befitting of the weather.

Bryce made the first move.

He lunged forward, swinging the pipe from his hip. It was an upward strike, his target's head being four inches above his own. In a telling move, the man not only reacted but did precisely what Bryce would have done—he stepped into the blow, reducing its force and placing the brunt of the impact on an armful of firewood.

Kindling flew across the ice-encrusted porch as the pipe struck a glancing blow.

Bryce tried to regain his balance, planning a second swing, but his feet skidded on the slick surface. He saw the man rear back with the ax, a lumberjack about to fell a tree with a single blow. The windmilling swing came straight at Bryce's head. He ducked, the blade nearly scalping him. Then a *thunk* as the ax embedded deep in a wooden support post.

Bryce swung the pipe in an uppercut motion, striking the man's extended arm and separating it from the weapon that remained lodged in the post. The big man spun toward Bryce with his arms wide, a wrestler's advance. He knew he couldn't grapple with a such a massive adversary, especially in his weakened condition. Bryce feinted left, then shifted right and low as the big man lunged toward him. He reached for Bryce's left hand, which still held the pipe. Instincts honed from years of hand-to-hand training remained in place. *Use the momentum you have.*

Bryce deflected the big paws and dropped the pipe. Using his good leg for support, he lashed a kick with his right heel. The pain on contact was excruciating, but he landed a solid strike, battering the man's left knee. His adversary staggered two steps, then stepped on a loose piece of firewood. His feet bicycled like a logroller on a river, and he went flying down the steps and crashed into a snow bank.

Bryce had to prepare for the next rush, but he could barely stand straight. Feeling his strength ebbing fast, he searched for the pipe but didn't see it. Mikhail scrambled up and stood. Six paces away, he was huffing like a plough horse at the top of a hill. He paused for a moment, standing a bit crookedly, and seemed to recognize his advantage.

Feeling his right leg about to buckle, Bryce saw only one chance. A half step to his left put him on the second of three wooden stairs. It also put his left arm in perfect position.

Bryce had never received formal training in what he was about to attempt, yet he'd won countless bets as an amateur. Deployed commandos recreated much as they worked, engaging in all forms of martial arts. Among them: the use of bladed weapons.

In one fluid motion Bryce reached back with his left hand, wrenched the ax from the post, and began to rotate—a blend of new movements for his nondominant hand. The motion mimicked that of a baseball pitcher, the one modification being a rigidly bent elbow. Like utilizing any weapon, the mastery of throwing axes required practice. In truth, Bryce's intent was to merely stun the man, followed by a rush down the steps to grab a nearby log, then strike a head blow before Mikhail regained awareness. If he was fast enough, it might work.

Bryce followed through as best he could and released the handle. Still moving forward, he reached for a two-foot log with a tapered end. A caveman's club.

As it turned out, he didn't need it.

The ax flew straight and true through twelve feet of frigid air, completing one perfect rotation about its lateral axis. The heavy blade met its target squarely center of mass, and sank deep, just below the right clavicle. The sound of the impact was nothing short of grisly—a muffled crack of bone, the wet slap of flesh yielding to metal. A guttural purge of air.

The great man seemed to waver for a moment, then he took a step back. He looked down at his chest questioningly, disbelievingly, saw the blade sunk to the hilt. Blood pulsed all around the wound, glistening in the dim light. His big right hand curled toward the handle, yet the limb seemed to malfunction, a swiping motion that never quite made contact.

The man looked at Bryce with glazed eyes, something between astonishment and horror. Blood was coursing from the wound, saturating his jacket and shirt, draining to the ground in an expanding pool of red. Mikhail blinked once, staggered another step, then fell back spread eagle into a pristine snow bank. His limbs flailed once, then twice, feebly, before finally going still. A snow angel from hell outlined in red.

Bryce staggered back and collapsed on the frozen steps. His lungs were heaving, his heart thumping. Half-naked, the subzero wind whipped snow in his face and bit into his exposed skin. It seemed almost purifying, made him feel incredibly alive. For the briefest of moments, he felt a sense of triumph. That was lashed away by the next gust of wind.

He hadn't won anything. Not yet. He'd simply survived the first step.

He grabbed the post and struggled to pull himself upright. His feet seemed frozen to the icy deck, and he felt a stabbing pain above his right eye—an aggravation of the existing injury.

He could just make out a small parking apron in front, but saw no vehicles of any kind. No car or truck, no ATV or snowmobile. His assumptions had been spot-on: the two details tag-teamed using a single vehicle. A vehicle that would likely arrive soon, delivering the change of shift. Four fresh men who might be more capable than these. Who might be wary if communications went unanswered between now and then.

No, he thought. *Staying here is definitely not an option.*

Snow sheeted across the barren landscape, and a distant image came to mind. A few Christmases back, standing on the back deck of their house in a swirling snowstorm. He, Sarah, and Alyssa had engaged in a full-blown snowball war. Laughter and exuberance. Not a care in the world.

Now Bryce looked out into a bleak Arctic night.

He saw no signs of life whatsoever.

Only a deep and impenetrable blackness.

58

A REALLY BAD FEELING

Troy Burke might have been old-school, but he never undervalued technology. It had become essential to his job in any number of ways: communications, evidence-gathering, and of course, keeping up with criminals who themselves leveraged technology to reach their nefarious ends. There was also the matter of legal process—FBI agents had to know what kinds of searches and evidence would stand up in a court of law. Which was why, as he stood watching EPIC go through its paces, he did so with a jaundiced eye.

"Do I have to explain how many laws you're breaking?" he asked.

Over the last twenty minutes, Claire and Atticus had performed an illegal wiretap on a phone in a nursing home in Virginia, pilfered records from a DOD database, and hacked into the tablet computer of a presidential candidate.

"Want us to stop?" Claire asked.

Burke said nothing.

"The fingerprint comparison is running," Atticus said.

As an alternative to DNA, Burke had suggested that a fingerprint match might be better for verifying Bryce Ridgeway's identity. As a method of correlating identical twins, it was much like DNA: siblings

displayed highly similar patterns, but with discernable variations. Bryce's true fingerprints had been
on file with the Army since his commissioning, and
Claire had no problem acquiring them. Then came
the bigger challenge: obtaining a comparison print
from his supposed twin.

Claire had suggested targeting a tablet computer,
recently issued to the candidate by his campaign, that
utilized a thumbprint as a security measure to unlock
its screen. EPIC, leveraging a secret NSA initiative,
quickly identified the tablet and determined that it
was cell enabled with a strong connection. From there
it was a matter of exploiting a known security flaw
to pry out what they needed. One thumbprint, reduced to its digital form, was right there for the cyber
taking.

Burke and Claire were looking over Atticus's
shoulder when the results flickered to the screen.

"There it is," she said. "Very similar thumbprints,
but not a perfect match."

"How accurate is the software you're using for
that determination?" Burke asked.

"We're actually using IAFIS," she said, referring
to the FBI's own Integrated Automated Fingerprint
Identification System.

Burke snorted a humorless laugh. "Of course you
are."

"Is that enough proof?" she asked.

Burke thought about it at length, trying to comprehend a case that was patently incomprehensible. He
saw a solid foundation to question Bryce Ridgeway's
identity. But what to do about it? The entire theory
was surreal, and none of the evidence they had so far
had been acquired through legally valid means. It was

a conundrum like none Burke had ever faced. Did he launch an investigation? Bring Alves in? Take it to his boss, Assistant Deputy Director Anne Fields, head of the D.C. Field Office?

An alert chimed on Claire's monitor. She checked it, and said, "It's Sarah calling my cell." Owing to the building's tight security, even Claire checked her cell at the door. Yet via EPIC, Atticus had rigged a remote repeater to advise her of inbound calls. She configured the system to shunt the call through secure VOIP software and put it to speaker.

Claire said, "Hey, Sarah. What's up?"

"It's Bryce, or whoever he is . . . he's got Alyssa!"

"Whoa, whoa," Claire said. "From the beginning."

Sarah went over her failed meeting with Walter, then explained how Bryce had picked up Alyssa with no coordination.

"I thought he was on the road," Claire said.

"He's supposed to be."

"Do you know where they are now?"

"I have no idea."

Claire flicked a finger toward Atticus who was already typing.

"Okay, we'll try to get a fix on them."

"I've tried calling them both. Neither answers."

Burke edged closer. Sarah was clearly distraught, and he didn't want to complicate things by joining the conversation. He scrawled a note on the pad on Claire's desk. *Tell her to go home—they might be there.*

Claire nodded. "Head home, Sarah. Hopefully that's where they are."

"All right. Call me if you hear anything. I have a really bad feeling about this, Claire. I keep thinking about that guy we saw at the condo—he's helping this imposter. He showed up right after we left, and now the condo's burned to the ground, the cameras are gone, and Alyssa is missing. I'm telling you, they know we're onto them."

"Okay, yeah . . . it looks that way. But we have to keep thinking straight."

"I tried to call Agent Burke but he didn't pick up. We need to tell him what's going on—we need his help." Sarah ended the call.

Claire and Burke exchanged a look. Before either could comment, Atticus broke in. "She's right. I show the tablet and the congressman's phone both local now. Looks like long-term parking at Reagan National Airport. I also came across a press release from the campaign." He read from his screen, "'Congressman Bryce Ridgeway is suffering from a minor case of the flu. He will be suspending travel for the next three days. A full and expedient recovery is expected, and all cancelled campaign events will be rescheduled.'"

Burke saw Claire looking at him imploringly.

"Okay," he relented. "It's time to kick this upstairs."

59

INTO THE TEETH OF A RUSSIAN WINTER

There was no question that all four men were dead. Ivan was the only one breathing when Bryce went back inside. Minutes later, he wasn't.

The air smelled of burned firewood and blood. When Bryce turned off the television, the only remaining sound came from a wall-mounted clock— something he'd never heard from his cell. It ticked away seconds like a metronome, the analog hands reading quarter past one. That aligned with Mengele's watch, which he'd seen a few hours ago, not to mention the deep twilight outside.

The heartbeat of the second hand weighed heavy.

Bryce had no illusions as to the seriousness of his situation. That he had just killed four men barely registered in the greater scheme of things. Russia had kidnapped a United States congressman, a virtual act of war. When Bryce considered the reason why—to hijack the highest office in the land—the word "virtual" was swept away. The stakes could not be higher.

The replacement guards were on the way, due to arrive later today. When they discovered his disappearance, not to mention four bodies, they would send word up the chain of command. The response was certain to be the greatest manhunt in Russia's history.

Which meant Bryce had to move.

Now.

Wearing nothing but grimy pajama bottoms, his first requirement had to be clothing. Moving through the room, he paused in front of a full-length mirror. What he saw was shocking. His right eye was partially closed, the surrounding orbit a terrible shade of black. His hair was matted in grime and blood, and two months of beard clung to his face like filthy blond moss. His emaciated ribs looked like they'd been tattooed by a paintball gun, all the mottled shades of pain. He probably weighed twenty pounds less than the 195 he'd been in November. And his scar count, substantial before his arrival, had risen astronomically.

Pavel's clothes turned out to be the best fit. Also the least bloody. The shirt was nearly his size, but he had to cinch the belt tight to keep the pants near his waist. It was the warmest he'd felt in two months.

The next chore was to determine precisely where he was.

This turned into a challenge. As a former Army officer, Bryce was accustomed to tactical maps spread out on tables or tacked to walls, topographical charts displayed on monitors. There was nothing of the kind, apparently, in SVR interrogation facilities. He turned over the bunk room and found three mobile phones. All had been turned off, as he suspected they had been since the team arrived days ago. Hoping to access a map application, he tried to bring them to life, one by one, but hit security screens in every case. He took them to the various corpses and tried to gain access using thumbprints and facial recognition. He succeeded in opening one—Pavel's—but saw what he feared. No cell signal whatsoever, no Wi-Fi. Which meant no position data.

Bryce moved on.

He checked the television and found it equipped with a basic satellite receiver, no connectivity available. Knowing they must have *some* form of communication, Bryce kept looking. He found it in a kitchen drawer—a sat-phone with two spare batteries. Unfortunately, the device required a six-digit code to unlock. He looked around and saw no sign of such a sequence in any common area—nothing scribbled on a notepad or the nearby wall trim.

The clock ticked louder.

He'd seen one clue regarding his position when he came back inside from the front porch. Above the front door was a makeshift sign, block Cyrillic letters on what looked like a piece of driftwood: Zubovka Beach Resort. It was the kind of black humor shared by soldiers everywhere—and also, apparently, by intelligence officers. Unfortunately, the name Zubovka meant nothing to him.

He went back to searching, and in a musty kitchen cabinet Bryce finally hit pay dirt: an old paper road map.

It was yellow with age, the ancient creases cracked. He went to the only table and swept aside a shipwreck of food cartons and dirty dishes, all of it clattering to the floor. Bryce spread out the map and saw that it covered most of northeast Russia. He easily found Murmansk, and this became his reference—he'd overheard his captors say that the city was a three-hour drive from the place they called The Dacha. Allowing for the condition of rural roads in Russia, he used a finger to scribe a rough hundred-mile arc. At the twelve o'clock position, on a large peninsula, he found the place called Zubovka. It was far removed from any kind of civilization. Indeed, on the whole of the peninsula, thirty miles long and fifteen wide, he saw but two other villages—one at either end, east and west, with Zubovka in the middle.

Bryce's Army-trained mind began building objectives. To begin, he had twelve hours until the second team arrived, perhaps a bit more. No amount of cleansing the scene would conceal his breakout, so he decided to leave immediately, get as much distance as possible between himself and The Dacha. Second, he had to find some manner of transportation.

He addressed the map, and saw the date of publication in one corner: 1962. Zubovka had barely registered back then, the smallest possible symbol, and Bryce knew that small towns and villages in Russia had been depopulating for decades. He also knew the SVR would seek out the utmost secrecy for a captive of his value. He guessed that Zubovka, if that's truly where he was, was likely a ghost town.

The only way to be sure was reconnaissance.

He concentrated on the map. If there was no transportation in the local area, he saw two alternatives: a village called Vayda Guba to the west, and in the other direction Tsypnavolok. Either could end up being no different from Zubovka, dead end roads on the top of the world. Of the two, however, Vayda Guba appeared larger, and had a small protected bay. It seemed the more likely to remain viable. Using the map's scale, he measured the distance to be twenty miles.

From there he measured another twenty miles, across open sea, to Norway. A small boat would be ideal if the weather broke. The bad news: the land route to the Norwegian border was twice as far, and required backtracking on the only road that accessed the peninsula. A road where he might well encounter a vehicle carrying the other four men who'd been making his life miserable. The road also introduced a tactical problem. The small land bridge connecting to the mainland was a natural choke point, less than a mile wide. When the replacement crew arrived, realized what had happened, they could easily shut down that escape route.

Bryce folded the map. He would deal with those problems later. Any conceivable escape began with one gauntlet: he had to walk into the teeth of a Russian winter.

He quickly began collecting the gear he would need. On a hook near the front door he found a heavy winter coat with a hood, ski gloves in the pocket. He retrieved a pair of winter boots from the body outside—the left was too large, but the right just fit over his still-swollen foot. Better yet, having ankle support seemed to aid his mobility. In the kitchen he discovered a flashlight and extra batteries. Bryce opened the door and stepped outside. He stood for a moment on the covered porch, saw Mikhail's barefoot body half-covered in snow.

What swirled beyond was enough to intimidate any man. An unyielding night filled with snow, ice, and wind. A vast expanse of enemy territory. For someone in his condition, with multiple injuries and minimal equipment, it bordered on suicide. *No*, he corrected. *Suicide is to stay here. Better to go down fighting.*

Bryce set out into the darkness. He used the flashlight for a time and found the connecting road. Once his eyes adjusted to the gloom, he switched it off to conserve battery power. He leaned into the wind, and adjusted his stride to minimize the pain in his bad foot.

He'd followed the road no more than a quarter mile when he encountered the skeleton of a collapsed building. Bryce circled the remains like a mourner rounding an open grave. All that was left were a few upright timbers, planks scattered around the perimeter like a derelict barn.

He came across two more buildings, both in the same condition, and where the road made its closest tangent to the sea he found the hulk of an old fishing boat rotting above the tideline. His greatest need was transportation, but the closest thing he found was a rusted and wheelless bicycle abandoned in a ditch.

He had deduced correctly: Zubovka, never more than the smallest of dots on a map, was merely the carcass of a long-dead fishing village.

And so his decision was made.

Bryce regarded the road, which looked different than it had on the map. *They always do*, he mused. It became the horizon of his life, an ever-changing, thirty-yard vista: the distance at which the raised dirt path disappeared in swirls of white. Beyond that lay the unknown.

Like all good officers, Bryce planned conservatively. He set out at a steady pace. By his best estimate, he had twenty miles to cover. And no more than twelve hours in which to do it. By then, his escape would surely be discovered. Under normal conditions, a simple undertaking. But now?

His gait was uneven, accommodating injuries new and old. But accommodate he did.

For two months Bryce Ridgeway had lived a tortured existence, his only companions pain and hope.

Which would prevail in the end?

The answer was unknowable. But he suspected it would come soon.

As it turned out, the real Bryce Ridgeway had less time than he envisioned.

Not fifteen minutes after he'd left The Dacha, the satellite phone on the kitchen counter began ringing. Ignored, it went off a second time ten minutes later. Almost immediately afterward, a backup phone Bryce had not discovered, high on a shelf in the bunk room, also trilled to no effect. A wave of sharp messages began chiming to each device. All went unanswered.

Getting no response from The Dacha, the replacement team from the SVR branch office in Murmansk grew increasingly concerned. Hoping for a simple explanation, but not willing to bet his career on it, the commander of the detail reported the loss of contact to agency headquarters in Moscow. Senior officers there, more worried about their careers than the situation in Zubovka, laddered the bad news up the chain until, at three o'clock that morning, the director of Russia's foreign intelligence service was gently shaken awake by the chief of his personal security detail.

His name was Arkady Radanov, a bald-headed bull of a man whose classically Slavic features had been dulled by age. At sixty-seven years old, all but twenty of them spent serving the various intelligence agencies of Mother Russia, Radanov was one of the few who'd outlasted three decades of purges. KGB, GRU, SVR—he had survived them all. That being the case, he was not particularly unsettled by the news from Murmansk. Losing communications with a remote interrogation site was not uncommon. Still, the message involved Operation Zerkalo, Radanov's crowning achievement. Thirty years in the making, it had finally reached its critical juncture, and he was not about to let it go off-rail.

The problem with being at the top of the pyramid, unfortunately, was the inability to shunt problems higher. Having no wish to wake the president of Russia in the middle of the night, Radanov reversed the flow of information. He ordered the interrogation unit in Murmansk to disregard the weather and make every effort to reach Zubovka to find out why their comrades weren't responding. Realizing this would take time, and recognizing how monumental the worse-case scenario could prove, Radanov dispatched a sideways message to his counterpart in military intelligence, the GRU. He knew this was a risk—the GRU commander, Stefanov, was every bit as cutthroat as he was—yet in the moment there seemed little recourse. If there was *any* problem involving Zerkalo, it had to be contained.

Within minutes an alert was generated, and a rapid-reaction team of Special Forces operators from the 420th Marine Recon was rousted. Located outside Murmansk, the unit was technically a subsidiary of the Northern Fleet, although control had long ago been commandeered by the GRU. For their part, the eight men who answered the call that morning cared little about command and control. Within twenty minutes of receiving the alert, the team was mustered in full combat rig on the nearby aviation tarmac. Without so much as a safety briefing, they boarded an idling Mi-24 Hind helicopter and disappeared into the churning night sky.

60

INTO A BLACK HOLE

It was a statement on the condition of her life that when Sarah was a block from her home she slowed to see who might be prowling out front. Last time it had been an uninvited FBI agent, and she'd instinctively hidden until he left.

She veered to the curb, and for the second time paused behind the Andersons' Chrysler minivan. The van, all but abandoned since their three kids had graduated and left home, was the perfect suburban hide. In truth, Sarah had been hoping to find a strange car in her driveway. Bryce's Tesla hadn't left the garage in weeks, and if he'd picked Alyssa up and brought her home, it would likely have been in a rental car. Or was a hired limo with a driver more likely? Night had fallen quickly, and in the glare of the streetlights Sarah saw nothing but an empty driveway. There were also no lights in the front windows. Her heart sank. She'd hoped Alyssa would be here, even if it meant dealing with the man who wasn't Bryce.

She put the car in gear, pulled out, and was turning into the driveway when something on the left caught her eye. Sarah braked to a stop. It took a moment to process what she was looking at: attached to the mailbox by what looked like a bungee cord was a small phone. The screen had blinked to life, and through the window she could hear a faint ring.

Transfixed, she cautiously put the car in park and got out. The phone kept ringing. She'd never seen the handset before—it looked like a cheap prepaid device. The pall of something ominous descended.

She approached the mailbox tentatively, unhooked the phone from the cord like she was defusing a bomb. She hit the green button, and said, "This is Sarah."

"I know." It was the voice she expected.

"Where's Alyssa?"

"She's safe."

"*Safe?* What does that—"

"Enough!" he barked. A voice so much like Bryce's. But the soul behind it was darker, malignant. "I'm not going to answer your questions—not yet. You need to listen and do exactly as I say. Do you understand, Sarah?"

"Yes," she said, forcing a resolve into her voice she didn't feel.

"Go back to the car and get your phone. Turn it off and drop it into the shrubs in front of the house."

Sarah stiffened. She half-turned, looked into the gloom up and down the street.

"Yes," the imposter said, "I'm watching you. Do exactly as I say."

Sarah went to the car, edged inside to retrieve her phone. As she did, she wriggled off her wedding ring. She walked slowly toward the front walkway, both hands on her phone as if fumbling to turn it off. She dropped it near the winter-brown legs of a hydrangea.

Sarah put the burner back to her ear. "All right, what now?"

"We need to meet."

"Where?"

He told her.

"But . . . why? It'll take over an hour to get there."

"I know."

Sarah hesitated, then said firmly, "No, not until I know Alyssa is all right."

A pause, then her daughter's voice. "Mom! I don't understand what Dad is—"

The call ended with the suddenness of a cracked whip.

Sarah let the phone fall limply to her side, the breath knocked out of her. Or maybe the life. Realizing she was being watched, she tried not to look defeated. Certainly she failed. She searched all around again, knowing she wouldn't see him but hoping Alyssa might see her. Or was she elsewhere? Perhaps there was another camera, one Claire hadn't found. Maybe the man with the baseball cap was nearby.

Sarah stood alone on her driveway for a full two minutes. She tried to think clearly, but felt like she was being pulled into a black hole by some malevolent force.

A void from which she might never escape.

The FBI's Washington Field office, owing to its size, was one of three detachments in the country headed by an assistant deputy director. Her name was Anne Fields, a displaced Californian whose Ivy League education and solid record in the field had put her on a fast track in management. Tall and fit, Fields was a handsome woman who dressed impeccably, and in the role of supervisor, Burke had always thought her a reasonable sort—an impression that ended when he walked into her office that night.

To begin, Burke had pulled her away from dinner

with her husband, claiming he needed to brief her on "a time-critical matter of the highest urgency." They met in her sixth-floor suite, the ADD wearing an evening dress, and displaying cleavage, that was far removed from her button-down norm. She sat behind her desk, all sequins and pearls, and told him to make his case in a stony *This better be good* tone.

Burke did his best. He detailed what he believed to be a plot targeting the highest office in the land. He explained Claire Hall's involvement, the evidence she'd gathered, and as far as Burke understood it, the capabilities of the technology she was leveraging, which included, and went far beyond, the FBI's own cyber arsenal.

When he finished, the ADD's eyes bored into him with laser precision. "Seriously? You're trying to tell me that Congressman Bryce Ridgeway is some kind of evil twin?"

"That's what his wife thinks. And there *is* evidence to support the theory."

"Given to you by some mad cyber scientist who happens to be Sarah Ridgeway's best friend?"

"I've seen the evidence. I'm convinced. The two sets of fingerprints don't match."

Fields was formulating a reply when Burke's phone vibrated. The ADD's office wasn't generally used for classified briefings, and therefore wasn't subject to electronic lockdown as were other parts of the building.

"It's Dr. Hall," Burke said. "Mind if I take it?"

She waved a hand as if shooing away a moth.

Burke's exchange lasted thirty seconds. After ending the call, he provided an update. "Dr. Hall hasn't been able to reach Sarah Ridgeway. Her assistant triangulated Sarah's iPhone to her house, and Hall went to check on her. Sarah wasn't home, but Hall found the phone under a bush near the front walkway. Someone used a sharp object to scratch a message into the screen protector. H-E-L-P."

Fields looked at him guardedly.

"On top of that, the Ridgeway campaign just announced they're cancelling all campaign stops for the next few days. The official statement says the candidate is under the weather. Nobody seems to know where he is, but apparently it's not home in bed."

The ADD's tone lowered an octave. "So, now you're suggesting that Sarah Ridgeway has gone missing?"

"I am. Possibly her daughter as well."

"And you think her husband is responsible."

Burke hesitated. "I can't go that far, but something strange is going on. Listen, if I'm wrong, I'll take the heat. But imagine what happens if we ignore this and I'm right. Bryce Ridgeway is taking this election by storm. He's going to be elected president."

Fields remained silent.

Burke doubled down. "I'm the lead on the investigation into the Veteran's Day bombing, and I'm telling you it's an absolute dead end. One bomber with no visible means of support, a third-tier jihadi who somehow put together an extremely intricate explosive device. Do you remember the briefing I gave you on the timer?"

"Some of it," she replied.

"There was a built-in delay in the trigger. At the time we didn't understand why, but now it makes sense—it gave Bryce Ridgeway, or whoever he is, a chance to intervene and make a name for himself. A heroic act in a very public place . . . one that was sure to be captured on video."

The ADD leaned back in her chair, contemplating.

Burke sensed a shift. He could almost see the risk analysis playing out in her head. If she took the matter higher and it turned out to be a flop, it would be a black mark. If she didn't pursue it, however, and Burke was right—that was a career ender.

"You can show me this supposed evidence?"

"Absolutely."

Another pause. "All right. I'll run it by the deputy director."

To Burke's surprise, in the next ten minutes things snowballed. He had come here wanting some backing from the field office, maybe a manpower bump and a few warrants. What he got was something else altogether. It required three phone calls, and Burke heard half of each conversation. The last one was to the FBI Director himself.

"Good evening, Director," Fields said. "I'm sorry to bother you at this time of night, but we've got a situation, something I thought you'd want to know about right away. It has to do with Congressman Bryce Ridgeway . . ."

She gave a one-minute synopsis of what Burke had told her, then listened for a time.

"Yes, sir," Fields responded. "I know this all sounds implausible, yet there is some evidence to suggest that the man purporting to be Bryce Ridgeway could be an identical twin. As outlandish as it sounds, Dr. Claire Hall has—"

The director cut Fields off there. He spoke at

length, and Fields was relegated to the likes of, "Yes, sir," and, "Of course." Then, "Absolutely, right away."

Fields put down her phone looking uncharacteristically shell-shocked. A fish whose pond had suddenly been drained. "The director wants us to meet him immediately. The J. Edgar Hoover Building. Oh . . . and he wants Dr. Hall to join us."

61

THE EDGE OF THE KNOWN WORLD

Bryce had known cold before. He'd suffered through the Army's Cold Weather Leader Course in Alaska, and later spent weeks training in the Canadian Rockies. This was on another level.

His lungs felt frozen, like he was inhaling dry ice. Every inch of exposed skin burned, nerve ends going numb with each gust of wind. It was pain on top of pain. He knew he had to keep moving, keep his muscles working. To stop in the open was to die. Unfortunately, the beatings he'd suffered had taken their toll, additives to his Arctic misery. Every step became a trial and his stride was uneven, his right boot dragging behind. He tried to take it as a positive when the pain in that foot gave way to numbness. The frigid floor of his cell seemed an oddly cozy memory.

Yet there was good news. Most important, he wasn't lost. The visibility had improved, enough that he could make out the surrounding wind-racked hills. According to his map, the only road to Vayda Guba tracked the coastline. He guessed it was a dirt road, although a blanket of snow and ice buried any trace of the surface. Fortunately, even in the darkness, the profile of the raised roadbed was clear. Also reassuringly, on his right was the constant twilight reflection of the Barents Sea. Beyond that his map ended, uncharted waters beyond. On an ancient mariners' chart, the border where dragons would be depicted—the edge of the known world.

Bryce didn't believe in dragons, but there was danger from that direction—with no terrain or forest to break the flow, the wind swept in from the sea at near gale force. The hood and sleeves of his parka fluttered helplessly. It was torture of a new kind, this tormentor indifferent, less sadistic than Mengele, but no less vicious. And no less lethal.

He tried to nail down his position using the map and terrain features, but the undulating coastline and featureless hills made it all but impossible. He regretted not retrieving Mengele's wristwatch before leaving—it would have allowed him to dead reckon. As it was, the distance and heading gleaned from the map were useless without time. How long had he been walking? Hours, surely.

He stumbled at the bottom of a depression, ice giving way under his numb right foot. Bryce spun and went down on one knee before stabilizing. He looked back accusingly and saw a gash in the ice, a seasonal channel that would carry the melt come spring. He struggled back to his feet, bones frozen, muscles aching. Each successive step seemed harder, his feet sucking into frozen muck.

His thoughts began to meander in a troubling way. In training, he'd learned that the onset symptoms of hypothermia varied from person to person. Every student had been forced to that edge to discover their personal indications. Bryce felt them now precisely as he had in Alaska: uncontrollable shivering, shallow breathing, mild confusion. The training exercise had ended there, warmth given to sustain life. Here he had only the promise of more cold.

A severe gust rushed up from the sea, nearly knocking him down. He set his head lower, tightened the hood around his chin. Out of the murky darkness, a shape materialized on the siding ahead. Other than the road, it was the first man-made object he'd seen in an hour. Its right-angle edges stood out against the curves of nature, and he recognized the remains of a tiny shed of some kind. It wasn't much bigger than a large doghouse; one side had collapsed, a pair of rotted planks clutching out of the snow like hands from a grave. Bryce went closer, and inside he saw derelict machinery—an ancient pump, perhaps. He also noted one intact corner backing to the sea. A rare windbreak.

Bryce hesitated.

He desperately needed a break, relief from the wind. But would a delay surrender whatever head start he'd gained? He told himself that if he could rest for ten, maybe fifteen minutes, he would rally and make better time, an investment with positive returns. It might have been true. Then again, it might have been his chilled brain malfunctioning. Either way, Bryce relented. He crawled inside a space barely big enough to cover his frostbitten body. The wind was cut instantly.

He dreamed of building a fire, but it never went beyond that.

For the first time in what seemed like days, the real Bryce Ridgeway closed his eyes.

Sarah had been driving for hours, yet she felt no trace of weariness. No heavy eyelids. No drifting thoughts. No caffeine necessary. She was wired on adrenaline. Running on hope.

Her initial instructions had been to drive to Middletown, Virginia. Then, shortly before arriving, the horrid little phone vibrated again. Amended instructions were given: a turn toward West Virginia, into the Monongahela National Forest.

The new route ran into thickening woodlands, the road lacing through knolls, curling left and right. Sarah understood what was happening: she was being isolated, pulled away from everything familiar. Home, Claire, her neighborhood. Perhaps even Agent Burke. Still, she never hesitated. She complied blindly, unfalteringly with every new directive. She would do whatever it took to get Alyssa back.

As she steered through the quiet hills, her mind kept looping back to the most vexing question: Where was the real Bryce? Sarah was not mystical by nature, yet she felt that if Bryce had been killed, his soul laid to waste, she would somehow know. Maybe it was false hope. Perhaps even denial. Whatever the source, she would not give up on the thought. Just as she would never give up on their daughter.

Ten miles into West Virginia she stopped for gas. Standing at the pump in the cool mountain air, her eyes alert, Sarah weighed going into the convenience store to borrow a phone. She could call 911. Or Claire or the FBI. The Imposter had specifically warned her not to contact anyone, but how would he know? This was how she referenced him now: The Imposter.

Her eyes drifted to cars at the other pumps, then across the parking lot and road. *Is he following me? Watching like he did outside the house? Was this whole mad journey only a way of making sure she was alone? Where would it end? What did he want?*

So many questions.

A repulsive memory struck: she recalled being intimate with The Imposter on the night of their date. Even then Sarah had sensed something wrong, but she could never have imagined the source of her misgivings. Did it count as being unfaithful? One more excruciating paradox. *One day*, she told herself, *I'll confess my sin to Bryce.*

Her thoughts turned back to the present. She wondered what Claire was doing. Could she be tracking her using EPIC? Sarah's Camry was eight years old, and as far as she knew it wasn't wired for GPS tracking. Still, Claire had shown her what EPIC could do: traffic cameras and toll footage to track license plates, even sort vehicles by makes and model. The system had helped build a map of The Imposter's movements, which in turn had led to the condo.

But would it work now?

Here?

Sarah clicked off the pump after putting a very slow two gallons into her half-full tank. In the end, she decided against trying to borrow a phone. She wouldn't do anything to put Alyssa at risk. She had to buy time, let the game play out. When she got back in the car and set out again, Sarah cracked the window. A chill wind swept in, heavy with the scent of forest and yesterday's rain.

I have to trust Claire to find me, she thought. *Just like Alyssa will be trusting me to come for her.*

62

CLOSER TO A LEGEND

Burke had been to the J. Edgar Hoover Building on a handful of occasions, most of them owing to proximity: the Washington D.C. Field Office was the nearest source of field agents who could be summoned to national headquarters for photo ops, award ceremonies, and on rare occasions, staffing the odd task force.

Never before had he been to the director's office.

The building was a monument to its namesake, the agency's founding director who'd planned, plotted, and conceived of its construction, yet not lived long enough to see its dedication.

Burke arrived with ADD Fields, who'd donned a sweater to moderate her evening dress. Claire Hall was right behind them. All three were corralled at the main entrance by an escort. IDs were checked, phones confiscated, and after everyone was guided through a security station they were whisked straight to the director's suite.

Robert Truman was waiting in a surprisingly modest office. The broad desk was backed by a single wall of shelves and cabinetry, and Burke saw at least four different communications devices, two of which he recognized. In an ode to secrecy that would have Hoover smiling down, the director's office was positioned centrally in one of the building's SCIFs—the secure areas where no electronic devices were allowed. Truman was a tall man, midsixties. His burly build and clean-shaven head would have looked right at home in a uniform with stars on the collar. It was rumored he had worked his way through college as a bouncer, and Burke thought it might be true.

To his surprise, after introductions, Truman began by addressing Claire. "I'm familiar with your project, Miss Hall, at least in a general way. I have to tell you, I wasn't a fan of giving you access to our databases. In the end, I decided it might one day lead to something worthwhile. Today is your chance to prove it."

"I'll certainly do my best," she said.

Truman swiveled toward Burke, a Howitzer being resighted. "All right, Special Agent Burke. Tell me what you've got."

Burke launched into the same briefing he'd given Fields an hour earlier. The director listened patiently, attentively, taking a few notes along the way. Burke had heard this about the man—despite his alpha-presence, he was an unusually good listener.

When Burke finished, the director leaned back in his chair, leather crinkling under his wide frame. His eyes shifted back to Claire. "Do you have anything to add?"

She cleared her throat. "I spoke to my assistant shortly before arriving. He's been using EPIC to locate everyone involved. We can't find Sarah Ridgeway or her daughter, Alyssa. Alyssa's phone has been turned off, possibly destroyed. A couple of hours ago we registered Sarah's phone pinging at her house, so I went to investigate. I found it under a bush in the front yard. There was a message scratched roughly into the screen protector."

"A message?"

"H,E,L,P."

Truman's great bullet headed tilted. "So you believe they've been abducted?"

"I suspect Alyssa has been. I'm not sure about Sarah. My assistant, Atticus, is pretty adept at tracking with EPIC. Sarah's car has no means of direct-locating—no OnStar or GPS. The best chance was to input a description of the vehicle, along with the plate number, and cross-check every possible feed. Tollbooths, traffic cameras, parking lots, Highway Patrol dash-cams. So far, nothing. If she's traveling on secondary roads, she might be hard to spot. Alternately, she could have parked out of sight and taken some other means of transportation. Of course, there's also the possibility that she, too, has been abducted."

The executive fingers tapped on mahogany, a virtuoso warming up. "And you've been leveraging this system of yours to research Bryce Ridgeway?"

"Yes. Roughly a week ago Sarah confessed to me that her husband's behavior was becoming erratic, and that he wasn't being truthful regarding his whereabouts. She saw a text message on his phone that led her to suspect he was having an affair." She hesitated, then added, "I offered to help, which I admit mingled my personal life with work—I took actions that were outside the charter of my project. But in light of Bryce's sudden high profile, and the fact that EPIC was about to be shut down . . . I threw caution to the wind."

Sweeping straight past her reservations, Truman asked, "In the course of your research, how far back did you go?"

"How far back?"

"A month, a year?"

"A couple of months in the beginning, then I expanded and went back almost a year. Ultimately, when Sarah and I became suspicious of his identity, I tried to track down his birth records."

"What did you find?"

"Enough to convince me that the birth record he'd been presenting his entire life is a forged document."

Claire exchanged a glance with Burke. Neither of them understood where the director was headed . . . but there *was* a destination.

Truman said, "Agent Burke mentioned this condo, the one that burned down under suspicious circumstances. He said you entered it the night before the fire, found it full of photographs and other records relating to Congressman Ridgeway."

"I've never seen anything like it," Claire said. She spent a few minutes detailing what they'd seen, the labeled photos, the computer files. She told him there had been live feeds to cameras in his own house and office—cameras which had since disappeared.

When she was done, the director went silent, increasingly thoughtful. Increasingly grim. Burke could almost see a decision matrix running in his head, branches going to places none of them could fathom. Fields hadn't said a word since the handshaking, a company-grade officer in a foxhole keeping her head down.

The director finally picked back up. "You said you found a discrepancy in Ridgeway's fingerprints—what they are today versus what's on record."

"That's right," Burke said.

"Did you pursue DNA?"

"Agent Burke and I discussed it," Claire said, "but

we reasoned that fingerprints would be easier to obtain. I have no doubt that if we checked DNA we'd get the same result. A similar profile, but not a precise match."

"Which would confirm our theory of identical twins," Burke added.

"Actually, I think you might find a bit more than that. I'd venture a guess that Bryce Ridgeway's DNA—whichever one you choose—would also not be a match to either of his parents."

Burke's eyes flicked to Claire and then Fields. He saw the same muted confusion in their expressions.

Truman, somehow, had leapfrogged them all. His expression went to something severe. He interlaced his hands on the blotter of his desk, a school principal about to set guidelines. "All three of you, in your various capacities, have high-level security clearances. What I am about to tell you goes beyond any of that. In truth, the factual basis is somewhat in question—there are shreds of hard intel, but it's closer to legend. I think that when you hear the story, you'll understand its relevance. I am reading you in, in part, because you've got a head start. But you also have unique assets under your control that might help me stop what could be a plot against our nation. If I'm correct, it's an attack more insidious than any we've ever faced. Our mission, in that case, would be to determine exactly who is behind it . . . and then end it once and for all."

63

IRONY FOR THE AGES

Lucy was spooning the last of a carton of apple sauce through Marge Goldberg's quavering lips when a familiar face appeared at the main entrance. Gently, she wiped Marge's mouth, and then went to greet him.

"Hello, Congressman!"

Bryce Ridgeway smiled broadly. "Hey, Lucy. Good to see you."

"I'm so glad you made it in—life must be crazy busy for you these days."

"You can't imagine. How's Dad?"

"Oh, about the same. Good days and bad."

"I'd like to ask a favor. It's his birthday next week and I'm going to be out of town. I know it's getting late, but I was hoping to take him out to dinner, then maybe for some ice cream—you know, that place down the street he likes."

"Oh, right. I know you've taken him there before." She checked her watch—seven o'clock. It was rare to take a resident out this late, but they weren't running a prison. *And if you can't trust a guy like Bryce Ridgeway to take his father out for ice cream . . .*

Lucy said, "I'm sure he'd love it! Come on, he's in his room. We'll have to get him ready."

Ten minutes later, the congressman was completing the sign-out log at the front desk.

Walter was in a wheelchair, and Lucy snugged up the zipper on his jacket. He looked befuddled, but calm. She turned to his son, and said, "Do you need help out to the car?"

"No, I can manage. We'll be back in an hour or two."

"Okay, I'm going off shift soon, so I may miss you."

"No problem. Thanks for everything, Lucy—I'll see you next time."

She watched Ridgeway wheel his father toward a sedan at the far end of the nearly empty lot. After helping him into the passenger seat, he returned the wheelchair to the portico. Catching Lucy's gaze, he gave her a broad smile.

The man playing Bryce climbed behind the wheel. Walter, sitting next to him, stared straight ahead. As they drove past the entrance, the candidate waved to Lucy, who was still watching. At the main road he turned right. A hundred yards farther on, he pulled into the empty parking lot of a medical complex that was shuttered for the night.

Walter turned to face him, and said, "God, that place is getting on my nerves."

His infirmity had vaporized. He still wore his eighty years, but his blue eyes were clear, his stooped posture straighter. He said in flawless Russian, "Tell me the latest, Sergei."

The younger man had to smile. He had not heard his true name since leaving Russia, nearly a year ago now. Even then it had been used sparingly, a consequence of the immersion training he'd undergone since childhood. A lifetime of preparation that was finally, stunningly reaching its payoff.

"Sarah's suspicions have advanced," he said. "I made every effort to minimize contact with her, but that strategy had its limits. To spend too much time away—that would have been suspicious in its own right. We always knew she presented the biggest risk."

"Along with the girl."

"Alyssa was easier. Teenage girls rarely seek time with their parents. Unfortunately, my sudden fame brought a rise in her own popularity. She parades me in front of her friends every chance she gets. I hadn't predicted that."

Walter said nothing.

"There is another complication. Sarah confided her concerns with someone else—someone who's proved exceptionally adept at digging into backgrounds."

"The FBI agent you mentioned?"

"No, he doesn't worry me," said Sergei. "It's Sarah's best friend, Claire. Apparently, she is some kind of government researcher, an expert at cyber surveillance. I suspect she's the one who uncovered the condo."

"Did Gregor deal with it?"

"Burned to the ground. It will look suspicious, but the ownership is well hidden. It can't lead anywhere."

"How will you deal with Sarah?"

"There was only ever going to be one way. It simply came sooner than expected."

"Natalia?" Walter asked. Natalia Volkov was their lone liaison at the embassy. Sultry-voiced and lethal she was the only one with knowledge of the operation who held formal diplomatic status.

"No, she has returned to Moscow. Even if she were here, we couldn't risk using an embassy asset. Colone

Radanov wanted to bring in a special SVR team. I told him no."

"You denied Radanov? The man who built the program?"

A satisfied smile. "He could hardly argue—I am soon to be the most powerful man on earth." Sergei's phone buzzed with a text. He read it, then began an extended back-and-forth.

Walter watched him closely. He seemed so familiar, yet was of course a stranger—not the young man he'd molded meticulously for thirty-five years. Walter had raised Bryce Ridgeway since infancy. Guided him as a child, sent him to the best schools, ensured he studied the right subjects. They'd had their differences like any "father and son." In truth, more than most given the elder's controlling instincts and the younger's stubbornness. The first major dustup involved marriage. Walter had hoped to steer Bryce toward a suitable union: a girl with money, pedigree, maybe a little political ambition of her own. Instead, he'd fallen for Sarah at Princeton. Walter had viewed their engagement critically, in part because they were so young, but also because he recognized Sarah for what she was—a smart and determined woman who might eventually create problems. Now those old worries were proving spot-on.

The greater disaster came when Bryce joined the Army. Walter had fought tooth and nail against it, trying to persuade Bryce that he could serve America far more effectively by attending a top law school, and thereafter going into government, rather than fighting jihadis on the front lines. He might as well have been talking to a stone wall. For reasons Walter never understood, the child he'd raised in the lap of privilege had turned into a patriot, a true believer in America.

Contradicting the destiny Bryce knew nothing about, it was an irony for the ages.

Never losing sight of the endgame, Walter allowed that if the boy never became a senator, he might at least reach a high rank in the Army. Radanov, certainly, could do something with that. Then fate had intervened. Bryce suffered injuries that forced him to leave the service. And there, finally, Walter had seen one last chance. Reluctantly, Bryce agreed to run for office, a telegenic veteran who won his congressional seat by a landslide. With that, the plan that was a lifetime in the making not only fell back on track, but transformed to exceed even Radanov's wildest dreams.

Walter's conversion had begun early in his diplomatic career, a combination of youthful recklessness and doctrinal ambiguity. A secure cable leaked in Paris, a meeting reported from Munich. On the surface, he was a young diplomat who talked a hard line against the Soviets. Deep down, however, his sympathies had long wavered. What began as ideological support for the communists graduated to receiving direct payments from them. Slowly, insidiously, a cavalier sympathizer morphed into a beholden agent. As Walter rose in the State Department, the KGB loosened its grip, watching and waiting. Their biggest move, as it turned out, came when he took over the mission in Prague. Marsha had been pining for a child, yet they'd been unable to conceive. Ever the opportunist, Radanov had learned of it and played his ace perfectly: the insertion into America of a sleeper agent like no other. The Ridgeways raised the child as their own. Over time, with the fall of the Soviets and the rise of the oligarchs, Walter's sympathies toward Russia declined. Only later was he told the rest of the plan. The boy would someday be replaced. By then, of course, it was hopeless—with the depths of his treason bottomless, Walter was fully committed.

Now he sat looking at a man he barely knew. One whose entire upbringing had been tailored for this moment.

Sergei ended his text exchange. "Sarah has been isolated. She's across the state line, in West Virginia."

"How will you do it?"

"I devised a contingency plan months ago—it's based on photographs from the condo. I only have to draw Sarah to the right place."

"How did you convince her to come?"

"The girl, of course."

Walter straightened. "You have Alyssa? Is that necessary?"

"You know it was inevitable."

"Where is she now?"

"Gregor is watching her."

Walter recoiled. He'd never liked the SVR man. But then, one didn't get to choose one's control officer. Gregor also provided Sergei's logistical support.

Sergei gestured up the road. "They are a few miles ahead. We will reunite the girl with her mother soon."

"It's too bad," Walter lamented. "As a granddaughter, I rather liked her."

"I might have warmed to her myself, given time. Unfortunately, raising children was never part of my curriculum."

The old man shook his head as if clearing out doubts. "No, of course—both of them."

"That was always the plan. I could not have fooled them forever."

"You're sure it can be done cleanly?"

"Trust me, I've given this great thought," said the ersatz son. "Their tragedy will become my gain."

"How so?"

Sergei grinned. "Come November, America's voters will weep tears of sympathy as they blacken the circle next to my name."

The weather was beginning to break when the helicopter arrived at The Dacha. The pilots were equipped with night vision gear, and the Hind was fully instrumented for flight in adverse weather. Even so, the wind was gusting, and low layers of cloud obscured much of the coastline.

The aircraft commander brought the Hind to a hover over the coordinates they'd been given. Unfortunately, the undercast was so solid he saw no sign of the building in question. The nearest break in the clouds was a mile west along the shoreline, and after circling the area twice he set down above the tideline on a broad gravel delta. The eight commandos in back, all in full combat rig, bundled out, organized, and set out on a steady run.

The captain in command got his first glimpse of the building minutes later. From a distance it looked simple enough—solid and square, the size of a residential home. He'd been briefed to expect no threat, yet the fact that his team had been called out was reason enough to think otherwise. That wariness ratcheted up considerably when the captain nearly stepped on a body outside the front door: a big man splayed on his back, covered in an inch of fresh snow.

He'd been told that only one prisoner was being held inside. Even so, seeing a closed front door and a dead man with a hatchet protruding from his chest, the captain was rightly cautious. Using hand signals to order the breach, he was the first man through the door, and a textbook clearing operation took less than a minute. At that point the commander lowered his weapon and initiated a call to headquarters using his tactical sat-phone. His report was every bit as concise as the clearing op: four bodies, no sign of the detainee.

While the captain took new orders, his men watched him guardedly. When the call ended, the senior NCO said, "Let me guess. Now we're supposed to find him?"

"We are. And we're going to get some help—apparently an entire brigade. By midday today, there will be more soldiers on this peninsula than seabirds." With that, the captain headed outside to organize the search.

Colonel Radanov had been on the other end of the call, and for the first time since being shaken out of a sound sleep, hours earlier, he truly began to worry. Yesterday he'd been on the cusp of the greatest espionage coup of all time.

And today? The rate at which it was unraveling seemed to double by the minute.

He now faced problems on two fronts.

The first had been brewing for days—the suspicious wife of Bryce Ridgeway. He'd assumed this to be a manageable difficulty. Indeed, one they would have to face eventually. Following his insertion, Sergei had done his best to keep a distance from those who knew Bryce Ridgeway best. He'd fired Mandy Treanor without consequence, and avoided certain friends on Capitol Hill. Marital distancing, however, was more problematic. Radanov knew the day would come when Sarah Ridgeway and her daughter became suspicious—they would recognize too many differences in Sergei. He'd hoped it wouldn't reach criticality until after the election. Now that it had, however, he was convinced that if the two could be eliminated convincingly, the problem might turn in their favor.

The issue of the real Bryce Ridgeway escaping was something else altogether: that was an unmitigated disaster. Radanov had regularly watched the interrogation videos, so he knew the man was in terrible shape. Still, the fact that he'd overpowered four SVR officers, then bolted out into a snowstorm, said something about Ridgeway. He was a soldier, a fighter. This Radanov had forgotten.

Now everything came down to the next few hours.

Sergei and Gregor could contain things in America.

Yet if Ridgeway couldn't be captured, if he somehow managed to reach the West . . . the greatest espionage triumph of all time would turn into the most profound failure.

And Radanov, after surviving so many decades of intelligence work, had no doubt who would be held responsible.

64

MIRROR

Bryce was startled from a deep sleep by an iron grip on his shoulder. He stiffened immediately, started to react, yet when his eyes opened he saw no apparent threat. Only a bleak panorama of snow sweeping across an elevated roadbed.

Tilting his head, he saw the source of the assault—a plank had blown off the shed wall and was wedged against his upper arm. He shrugged it away and sat higher, looking guardedly outside.

How long had he slept? An hour? Three? He had no idea.

He squirmed out of his hide, injuries new and old protesting every movement. The mere act of standing was a new adventure in pain. He instantly felt the slicing wind. On first glance, the scene appeared unchanged: low hills covered in snow, a wind-whipped sea to his right. Yet something seemed different, and it took a moment to realize what it was. The weather. The storm that had been howling was beginning to ease, and there was perhaps a bit more light. Bryce saw breaks in what had been solid darkness above, stars in the gaps that looked remarkably bright. It reminded him of hiking last summer with Alyssa, a rare father-daughter trek into the Appalachians. A full week of talking and bonding . . . and every night the stars.

He dropped back into the protection of the shed,

fished out his map and flashlight. Cupping the light in his palm, he tried to correlate one of the repetitive coves on the map to what he'd seen outside. It was hopeless.

The break had been necessary but he could not allow more. Bryce set out again with the sea to his right, head down and plodding onward. The terrain was rough: lichen-covered rock and ice, a few sturdy clumps of brown grass defying the wind. In the dim light he saw the road bend seaward, then curve back toward the crest of a hill. A mile distant, perhaps a bit more.

His foot was stiff, but the more he moved the better things got. The cold remained intense, and if for no other reason than to keep his mind engaged, Bryce prioritized his next steps. Transportation was his most vital need, some method to span either twelve miles of sea or forty over tundra. Food and shelter would be nice, but he couldn't waste time—a search would commence soon, and it was a net he'd have little chance of evading. Not for the first time, the date in the corner of his map weighed heavy: 1962. Would the place called Vayda Guba even exist more than sixty years later? Or had it suffered the same fate as Zubovka, a tiny fishing village forsaken and gone to rot?

He made his way up the hill, but at the crest was dispirited: he saw only treeless tundra ahead, and in the distance another hill. The cycle repeated, a seemingly endless series of coves swept by the wind, battered by the sea. His head hurt, and he tried to snug the jacket's hood. When his thoughts strayed, he always fought back to the same base: Sarah and Alyssa. If there was an imposter taking his place, would the two people who knew him most intimately realize it? He decided they would. From there his thoughts spiraled. The pretender would be prepared for such a contingency, and would likely deem his wife and daughter expendable, just as he had been.

Bryce put his head down, forcing away the self-defeating notion.

He plodded through slush and mud, the icy wind stinging his exposed flesh. The gloves were a godsend, the boots a necessity. After the fourth hill the road carried toward a saddle between two rocky promontories. His legs were like anchors, and twice he stopped and bent low, his hands on his knees like a winded runner. Finally, Bryce reached the crest, and there he saw a sight that sent his spirits soaring.

A town lay before him . . . and it appeared to be inhabited.

On closer inspection, the word "town" was generous. Bryce saw an anemic collection of gray buildings bunkered in a narrow cove. The structures looked sullen and weary, a shoddy collection of clapboard siding and warped roofs that appeared to have been taken from the same source—perhaps the hull of a derelict ship repatriated from sea to land. It had the aura of a settlement that had stood for a hundred winters, yet whose odds of surviving another was in question. Against the backdrop of barren taiga and a storm-whipped sea, it was a vision of despair. A tiny clutch of souls, lost to time, surviving the elements. Awaiting better days that would never come.

Bryce stood still for a time, studying the little village. Tendrils of smoke curled from a few chimneys only to be swept to oblivion by the wind. The faint odor of burned wood was unmistakable. He saw no one outside, yet a few of the windows were glowing, defiant squares of yellow in the tireless twilight. From the crest of the hill he studied the land, searching for the best approach. He had freed himself from The Dacha, then walked for hours through a fierce Russian winter. Now he had but one last hurdle to cross.

That spark of hope was dashed in the next instant.

Bryce heard it before he saw it. Somewhere in the distance a distinctive sound, one that any soldier would recognize. On most days a resonance that portended good news. The bass *whup whup whup* of an approaching helicopter.

On this day it was nothing less than a mortal threat.

Caught in the open, with no viable cover, Bryce prayed he could still run.

Burke and the others sat in silence. Thinking they'd come to brief the director on an implausible threat to America, Truman had turned the tables completely. He was now divulging a story that gave foundation to it all.

"When I first became director, four years ago, my predecessor provided a number of transitional briefings. Most were what you would expect. His view of day-to-day operations at the agency, updates on ongoing operations. On the last day we shared a casual lunch in this office, and in the course of it he relayed a story. As I said, it was steeped more in agency lore than any kind of hard intel, a tale that had been passed down over the years. Still, like those before him, he thought it wise to keep the legend alive.

"It began in the mid-1980s, at the end of the Cold

War. Reagan had upped the ante with an avalanche of military spending, and while the Soviet Union tried to keep up for a time, their economy could never support such expenditures. Gorbachev talked of Perestroika, of democratization and opening to the West. None of this, mind you, was lost on the senior officers in Russia's military and intelligence services. They knew changes were coming—big changes—and many began to plan for the future.

"In the years leading up to the fall of the Berlin Wall, senior KGB officers devised a host of schemes— this much is well documented. Most were self-serving, operations to squirrel away money in Switzerland, or align themselves with politicians who they thought might survive the purge. Yet there were a hardened few who believed that democratization would be nothing more than a temporary setback. They were convinced the Soviet state would make a resurgence, and committed to operations that would survive the turbulence and seed long-term strategies. One of the most outlandish was Operation Zerkalo."

Truman rose and stepped back to lean on the cabinet behind him, a shift to informality that emphasized what was coming.

"The details have long been vague," he continued, "little more than hearsay, really. We've never interviewed anyone directly tied to the program, nor have we acquired any documents to prove it even existed. In the years after the fall, however, two high-level defectors independently made mention of Operation Zerkalo.

"The concept, in essence, was simple. Pairs of identical twins born in Russia were seized by the state, and the parents were told that the children hadn't survived birth. Most were male, yet there were female pairs as well. While the infants were cared for in a secure location, the KGB quietly researched American couples who might have leanings toward adoption. Of course, the adoption of Russian infants, which became popular during the nineties, was strictly prohibited during the Soviet era, which makes Operation Zerkalo all the more incredible. It supposedly focused on wealthy and influential Western families who were childless, in particular those who were overseas in corporate or diplomatic postings. Select individuals were approached, and the subject of adoption discreetly brought up. On this point we have verifiable evidence—at least three former State Department employees, along with two individuals posted to Europe with Fortune 500 companies, are on record as reporting contacts regarding the adoption of a Russian infant. None of these ever advanced to the state of negotiation, but it was presented as a for-profit venture—X-amount of money for a healthy child."

"Singular?" Burke inquired.

"Precisely. As the legend goes, one of the twins would be placed with a family of privilege in the hope that he or she would one day rise to a position of prominence in politics, industry, or the military."

"And the second child?" Fields asked.

"That's where the scheme gets murky. As the story goes, the twins held back were sent to a secret state-sponsored school. Language, customs, education—they were effectively raised as Americans, tracking as closely as possible to the upbringing of their respective twins, all while being indoctrinated by the KGB. Once the program had begun, the few who were aware of its existence went to great lengths to keep it active during the upheaval of the nineties. 'The Institute,' as it was referred to in one debriefing, was somewhere deep in Siberia, funded by secret overseas accounts and largely forgotten. By the late nineties Putin had begun his rise, along with a newly empowered SVR. At some point, Operation Zerkalo could have been assimilated by the new regime—assuming it ever existed at all."

Truman paused to let it all sink in.

"That's a very long-term play," said Claire.

"True," Truman agreed. "But then, the Russians have always had us beat on that count. Our politicians never think beyond the next election cycle. Those in power in Russia, on the other hand, particularly during the Soviet era, expected to remain in place for life."

The director put his hands on the back of his chair.

"Until today, I doubted any of this was true. The least dubious defector we interviewed claimed that roughly forty such adoptions took place in the years before Perestroika. He said most of those placed were expected to fail—the children of privilege in America don't always turn out well. Some would struggle academically, others get involved with drugs. A few could be expected to attain marginal success, yet never reach high office or a corporate boardroom. It was all a game of odds—the chance that one or two might present a spectacular opportunity. And if that did come to pass, then the successful twin might be . . ." Truman let his words trail off.

"Replaced at the opportune moment," Claire finished.

Truman nodded. "That was apparently the endgame. The direct installation of moles into the highest seats in America. For twenty years this tale has been passed down from one director to another, a cautionary suggestion to keep an eye out for men and women who attain high positions, yet who show an unnatural allegiance to Russia." He put his gaze squarely on ADD Fields. "Honestly, until you called me tonight, I'd always thought it nothing more than a bit of colorful agency lore. Yet the moment you mentioned the possibility of Bryce Ridgeway being replaced by an identical twin . . . the threat became very real."

"Where do we go from here?" Fields asked.

"If Bryce Ridgeway is a product of Operation Zerkalo, it shouldn't be difficult to prove using DNA. The immediate problem involves his wife and daughter. If he *is* a Russian agent, and views them as a threat— they could very well be in danger. We have no choice but to act."

There could be no dissent.

The response formed quickly. Claire was assigned to search for Sarah and Alyssa using EPIC. Truman and Fields would leverage FBI assets. Burke was tasked to lead the response once they were located—a helicopter with a tactical team would be placed on alert.

With Truman on the phone issuing orders, Burke pulled Claire aside. "You said you found Sarah's phone, right?"

"I did."

"Where is it now?"

"Out in my car."

"I'd like to see it before you go."

"Sure."

The director finished his call. "All right, let's get on this."

As the three guests headed for the door, it was

Burke who paused. He turned to the director, and said, "The name, Operation Zerkalo . . . any idea what it means?"

"I once wondered the same thing," Truman replied. "Zerkalo is Russian for 'mirror.'"

65

NOT EVEN A DAMNED ROWBOAT

Sarah drove onward, steady and true. She'd been getting regular instructions, the horrid burner ringing to give changes to her route. The Imposter's voice, both foreign and familiar, gave away nothing. He implied she was being followed. Then again, that might only be what he wanted her to think. Subterfuge was not Sarah's strong point. Or perhaps he was only trying to drive her to the edge of sanity.

If so, it wasn't working.

In truth, her focus was sharpening with each passing minute. For the first time, she thought she might understand what Bryce had felt during deployments. He'd often talked about operating "in the zone," a state of hyperawareness in which the world narrowed to the mission at hand. Sarah was not trained for battle, yet her sense of mission was laser-like.

She was going to reach Alyssa.

Deliver her to safety.

Nothing else mattered.

A cluster of lights appeared ahead: a few houses along the road, a dated strip mall anchored by a dollar store. Sarah sensed she was nearing an end, approaching whatever rendezvous they were luring her toward. She checked the rearview mirror, saw no cars behind. A short distance ahead, on the right, she saw what she needed.

For the third time that night, she pulled into a gas station.

In the parking garage outside the J. Edgar Hoover building, Claire popped the glove box in her car. She pulled out Sarah's phone and handed it to Burke.

He examined the screen under the car's dome light and saw the HELP message inscribed clearly. He woke the phone by tapping the face, but couldn't get past the home screen. "Do you think EPIC could bypass the security?"

"I'm sure it can . . . but that would take time we don't have."

Burke nodded. "Yeah, I imagine our techs could do it as well. But the same problem."

He turned the phone in his hand and looked at the back and sides, saw nothing of note. Then he looked a second time at the screen. The HELP message took up nearly the entire display, but with the handset at an acute angle he noticed more scratches in the lower right corner—smaller and less defined, but apparent now with the screen backlit. He put on his readers and studied it. "Look at this," he said, showing Claire. "Do those marks not look similar . . . maybe scratched in with the same sharp object?"

She saw what looked like an awkward letter S, and a line that bisected it vertically. "The screensaver is pretty beat up . . . I saw that but figured it for random damage. It almost looks like a . . ." her voice trailed off and she looked at Burke.

"A dollar sign," he said. "But what would that mean?"

Claire broke into a smile. "Sarah knows what EPIC can do. She knows it can track a credit card."

Burke understood immediately. "Which she could use to tell us where she is."

"Probably already has."

"I'll get Truman's approval to track the transactions on all her cards."

Claire countered with, "EPIC is faster—and it doesn't need any approval."

Bryce ran down the road with all the grace of a lame cow. His boots skated on icy gravel and the wind was unrelenting. The community ahead consisted of no more than twenty buildings. Roughly half had lights in the windows, most of them clustered in a swale near the harbor—the residential district. The remaining structures ringed the perimeter at random distances—work sheds and warehouses, many sided by crab traps, nets, and equipment.

The building Bryce was aiming for was isolated from the rest. It looked like a barn, a square and windowless place with high walls and a softly gabled roof. The size of a two-story house, it was a quarter mile away from the rest of the village. In that moment, however, it had one highly appealing feature—against the barren landscape, it was the nearest concealment.

Bryce reached the building in a final breathless surge. He threw his back against the outer wall and paused to listen. The thrum of rotors was clear. The helicopter was closing in, although scanning the dark sky he saw no sign of it. He'd once been something of an expert on rotorcraft, able to differentiate models based on their unique sounds. All he could say about this one was that it was big. He never doubted it was a military item—and by extension, never doubted that it was looking for him. A HIND or a HIP, either of which would presumably be equipped for infra-red search. Even cold and shivering, his body would stand out like a moon in the night sky against the frozen taiga.

Bryce couldn't risk moving without knowing where the chopper was. He edged to the corner of the building and peered around. The wind slapped his face like an icy hand. Still seeing no sign of the helicopter, he studied the little village. It was three hundred yards distant, down a long flat glade leading to the top of the harbor. He saw a small network of docks, and nearby, fifty oil drums were stacked like canned food on a supermarket endcap. His eyes fought the gloom, searching for a way out. What he saw caused his spirits to sink. There were only two boats in sight, a pair of modest fishing trawlers. Both had been hauled above the tideline for winter dry dock. He saw nothing in the ice-edged waters of the harbor. No skiff, no runabout, not so much as a damned rowboat.

"What the hell kind of fishermen are they?" he muttered.

Bryce had reckoned a boat would be his best chance of escape—the Norwegian coast was a mere twenty miles away over open water. A small craft would be risky in high seas, but risk was an increasingly relative term. The only other escape involved stealing a car or truck for a forty-mile cannonball run toward the border, with a narrow choke point along the way. Surveying the village, he discerned only two vehicles: an old sedan covered in snow and a beaten pickup truck with a tarp over the cab. Neither looked promising. He was wondering if there might be something else, an ATV in one of the sheds, another truck behind a building, when a flicker of light caught his eye.

The cloud cover had parted in the sky to his right, and a pair of red and green navigation lights flickered through the mist. Bryce was vulnerable where he stood: a lone human shape backed against a frozen wall. Like a man facing a firing squad. He rushed toward the far corner and stumbled behind the building. Bryce kept going and peered around the next corner, a diagonal from where he'd begun. He watched the helicopter make a lazy circle over the village, the pilots searching for a place to put down.

Had they spotted him?

No, he decided. If they had, the pilot would have landed on the long flat tract near the barn. Still, the reason for their coming was obvious. His escape had been uncovered, and they'd made the same calculations he had: Vayda Guba was the closest thing to civilization on the peninsula, the nearest place to find transportation. A search was about to begin. They'd start in the village, then move to the outbuildings. He had time, but not much.

He refocused on the building beside him. He hadn't noticed any windows, but to his right was a weathered entry door. Bryce ventured another look around the corner and studied the wall that faced town—it was the only side he'd not yet seen. He saw what he expected: two large swinging doors, implying a barn or a storage garage.

The chopper pilot picked his spot, the aircraft's rotors beating thunderously as it settled onto a clear zone north of town. Bryce identified the aircraft as a HIND D, a rugged, all-purpose military model that had seen action around the world. Most variants bristled with armaments, and on this one he distinguished a chin-mounted gun. Yet it had likely been scrambled on short notice, tasked to deliver a search team. Which meant it might or might not be packing live ordnance. Unfortunately, the soldiers inside most assuredly would be.

As the helicopter touched down its rotors churned a small storm, snow and dust swirling into the gray-shaded morning. In the wash of the aircraft's lights, Bryce counted eight men as they dropped out the side door. They quickly organized using hand signals he recognized from his infantry days. It was a decent plan: split into two groups, flank either side. Search every building, working toward the center.

Lights snapped on in virtually every shack, fishermen and their wives wondering what all the ruckus was about. *They're about to find out.* Fists began pounding on doors. Any that didn't open would be breached. Once the cluster of homes had been cleared, only the outbuildings would remain.

Not much time at all.

Bryce looked beyond the barn, saw nothing but dark, featureless hills. The wind had abated, yet stands of tough brush lay bent shoreward, wary of the irritable sea. The only man-made object in that direction was a flagpole of some kind: jutting from the ground, it was ten feet high, and an empty metal ring at the top danced in the wind. It seemed vaguely familiar, but Bryce moved on.

He studied the barn, praying it held some way out. The odds were against it: if there was a vehicle inside, it would most likely be a tractor or a forklift, either useless for a forty-mile dash at the height of winter. He moved to the door and put his hand on the simple handle. It turned freely—locks were unnecessary at the end of the earth—yet when he pushed the door it seemed frozen shut. As it turned out, quite literally. The threshold at his feet was encased in two inches of snow and ice. He kicked to clear the worst of it away, and on his second push the door budged. With a final shove, using his good shoulder, the door scraped open.

Once inside, the relief from the wind was immediate. In near darkness Bryce saw only shadows at first. He felt the wall for a light switch, not even sure if the place had power. He felt a toggle, but hesitated. Flicking it on would be a mistake—even from where he stood he could see cracks at the edges of the big main doors. Turning on lights would be like putting a spotlight on the barn. He pulled out his flashlight, switched it on, and took another step inside. He swept the beam forward into the cavernous interior.

What he saw froze him in his tracks.

66

MISERABLE PROSPECTS

Sarah navigated the dirt road as if it were a minefield. Twin muddy tracks were barely visible in the bouncing high beams, and both sides were choked with thick forest, the canopy above sealing an evergreen tunnel. She glanced for the hundredth time at the rearview mirror, but saw only deepening shadows behind. Sarah hated how things were playing out. She was alone and vulnerable. But what choice did she have?

The final call had directed her here, away from the main highway and onto the access road for a hiking trail—it was actually familiar, although she'd never been here at night. The sign a mile behind her had been clear: a stick figure with a backpack, the name of the trailhead. At this hour, of course, there would be no hikers—only a soulless imposter who looked very much like her husband. And with any luck, her daughter.

He'd told her the meeting point was a mile and a half from the highway, and having tripped the odometer, Sarah knew she was getting close. The road begged for four-wheel drive—the potholes looked like bathtubs after the recent rains. She prayed her milquetoast Camry didn't hang up a wheel.

Sarah wasn't tactically-trained, but she was married to someone who was—or at least had been. At every decision point since leaving her home, she'd asked herself one recurring question: How would Bryce handle this?

She could almost hear his voice in her head: *Control what you can, then use it.*

At that moment, she controlled the car. When she reached the meeting point, she would leave it running, parked with the best chance for a getaway. She had the high beams on to avoid the worst craters in the road, yet also to blind anyone ahead.

What else?

Use all your senses.

She ran down all four windows. Cold air swept inside and mud splashed up from the tires. All the same, it would enhance her ability to hear and smell.

Sarah slowed, the odometer shouting that she was nearly there. The canopy began to thin, the stars above flickering like fireflies. A half-moon prowled behind broken clouds. She rounded a gentle curve and the forest gave way on one side. She braked to a sudden stop. A hundred feet ahead were a row of brilliant lights. Four sources, arranged horizontally.

Two cars.

They, too, had their brights on.

"She made three gas purchases tonight." Claire's voice came over a speaker-phone in Truman's office.

Truman and Burke had discussed shifting to the Strategic Information and Operations Center, but given the delicacy of what they were doing, the director didn't want to brief in the entire SIOC staff. Fields was in a side office working logistics: the tactical team and helicopter from the Critical Incident Response Group.

"Where were the hits?" Burke asked.

"One in Virginia, two just over the state line in West Virginia. I also nailed her car from a couple of traffic cams and some private CCTV footage. I fused everything together on a map—I'll transfer it to the network we set up."

Burke and the director waited behind a monitor they'd linked securely to EPIC's servers. The map arrived, and Burke saw a solid red line that ran from Sarah's house into West Virginia, time stamps at various points along the way. The last known location: twenty minutes ago, she was on a minor highway in the Monongahela National Forest.

"Okay, that's where I'm headed," he said.

"There's one more thing you should see," said Claire. "It's a clip from a gas station camera."

Burke and Truman waited, and soon a short video downloaded and began to play. Sarah was at a gas pump, and after hanging up the nozzle she popped the car's trunk and leaned inside for nearly a minute.

"I can't tell what she's doing," Claire said. "The trunk lid blocks the view. I've already checked and there aren't any better angles. You guys have any ideas?"

Burke shared a look with Truman, then said, "No clue."

"Okay, I'll do my best to keep tracking her."

One of Truman's secure lines rang, and he picked up. After a brief conversation, he said to Burke, "The Blackhawk with the CIRG team will be landing shortly. I told them you have operational command. They have good comm—I'll forward any updates that come in."

Without another word, Burke rushed for the door and was gone.

As Bryce stood staring, bits of what he'd seen in the last ten minutes suddenly coalesced. The flat glade outside, the metal pole that wasn't a flagpole. A barn that wasn't a barn. The glade was a runway, the pole the frame of a wind sock. And the barn, of course, was a hangar.

In front of him was the reason for it all: an airplane.

The craft was small and basic, a single engine machine with a cargo door on one side. It looked rugged and worn, and was clearly a Western-built model—manufacturing general aviation aircraft had never been a priority for Russia. Whatever it was, Bryce saw one conspicuous difference from any airplane he'd ever seen: attached beneath the wheels were a pair of skis.

Bryce knew a good bit about airplanes. His father had funded flying lessons when he was a teen, and later, on downtime between deployments, he'd finished up his pilot's license. Altogether, he had roughly two hundred hours in small aircraft—Piper Cubs, Cessna trainers, Beechcraft. He was nowhere near a professional, but he knew his way around a cockpit. Enough to know his limitations.

Rival thoughts began battling in his head.

I haven't flown in two years.

Then again, before today I'd never escaped from prison.

He went closer, ran the flashlight over the airplane from nose to tail. The paint might once have been white, but in the dim, dank hangar it seemed a mottled gray. The prop looked fine, and a drip pan beneath the engine held a pint of greasy black fluid. The fat tires were attached to what looked like two giant water skis. Bryce had never seen such a configuration, although he knew it was an option for winter operations. The closest he'd ever come was a few hours in a seaplane owned by a family friend, splashing down in the reservoirs of southern Virginia.

On the fuselage he saw AVIAT, a name that sounded familiar. He opened the left-hand door and trained his light on the instrument panel. It was very basic: attitude, airspeed, heading. Oddly, while the gauges were marked for Western units—feet, miles, and pounds—the switches and controls had been labeled in Cyrillic with what looked like permanent marker. He recognized a few words, but his Russian had never been technical in nature. He easily picked out the ignition switch and saw the key in place. Not at all uncommon. *Who would come here to steal an airplane?*

Bryce was absorbed by the obvious possibility. Twenty miles *over* open ocean? He could reach freedom within minutes. But was it possible? He couldn't be sure the airplane was even operational, but he decided there was a good chance. Rigged with skis, it was probably the village's winter supply line. Or at the very least, its ambulance for medical emergencies.

What about the weather? He wasn't trained to fly on instruments, which meant he had to stay clear of the clouds. Even if he knew what he was doing, the airplane wasn't equipped for it. Yet the weather *had* begun to break. Would that trend continue? Was there enough twilight to see the horizon, the only reference to keep him from spiraling into the sea?

A shout from outside broke his spell, carried on the wind across five hundred yards of flat terrain. Bryce couldn't make out the words, but the tone was one of authority. He could easily fill in the dialogue.

"He's not here!"

"Keep looking!"

There were too many questions, no time for answers. If the airplane ran, it was his best chance—which only emphasized his miserable prospects. In a pocket on the airplane's door he found a laminated card printed in Russian. The title: Pilot Checklist.

Bryce skipped past the preflight portions, some of which he couldn't even translate, and found the first relevant step.

Battery . . . On

His finger went to a red rocker switch on the lower left instrument panel. He snapped it to the ON position and in the confines of the great hangar it echoed like a gunshot.

Nothing happened.

67

VARIABLES

Sarah squinted against the brightness. Just in front of the two cars ahead she saw a gathering of shadows. Silhouettes in the footlights of a nightmare. None of them moved.

Her eyes adjusted, and she discerned four distinct profiles, two of which were agonizingly familiar. One she wanted to hold forever. The other she would happily kill.

She got out of her car slowly, every sense on alert. Were there others behind her? In the trees to her left? She took a few deliberate steps to put herself in front of her car, forcing them to endure the same visual handicap she was facing.

"Hello, Sarah." The voice so wretchedly intimate.

"Alyssa?" Sarah called out, ignoring his greeting.

"Mom!"

A dagger in Sarah's heart. "It's okay, baby."

The four began walking toward her. Three moved slow and steady, while Alyssa was wrestled ahead in a frog-march. Sarah didn't move, letting them come to her.

Her eyes swept left and right, taking in every nuance. She had been here with Alyssa and the real Bryce twice before, a challenging day hike. To the left was solid forest, wintering evergreens all the way to the highway. On the right, the road gave way to a small parking apron bounded by a semicircle of timbers to delineate the edge. Beyond that, she remembered, was a void, the mountain falling away steeply. In the faraway valley she saw a few lights, the brooding shadow of the next ridgeline. A hip-high sign in the parking area looked vaguely familiar, something informational—trail rules, or maybe a description of the scenic overlook.

The Imposter and his entourage covered half the distance before stopping. She could see them more clearly now. Her tormentor stood easy, although she thought he looked different. No longer emulating her husband's military bearing, but more the casualness of a gunslinger who was certain he had the fastest draw. Next was the man holding Alyssa—Sarah couldn't be sure, but she thought it might be the man in the baseball cap she and Claire had seen outside the condo. One hand gripped her daughter's arm, the other held a handgun.

All of that was predictable. What put Sarah's thoughts into a tailspin was the man on the right. She'd sensed familiarity earlier, but now his face was clear in the wash of her own headlights. A man that she hadn't seen upright without a walker for two years, stood before her looking perfectly poised and alert.

She stared at him slack-jawed. *"Walter?"*

"Yes, Sarah. I know this must come as a shock." His speech was clear and succinct, lunch at the country club.

Just when Sarah thought she'd grasped the worst, she felt herself plunging into an abyss of conflicting memories. Walter's lifelong drive to push Bryce into politics, the depth of his contacts in D.C. Then, when Bryce finally took the father's path, a sudden mental collapse. Walter had been isolated ever since, out of the game and forgotten. Until now. The Imposter had taken his son's place, and now the father stood casually by his side. In another revelation, it occurred to Sarah what she *hadn't* seen at the condo that night: there hadn't been a single photograph of Walter.

"You knew about . . ." Sarah's thoughts stuttered. "No . . . you *planned* all of this."

"I can't take credit," he said, a verbal smirk. "Yet it *has* worked out brilliantly." Walter spoke in a low voice, his tone befitting a eulogy. He told her about his communist leanings, his recruitment by the KGB. "One year into my assignment in Prague, I was approached by my handler with an unusual opportunity: the chance to adopt a Russian child. Marsha and I had been trying to conceive for years, but we were never so blessed. That's how Bryce came into our lives. I committed to raising him well, the right schools and opportunities. I spoke Russian to him at home, encouraged him to study the language and culture. I hoped he might develop views similar to my own. This replacement strategy, however, I knew nothing about that. Not in the beginning. When it was finally explained to me, I admit I had reservations. But look at what we're on the brink of accomplishing!"

"You could sacrifice your own son?"

Walter hesitated.

Alyssa lunged at Walter, but was restrained by the man holding her. "You're monsters!" she shouted. "All of you!"

"Where is Bryce?" Sarah demanded.

An exchanged glance, and The Imposter picked up, "Far from here."

"He's alive?"

"Let's just say, you won't be seeing him again. Enough of this—I have a campaign to run."

"There's no way you can keep this charade going," Sarah said.

"Oh, I think I can. It's something I've been planning my entire life." He closed in on Alyssa, as did Walter. Each of them took an arm, freeing the man with the gun who started walking toward Sarah.

She backed away, rounding the far side of the car. The man didn't track her movement, but instead went to the driver's door and climbed in. The car was still running, and Sarah sensed a mistake. She watched helplessly as the gunman pulled the car forward into the semicircular parking area, the front bumper nosing tight to the timber-lined edge.

Standing alone in the road, Sarah felt vulnerable, a flushed animal caught in the open. She had no delusions—she'd seen this movie before, knew how it ended. Perhaps not the precise means, but the endgame was clear. She and Alyssa were to be killed. They had become a risk to the entire psychotic scheme. Sarah needed to do something to change the equation, to put them off their game. But not by using what was cuffed up the right-hand sleeve of her jacket.

Not yet.

"You seriously think you can pull this off?" she said. "It's not only Alyssa and me. Claire knows everything. She—"

"Claire can be dealt with," The Imposter interrupted. "She's not the only one with cyber skills. Gregor, here, has very good connections. People who are uniquely capable when it comes to information warfare."

"Russia?"

He let go of Alyssa's arm, leaving her with Walter, and began moving toward Sarah. She squinted against the headlights, watching his every step. The man with the gun was standing next to the Camry, the engine still running. Sarah was beginning to understand.

She asked herself the question she'd been asking all night. *What would Bryce do . . . ?*

Surprisingly, an answer came.

One that was crystalline in its clarity.

68

NOT MUCH OF A PLAN

Bryce closed his eyes, the defeat crushing. No lights, no spinning instruments. No sign of life whatsoever after turning on the airplane's battery. He felt suddenly immobile, weary, overcome by the inevitable.

Keep going, he told himself. *Find another way.*

He backed out of the cockpit, lighthoused his beam around the barn's perimeter. The idea of hiking forty miles through freezing cold, in his present condition, all while being hunted, wasn't realistic. He needed some means of transportation. A car, a motorcycle. Even a damned bicycle.

He saw nothing.

Workbenches and equipment lined the walls. A pile of old farm implements lay rusting in one corner, a pitchfork pointed skyward. Then his eye snagged on the most ordinary of sights in any workroom: running from a wall-mounted electrical socket, an extension cord snaked toward the airplane. He traced it using the beam: beginning at the wall, around the propeller, then upward through a cracked panel on the engine cowling. Bryce lifted the panel, and what he saw inside was nothing short of salvation—a trickle charger clamped to a battery with disconnected cables.

He quickly unclamped the charger, and when he reconnected the positive cable to the terminal a spark lightninged between the two. *Because I left the battery switch on.* Bryce backed off and checked the cockpit, saw an array of instrument background lights and radios warming up.

"*Well hoo-damned-rah,*" he whispered.

More shouting in the distance. His window of opportunity was closing fast.

He found a wrench on a workbench, tightened the battery cables, then threw the charger clear. He circled once around the airplane, quite literally looking for red flags—any gust locks or safety devices would have a REMOVE BEFORE FLIGHT flag attached.

Or is that not a Russian thing?

He found none until he reached the cockpit. There a pin with a red flag secured the control stick in a neutral position. He pulled the pin and threw it behind the seat. Bryce checked the fuel gauges—a Russian word he knew—and saw half-full tanks. He had no idea how much that was, but it would surely take him twenty miles.

For the first time he noticed what was under the skis—a pair of standard wooden pallets had been modified with a system of rollers. To one side he saw a tow bar, and he visualized how it would work. The plane would be connected to a truck or a tractor by the tow bar, then pulled out of the hangar on the roller system. Bryce had neither a truck nor the time. The floor in front of the airplane was compacted earth, and he saw no obstructions between the airplane and the doors. The wings would have perhaps five feet of clearance on either side. *If it can ski over snow,* he reasoned, *with enough power it can ski over twenty feet of frozen dirt.*

Everything was taking shape, but one important

decision remained. Which came first: opening the doors or starting the engine? Both were sure to alert the soldiers outside. He decided the engine would be less obvious—with any luck the noise would be drowned out by the HIND which was still idling near the village.

Bryce climbed into the cockpit and looked over the instrument panel. He studied the gauges and switches, with their Cyrillic labels, and their Western scales and units. Manifold pressure, engine RPM, carburetor heat. The communications and navigation control heads were the least decipherable. Also, the least necessary. He didn't plan on talking to anyone, and didn't need to navigate to an airport. All he had to do was fly west for ten minutes and find Norway. At that point, any frozen lake would do as a landing strip.

This flight would be unlike any he'd ever undertaken. There would be no preflight planning, no precautionary ground checks. No flight plan or air traffic control tower. He had an engine and a propeller, a control stick connected to the flight controls. Fuel? Probably. Weather report? Look out the barn door, check the broken wind sock.

It was back to basics. A magnetic compass and a throttle.

Head west, go fast. Don't talk to anyone.

Altogether, not much of a plan. But it was his only chance to get home.

69

SEAT OF HIS PANTS

Bryce went through the checklist methodically. The procedures card was a simple laminated item, labeled Aviat A-1B. Bryce had heard of the type, but certainly never flown one.

"An airplane's an airplane," he told himself hopefully.

The runway, if three football fields of frozen taiga was worthy of the term, began directly outside the doors. The wind was coming off the sea, which was in his favor—the takeoff run would be a straight shot directly over town. After that, head to sea, a slight left turn, and start looking for Norway.

On the downside, he would have to fly directly over the squad searching for him. He wondered how they would react. Would they take the time to consider who was in the airplane? Or would they simply assume the worst and start taking potshots? And what of the HIND, still sitting in a clearing with its engine idling? Would the pilots take up pursuit? Bryce didn't know the top speed of an Aviat A-1B, but he suspected it was considerably less than that of a turbine-powered combat helicopter.

In the easiest decision he'd made all day, he elected to keep the airplane's exterior lights off, better to blend in with the Arctic gloom.

With everything prepared, he went through the start sequence:

Mixture—Rich
Carb Heat—Off
Prop—Clear
Master—On

Bryce engaged the starter. The engine coughed and the propeller spun. The engine didn't catch, which he figured wasn't unusual for a cold-soaked machine. He paused a beat, then tried again. This time a sputter, a puff of smoke, before everything ground to a stop. He closed his eyes, knowing what was at stake. A third try. The prop spun, another cough, then a chugging rhythm as the engine caught idle with all the charm of a top-fuel dragster.

Wasting no time, Bryce clambered out of the cockpit and hurried toward the doors. He started with the left side, leaning into it. The door didn't budge. He looked down, saw bolts seated into sleeves in the ground—something he should have checked before. He heard shouting outside, an alarm being raised.

He reached down and tried to lift the locking bolt, but it was frozen in place. His weak right hand was little help. Desperate, he hobbled to the workbench and found a hammer. As he was reaching for it, he saw a bigger one. He hauled the minisledge over, and with a haymaker swing gave the locking bolt a mighty whack. The bolt gave way, its bracket parting from the splintered wood. A kick freed it completely, and he gave the same treatment to the right-hand door. The hinges turned out to be in decent shape and the doors swung open freely, the only resistance being the gusting wind.

After the second door was clear, he chanced a look toward town. There were lights on in nearly every building, and the helicopter's searchlight was sweeping the docks. Framed against the dead-black Barents Sea at twilight, the village stood out like Times Square. Then he saw the inevitable—a member of the search team pointing toward the hangar.

Bryce rushed back to the cockpit, and without so much as fastening his lap belt he goosed the engine. Things didn't go as planned. The Aviat jumped ahead, the skids sliding off the crates, but the moment it hit dirt the right ski seemed to grab. The nose jerked sideways before straightening. In any conventional airplane he would have some manner of directional control. A steerable nosewheel, or at least differential braking. A tail-dragger riding skis offered none of that. The only way to steer on the ground was to use the rudder on the tail, and that was useless until he gained more speed.

Knowing he was committed, Bryce watched helplessly as the plane accelerated on an angle toward the right-hand door. The wingtip clipped the door, nearly jolting Bryce out of his seat, but then the little airplane bounded outside in the general direction of the runway. The skis hit snow, and the decrease in friction brought a marked acceleration. Using his palm, Bryce firewalled the throttle. The engine roared and the airframe shuddered over the lumpy surface.

Bryce realized he'd neglected the Before Takeoff checklist, normally performed after engine start but before taking the runway. With no time, he ad-libbed what seemed important, lowering the flaps to full extension. The airspeed came off the bottom peg—thirty knots and rising. He stepped on the rudder pedals, thankful that the needed correction was to the left—his more useful leg. Directional control began coming alive. By the time the airspeed reached forty knots, he was centered on the snow-clad strip. Since the airplane had a tailwheel, he pushed the control stick gently forward. The nose lowered slightly, giving more acceleration.

Fifty knots.

A crosswind gust hit hard, and Bryce had the sensation of skiing down a mountain—barely in control and skidding sideways, but still accelerating. The Aviat bounced and buffeted, and soon its wings were gripping the air. He tried to hold the nose straight using the rudder. At the end of the glade, a hundred yards ahead, he saw three men at the edge of town. Two were raising their weapons—as if to answer his earlier question.

He felt the skids lift momentarily, followed by a bounce. Finally he was airborne. The men were fifty yards away now, their rifles shouldered. Bryce could think of only one defense. He pushed the nose lower and flew straight at them—a strafing pass without a gun from ten feet in the air, a buzz-saw propeller leading the way. He saw barrels settle on him in an absurd game of chicken, then the blink of muzzle flashes. Bryce ducked instinctively, and the forward windscreen shattered in one corner. He popped his head back up to hold the collision course.

At the last moment the soldiers flew aside as if parted by Moses. The little Aviat shot past only feet above the ground, one ski tapping the permafrost. As soon as he was past the soldiers, Bryce hauled back on the control stick. The airspeed had been building, and the airplane shot skyward like a raptor catching a thermal. He raised the flaps and looked over his shoulder, saw more sparkling muzzle flashes that quickly faded.

Bryce referenced the compass and turned west, leaving the throttle at maximum power. He looked back again, and in the dim light saw figures running toward the HIND. They would probably pursue him, and might even call to have air defense fighters scrambled. Bryce's best ally was speed. If he could reach Norwegian airspace, only minutes ahead, he knew they couldn't follow.

He turned back forward, and as he did the Aviat was swallowed by a cloud. The dim horizon, his only reference to the world, disappeared instantly. The little airplane shot ahead at speed, rushing into the misty void. There was suddenly no up or down. No sky or earth. The loss of his only attitude reference conspired with what had been an abrupt movement of his head. The sum result: Bryce became completely disoriented.

He looked at the instruments but they were little help. The attitude indicator showed a steepening turn, but he'd never initialized it on the ground. Was it even accurate? The airspeed was increasing, the compass spinning wildly. The seat of his pants told him he was flying straight and level. The instruments screamed otherwise. If he'd ever had the training to decipher it all, if he had experience flying on instruments, he might have had a chance.

Then, in an instant, the Aviat broke out of the clouds. The windshield was filled completely by a windswept black sea.

70

ABSOLUTE VICTORY OR SMASHING DEFEAT

There is a bond between mothers and daughters that others will never know. Sarah had always felt hers with Alyssa was uncommonly strong. Moments of teen angst aside, she sensed ties to her daughter that transcended normal means of communication. A mere look could convey moods and requests. A gesture might imply urgency. It worked in both directions, their unshakable attachment.

Sarah was very much counting on that connection now.

The Imposter stopped a few feet away, to her left, but made no attempt to come closer. More like a dog herding a stray sheep.

"Move to your car," he said.

Sarah started out slowly, angles and distances running in her head. When she reached the closest point to Alyssa, she gave her daughter a straight-on look. Knowing and purposeful. *Be ready.*

Alyssa responded with the same. *I am.*

The Imposter followed, a few steps behind. The man named Gregor was near her car. As she approached, he opened the driver's door and stood with all the patience of a waiting chauffeur. The car was running, and as Sarah neared she got a better look at what was beyond: just past the ankle-high timber rail, a gorge hundreds of feet deep. So there was the plan.

Get them both in the car, send it over. Lethal without a doubt, and plausibly an accident.

Sarah had her own plan, but it was little more than a prayer. She felt like she was going over Niagara Falls in a barrel—committed to either absolute victory or smashing defeat. She straightened her right arm, and the tire iron in the sleeve of her jacket dropped slightly. The wrench fitting at the bottom fell cupped in her hand. Sarah had never before imparted violence on another human. But then, never before had her daughter's life been threatened.

This is exactly *what Bryce would do.*

Passing the Camry's back bumper, she shifted, keeping her right arm hidden from Gregor. The gun was in his right hand, but pointed down, his arm at his side.

Nearing the back door, Sarah let the iron slide into the open and caught its end in a solid grip. One step later she made her move. She swung with all her might. The surprise in Gregor's wide eyes was evident, and he wasn't quick enough to stop the blow. The bar struck him squarely in the forehead.

"Run, Alyssa!" she shouted. *"Take one of the cars!"*

Gregor went down like a sack of wet cement, smacking the ground and clutching his head with both hands. The gun was gone, but Sarah couldn't say where. She turned and saw The Imposter rushing toward her. She took a swing at him, more wild than anything targeted. He partially blocked it, but caught a blow to the ribs. It was enough to stop his advance and he stumbled into the fender. Knowing she could never fight both men, and penned in by geometry, Sarah took the only way out. She dove into the car and panic-crawled across the front seats. Someone grabbed her ankle, but she kicked free and pushed the opposite door open. Sarah threw herself to the dirt on the far side, then looked back to see The Imposter crawling through after her. She got to her knees and slammed the door shut as hard as she could. A howl of rage as it struck him squarely in the face.

Sarah scrambled to her feet and ran.

Alyssa did her part. The instant her mother struck the first blow, she locked eyes with the man she'd always thought to be her grandfather. His bony hand tightened on her arm, but it was a weak grip. Alyssa was no more a trained fighter than her mother was, yet she was young and strong—and also perfectly comfortable with physical contact. She played defender on her soccer team, which made her an expert at using her body to put others off balance.

She pulled away slightly to alter Walter's center of gravity, then lunged in low with a wicked hip-check. The robustness Walter had shown all night evaporated, and an eighty-year-old man went sprawling into the dirt.

Alyssa ran toward the two strange cars—her speed was also honed from soccer. Both vehicles were running, and she chose the nearest, a sedan like a million others. She threw the door open and clambered in. None of the gauges and instruments resembled the Camry—the only car she'd ever driven. The shift lever and accelerator looked the same, though, and after yanking the door closed she slammed the car into gear.

She looked ahead and saw Walter limping toward her in the twin beams. Alyssa stepped on the gas, more than she meant to in her excitement. The car leaped forward like it had been shot from a cannon. She tried to steer away from Walter, but the left side skidded toward him. At the last moment he jumped clear, tumbling into the dirt a second time.

Alyssa got things under control and steered toward the access road. A series of loud bangs echoed from outside and the car's back window exploded, shards of glass flying through the interior. She screamed, but kept accelerating.

Soon the car was swallowed by a tunnel of dark forest.

Sarah watched everything play out as she ran. The car Alyssa had taken disappeared around the bend. She feared the worst when she heard the shots, but the car's motor carried on, fading but reassuringly steady—her daughter's foot firmly on the accelerator. Sarah threw a glance back and saw The Imposter gesturing and shouting instructions. Gregor peeled off and staggered toward the second car with Walter.

The man who was not her husband stood holding his nose with a hand, blood streaming down his face. He set his hate-filled eyes on Sarah and began sprinting toward her.

71

INESCAPABLE GEOMETRY

t wasn't so much flying as a startle reflex. Recognizing a near-vertical dive, Bryce heaved the control stick back between his knees, hitting the stop with so much force he was afraid he might have broken it. With the stick planted in his lap, he watched helplessly, mesmerized by the black-and-white maelstrom ahead—the Barents Sea filling the front windscreen, an explosion of windswept water and foam.

Bryce had no idea what the G-limit was for an Aviat rigged with skis. Whatever the number, he surely exceeded it. The nose began to rise and he was pressed into the seat by the accelerative forces. The sea seemed close enough to touch, white breakers giving texture to undulating mountains of black water. When the little airplane leveled off, it seemed to be skimming across the surface, choppy ridgelines looming on either side.

His heart pounding, Bryce began a climb. He looked up, and in the dim light saw the clouds that had nearly gotten the better of him: a solid deck hanging like a shroud above the unruly sea. Desperate to avoid a repeat, and with adrenaline still pumping, he shoved the stick forward to level off and was reminded he hadn't buckled in—not a priority in the chaotic moments before takeoff. His head struck the ceiling, jamming his neck sideways. He blinked away the pain, stunned, and for a brief moment saw dirt rising from the floor. A broken pencil appeared out of nowhere and seemed to float in midair.

Finally, he got the airplane under control, the rollercoaster ride over. He leaned forward and scanned outside, desperate for references in the gloom. He was established in clear air, but only just—trapped between the roiling sea and a solid cloud deck a few hundred feet above. It was all Bryce could do to keep oriented, the horizon barely discernable in the scant light.

Gusty winds jostled the Aviat mercilessly. Bryce referenced the white-streaked sea, and realized there was a terrific crosswind from the north—his flight path was skidding sideways relative to his heading. He corrected with a turn, trying to keep his track as close as possible to due west. He hoped the weather wouldn't deteriorate as he approached the shores of Norway. If he could hold what he had, he would reach Norwegian airspace in a matter of minutes. A sprint to an invisible finish line.

There, surely, he would be safe.

Bryce would never know the scope of the upheaval behind him. The Hind got airborne quickly, flying through clouds less than four miles in trail. The pilots radioed headquarters and explained the situation. Radanov, having already inserted himself into the mix, spoke directly with the Russian Air Force's Western Military District Headquarters in Saint Petersburg.

Skeptical air defense commanders there did what they could. Fighters were scrambled from two separate bases in the hope of shooting down a tiny ski-plane. The problem was that both were over a hundred miles away. The few minutes it would take to get the jets airborne, combined with the distances involved, created an inescapable geometry—numbers and angles that even flying at twice the speed of sound could not overcome.

It quickly became apparent that the only aircraft with any chance of intercepting the fugitive was the Hind. Unfortunately, helicopters were not equipped with either radar or the armaments required for all-weather air-to-air engagements. The Hind's only available weapon was a Yak-B 12.7mm rotary cannon, which was intended for air-to-ground use. Yet there was one bit of good news: an air defense radar sector had picked up the little airplane and was tracking it nicely. They could vector the Hind in for an intercept, although not before reaching Norwegian airspace which, by then, was only a few miles in front of the Aviat.

Radanov made a convincing case to a senior officer in Saint Petersburg that both their careers were at stake. His conviction was such that Radanov, in essence, made a decision that was not customarily his to make.

They would shoot the little airplane down regardless of where it fell.

Alyssa drove as fast as she dared on the potholed dirt road—she'd never before driven on anything besides pavement. The unfamiliar car bounced and jolted like a bucking horse, and she held the wheel white-knuckled, more hanging on than steering. She'd never been so frightened in her life, yet her fear was overridden by determination.

Her mother's life was as stake. She *had* to get help.

She shook away tears, focusing on what was ahead. To begin, Alyssa assumed she was being followed. *How much farther to the main road?* She'd tried to pay attention when the man named Gregor brought her here, and she was sure there were no turns before reaching highway. A right turn there would take her back the way they'd come: a few miles of two-lane highway leading to a bridge, and then a small town beyond that. If she could reach the town she could flag someone down—a policeman, a store clerk, *anyone*—and call for help.

Finally, the darkness of the forest gave way and the main road appeared. Without stopping, she glanced left, saw no oncoming traffic, and ran the second stop sign of her life—this time in a stolen car. Alyssa tried to accelerate through the turn. The engine revved but nothing changed, as if the car was hesitating. She pressed the harder accelerator, and all at once the tires hit asphalt and everything took hold. The car slewed sideways, and she tried to correct but ended up straddling the centerline. A pair of oncoming headlights appeared out of nowhere. She swerved right, just missing an SUV that flew past, horn blaring. Out of control, Alyssa's car spun a half circle, ending at a dead stop and pointed in the wrong direction.

The SUV kept going.

Alyssa cursed. After a careful look in both directions, she U-turned to get back on track. She was stepping on the accelerator, this time more guardedly, when a pair of headlights flickered out of the forest behind her.

Broken light sputtered through the trees, more emphasizing the blackness than illuminating what was

around her. Sarah ran as fast as she dared on the familiar trail. She'd found the trailhead easily, and took
off on a slight downhill grade. Having been here before, she remembered two parallel switchbacks in the
first section, and so she went off trail, twice scooting
on her hands and bottom down a pair of wet inclines.
With any luck, gaining separation.

There had been no choice but to run—doing so
forced the three men to divide, giving Alyssa that
much more chance. She'd seen Walter and Gregor get
into a car and give chase, but Alyssa had a good head
start. The thought of her driving alone, at night, and
through a forest, would have seemed inconceivable a
week ago. Now it was their best hope for survival.

The final tally: one man was now behind her. The
Imposter who'd ruined their lives. She heard him now
and again, stampeding along the trail. Trying to track
her. Find her. Kill her.

Sarah kept moving, trying to recall what was
ahead. The idea of going into the woods crossed her
mind, but it would slow her progress considerably,
allow him to close the gap. If he got too close, got
within sight, there might be no escape.

She reached a straight section of path she remembered well. In days past it had been memorable for
the view: on the right a vertical granite wall clawed
up the mountain, and to the left was a sheer drop of
hundreds of feet. The path ran straight and true for
at least a hundred yards, and Sarah realized too late
that she would be easily seen on the straightaway. She
stopped and listened, heard him coming on a dead run.

She spun a circle, desperate. The recent rains had
carved a gap in the earthen wall to her right. Sarah
pressed herself into the crevice, squirming to conceal

as much of her body as possible. With the footsteps closing in, she willed herself to stillness, to silence. She pulled in one last lungful of cool night air.

Death was never more than one breath away.

To Sarah it had never seemed closer.

ONE FROZEN IMAGE

Alyssa saw a road sign fly past: SPEED LIMIT 45 MPH. She checked the speedometer and saw that she was doing seventy. Almost twice as fast as she'd ever driven in her life. *Where's a cop with a radar gun when you need one?*

Far more concerning than the speed was what she saw in the mirror: headlights closing in fast. She felt like she was barely in control, every touch of the wheel magnified. There was little traffic on the two-lane road, but the occasional car passed in the opposite direction in a blur. Ahead she saw the iron-lattice frame of the bridge in the distance.

The car was right behind her now, nearly on her bumper. It swerved abruptly into the opposing lane and pulled beside her. Alyssa shot a glance across, saw the man she'd always called *grandpa*. His gaze was oddly fearful. Her eyes went back to the road and she saw another set of headlights approaching in the opposite direction, midway across the bridge. The lights of the town were clear beyond.

With the car hovering next to her, Alyssa didn't know what to do. Go faster? Hit the brakes? Suddenly the car swerved and they collided. Sparks flew between them, and she felt her car slew into a terrible fishtail. She screamed but kept driving, fought the skid and somehow kept control. She'd lost speed but was still on the road.

The car closed in for a second sideswipe, but then had to back away for the oncoming headlights. Alyssa stomped the accelerator until it hit the floor.

Gregor was driving, Walter in the passenger seat.

They'd been forced to back away for the approaching headlights, a set of wide-spaced beams with a higher row of amber lights—a mid-sized truck that might not give way.

"The next one will do it," Gregor said. "We'll take her on the bridge."

Walter said nothing. He looked ahead and saw it, a squat iron-framed overpass above a deep ravine. His mind remained locked on one frozen image— moments ago, Alyssa's face. The sweet girl he'd watched grow up, blossom into a beautiful young woman, was wearing a horrified expression he could never have imagined.

The bridge was getting close, the truck about to pass. Walter simply couldn't shake the image.

"And all for what?" he said in a low voice.

Gregor glanced at him questioningly. "What?"

Walter lunged for the wheel and seized it with both hands.

"No!" Gregor shouted.

The car veered left into the oncoming lane.

The truck driver did his best, a last-ditch swerve to avoid the head-on collision. Its heavy bumper clipped the sedan's rear fender, sending it careening off the road on the far side. The sedan struck the guardrail at nearly seventy miles an hour. It vaulted airborne, flew over an embankment, and disappeared into the ravine.

Sarah remained motionless, every sense on alert.

The footfalls came near, then their pattern suddenly changed. A purposeful run became a hesitant jog. The Imposter still coming, but wary.

Then she heard the reason: the faint sound of a helicopter thrumming in the nearby valley. The heavy boots paused a few steps away. He was panting from the exertion. Sarah couldn't see him, but she felt his presence. Sensed his indecision.

Her body was pressed hard into the earthen crevice. Every inch of concealment taken, every bit of vegetation curtained between them. With her hands flattened against the wall she noticed a protrusion under her right palm. Ever so cautiously, her fingertips traced a softball-sized rock. It was lodged in the mud but loose. Sarah tried to work it free silently.

He started moving again, cautiously, and finally she saw him, a watchful shadow on the narrow path. Sarah cursed the helicopter—if it hadn't come he would have run straight past, allowing her to double back to the parking area. If he didn't keep going she would have to confront him, here and now: he was a threat to Alyssa and had to be stopped.

He paused again, this time directly in front of her. The sound of the helicopter grew and he stood scanning the valley with his back to her. Sarah pried the rock free, but as it gave way bits of earth dislodged. The tiniest of avalanches. The slightest of sounds.

But it was enough.

His posture stiffened and he began to turn.

Sarah lunged and swung the stone, aiming for his

head. He raised an arm and the rock struck his temple at half-strength. The Imposter was stunned but still on his feet. She lost her grip on the stone and it tumbled toward the ledge. Sarah hurled herself in desperation, putting her arms on his chest and driving him toward the drop-off. His advantage in size stalled her momentum. With one backward step he could seize control. But it was a step he didn't have.

His back boot found nothing but air.

His arms windmilled once, and he grabbed the only thing within reach—Sarah's jacket. In a reversal of what had happened at the Watergate, he clawed her in a frantic grip. Sarah, however, reacted differently than he had that day. Without hesitation, thinking only of Alyssa's safety, she didn't resist his pull. She let herself fall with him toward the abyss.

"No!" he shouted, his free hand flailing. "Help—"

They went over as one, joined by his hand. Sarah's last points of contact were her feet dragging across the earth. Nearing the precipice, her right foot encountered resistance. She stiffened that leg, shifted her weight, and the toe of her shoe caught on something firm.

His hand gave way, releasing her jacket.

Sarah caught one glimpse in the dim light, what seemed like a snapshot: the so-familiar face free-falling into darkness. She was right behind him, mirroring his fall, when her foot wrenched to an abrupt stop. Her upper body pivoted and she slammed face-first into the ledge, bent at the hips, her torso upside down. But there she remained.

Her ankle, twisted painfully, was caught in what felt like a vise. Sarah clawed at the rock wall and found the tiniest of handholds, a fissure in the stone face.

She twisted cautiously, and her other hand seized the trunk of a cliffside sapling. With three points of contact, things stabilized. She looked up and saw her foot snagged beneath a thick root, probably exposed in the recent rains. Her shoe was gone, and she wriggled her bare foot deeper into the cleft. Tiny plots of earth skittered down the hillside, yet inch by inch she began working her way upward.

Finally, Sarah reached the path, breathless and bruised. She looked down into the blackness, searching for any trace of The Imposter.

She saw and heard nothing.

73

SMOLDERING HEAP

Yes!" Bryce shouted to no one when the coastline came into view.

At first, it was little more than a shadow. A variance in the texture of the sea. Then a necklace of white water materialized along the beach, and hills emerged to complete the picture.

"All I need now is a place to put down," he whispered.

The weather was marginally better—he was flying at five hundred feet, the hard deck of clouds having risen. The horizon was clearer, visibility improving. Bryce was scanning the coastline, searching for a few flat acres in which to set down, when a flash of motion on the left caught his eye.

The Hind came out of the clouds like a raptor from hell. It was less than a mile away, pointed right at him. A sparkle beneath the cockpit Bryce instantly recognized as muzzle flashes. By some instinct he didn't understand, he rolled left and pointed his little airplane directly at the threat. The combined closure of the aircraft became extreme, and before the chopper could get off another shot, its pilot faced the reality of a midair collision. Bryce could actually see two visored helmets as the aircraft flashed overhead. He reversed back right, his head on a swivel to reacquire the Hind.

It was a dogfight he could never win: an unarmed, light utility aircraft against an armored combat helicopter. Bryce wasn't surprised they'd found him. He was stunned, however, that the Russians had followed him into Norwegian airspace. Absolutely astounded they were trying to shoot him down here. Then he recalled what was at stake—for everyone.

The Hind was repositioning on his right, setting up for another pass. The big machine could probably ram him with its undercarriage if it came to that. Bryce realized his only chance was to get on the ground. He dove for the beach, having no idea what kind of surface he would find. Sand, rocks, solid ice. Whatever it was, it was about to take a crash landing.

Against every "fight-or-flight" survival instinct, he pulled the throttle back in order to slow. He looked back and saw the Hind bearing down, closing in for the kill. Bryce jerked the Aviat into a steep left turn, then reversed and went harder to the right. It was pure instinct, like running across a battlefield—never move in a straight line. He kept slowing, while the Hind was accelerating and closing in fast. The chopper looked massive over his shoulder. When the pilot fired, Bryce had the Aviat in a steep left turn no more than a hundred feet above the ground.

He felt the bullets strike home. Battering the delicate airframe, causing it to shudder. The left wing dropped farther, its tip nearly scraping the rocky beach. Bryce fought the controls for all he was worth, muscling the stick and rudder. The Hind blew past directly overhead, the roar of its engines and downdraft of its rotors adding to the maelstrom. The beach of rounded stones became a blur, and the left wingtip snagged the earth. The nose slammed down hard and Bryce flung his arms up protectively. The Aviat slammed down in a shriek of tearing metal and flying glass.

Then everything went black.

"Norwegian F-16's are airborne," said the general from air defense headquarters. "I am ordering the chopper out!"

"No!" Radanov shouted into his handset. "We must be certain!"

"I cannot risk it! We have already committed multiple violations of international law."

"Then one more will not matter. I would call the president if there was time, but I can assure you he is not a man who appreciates half-measures."

Radanov waited for what seemed an interminable amount of time. In the end, no argument came.

The pilot nearly had the Hind back in Russian airspace when the order came to make one last attack run. He explained that there was nothing left but wreckage, yet the orders were only reiterated. Grumbling, he turned back.

Once settled on the reciprocal course, his eyes flicked upward—they would soon not be the only ones in these skies carrying weapons. He easily found what was left of the little aircraft; a heap of crumpled metal rocking lazily in the shore break. The wreckage wasn't in flames, but smoke spewed from the engine. He slowed to hover a mere fifty meters away—a perfectly stable platform, at point-blank range, for the weapons officer in front of him.

The gun had six hundred rounds remaining. Thirty seconds later, after a series of extended bursts, the ammo drum was empty. The high-explosive incendiary rounds brutalized the wreckage, fragments of metal and ricochets spewing in all directions. By the time they were done, no piece of the airplane larger than a car door remained.

The Hind turned away from the smoldering heap, set an easterly course, and fast disappeared into the mist.

74

FLOTSAM

Anders Nystrom, in all his nine years, had never seen anything like it.

The towheaded boy was standing alone on the rocky beach, his down jacket fluttering in the wind. After being kept in the house for two days by the storm, his mother had finally allowed him outside to comb the beaches this morning.

Anders knew these shores like his own backyard, having been born and raised in the nearby village of Skallelv. He particularly loved the beaches during rough weather, reveling in the strength of the sea and the edge of the wind. More to the point, he looked forward to the curiosities washed up by the big blows. His mother was enamored with driftwood, but Anders preferred the man-made flotsam gifted by the sea. Colorful buoys broken away from traps, lumber washed overboard from cargo ships, the odd derelict rowboat or hatch cover. He'd once found an entire shipping container washed up on the beach—as it turned out, full of red and blue picnic coolers.

Yet never had anything approached what Anders was looking at now.

The ruckus from the next cove had gotten his attention instantly. Noises unlike anything he'd ever heard, great explosions like the thunder of breaking waves during the worst storms. He'd run to the point to see what was happening, and on the way there he was sure he heard a helicopter—the Coast Guard flew by regularly, although this one sounded different. The helicopter sound faded, and when he finally reached the point Anders saw but one peculiarity in South Cove: wavering in the surf, a smashed and smoking machine of some kind.

He sprinted down the hill and along the beach. Anders drew to a stop ten meters away, mesmerized by the thrashed pile of wreckage. A few bits and pieces reminded him of an airplane, but given the degree of pulverization, he couldn't be sure. He stared for a time as the remains rose and fell, riding the surf's rhythmic carriage.

Then a misplaced sound diverted his attention.

Anders looked above the tideline, and with a start he saw what he hadn't at first. Beside a small rock outcropping, half-hidden beneath a drift of icy seaweed, lay the unmistakable figure of a man. Anders moved closer, quickly at first, but then more cautiously. The figure didn't move, and he stopped a few paces away. He saw blood on the shirt and pants, limbs that seemed arranged awkwardly. He assumed the man was dead: some shipwrecked soul, a victim of the storm. He'd never seen a dead person.

Bravely, Anders went closer, and he looked for the one thing that might prove the point. To his surprise, he saw the opposite: the man was definitely breathing.

Without hesitation, he broke into a run and headed for home.

He had to tell his mother.

The helicopter carrying Burke and the rapid response team was circling when the 911 call from Alyssa

arrived. It took three minutes for it to be routed to the
FBI command center, where no less than the director
himself began coordinating a response. With the West
Virginia Highway Patrol blockading the road in both
directions, the pilot landed on the highway south of
the bridge.

Burke quickly located Alyssa, who explained what
had happened. Based on her account, and acting as
on-scene commander, Burke dispatched a burgeoning army of law enforcement personnel. He sent local
sheriff's deputies to the scene of a car crash near the
bridge, telling the officers to proceed with caution.
Keeping Alyssa with him, Burke led a small convoy of
highway patrol vehicles into the nearby forest. They
arrived at the head of the hiking trail to find Sarah
Ridgeway walking out of the woods.

On first glance she looked traumatized, but her
relief was instantaneous when she caught sight of
her daughter. Burke held back to let the reunion run
its course. Sarah Ridgeway and her daughter flew
into each other's arms, locking so tight they seemed
to become one. He allowed a full minute before asking Sarah what had become of the imposter. When
she told him, Burke decided the immediate crisis had
ended.

Longer term worries, however, quickly took hold.

He backed away from the mother and daughter,
and called Truman. His conversation with the FBI
director lasted five minutes, Burke mostly listening.
When the call ended, he made his way back to the bit-
tersweet reunion.

"I just talked to headquarters," he said, ushering
them a discreet distance away from a clutch of highway patrol officers. "I'm glad you're both safe, but we

have some unusual considerations going forward. The three of us have to be very careful."

"Careful in what way?" Sarah asked, her over-taxed mind not capable of nuance.

"We are in a very precarious situation. The director wants to meet with you both."

"The director of the FBI? Now?"

"I know it's been a long night, but I'll explain on the way. Claire will be there as well. I've got a helicopter standing by. For the moment, it is very, *very* important that you don't talk to anyone about what's happened."

"A helicopter?" Alyssa said, mirroring her mother's edge.

Sarah drew her daughter closer, seeming to catch what Burke was saying. "It's okay, baby. I know you've been through a lot, but we're safe. Agent Burke is right."

Alyssa seemed to think about it, and then in an uncertain voice, said, "Mom . . . where's Dad?"

She pulled her daughter closer still. "I wish I knew, sweetheart. I really wish I knew."

The tragedy of timing over the next twelve hours was nothing less than Shakespearian.

At eight o'clock the next morning, the FBI issued a press release announcing the tragic and untimely death of Congressman Bryce Ridgeway. Both sparse and vague on detail, the story line invoked a hiking accident in West Virginia, and verified that his family was with him in the final moments—elements of truth, tortured as they were. Within an hour the Ridgeway home was surrounded by news crews desperate for some sign of the widow and daughter, who were in fact bunkered safely in the home of a close friend.

At noon that day, Claire opened the door of her townhome to find FBI Director Robert Truman and Agent Burke. "We need to talk to Sarah and Alyssa," Truman said.

"They're asleep."

Truman shouldered in uninvited. "It's very important—they'll want to hear this."

Five minutes later a groggy mother and daughter were together on the couch, the others crowded into various chairs. "What's this about?" Sarah asked.

"We received word this morning of certain signal intercepts—they were obtained last night by the National Security Agency. NSA routinely monitors electronic communications around the world, but yesterday there was an unusual spike of activity. A highly irregular military operation took place along the extreme northwestern border of Russia. In the end, an airplane was shot down—it crashed on a beach in northern Norway."

"All right," Sarah said, "but what does that have to do with us?"

"The Russian Air Force was apparently operating in conjunction with the SVR, their foreign intelligence service. They were trying to prevent a light aircraft from escaping Russian airspace. The intercepts made clear that this was an extremely high-risk operation—orders were given to shoot down a civilian airplane inside another country's airspace. Not unprecedented, but *very* risky."

Sarah's expression began to shift. She no longer looked weary. "Are you saying—"

The director held up a hand to stop her. "The only certainty is that there was a survivor from the crash. He was severely injured, and is being airlifted as we speak to a regional medical center. We've only got a few pictures to go by, but yes . . . we think it might be Bryce."

Mother and daughter locked eyes.

Without another word, tears of joy began to flow.

75

NEVER LET GO

Forty-eight hours after the chaos on the bleak shores of northern Norway, a Gulfstream 650 business jet touched down two hundred miles west in Hammerfest—the northernmost town of any size in the world. The jet taxied to the executive terminal, and there a limousine, arranged by the Norwegian Intelligence Service as a courtesy to its American counterpart, collected three occupants.

A man, a woman, and a teenage girl were delivered directly to the regional hospital. At a side entrance they were met by an officious officer, also of the NIS, who led them to an isolated room on the third floor. The two women braced themselves, arm-in-arm, before following a nurse inside room 37. Burke heard a chorus of muted shrieks as the door closed. Not anything worrisome—more the exhalation of pent-up faith. Something none of them had ever relinquished.

The NIS man introduced Burke to a doctor, and they exchanged pleasantries.

"Has his condition changed?" Burke asked.

"He is stable," said the doctor in effortless English—he was eyeing the NIS man, who'd receded into a shadow in a building that held few. "He was airlifted here from a clinic in the east two days ago. When he arrived, honestly, I didn't think he would make it. He had a most irregular array of injuries. Recent trauma, as one might see from an automobile crash, but also multiple injuries that looked older. The sort of damage that one might classify as . . . intentionally inflicted by others."

Burke nodded, yet offered no explanation.

"Can you enlighten me as to how he arrived here?" the doctor asked.

"I wish I could, but I'm under strict orders."

The doctor frowned, but didn't press—it was the answer he'd been getting all along. "Does he have a name?"

Burke smiled thinly. "We're trying to work that out."

The doctor looked at him skeptically.

"I can tell you he's American," Burke said, perhaps with a trace of pride.

"Well, whoever he is, he's damned tough. That is a good thing—he faces a long path to recovery. His cranial and facial injuries are severe. Many surgeries will be required. His right arm has serious damage, both new and old. His right foot will never be the same."

"You may be right, Doctor. But I can tell you his tenacity has surprised a lot of people, myself included."

"I understand you wish to transport him home?"

"As soon as possible. Our aircraft is configured as a medical transport, all the necessary equipment and an in-flight nurse."

The doctor sighed. "Very well. I think he should have one more night with us. Barring setbacks, however, and assuming he will have proper care enroute . . . I could release him tomorrow."

"Thank you."

The doctor went about his rounds.

Burke decided it was time. He opened the door softly and stepped into the room. Bryce, Sarah, and Alyssa Ridgeway were knotted in each other's arms. It looked for all the world like they would never let go.

76

THE VEIL

One week later

The death of Congressman Bryce Ridgeway assumed the proportions of a national tragedy. By consensus opinion, he was twice a hero: first for having bled for his country, and more recently for giving it hope. Virtually overnight, Ridgeway had ascended to the Beltway's version of a saint . . . JFK without the inauguration.

While the details remained vague, an account of the congressman's death on a West Virginia hiking trail was given by no less than President Connolly himself. By consensus opinion, it was one of the president's better moments. There were no political overtones whatsoever, the incumbent granting the high road to a warrior and statesman who had departed before his time.

The memorial service could not be held anywhere but Arlington. In those gentle hills beside the Pentagon, where so many American presidents and heroes lay, Ridgeway was put to rest with all the accordant honors. On an unusually clear winter morning, an escort platoon with horse-drawn limber and caisson delivered the casket, trailed by a riderless horse. A nineteen-gun artillery salute highlighted the affair, two short of what might have been—twenty-one guns, artillery, was reserved for duly-elected presidents. In attendance were dignitaries, ambassadors, Ridgeway's brothers from the Army, and a good percentage of his more shaded brethren from Capitol Hill. Two former presidents paid their homage, as did nine foreign heads of state. The spectacle was carried live on every news network and many overseas.

Like those around her, the widow was dressed in black, and, in a throwback style that would set a seasonal trend in mourning, she went to the trouble of wearing a full black veil. Everyone understood, in light of her grief, just as they made allowances for the absence of Bryce Ridgeway's distraught daughter. The tears for her father, undoubtedly, had proved incapacitating.

The ceremony went through its rigid paces, culminating with the widow being given a folded American flag. After the final note of taps was played, mourners of sufficient social rank paid their respects to the widow, many of them adding condolences for the sudden, and nearly concurrent, loss of her father-in-law. The death of Walter Ridgeway, at least, had been a foreseeable event in light of his long decline.

When the receiving line finally finished, a hard day reached its end.

Or nearly so.

The most telling moment of the entire affair was in fact noticed by no one, nor recorded by any cameras. With the crowd dispersing and news networks going back to studio coverage, the widow discreetly went graveside for a final moment with the earthly remains of her husband. In that moment, the veil played an uncharacteristically critical role when, as the widow leaned solemnly toward the grave, it obscured her face as she spat on the polished silver casket.

The end of Arkady Radanov, compared to the official fate of Bryce Ridgeway, could not have been more different in either method or ritual.

Following the twin debacles in Zubovka and Washington, Radanov had gone into the professional equivalent of a fighter's crouch. He was summoned immediately to Moscow, yet instead of the expected basement grilling at the hands of his younger SVR colleagues, many of whom would have relished the opportunity, he was installed in a posh suite at the Kadashevskaya Hotel. There he remained for two days. Fine meals were brought to his room, which he enjoyed in the imperious company of an ice-clad Moscow River.

The summons came on the third day: an invitation to meet with the president and provide his version of recent events. In truth, Radanov couldn't imagine there was much to be said. He had briefed the president on Operation Zerkalo a number of times over the years, most recently three weeks ago, and had always sensed enthusiastic support. The prospect of installing a mole as president of the United States would be a coup unsurpassed in the annals of espionage, and beyond that, it played straight to the Russian president's black and scheming heart. Now however, Zerkalo was at an end: the mission had failed, and the Americans damned well knew it.

Radanov, like the man across the river, he was sure, had been watching Western news reports for any signal, any shred of evidence to answer the trillion-dollar question: How would the Americans respond to such a grievous breach of sovereignty? He suspected—as it turned out, rightly—that Russia's military, including its strategic nuclear forces, had been placed on high alert. Yet now, finally, the president wanted to see him, and for the first time in days Radanov was buoyed. The fact that he was being called to the Kremlin's ornate red carpet this morning implied that decisions had been made in both hemispheres. Decisions that might, conceivably, work in his favor after all.

After a sumptuous breakfast, he dressed in his best suit for the meeting across the river. It was a rare sunny day in January, bitter cold but with little wind. He left the hotel and walked directly to the Bolshoy Kamenny Bridge, the nearest crossing to reach the Kremlin.

Radanov kept a leisurely pace across the bridge, the warmth of the sun penetrating his heavy overcoat. He never saw the man in the black jacket behind him, or the gun he lifted from his pocket. The bullet traveled less than three feet before entering Radanov's head, and he was dead before he hit the ground—a presumption the assassin did not allow. He issued two more rounds, just to be sure, then walked calmly away and disappeared into a subway entrance two blocks distant.

Because the murder took place in broad daylight, and virtually in the shadow of the Kremlin, there was no shortage of witnesses. The president that night expressed mild outrage that a high-ranking official could be gunned down in the heart of Moscow. He promised an investigation, yet in the weeks that followed no suspects were mentioned by the police. Nor was any usable CCTV footage ever produced—this despite the fact that the crime had occurred in the most closely monitored square mile in all of Russia.

In the end, the investigation came to naught.

For Arkady Radanov there were no military honors, no sounding artillery. His body was cremated in the basement of a nearby prison, long ago configured for such tasks, and his ashes flushed ingloriously down a toilet.

BACK FORTY

Six months later

Claire was nine miles outside Telluride, Colorado. Seemingly a million from Washington D.C.

The mountains were spectacular in late spring, twelve-thousand-foot peaks holding a cap of snow on their crests. The air sweeping in through the open window was dry and pleasant, far removed from the warming eastern seaboard.

She slowed the rental car as the GPS route neared its end. A right turn into the forest loomed ahead. She saw the road, yet there was no way to be sure it was the right one. The reason was obvious: a municipal work crew was installing a new sign at the corner. The metal pole was being set, yet the street name had not been attached.

Claire turned onto a dirt road that was in decent shape. Half a mile later, rounding the side of a minor hill, a ranch-style residence came into view. It was single-level and solid, with wood-plank siding and a great stone chimney. A broad front porch ran the width of the home.

Sarah was waiting by the door.

Claire pulled to the top of a gray-gravel parking apron and waved. They met in a hug midway to the house.

"God, I missed you," Sarah said, standing back to regard her friend.

"You too. But it's a long damned way to come for coffee."

"The least I can do is make good on it."

They climbed to the porch where Sarah had a tray waiting—Claire had called from the airport to say she'd arrived. While she poured, Claire studied her friend; they'd not seen one another since the day after the funeral. She noted a few changes: Sarah had cut her hair short and she looked fitter. There was more color in her skin tone. A far cry from the stressed-out "widow" she'd last seen.

"Where's Bryce?"

"He and Alyssa took the truck out back—they've been mapping the old fence line."

"How western."

"We're rolling with it."

"How's his recovery going?"

"As well as can be. The surgeries took three months. He looks different, which I guess is a good thing. He's walking pretty well—the doctors are amazed. They told him he'd be on a walker the rest of his life, but he's already got it down to a cane, and that's only on uneven ground."

"That's my Bryce."

"Yeah, mine too."

Sarah handed over a full mug.

"So, what's it like to disappear?" Claire asked.

"Surprisingly . . . liberating. After what happened, we really didn't have any choice. We met with President Connolly, and he was decent about it. He said he would support whatever choice we made, but that going off-grid was probably the best option for everyone. If what the Russians did came to light, it could shake the faith in our democracy."

"And there would be some pretty loud shouts for war with Russia."

"I think the president said something along those lines. For the three of us it was an easy choice. Alyssa and I could have stayed in Virginia, but for Bryce there was no option—he was a dead man walking. The FBI gave us all a fresh start—identities, a place to live, small nest egg." She looked out over the hills. "People out here mind their own business—which is easy, I guess, when your nearest neighbor is half a mile away. As far as disappearing, Bryce was the main concern. I was never active in the campaign, and the press kept Alyssa out of the fray. He was the only who might get recognized."

"And has he been?"

"We go into town a few times each week. So far there haven't been any double takes or awkward questions. The longer we stay, the easier it should get."

"And Alyssa? How is she handling it?"

"It surprised me, but she was the one who pushed to come here. She wanted to do it for her father, one hundred percent. She misses her friends, of course, but the local high school is good and the kids have been friendly. She's starting to think about college, and we even found a club soccer team in need of a solid defender."

"Sounds like she's adjusting."

"I think maturing is more like it. She knows what's at stake—what happened during those two months is something we can never confide to anyone. She's convinced this is the best situation for her father. She put his needs above her own, and I'm really proud of her for that."

After a short silence, Sarah said, "What about you? Last I heard, EPIC was getting a second look."

"A lot more than that. The president himself got involved, and FBI Director Truman is working on long-term funding. I expect there will be a few more legal boundaries for EPIC 2.0—we were pressing the edge, probably going beyond. But we proved the concept."

"Glad to hear it."

"So was Atticus."

The sound of tires over gravel rose from behind the house, and soon a beaten pickup truck rounded the corner. Alyssa was at the wheel, and she pulled in next to the rental car.

Claire watched them get out. Alyssa was little changed, albeit decked out in jeans and boots instead of the athletic wear that had long been her standard. She looked happy and waved enthusiastically. Claire waved back.

Bryce was another story. She hadn't seen him—not the *real* Bryce—since last fall. He did look different. There was scarring on his face, a slight misalignment in his stance—his right shoulder looked frozen in place. His hair was longer, lighter from the sun, and a week's growth of beard altered the visage even more. He moved with an uneven stride, tentative but determined, and leaned heavily on his cane as he made his way up the steps.

Claire took a heartfelt hug from Alyssa. Bryce came closer, and she saw the familiar eyes. Then, of course . . .

the signature smile. The one that that had captivated Sarah so many years ago. And more recently, America.

"Good to see you, Claire. I never got around to properly saying thanks."

Claire hugged him gingerly, as if worried he might break. He hugged her back in a way that assured her he wouldn't.

The reunion began on the porch, but by late afternoon they moved inside as a cool drizzle started to fall. Sarah and Alyssa worked on dinner, and Bryce busied himself hauling armloads of firewood inside. Claire thought he seemed to get stronger with each trip.

As Bryce began building a fire, Claire's phone buzzed. She pulled it from her pocket, read the message, and said, "Typical."

"What's up?" he asked.

"The airline lost my bag. Apparently it arrived, but they can't deliver it until tomorrow." She pocketed her phone. "I'll have to drive to the airport and pick it up."

"I can take you," Bryce said.

Ten minutes later they were in the pickup, Bryce behind the wheel. "I only started driving a few weeks ago—my right foot wasn't up to it until then."

"Looks like you're making good progress."

He pointed out a few landmarks on the property, a small barn and a smokehouse. Bryce explained his plans for the back forty: an upgraded fence, clearing some deadwood, and eventually a few horses. He'd also designed a back patio with a view of the mountains, complete with a fire pit and gazebo.

"You going to do all that yourself?" she asked.

"Why not? It'll take some time, but I'm in no hurry."

Claire regarded him thoughtfully.

He caught her looking. "What?"

"I was thinking about where you were last year. Do you have any regrets? What might have been?"

"Serving in Congress?" He laughed and shook his head. "Been there, done that. I miss the Army more."

She looked at him questioningly. "I was actually thinking more about the presidency."

He shot her a level gaze. "Honestly . . . I don't think about it. That was my father's dream, not mine."

Claire nodded and looked out the side window. The rain was tapering off, and she saw the half-cut sun falling behind a mountain on the right.

When they reached the main road, Bryce paused for a passing car. Claire noticed the work crew was gone, and she looked up at the newly installed sign. The street's name brought a smile to her face.

Tenacity Lane.

ACKNOWLEDGMENTS

Deep Fake is a departure from my usual David Slaton series, and was written during the lockdown days of COVID-19. I am deeply thankful to have a publisher who allows me to occasionally go off-script, which, as any writer who has done so will attest, is something near therapy.

Much appreciation to my editor, Bob Gleason, who has long championed my stories at Tor, and whose insights and suggestions are invariably spot-on. Thanks also to Robert Davis for being such an agreeable mentor—I feel like each book we build together gets easier. To Robert Allen and Katy Robitzski at Macmillan Audio, my sincere gratitude for all you do. To Eileen Lawrence and Libby Collins, your efforts in getting the word out are enduringly appreciated. And of course, thanks to Linda Quinton whose stewardship at Forge is steady as ever.

Much appreciation to my agent, Susan Gleason, for your longtime support and encouragement. Thanks also to the board of International Thriller Writers for carrying the organization through difficult times. ThrillerFest XVII was a smashing success, and it was fantastic to reconnect with so many friends. Jeff Wilson, Mark Greaney, Brian Andrews, Simon Gervais, Brad Taylor, Tony Tata, Heather Graham, Jack Stewart,

Chris Hauty, Don Bentley—you made it better than ever.

James Abt, the man behind the curtain at Best Thriller Books, has proved himself one of savviest promoters in the business. BTB has also assembled a stellar lineup of reviewers. Todd, Ankit, Derek, Chris, Sarah, Steve, Stuart, Kashif, David: your words and opinions are truly valued. I also enjoyed talking thrillers with David Temple of *The Thriller Zone* podcast, and Mike Martini of the *No Limits: Mitch Rapp Podcast*. You truly are the experts.

And as always, much gratitude to my family for their support, advice, and tolerance. Without you I would have no stories to tell.